Dark Desire

Christine Feehan

Thorndike Press • Waterville, Maine

Published in 2004 by arrangement with Leisure Books,
a division of Dorchester Publishing Co., Inc.

Thorndike Press® Large Print Romance.

The tree indicium is a trademark of Thorndike Press.

The text of this Large Print edition is unabridged.
Other aspects of the book may vary from the original edition.

Set in 16 pt. Plantin by Al Chase.

Printed in the United States on permanent paper.

Library of Congress Cataloging-in-Publication Data

Feehan, Christine.
    Dark desire / Christine Feehan.
      p. cm.
    ISBN 0-7862-6785-2 (lg. print : hc : alk. paper)
    1. Carpathian Mountains — Fiction.   2. Women
physicians — Fiction.   3. Immortalism — Fiction.
4. Large type books.   I. Title.
PS3606.E36D355 2004
813'.54—dc22   2004047384

For my father, Mark King, who taught me there are many kinds of heroes in the world. For my agent, Helen, who refused to give up on my Carpathians. Special thanks to Allison Luce and my daughter Billie Jo Feehan who fell in love with Jacques and gave many helpful suggestions. And of course for my son Brian who had to read the action scenes many, many times for me.

As the Founder/CEO of NAVH, the only national health agency solely devoted to those who, although not totally blind, have an eye disease which could lead to serious visual impairment, I am pleased to recognize Thorndike Press* as one of the leading publishers in the large print field.

Founded in 1954 in San Francisco to prepare large print textbooks for partially seeing children, NAVH became the pioneer and standard setting agency in the preparation of large type.

Today, those publishers who meet our standards carry the prestigious "Seal of Approval" indicating high quality large print. We are delighted that Thorndike Press is one of the publishers whose titles meet these standards. We are also pleased to recognize the significant contribution Thorndike Press is making in this important and growing field.

Lorraine H. Marchi, L.H.D.
Founder/CEO
NAVH

* Thorndike Press encompasses the following imprints: Thorndike, Wheeler, Walker and Large Print Press.

Chapter One

There was blood, a river of it running. There was pain, a sea he was floating in. Would it never end? A thousand cuts, burns, the taunting laughter telling him it would go on for all eternity. He could not believe he was so helpless, could not believe his incredible power and strength had been drained from him, leaving him reduced to such a pitiful state. He sent mental call after call out into the night; none of his kind came to help him. The agony continued, went on relentlessly. Where were they? His kin? His friends? Why wouldn't they come to him and end this? Had it been a conspiracy? Had they deliberately left him to these butchers who wielded their knives and torches with such delight? It had been someone he knew who had betrayed him, but the memory was curiously fading, obscured by endless pain.

His tormentors had somehow managed to capture him, paralyze him so that he could feel yet not move, not even his vocal cords. He was totally helpless, vulnerable to the puny humans tearing his body apart. He heard their taunts, the endless questions, felt the rage in them when he refused to acknowledge their presence or the pain they inflicted on him. He wanted death, welcomed it, and his eyes, cold as ice, never left their faces, never blinked, the eyes of a predator waiting, watching, promising retaliation. It maddened them, but they refused to administer the finishing blow.

Time no longer meant anything to him, his world had become so narrow, but at some point he felt another's presence in his mind. The touch was far off, female, young. He had no idea how he had inadvertently connected with her, his mind melded to hers so that she was sharing his torment, every scorching burn, every cut of the knife, draining his blood, his life force from him. He tried to remember who she might be. She had to be close to him if she shared his mind. She was as helpless as he was, enduring the pain with him, sharing his agony. He tried to close himself off from her, the need to protect her paramount in him, yet he was far too weak to block his mental thoughts. His pain poured out of him, a raging torrent, flowing straight to the female sharing his mind.

Her anguish hit him like a powerful blow. He was, after all, a Carpathian male. His first duty was to protect a woman above his own life at all times. That he should falter so added to his despair and sense of failure. He

8

caught brief images of her in his mind, a small, fragile figure huddled in a ball of pain, trying desperately to hang on to her sanity. She seemed a stranger to him, yet he saw her in color, something he had not seen in centuries. He couldn't send either of them to sleep to save both of them from this agony. He could only catch fragments of her thoughts as she desperately tried to call out for help, tried to decipher what was happening to her.

Droplets of blood began to seep from his pores. Red blood. He clearly saw that his blood was red. It meant something important, yet he was confused, unable to discern why it was significant and what it meant. His mind was becoming hazy, as if a great veil were being drawn over his brain. He couldn't remember how they had managed to capture him. He struggled to "see" the image of the one of his own kind who had betrayed him, but the picture would not return to his mind. There was only pain. Terrible, endless pain. He could not make a sound, even when his mind shattered into a million fragments and he could no longer remember what, or whom, he was struggling to protect.

Shea O'Halloran lay curled up on her bed, the lamp providing her just enough light to read her medical journal. She covered page after page in mere seconds, committing the material to memory as she had done since she was a child. Now she was completing her residency, the youngest resident on record, and it was an exhausting ordeal. She hurried to finish the text, wanting to get some rest while she could. The pain hit her unexpectedly, slamming into her with such virulence that she was thrown off the bed, her body contorting with the force. She tried to cry out, to crawl blindly toward the phone, but she could only writhe on the floor helplessly. Sweat beaded on her skin; smears of crimson blood seeped through her pores. The pain was like nothing she had ever experienced, as if someone were cutting her flesh with a knife, burning her, torturing her endlessly. It went on and on — hours, days, she didn't know. No one came to help her, and they wouldn't; she was alone, so private that she had no real friends. At the end, when the pain ripped through her as if a hole the size of her fist had opened in her chest, she lost consciousness.

When he thought his tormentors were through with him, would end his suffering, give him death, he discovered what true hell really was. Gut-wrenching agony. Evil faces above him. A sharpened stake poised over his heart. A beat of time, a second. It would end now. It had to end. He felt the thick wooden point drive into his flesh, tearing a huge hole through muscle and sinew. The hammer fell hard on the end of the stake, driving it ever deeper. The pain was beyond anything he had ever imagined. The female sharing his mind lost consciousness, a mercy for both of them. He continued to feel every blow, the huge peg separating his flesh, penetrating his insides while blood spurted like a geyser, further weakening him. He felt his life force fading away, his strength so drained now that he was certain he would die. He reached for death. Embraced death. But it wasn't to be. He was a Carpathian male, an immortal, one not so easily disposed of. One whose will was strong and determined. A will that fought death even when his body begged for an end to his suffering and existence.

His eyes found them, the two humans. They were covered in his blood, red sprays across their clothes. He gathered his strength, the last of it, and captured their gazes with his mesmerizing stare. If he could just hold them long enough to turn their own evil back on them. One cursed suddenly and jerked his companion away. Quickly, they covered his eyes with cloth, no longer able to stand the dark promise in the deep pits of suffering, afraid of his power, although he was so helpless before them. They laughed as they chained him into the coffin and lifted it upright. He heard himself scream with the pain, but the sound was only in his mind, echoing sharply, locked away, mocking him. He forced himself to stop. They couldn't hear him, but it didn't matter to him. He had a shred of dignity left. Self-respect. They would not defeat him. He was Carpathian. He heard the dirt hitting the wood as they buried him in the wall of the cellar. Each shovelful. The darkness was complete. The silence took him like a blow.

He was a creature of the night. The dark was his home. Yet now, in his agony, it was his enemy. There was only pain and silence. Always before, he was the one who chose whether to stay in the darkness, in the healing soil. Now he was a prisoner, locked away, with the soil just out of reach. Comfort should have been his, was near, yet always the wood of the coffin prevented his body from touching what would eventually have healed his wounds.

Hunger began to invade his world of agony. Time passed, meant nothing. Only the terrible, relentless hunger that grew until it became his entire world. Agony. Hunger. Nothing else existed for him anymore.

He found, after some time, that he could put himself to sleep. But the return of this gift meant nothing anymore. He remembered nothing. This was his life. Sleep. Wake only when an inquisitive creature strayed too close. The rush of agony consuming him when his heart beat. Conserving as much strength as possible to try to draw food to him. Sources were few and far between. Even insects learned to avoid the place of darkness and the malevolent creature who dwelled there.

In the endless moments that inched past during his waking agony, he would whisper his name to himself. *Jacques.* He had a name. He was real. He existed. He lived in hell. He lived in darkness. The hours turned into months, then years. He could no longer remember any other way of life, any other existence. There was no hope, no peace, no way out. There was no end. Only the darkness, the pain, the terrible hunger. Time continued to pass, meant nothing in his limited world.

His wrists were manacled so that he had little room to maneuver, but every time a creature came close enough to awaken him, he scratched at the walls of his coffin in a vain attempt to get out. His strength of mind was returning so that he eventually

13

could coax his prey to him, yet only enough to barely survive. There was no way to regain his power and strength without replacing the huge volume of blood he had lost. There was no creature underground big enough to do that. Every time he woke, moved, fresh blood would drip steadily from his wounds. Without the necessary amount of blood to replace his loss, his body could not heal itself. The circle was endless, hideous, an ugly cycle that would last for all eternity.

Then the dreams began to intrude. Waking him when he was starving, without a way to fill the void. A woman. He recognized her, knew she was out there, alive, no manacles, not buried beneath the earth but able to move freely around. She was just out of his mind's reach, yet he could almost touch her. Why didn't she come to him? He could summon up no face, no past, only the knowledge that she was out there somewhere. He called to her. Begged. Pleaded. Raged. Where was she? Why wouldn't she come to him? Why did she allow his agony to continue when even her presence in his mind would ease the terrible sense of isolation? What had he done that was so terrible that he deserved this?

Anger found its way into his world.

Hatred, even. In the place of a man a monster grew, deadly, dangerous, grew and thrived on the pain, became a will impossible to crush. Fifty years, a hundred — what did it matter if he traveled to the very gates of hell for revenge? He already resided there, imprisoned in it every waking moment.

She would come to him. He vowed it. He would bend his will to finding her. And once he found her he would become a shadow in her mind until he was familiar enough with her to force his will on her. She would come to him, and he would have his revenge.

Hunger gripped him each time he woke, so that pain and hunger melted together and became the same. Concentrating on finding the path to the woman, however, saved him some agony. His focus was so complete that he could actually block the pain for a short while. First it was only seconds. Then minutes. Each time he woke, he bent his will toward finding her; there was nothing else to do. Months. Years. It didn't matter to him. She could not escape him forever.

The first time he touched her mind, it was such a shock after all the thousands of fruitless tries that he immediately lost contact. And the rush of elation caused a bright red spray of blood to erupt around the stake buried deep within his body, draining his remaining strength. He slept a long time in an attempt to recover. A week perhaps. A month. There was no need to measure time. He had a direction now, although she was far away from him. The distance was so great, it took his full concentration to focus and reach for her across time and space.

Jacques tried again when he woke. This time he was unprepared for the images in her mind. Blood. A small human chest ripped wide open. A pulsating heart. Her hands were immersed inside the chest cavity, covered in blood. There were others in the room with her, and she was directing their movements with her mind. She seemed unaware that she was doing so. Her focus was completely on her horrendous task. The ease with which she directed the others suggested that she did so often. The vivid pictures were horrible, and he knew she had been part of the betrayal, was part of those torturing him. He nearly lost the contact, but his indomitable will kicked in. She would suffer for this. Really suffer for this. The body she was torturing was so small, it had to be a child.

The operating room was dimly lit, just the way Dr. O'Halloran liked it; only the body on the table had a bright light shining down on it.

16

Her unusually acute hearing picked up voices outside the room: a nurse consoling the patient's parents. "You're lucky Dr. O'Halloran is working tonight. She's the best there is. She has a gift. Really. When there's no chance at all, she still pulls them out. Your little boy couldn't be in better hands."

"But he looked so awful." That was the terrified, already grieving mother.

"Dr. O'Halloran has been known to work miracles. Truly. Have faith. She just never stops until she saves them. We think she wills them to live."

Shea O'Halloran couldn't have any distractions right now, certainly not a nurse promising parents she could save this child with his chest crushed and his internal organs a jigsaw puzzle. Not when she had spent the last forty-eight hours solid doing research, and her body was screaming at her for sleep and nourishment. She blocked out all noises, all voices, and focused completely on the task at hand. She would not lose this little boy. She wouldn't. It was that simple to her. She never gave herself any other choice, never allowed any other thought into her mind. She had a good team, knew they worked well with her, meshing like a finely tuned machine. She never had to look to see if they were reacting to what she wanted or needed; they were always there for her. If she

17

was able to save her patients, where others couldn't, it wasn't by her efforts alone.

She bent closer to the little boy, pushing out everything but her desire for this child to live. As she was reaching to take the instrument her nurse was handing her, something struck at her. Pain gripped her, consumed her, sweeping through her body like a terrible fire. She had felt such agony only one other time, a couple of years earlier. She had never managed to discover what had been wrong with her. The pain had simply disappeared after nearly twenty-four hours. Now, with a child's life hanging by a thread, depending upon her skills, she did not have the luxury of fainting. Agony gripped her, twisted her insides, and took the breath from her lungs. Shea struggled to control herself; years of forcing her mind to remain under strict discipline stood her in good stead. As she did with every other distraction, she forced the pain out of her mind, took a deep breath, and concentrated on the child.

The nurse closest to her regarded the doctor with complete shock. In all the time she had worked with O'Halloran, admiring her, almost idolizing her, she had never seen the surgeon lose her focus, not even for a second. This time, Shea had stood perfectly still — a few heartbeats, that was all — but the nurse couldn't help noticing because it was so unusual. Her hands had trembled, and she had broken out in a sweat. Automatically the nurse reached up to wipe the moisture from the doctor's forehead. To her horror, the cloth came away stained with blood. Droplets were beading up, seeping through her pores. The nurse wiped the surgeon's forehead a second time, attempting to hide the cloth from the others. She had never seen anything like it.

Then Shea was once more herself, snapping instantly back to attention. The nurse swallowed all her questions and returned to work, the images of what Dr. O'Halloran needed coming into her mind so fast, she had no time to think about the strange phenomenon anymore. She had long ago become used to knowing what the doctor needed before she asked for it.

Shea felt an unfamiliar presence in her mind, felt the dark malevolence beating at her for one more heartbeat before she closed it out; then her attention was completely taken up with the child and the shredded jumble that was his chest. He would not die. She would not allow it. You hear me, child? I'm here with you, and I will not let you die, *she silently vowed. She meant it. She always meant it. It was as if part of her merged with her patients and somehow managed to keep them alive until modern medicine could kick in.*

Jacques slept for some time. It didn't

19

matter to him how long it had been. Hunger was waiting. Pain was waiting. The treacherous heart and soul of a woman were waiting. He had an eternity to gather what strength he could, and she could never escape him now that he knew the mental path to her mind. He slept the sleep of immortals, his lungs and heart stopped as he lay in the earth, his body close to the soil it so desperately needed to aid healing, yet a thin layer of wood away. When he awakened, he scratched at the walls of his coffin patiently. He would reach the healing soil someday. He had managed to make a small hole to coax his prey to him. He could wait. She would never escape him. She was his single-minded purpose.

He haunted her. Day or night. It didn't matter to him. He no longer knew the difference when it had mattered so much before. He lived to try to appease his ever-present hunger. He lived for revenge. For retribution. He lived to make her life a living hell during his waking hours. He became good at it. Taking possession of her mind for minutes at a time. It was impossible to figure her out. She was so complex. There were things in her brain that made little sense to him, and the few moments he could stay awake without losing his precious remaining blood did not give him sufficient time to understand her.

There was the time she was frightened. He could taste her fear. Feel her heart pounding so that his own matched the terrible rhythm. Still, her mind remained calm in the center of the storm, receiving quick, brilliant flashes of data she processed so quickly that he nearly missed them. Two strangers were hunting her. Taunting her. He also saw an image of himself, his thick hair hanging in strands around his ravaged face, his body savaged by brutal hands. He clearly saw the stake driven deep within his tissue and sinews. It flashed for a moment in her mind, there was the impression of grief, and then he lost contact.

Shea would never forget their faces, their eyes, and the smell of their sweat. One of them, the taller of the two, couldn't take his eyes from her. "Who are you?" She stared at them, wide-eyed, innocent, totally harmless. Shea knew she looked young and helpless, too small to give them trouble.

"Jeff Smith," the tall one said gruffly. His eyes devoured her. "This is my partner, Don Wallace. We need you to come with us and answer a few questions."

"Am I wanted for something? I'm a doctor, gentlemen. I can't just pick up and go. I'm due

21

in surgery in an hour. Perhaps you could arrange to ask your questions when my shift is over."

Wallace grinned at her. He thought he looked charming. Shea thought he looked like a shark. "We can't do that, Doc. It isn't only our questions, there's an entire committee looking to talk with you." He laughed softly, a film of perspiration on his forehead. He enjoyed inflicting pain, and Shea was altogether too cool, too haughty.

Shea made certain her desk was solidly between her and the men. Taking great care to move slowly and appear unconcerned, she glanced down at her computer, typed in the command to destroy her data, and hit the enter key. Then she picked up her mother's diary, and slipped it into her purse. She accomplished everything easily, naturally. "Are you certain you have the right person?"

"Shea O'Halloran, your mother was Margaret 'Maggie' O'Halloran from Ireland?" Jeff Smith recited. "You were born in Romania, your father is unknown?" There was a taunting note in his voice.

She turned the full power of her emerald eyes on the man, watched coolly as he squirmed uneasily, as he became consumed with desire for her. Smith was far more susceptible than his partner was. "Is that supposed to upset me, Mr.

22

Smith? I am who I am. My father has nothing to do with it."

"No?" Wallace stepped closer to the desk. "Don't you need blood? Crave it? Don't you drink it?" His eyes glowed with hatred.

Shea burst out laughing. Her laughter was soft, sexy, a melody to listen to forever. "Drink blood? Is this some kind of joke? I don't have time for this nonsense."

Smith licked his lips. "You don't drink blood?" His voice held a hopeful note.

Wallace looked at him sharply. "Don't look into her eyes," he snarled. "You should know that by now."

Shea's eyebrows shot up. She laughed again softly, inviting Smith to join her. "I occasionally require a transfusion. It isn't uncommon. Haven't you ever heard of hemophilia? Gentlemen, you are wasting my time." Her voice dropped even lower, a soft seduction of musical notes. "You really should leave."

Smith scratched his head. "Maybe we've got the wrong woman. Look at her. She's a doctor. She's nothing like the others. They're tall and strong and have dark hair. She's delicate, petite, a redhead. And she goes out in the sunlight."

"Shut up," Wallace snapped. "She's one of them. We should have gagged her. She's turning you with her voice." His eyes slid over her, making her flesh crawl. "She'll talk." He grinned evilly. "Now I've scared you. It's about time. You'll cooperate, O'Halloran, the hard way or the easy way. Actually, I prefer the hard way."

"I'll bet you do. Just what do you want from me?"

"Proof that you're a vampire." Wallace hissed.

"You've got to be kidding. Vampires don't exist. There's no such thing," she goaded, needing information and willing to acquire it from any source, even if it meant prompting men as sick as these two.

"No? I've met several." Wallace grinned his evil grin again. "Perhaps a friend or two of yours." He threw several photographs onto the desk, his eyes daring her to look at them. His excitement was palpable.

Keeping her face blank, Shea picked up the pictures. Her stomach lurched, bile rose, but her training didn't let her down. The photographs were numbered, eight of them in all. Each of the victims was blindfolded, gagged, manacled, all in various stages of torment. Don Wallace was a butcher. She touched a fingertip to the one tagged with a number two, experiencing a sudden, unexpected wrench. A boy no more than eighteen.

Quickly, before tears could well up, she

24

flipped through the rest of the photographs. Number seven was a man with a mane of jet-black hair — the man haunting her dreams! There was no denying it. No mistake. She knew every angle and plane of his face — the well-cut mouth, the dark, expressive eyes, the long hair. Anguish welled up. For a moment she felt his pain, a sharp agony of mind and body driving out all sane thoughts until there was only room for pain, hatred, and hunger. She brushed the pad of her thumb over the tormented face lightly, almost lovingly. A caress. The pain and hatred only grew stronger. Hunger became all consuming. The emotions were so strong, so alien to her nature, she had a strange feeling that something or someone was sharing her mind. Disoriented for a moment, Shea dropped the photos onto the desk.

"It was you two in Europe a few years back, the 'vampire' killings, wasn't it? You murdered all those innocent people." Shea made the accusation calmly.

Don Wallace didn't deny it. "And now I've got you."

"If vampires are such powerful creatures, how did you manage to kill so many of them?" Sarcasm dripped deliberately to egg him on.

"Their males are very competitive." Wallace laughed harshly. "They don't like one another. They need women, and they don't like to share.

They turn on each other, place someone into our hands. Still, they are strong. No matter how they suffer, they never talk. Which in some ways is fine, since they can mesmerize with their voices. But you'll talk, Doc. I'll have all the time in the world with you. Did you know when a vampire's in agony, it sweats blood?"

"Surely I would know that if I were a vampire. I've never sweated blood in my life. Let's see if I have this straight. Vampires stalk not only humans but also each other. The males betray one another to you human butchers because they need females. I thought they could just bite women and turn them into vampires." Sarcastically she was ticking off each item on her fingers. "You want me to believe I'm one of these fictitious creatures, so powerful that my voice alone can enslave this strong man here." Deliberately she gestured toward Jeff Smith, flashing him a gentle smile. "Gentlemen, I'm a doctor. I save lives every day. I sleep in a bed, not in a coffin. I am not the least bit strong, and I have never sucked anyone's blood in my life." She glanced at Don Wallace. "You, however, admittedly have tortured and mutilated men, even murdered them. And evidently you derive great pleasure from this. I don't believe you two are cops, or officials of any law-abiding agency. I think you are the monsters." She turned her emerald eyes back to Jeff

26

Smith, her voice low, seductive. "Do you really think I'm a danger to you?"

He seemed to be falling forward into her beckoning gaze. He had never wanted a woman more. He blinked, cleared his throat, and stole a slow, calculating look at Wallace. Smith had never noticed that greedy, cold look on his partner's face before. "No, no, of course you're not a danger to me or anyone else."

"Damn it, Jeff, let's get her and get the hell out of here," Wallace snarled, the need to teach her who was in charge riding him hard.

Emerald eyes slid over Smith, fastened on his mesmerized gaze. She could feel his desire, and she fed it, fed his fantasies of her welcoming his attentions. She had learned at a very young age that she could get into people's minds, manipulate their thoughts. Initially it had terrified her to wield that kind of power, but it was a useful tool in the O.R., and it was useful now, when she was threatened.

"Don, why don't they just turn human women? That would make sense. And why did the vampire just quit helping us? We left the area in a big hurry, and you never did tell me what went wrong," Smith said suspiciously.

"Are you trying to say one of these male vampires actually helped you in your campaign to kill others and that's how you were so successful?" Shea asked, a little sneer of disbelief in her voice.

"He was nasty, vengeful. He hated the kid, but he particularly despised this one here." Smith tapped the photograph of the man with the long black hair. "He wanted him tortured, burned, to feel it."

"Shut up," Wallace snapped. "Let's get it over. She's worth a hundred thousand dollars to the society. They want to study her."

Shea laughed softly. "If I truly was one of your mythical vampires, I should be worth far more than that to your 'research' committee. I think your partner is holding out on you, Mr. Smith."

The truth was there to read on Wallace's face. When Smith turned to confront him, Shea made her move: she leapt out the window, landed on her feet like a cat, and ran for her life. She had no personal items she was concerned about, no favorite memento. Her one regret was the loss of her books.

When he felt her fear, Jacques experienced the need to protect her. The urge was as strong as his desire to revenge himself. Whatever he had done, and he was the first to admit he couldn't remember, he couldn't possibly deserve such a horrendous punishment. Once again sleep overtook him, but it was the first time in months he had not filled her body with his pain or possessed her mind for a few seconds, ensuring that she felt his dark anger and promise of retribution. This time he hadn't punished her. Only he had the right to put fear into her mind, into her fragile, trembling body. She had looked upon his image with a mixture of puzzlement and regret. Did she think he was dead and it was his damned soul haunting her? What went on in the head of a treacherous woman?

Time continued endlessly. Wake when a creature strayed near. Scratch and claw at the decaying wood. Eventually the cloth over his eyes rotted until it fell away from him. He had no idea how long he had been there. It made no difference to him. Dark was dark. Isolation, isolation. His only companion was the woman in his mind. The woman who had betrayed him, forsaken him. At times he called to her, ordered her to come to him. Threatened her. Pleaded. Perverse as it was, he needed her. He was already deranged; he accepted that. But this total isolation was making him completely mad. Without her touch, he would be lost to the world, not even his will keeping him going. And he had a need to live: retribution. He needed her as much as he loathed and despised her. As twisted as their relationship was, he needed the moments of companionship.

She was physically closer to him now, not an ocean away. She had been so far away from him, he could barely make it across the distance. But now she was much closer. He renewed his efforts, calling her at all hours, striving to keep her from sleep.

When he could manage to get past the pain and hunger and simply remain quiet, a shadow in her mind, she intrigued him. She was obviously intelligent, brilliant even. Her method of thinking was like that of a machine, processing information at incredible speed. She seemed to be able to push aside all emotion; perhaps she wasn't capable of feeling emotion. He found himself admiring her brain, her thinking patterns, the way she focused wholly on her work. She was researching a disease, seemed obsessed with finding a cure. Perhaps that was why he often found her in the dimly lit room, covered in blood, her hands buried deep within a body. She was conducting experiments. It didn't excuse the abomination of what she was, but he could admire her single-minded purpose. She was able to put aside her need for sleep, for sustenance, for long periods. He felt her need, but she concentrated so wholly on what she was doing, she didn't seem to recognize her body's cries for normal care.

There seemed to be no laughter in her life, no real closeness to anyone. That was odd to him. Jacques was unsure when that began to bother him, but he found it did. She had no one. She concentrated only on what she was doing. Of course, he would not have tolerated another male's presence in her life; he would have sought to destroy any other that came near her. He told himself it was because whatever male came near her must be in on the conspiracy to make him suffer. He often resented wanting to talk to her, but she had an interesting mind. And she was everything to him. His Savior. His tormentor. Without her presence, without touching her mind, he would have been completely insane, and he knew it. She unwittingly shared her strange life with him, gave him something to concentrate on, a companionship of sorts. In a way it was ironic. She thought him locked underground. She thought herself safe from his vengeance. But she had created the monster, and now she was keeping him going, his strength growing with his every touch to her mind.

He found her again a month later, perhaps a year later, he didn't know, didn't care. Her heart was pounding in fear. So was his. Perhaps the overwhelming intensity of her emotion woke him. The pain was excruciating, the hunger engulfing him, yet his heartbeat was frantically matching hers, and he could not find enough lung power to breathe. She feared for her life. Someone was hunting her. Perhaps the others who had helped betray him had now turned on her. He gathered himself, waited, blocking out pain and hunger as he had learned over the years to do. No one would harm her. She belonged to him. Only he could decide whether she lived or died, no one else. If he could manage to "see" the enemy through her eyes, he could destroy them. He felt his power swelling in him, his rage so intense, so potent at the idea that someone might take her from him that it astonished him.

The picture was clear. She was in a shelter of some kind, clothing and furniture overturned all around her as if there had been a fight or someone had searched her belongings. She was running through the rooms, grabbing a few things along the way. He caught glimpses of wild red hair, silky soft, vibrant. He wanted to touch that hair. To sink his fingers into its thickness. To wrap it around her neck and strangle her with it. To bury his face in it. Then the image was gone, his strength drained, and he slumped impotently in his prison, unable to reach her, to help her, to see that she was safe. That added to his torment of agony and hunger. That added to the debt she already owed him.

He remained quiet and slowed his heart until it barely beat, only enough to allow him to think, to gather himself for one last try. If she survived, he was going to bring her to him. He would not allow any more attempts on her life. If she lived or died, it was to be his decision alone. *Come to me, come here to me. The Carpathian Mountains. The remote, wild regions where you should be, where your home is, your people are. Come to me.* He sent the call, filled her mind with the compulsion. It was strong. The strongest he had been able to accomplish. It was done. It was all he could do without further endangering his own life. So close to his goal, he would not take any foolish risks.

They had found her again. And again Shea O'Halloran ran for her life. She had been more careful this time, now that she was aware she was being hunted. She had plenty of cash hidden in various locations; her truck, a four-wheel drive, had a camper shell, so she could live in it if necessary. She kept essentials packed so all she had to do was grab a bag and run. Where this time? Where could she go to lose them? She was driving fast, racing from those who would dissect her like an insect, those who looked upon her as something less than human.

She knew she had little time to live. Her strength was already wearing down. The terrible disease was taking its toll, and she was no closer to finding a cure than when she'd started. She had most likely inherited the illness from her father. The father she had never met, never knew, the father who had abandoned her mother before Shea was even born. She had read her mother's diary so many times. The father who had stolen her mother's love, her very life, so that she was a mere shadow, not a real person anymore. The father who didn't care in the least for her mother or herself.

She was already driving in the general direction of the Carpathian Mountains, her father's birthplace. The land of superstition and myth. The rare blood disorder she suffered from could very well have originated there. Suddenly she was excited, focusing her mind completely on the data so that she pushed aside fear. This had to be the origin. So many vampire myths had begun there. She easily recalled every detail of every story she had ever read or heard. She could be on the right trail at last. The evidence had been in her mother's diary all along. Shea was disgusted with herself for not recognizing it sooner. She had developed such an aversion to the idea of her father or any of his family, she hadn't stopped to consider tracking her own roots to find the answers she was seeking. Her mother's diary. She knew every tragic entry by heart.

I met him tonight. The moment I saw him I knew he was the one. Tall, handsome, with mesmerizing eyes. His voice is the most beautiful thing I have ever heard. He feels the same way about me. I know he does. It is wrong, of course — he is a married man — but there is no way out for us. We cannot be apart. Rand. That is his name — foreign, like him, like his accent. The Carpathian Mountains are his home. How could I have ever existed without him?

His wife, Noelle, gave birth two months ago to a boy. I know he was bitterly disappointed. For some reason, it is important he have a female child. He is with me all the time, even though I am often alone. He is in my mind, talking to me, whispering how much he loves me. He has a strange blood disorder and cannot go out into the sun.

He has such strange habits. When we make love, and you can't imagine how glorious it is, he is in my mind as well as my heart and body. He says it is because I am psychic and so is he, but I know it is more. It has something to do with his need to drink my blood. There. I wrote it where I could not say it aloud. It sounds awful, terrible, but it is so erotic, the feel of his mouth on me, my blood in his body. How I love him. There is rarely a mark unless he wishes to brand me as his. His tongue heals wounds quickly. I have seen it, like a miracle. He is a miracle.

His wife, Noelle, knows of me. He has told me she will not allow him to leave her, that she is dangerous. I know this is true because she threatened me, threatened to kill me. I was so afraid. Her eyes glowed red, and her teeth gleamed at me like an animal's, but Rand arrived before she could hurt me. He was furious, so protective of me. I know that he tells the truth when he says he loves me; I could tell by the way he spoke to her, commanding her to leave. How she hates me!

I am so happy! I am pregnant. He

doesn't know yet. I haven't seen him in two nights, but I'm certain he would never leave me. His wife must be protesting his leaving her. I hope the child is female. I know he wants a daughter desperately. I will give him the one thing he has always wished for, and Noelle will be in his past. I know I should feel guilt, but I cannot when it is obvious to both of us that he belongs with me. Where is he? Why doesn't he come to me when I need him so desperately? Why has he gone from my mind?

Shea cries constantly. The doctors are excited over her strange blood results. She needs transfusions daily. God, I hate her; she keeps me tied to this empty world. I know he is dead. The day Noelle came to see me, he returned alone for a few wonderful hours. He told me he was going to leave her. I believe he tried. He simply vanished, out of my mind, out of my life. My parents thought he left me because I was pregnant, that he used me, but I know he is dead. I felt his terrible agony, his grief. He would come to me if he could. And he never knew of the child. I would have joined him, but I had to give his daughter life. If his wife murdered him, and I am certain she is capable, he will live on through me, through our child.

I have brought her to Ireland. My parents are dead, and I have inherited their properties. I would have given her to them, but it's too late now. I cannot join him. I can't possibly leave her when so many ask questions about her. I'm afraid they will try to kill her. She is like him. The sun burns her easily. She needs blood as he did. The doctors whispered so much about her and stared at me in such a way, I was afraid. I knew I had to disappear with her. I won't allow anyone to harm your daughter, Rand. God help me, I cannot feel anything. I am dead inside without you. Where are you? Did Noelle murder you as she swore she would? How can I live without you? Only your daughter keeps me from joining you. Soon, my darling, very soon I will be with you.

Shea let her breath out slowly. Of course. It was there in front of her. *She needs blood as he did.* She had inherited the blood disorder from her father. Her mother had written that Rand actually took her blood when they were making love. How many people had been persecuted and had a stake driven through their heart just because no one had found the cure for their terrible disease? She knew what it was like to suffer such a thing, to loathe oneself and fear discovery. She had to find the cure; even if it was too late for her, she had to find the cure.

Jacques slept for a long time, determined to renew his strength. He woke only to feed briefly, to assure himself that she was alive and nearby. He contained his elation so that he would lose no more blood. He needed his strength now. She was so close, he could feel her. She was within a few miles of him. Twice he "saw" her cabin through her eyes. She was fixing it up, doing the things women did to make a rundown shelter a home. Later, Jacques began to awaken at regular intervals, testing his strength, drawing animals to him to give him much-needed blood. He haunted her dreams, called her continually, kept her awake when her body desperately needed sleep. She was already fragile, half-starved, weak from lack of feeding. She worked day and night, her mind filled with problems and solutions. He ignored all that to keep at her so that she would be so tired, he could easily hold her under compulsion to do his bidding.

He was patient. He had learned patience.

He knew he was closing in on her. He had time now. There was no need to hurry this. He could afford to grow in strength. From his dark grave he stalked her, every touch of his mind to hers making the connection between them that much stronger. He had no real idea of what he was going to do to her once she was in his hands. He wouldn't kill her right away; he had spent so long in her mind, it sometimes seemed as if they were one. But she would surely suffer. Once again he sent himself to sleep to conserve the remaining blood in his veins.

She was asleep at her computer, her head resting on a stack of papers. Even in her sleep, her mind was active. Jacques had learned many details about her. She had a photographic memory. He learned things from her mind that he had either forgotten or perhaps had never known. He often spent time studying before he subjected her to his harassment. She was a source of knowledge for him, knowledge of the outside world.

She was always alone. Even the flashes of long-ago memories he caught were of a small child isolated from others. He felt as if he knew her intimately, yet he really knew nothing personal about her. Her mind was filled with formulas and data, with instruments and chemistry. She never thought about her appearance or anything he would expect a woman to think about. Only her work. Anything else was quickly banished.

Jacques focused and aimed. *You will come to me now. You will not allow anything to stop you. Awaken, and come to me while I am resting and waiting.* He used every ounce of strength he possessed to embed the compulsion deep within her. He had forced her several times over the last two months or so to walk toward him, to be drawn through the darkened forest in the vicinity of his prison. Each time she had come his way as he had bidden her, but her need to complete her work had been so strong in her, she had eventually turned back. This time he was certain he had enough strength to force her compliance. She felt his presence within her, recognized his touch, but she had no real idea that they were linked. She thought of him as a dream — or rather, a nightmare.

Jacques smiled at that. But there was no amusement in the white flash of his teeth, only the promise of savagery, the promise of a predator stalking its prey.

Shea jerked awake, blinked to bring the room into focus. Her work was scattered everywhere, the computer on, the documents she had been studying a bit crumpled where her head had rested on them. The dream again. Would it never stop, leave her in peace? She was familiar with the man in the dream now, his thick mane of jet-black hair and the touch of cruelty around his sensuous mouth. In the first few years she had been unable to see his eyes in that nightmare dream, as if perhaps they were covered, but the last couple of years he had stared at her with black menace.

Shea shoved at her hair, felt the little beads of perspiration gathered on her forehead. For a moment she experienced the strange disorientation she always did after the dream, as if something held her mind for just a heartbeat of time, then slowly, with great reluctance, released her.

Shea knew she was being hunted. Where the dream was not reality, the fact that someone was stalking her was true. She could never lose sight of that, never forget. She would never be safe again, not unless she found a cure for herself and the handful of others who shared the same rare disease. She was being hunted as if she were an animal with no emotions or intelligence. It didn't matter to the hunters that she spoke six languages fluently, that she was a skilled surgeon, that she had saved countless lives.

The words on the paper in front of her

blurred, ran together. How long had it been since she had really slept? She sighed, swept a hand through her thick, waist-length, silky red hair, shoving it away from her face. She pulled it back rather haphazardly and, as always, secured it with whatever happened to be handy.

She began to review the symptoms of her strange blood disease. To catalog herself. She was small and very delicate, frail almost. She looked young, like a teenager, aging at a much slower rate than a normal human. Her eyes were enormous, vividly green. Her voice was soft, velvety, often called mesmerizing. When she lectured, most of the students were so enthralled by her voice, they remembered every word she spoke. Her senses were far superior to others of the human race, her hearing and sense of smell extremely acute. She saw colors more vividly, registered details most humans missed. She could communicate with animals, jump higher and run faster than many trained athletes. She had learned at an early age to hide her talents.

She stood up, stretched. She was dying slowly. Every minute that ticked by was a heartbeat less in the time she had to find the cure. Somewhere in all these boxes and reams of paper, there had to be a solution.

Even if she found the answer too late for herself, she could prevent those like her from the terrible isolation she had felt all her life.

She might age slowly and have exceptional abilities, but she paid a high price for them. The sun burned her skin. Although she could see clearly on the darkest night, her eyes had a hard time in the light of day. Her body rejected most foods, and worst of all, she had to have blood every day. Any blood. There was no blood incompatible with hers. Animal blood kept her alive — barely. She desperately needed human blood, and only when she was close to collapse did she allow herself to use it, and then only by transfusion. Unfortunately, her particular disease seemed to require oral transfusions.

Shea flung open the door, inhaled the night, listened to the breeze whispering of fox and marmots, of rabbits and deer. The cry of an owl missing its prey and the squeak of a bat sent blood rushing through her veins. She belonged here. For the first time in her lonely existence, she felt a semblance of peace.

Shea wandered outside to her porch. Her snug blue jeans and hiking boots were fine, but her thin T-shirt would not stave off the cold of the mountains. Snagging her sweat-shirt and hiking bag, Shea hurried out to the beckoning land. If only she had known of this place earlier. She had wasted so much time. Just a month ago she had discovered the healing properties in the soil here. She had already known of the healing agent in her saliva. Shea had planted a garden, vegetable and herb. She loved working in the soil. Quite by accident she had cut herself, a rather deep and nasty gash. The earth seemed to ease the pain, and the cut was nearly closed by the time she finished working.

She began to wander aimlessly along the trail, wishing her mother could have experienced this place of peace. Poor Maggie. Young. Irish. On vacation for the first time in her life, she had met a dark, brooding stranger, one who had used her and discarded her. Shea shook her head, tears welling up; she refused to shed them. Her mother had made her choice. One man. He had become her life to the exclusion of everything else. To the exclusion of her own flesh and blood, her daughter. Shea had not been worth the effort of trying, of living. Only Rand. A man who had deserted her without thought, without warning. A man who had passed on a disease so vile, his daughter had to hide it from the rest of the world. And Maggie had known. Yet Maggie hadn't bothered to research it or even to ask questions of Rand to find out just what her daughter would be facing.

Shea stooped to grasp a handful of soil, then let it trail through her fingers. Had Noelle, the woman her mother had named as his wife, been as obsessed with Rand as Maggie had? It sounded very much as if she had. Shea had no intentions of ever taking a chance that she shared her mother's failings. She would never need a man so much that she would neglect a child and eventually kill herself. Her mother's death had been a senseless tragedy, and she had abandoned Shea to a cold, cruel life without love or guidance. Maggie had known her daughter needed blood; it was all there in the diary, every damning word. Shea's fist clenched until her knuckles turned white. Maggie knew Rand's saliva carried a healing agent. She had known that, yet she had left it to her daughter to find out on her own.

Shea had healed herself countless times as a child while her mother stared dully out a window, half-alive, never once hearing a toddler's cries of pain when she fell learning to walk and run, learning everything alone. She had discovered the ability to heal small cuts and bruises with her tongue. It had taken a while before she realized she was unique in such a thing. Maggie had been an emotionless robot, caring for the barest minimum of Shea's physical needs and none of her emotional ones. Maggie had killed herself the day Shea turned eighteen. A low sound of sorrow escaped Shea's throat. It had been terrible enough to know she had to have blood to exist, but to grow up knowing her mother couldn't love her had been devastating.

Seven years ago, a kind of madness had swept Europe. It had seemed so laughable at first. For eons uneducated, superstitious people had whispered of the existence of vampires in this region her father had come from.

It now seemed probable that a blood disorder, perhaps originating here in the Carpathian Mountains, had been the basis of the vampire legends. If the disease was indigenous only to this region, wasn't it possible that those persecuted down through the ages had suffered from this condition Shea's father and she shared? Shea's excitement had set in at the prospect of studying others like herself.

Then the modern-day "vampire" killings had swept through Europe like a plague.

Men mostly, murdered in ritual vampire style, stakes through the heart. It was sickening, repugnant, frightening. Respected scientists had begun to discuss the possibility of vampires being real. Committees had been formed to study — and eliminate — them. Evidence from some earlier source, combined with samples of a female child's blood — hers, Shea was certain — had raised further questions. Shea had been terrified, certain those murdering in Europe might try to find her. And now, indeed, they were attempting to track her down. She had had to abandon her country and her career there to pursue her own line of research.

How could anyone in these educated times believe in such nonsense as vampires? She identified with those murdered people, certain she shared the same blood disorder. She was a doctor, a researcher, yet up until now she had failed all its victims, fearful of the discovery of what she thought of as her loathsome little secret. It angered her. She was gifted, brilliant even; she should have unlocked the secrets of this thing long ago. How many others had died because she hadn't been aggressive enough in her search for data?

Her guilt and fear now fed her wild, exhaustive sessions of study. She accumulated everything she could find on the area, the people, and the legends. Rumors, supposed evidence, old translations, and the latest newspaper articles. She rarely ate, rarely remembered to give herself transfusions, rarely slept, always searching for that one piece of the puzzle that would give her a trail to follow. She studied her blood endlessly, her saliva, her blood after animal intake, after human transfusions.

Shea had reluctantly burned her mother's diary; she would never forget a single word, but she still felt the loss of it deeply. Her bank account, however, was substantial. She had inherited funds from her mother, and she had made good money in her profession. She even owned property in Ireland that rented out for a sizable amount. She lived frugally and invested wisely. It had been easy enough to move her money to Switzerland and lay a few false trails through the Continent.

From the moment she had entered the range of the Carpathian mountains, Shea felt different. More alive. More at peace. The unrest, the sense of urgency in her grew, but she felt as if she had a home for the first time in her life. The plants, the trees, the wildlife, the very earth itself felt a part of her. As if somehow she was related to them. She loved breathing the air, wading in the water, touching the soil.

Shea caught the scent of a rabbit, and her body stilled. She could hear its heartbeat, feel its fear. The animal sensed danger, a predator stalking it. A fox; she caught the whisper of fur sliding through the underbrush. It was wonderful to hear, to feel things, to not be afraid of hearing things others couldn't. Bats wheeled and dipped, diving at insects, and Shea raised her face to the heavens, watching their antics, taking pleasure in the simple show. She began to walk again, needing the exercise, needing to put the weight of responsibility from her shoulders for a time.

She had found her cottage, the barest bones of a home, and over the last few months had turned it into a sanctuary. Shutters blocked out the sunlight during the day. A generator provided the lights and necessary power for her computer. A modern bathroom and kitchen had been the next priority. Slowly Shea had acquired books, supplies, and everything needed for the emergency care of patients. Though Shea hoped never to have to use her skills here — the fewer people who knew of her existence, the better off she was and the more time she could devote to her valuable research — she was, first and always, a doctor.

Shea entered the thick forest of trees, touched their trunks reverently. She always kept a supply of blood on hand, using her hacker skills when necessary to tap into blood banks in ways that allowed for payment but preserved her anonymity. Still, that required monthly trips, alternating among the three villages within a night's travel of her cabin. Lately she had grown so much weaker that fatigue was a major problem, and bruises were refusing to heal. A craving in her was growing, an emptiness begging to be filled. Her life was drawing to a close.

Shea yawned. She needed to go back and sleep. Normally she never slept at night, saving her down time for afternoon, when the sun took the heaviest toll on her body. She was miles from her house, in deep forest, high in the remotest part of the mountains. She came this way often, drawn inexplicably to the area. She felt restless, an almost overwhelming sense of urgency. She needed to be somewhere, but she had no idea where. When she analyzed how she felt, she realized that the force urging her onward was almost a compulsion.

She had every intention of turning around

and going home, but her feet continued along the uphill path. There were wolves in these mountains; she often heard them singing at night. There was such joy in their voices, such beauty in their song. She could touch the minds of animals when she chose, but she had never attempted such a thing with a creature as wild and unpredictable as a wolf. Still, their nightly songs almost made her wish she might encounter one now.

She continued to move forward, pulled toward an unknown destination. Nothing seemed to matter but that she continue moving upward, always higher, into the wildest, most isolated area she had ever been in. She should have been afraid, but the farther she got from her cabin, the more important it seemed for her to go on.

Her hands went up absently, rubbing at her temples, her forehead. There was a curious buzzing in her head. Strange how hunger gnawed at her insides. It wasn't normal hunger; it was different. Again she had the strange feeling that she was sharing her mind with another being and the hunger was not really hers. Part of the time it seemed as though she was walking in a dream world. Tails of mist wound around the trees, hovered above the ground. The fog was beginning to thicken a bit, the air temperature dropping several degrees.

Shea shivered, ran her hands up and down her arms. Her feet picked a path, missing rotting logs. She was always astonished at how silently she could move through this forest, instinctively avoiding fallen twigs and loose rocks. Something rippled in her mind. *Where are you? Why do you refuse to come to me?* That voice was a venomous hiss of fury. She stopped, horrified, and pressed both hands to her head. It was her nightmare, the same voice calling to her, echoing in her mind. The nightmares were coming more often, haunting her sleep, disturbing her waking hours, creeping into her consciousness at all hours. Sometimes she thought she might go mad.

Shea approached a rippling stream. Stepping stones, vibrant splashes of color, flat and welcoming, paved her way across the crystal-clear water. The stream was icy cold when she bent to idly trail her fingers in it. The feel was soothing.

Something compelled her forward. First one foot, then the other. It was madness to go so far from her cabin. She was too many hours without sleep. She even considered she was sleepwalking, she felt so strange. Shea paused near a small clearing and stared up at the starlit sky. She didn't even realize she was moving again until she had crossed the clearing and was in a thick grove of trees. A branch snagged in her hair, forcing her to stop again. Her head felt heavy, her mind clouded. She needed to be somewhere desperately, but she didn't know where. Listening didn't help. With her acute hearing, she would have heard if any person or creature was hurt or in trouble. Shea sniffed the night air. She would probably get lost and be caught out in the open and the sun would fry her. She would deserve it for this stupidity.

Although she laughed at herself, the feeling was so powerful that Shea walked on, allowing her body to ramble where it wanted to go. An almost nonexistent path, heavily grown over, weaved in and out of brambles and trees. She followed it faithfully, intrigued now, wondering what could draw her away from her research. Woods gave way to a higher meadow. She crossed the open field, and her pace began to pick up as if she had a purpose. At the far end of the meadow, a few scattered trees looked down on the remains of an old building. It had been no small cabin but a good-sized home, now blackened and crumbling, the forest creeping back to take what had once belonged to it.

She walked along the structure's perimeters, certain something had brought her to this place but unable to identify the reason. It was a place of power, she could feel that, but for what or how to use it, she had no idea. She paced, her body restless, a relentless pressure in her mind, as if she were on the verge of a great discovery. Squatting low, she let her hands run idly through the soil. Once. Twice. Her fingers found timber beneath the dirt. Shea's breath caught in her throat, and her pulse jumped with excitement. She had discovered something important. She was certain of it. Carefully brushing away the topsoil, she uncovered a large door, six feet by four with a solid metal pull. It took all her strength to lift it, and she had to sit still for a few moments to catch her breath and summon the nerve to look into the hole. Rickety steps, rotted and cracked with age, led downward into a large room. A moment of hesitation and Shea went, her body and mind pulling her when her brain wanted to be more cautious.

The walls of the cellar were constructed of earth and crumbling stone. No one, nothing, had disturbed the place in years. Shea's head went up alertly, eyes scanning the area quickly, senses flaring out, looking for danger. There was nothing. That was the trouble. It was totally silent. Eerily so. No night creatures, no insects. No animal tracks in the dirt. She could not detect so much as a rat scurrying or the shine of a spider's web.

Her hand of its own accord began to skim along a wall. Nothing. Shea wanted out of there. Some sense of self-preservation urged her to leave. She shook her head, unable to depart even though the place distressed her. For one horrible moment, her imagination overtook her, and she felt something watching her, lying in wait, dark and deadly. It was so real that she nearly ran, but just as she turned, determined to flee while she had the chance, her fingers found more wood beneath the earthen wall.

Curious, Shea examined the surface. Something had been deliberately covered up here. Age had not mounded the earth this way. Unable to stop herself, she dug away handfuls of soil and loose rock until she uncovered a long strip of rotting wood. Another door? It was at least six feet high, maybe more. She dug in earnest now, carelessly throwing clumps of dirt behind her. Then her fingers brushed something ghastly.

She recoiled, leaping back as dried little carcasses fell to the ground. Dead rats.

Hundreds of withered bodies. Horrified, she stared at the rotting box she had uncovered. The remaining dirt holding it in place shifted, and the box fell forward, part of its lid giving way. Shea backed all the way to the stairs, alarmed at her find. The pressure in her head increased until she cried out with the pain, falling to one knee before she could climb the steep, rickety stairs leading out into the fog-filled night.

Surely it wasn't a coffin. Who would bury a body upright in a wall that way? Something — morbid curiosity, some compulsion she couldn't overcome — forced her feet back to the box. She actually tried to stop herself from moving forward, but she couldn't. Her hand trembled as she reached out gingerly to shove off the rotting lid.

Chapter Two

Shea stood frozen, for a moment unable to breathe or even think. Was the answer in front of her in all its stark ugliness? Was this thing, tortured and mutilated, her future, the future of those like her? She closed her eyes briefly, trying to shut out the reality. The brutality of mankind to do this. Tears welled up for the pain and suffering this creature had endured before his death. She felt responsible. She had been given such special gifts, yet she had been unable to unlock the secrets to the disease that condemned those who suffered as she did.

She took a breath, made herself look. He had been alive when his attackers sealed up the coffin. He had scratched at the wood, eventually working a hole in the side of it. Shea stifled a sob, feeling a kinship for this poor murdered man. His body was covered with a thousand cuts. A wooden stake, as big around as a man's fist, had been driven through his body near the vicinity of his heart. Whoever had done it needed a lesson in anatomy. She sucked in her breath, appalled. What he must have suffered!

His hands and ankles were manacled; rotting, dirty rags lay in strips across his chest like those of a mummy. The doctor in her took over to allow a closer clinical study. It was impossible to tell how long he had been dead. By the condition of the cellar and the coffin, she would have guessed a number of years, but the body had not yet started to decompose. Lines of agony still creased the man's face. His skin was gray and stretched tightly over the bones. The signs of suffering were stamped on that face, harsh and merciless.

And she knew him. He was the man in her dreams.

Although it seemed impossible, there was no mistake; she had seen him enough times. And he was the man in the photograph Don Wallace had shown her. Though it all seemed out of the realm of possibility, she felt linked to him, felt she should have saved him. Grief was welling up, real grief. Shea felt as if a part of her lay dead in the coffin.

Shea touched his dirty, raven-black hair with gentle fingers. He must have had the same rare blood disorder as she had. How many others had been hunted, persecuted, tortured, and murdered for something they were born with? "I'm sorry," she whispered softly, meaning it. "I failed all of us."

A slow hiss of air was her only warning. Eyelids snapped open, and she was staring into eyes blazing with venomous hatred. A burst of strength shattered one rusty manacle, and a hand fastened around her throat with a grip like a vise. He was so strong, he cut off her airway, so it was impossible even to scream. Everything seemed to swirl, black and white rushing to overtake her. She had just enough time to feel regret that she would be unable to help him, to feel searing pain as teeth tore into her exposed throat.

Let it happen fast. Shea didn't struggle; she knew it was useless. In any case someone owed this tormented creature something, and she had long ago accepted death. She was terrified, of course, but strangely calm. If she could somehow give him a measure of peace, she wanted to do so. Guilt for not finding a cure was uppermost in her mind. And something else, something elemental, as old as time itself. The need to save him. The knowledge that he must live and that she was willing to offer up her life for his.

Shea woke dizzy and weak. She had a headache, and her throat was so sore that she was afraid to move. She frowned, unable to recognize her surroundings. She heard herself moan. She was lying in the dirt, one arm locked behind her, something tight around her wrist. She tugged to get her arm back, but the band tightened, threatening to crush her fragile bones. Her heart jumped, and with her free hand she touched her throat, remembering. Her neck was swollen and bruised. There was a wound, too, torn and aching. Her mouth felt odd, a faint coppery taste coating her tongue.

She had lost too much blood, she knew immediately. Her head was splintering, fragmenting as the pressure increased. She knew the creature was responsible, attempting to get inside her mind. Moistening her lips carefully, she inched backward, closer to the coffin, to take the pressure from her arm. His fingers still encircled her small wrist like a handcuff, a vise that threatened to crush her bones if she made one wrong move. Another moan escaped before she could prevent it. She wanted to believe this was a nightmare. Steeling herself, Shea turned her head slowly to look at him.

The movement was intensely painful, taking her breath away. Her eyes locked with his. Involuntarily Shea struggled, tried to get away. His eyes, as black as night, burned at her. Fierce hatred, venomous rage, were concentrated in the soulless depths. His fingers tightened, crushing her wrist, locking her to him, dragging a cry of pain and fear from her bruised throat. Her head pounded.

"Stop!" Shea's forehead cracked against the side of the coffin in her struggles. "If you hurt me, I can't help you." She raised her head to meet those black eyes. "Do you understand? I'm all you've got." She forced herself to hold that black gaze. Fire. Ice. He had the most frightening eyes she had ever encountered. "My name is Shea O'Halloran. I'm a doctor." She repeated it in several languages, gave up when his eyes continued to burn at her. He seemed to have no mercy in him.

Not soulless. An animal. Trapped. Hurt. Confused. A predator dangerous beyond belief, reduced to a helpless shell. "I'll help you if you let me," she crooned softly, as if coaxing a wild animal. She used the power of her voice shamelessly. Hypnotic, gentle, soothing. "I'll need tools and a vehicle. Do you understand?"

She leaned over him, her free hand gingerly touching his mutilated chest. Fresh blood was seeping around the stake, leaking from his many other cuts as if they were recent. His wrist had a fresh, ragged tear in it that she was certain had not been there earlier. "My God, you must be in terrible pain. Don't move. I can't take that stake out until I get you back to my cabin. You'll bleed to death." Shockingly, his color was slightly better.

The creature released her slowly, reluctantly, his gaze never leaving her face. His hand reached down to scrape up the earth, bring it to the terrible wounds. Of course! The soil. She helped him, scooping up handfuls of the richest dirt to spread over his cuts. There were so many. After the first handful, he lay still, conserving his energy, his gaze fastened on her like a brand. He never blinked, his dark eyes never once wavering.

Shea glanced upward toward the cellar entrance nervously. Much time had passed while she was unconscious. The sun would be coming up soon. She bent over him, stroked back his hair gently, a strange tenderness stealing over her. For some unexplained reason she felt drawn to this poor creature, and the sensation was far stronger than her natural compassion, her need as a doctor to help. She wanted him to live. He had to live. She had to find a way to take away his terrible pain. "I have to get some things. I'll hurry as fast as I can, but I'll come back, I promise." She rose to her feet, turned to go, taking one step.

He moved so fast that he was a blur, his

hand clamping around her neck, jerking her off her feet so that she fell across him. His teeth ripped at her exposed throat, the pain excruciating. He fed voraciously, a wild animal out of control. She struggled against the pain, against the futility of what he was doing. He was killing the one person who could save him. Her hand, flailing blindly, found his jet-black hair. Her fingers tangled in the dirty, thick mane, remained there when she slumped nearly lifeless across his upper chest. The last thing she heard before she passed out was his heartbeat. Shockingly, her own heart tried to follow the steady, strong rhythm.

There was silence, then a gasping wheeze as her body struggled for survival. The creature stared dully at her limp, slender body. The stronger and more alert he became, the more pain washed over him, consumed him. He raised his free hand, bit his wrist, and forced the gushing wound over her mouth for the second time. He was uncertain what was happening around him, the pain was so intense. He had been buried for so long, he could not remember seeing anything in his lifetime but shades of gray and black. Now his eyes hurt from the vivid brightness of the colors surrounding him. He had to escape the kaleidoscope of hues, the pain increasing every moment and unfamiliar emotions threatening to drown him.

Shea woke slowly, facedown in the dirt. Her throat was raw and throbbing, the same sweet, coppery taste coating her mouth. She was sick and dizzy, and instinctively she realized the sun was at its peak. Her body felt like lead. Where was she? She was cold and disoriented. Shea pushed herself to her knees, then had to lower her head to avoid fainting. She had never been so weak, so helpless. It was a frightening feeling.

Awareness hit, and she scrambled on all fours across the dirt floor. With her back to the wall and the width of the room between them, she stared in horror at the coffin. He lay as if dead. No discernible heartbeat or respiration. Shea pressed the back of one shaking hand to her mouth to keep a sob from escaping. She was not going near him again, dead or not. Even as the thought came, as intelligent as it was, she still felt the need to find a way to help him. Something in her could not let it go.

Maybe she was wrong about the blood disorder. *Was* there such a thing as a vampire? He used his teeth; his incisors were sharp and must have an anticoagulant agent, just as his saliva must have a healing agent. She rubbed her pounding temples. The need to help him was compelling, overwhelming, so intense that she felt obsessed. Someone had taken their time torturing this man, derived pleasure from his suffering. They had inflicted as much pain as they could and then buried him alive. God only knew how long he had endured such a terrible thing. She had to help him whatever the cost to herself. It was inhumane to consider leaving him in such a state. It was more than she could bear.

With a sigh she pulled herself into a standing position, then leaned against the wall until the cellar stopped spinning. Vampire or human, she could not leave him to suffer slow starvation and death. He was in terrible pain; it was obvious he didn't understand what was happening. He was trapped in a world of agony and madness. "It is obvious you are out of your mind, Shea," she whispered aloud. She knew what she was experiencing was more than compassion and the need to heal. Something incredibly strong in her was committed to ensuring his survival. In a bizarre way she had lived with this man for years. He had been with her at all hours, sharing her mind, calling to her, begging her to come release him. She had left him here in this place of suffering and madness because she had not thought he was real. She would not fail him again.

The sun was blazing in the sky. If he suffered the same lethargic effects as she did, he was probably in a deep sleep and would not wake until sunset. It was go now or risk another attack if he awoke. The sun was going to burn her skin. She found her bag, rummaged for her dark glasses.

Crossing the meadow was a kind of hell. Even with dark glasses, the light hurt her eyes, kept them watering so that her vision was constantly blurred. Unable to see the uneven ground clearly, she fell several times. The sun beat at her, relentless in its assault. In the shadow of the forest, the trees provided some relief. But by the time she reached her cottage she hadn't a square inch of skin that wasn't bright red or blistering.

Once at home she examined her swollen neck and throat, the terrible bruises and ragged wounds. She looked grotesque, a hideous lobster, beaten and battered. Shea smeared aloe vera over her skin, then, working quickly, gathered tools, instruments, and ropes, arranging them in her truck. The windows in the camper were already blackened, but she would need to cover him to get him into the truck. She returned for a blanket.

A wave of dizziness drove her to her knees. She was very weak. She needed a transfusion desperately. If she was to save this man, she must first save herself. It had taken a couple of hours to make the trek back to the cottage, and she hated wasting more valuable time. Still, knowing she had no choice, she set up a transfusion, using one of the units of blood she kept on hand. It seemed to take forever, each minute dragging by feeling like an hour, giving her too much time to worry, to wonder.

Was the coffin too near the opening to the cellar? Why hadn't she noticed? If she had left him where the sun would touch him, he was burning alive while she was attending to what amounted to minor inconveniences. Oh, God, why couldn't she remember? Her head ached, her throat was raw, and most of all she was terrified. She did not want to feel his hand wrapped around her throat again. She did not want to think that she could have been so insensitive as to leave him where the sun might reach him. The thought made her physically ill.

Finally transfused, Shea quickly prepared the cabin for the surgery ahead, laying out instruments to remove the stake and sutures to repair the damage. At least she had blood to give him. She didn't allow herself to think further about the task before her as she drove back to the blackened ruins.

The sun was sliding toward the mountains by the time she positioned the truck in front of the cellar entrance and, using the winch, lowered cable into the hole. Taking a breath, afraid of what she might find, Shea made her way down the rickety stairs. Instantly she felt the impact of those burning eyes. Her heart thudded fearfully, but she forced herself to cross the floor until she was standing just out of his reach. He was watching her with a predator's unblinking stare. He had awakened alone, still trapped. Fear and pain and intolerable hunger clawed at him. His black eyes fastened on her face in accusation, in rage, with the dark promise of retaliation.

"Listen to me. Please try to understand." She was so desperate, she used sign language as she spoke. "I need to get you in to my truck. It's going to hurt you, I know. If you're like me, drugs won't work on you." She was beginning to stammer, his unblinking stare unnerving her. "Look," she said desperately, "I didn't do this to you. I'm really trying my best to help you."

His eyes commanded her to take a step closer. She brought a hand up to shove at her hair and found she was trembling. "I'm going to have to tie you in so when I hook the cable to the . . ." She trailed off, bit her lip. "Quit staring at me that way. This is hard enough."

She approached him cautiously. It took every ounce of courage she possessed to step to his side. He could smell her fear, hear the frantic beat of her heart. There was terror in her eyes, in her voice, yet she came to him. He was not forcing her compliance. The pain made him weak. He chose to conserve his energy. It astonished him that she came to him despite her fear. Her fingers were cool on his skin, felt soothing in his filthy hair. "Trust me. I know I'm asking a lot, but this is all I could figure to do."

The eyes, black ice, never left her face. Slowly, trying to avoid alarming him, Shea padded the area around the wooden stake with folded towels, hoping that moving him wouldn't kill him. She covered him with a blanket to protect him from the sun. He simply watched her, seemingly uninterested, yet she knew by the way he held himself, that he was coiled and ready to strike if there was need. When she would have secured him in the coffin to minimize jarring and bleeding, he caught her wrist in the viselike grip she was becoming so familiar with.

The photographs Don Wallace and Jeff Smith had shown her two years earlier had pictured some of their victims with blindfolds and gags. She couldn't deny that this creature looked exactly like the man in her dreams, like the man in their photograph, yet surely he couldn't have survived seven years buried in this cellar? There were rags in the coffin. A gag? A blindfold? Her stomach somersaulted. Even to protect his eyes she could not blindfold him. She could not duplicate anything those murderers had done to him. His filthy hair was very long, tangled, and falling around his face. She had a strong need to brush it away from his cheeks, to touch it with gentle fingers, to stroke away the last seven years with a caress.

"Okay, I'll leave your arm free," she soothed. It was difficult to remain still, waiting for his decision, her eyes held captive by his burning gaze. It seemed an eternity. Shea could feel his rage seething just below the surface. Every second that ticked by made it more difficult to keep her courage. She was not altogether certain he was sane.

Reluctantly, finger by finger, he released her. Shea didn't make the mistake of touching his arm again. Very carefully she hooked the cable to the handle at the head of the coffin. "I have to put this over your eyes. The sun is sinking, but there's enough light to blind you. I'll just lay it across; you can take it off at any time."

The moment she laid the cloth across his eyes, he ripped it off, fingers shackling her wrist in warning. His strength was enormous, nearly crushing her bones, yet she had the feeling it wasn't his intention to hurt her. He had drawn a clear line for her, what was acceptable to him and what was not.

"Okay, okay, let me think. No cloth." Her tongue found her lower lip; her teeth followed. His black gaze simply watched her, followed the movement of her tongue, came back to her vivid green eyes. Watching. Learning. "I know. You can use my glasses until I get you into the camper." She placed the dark glasses very gently on his nose. Her fingers stroked his hair in a little caress. "I'm sorry, this is going to hurt."

Shea took a cautious step backward. It was worse not seeing his eyes. Another step. His mouth twisted in a silent snarl; white teeth gleamed. She ran a split second before his arm snaked out with blinding speed. His nails ripped a deep furrow in her arm. She cried out, clutched her arm, but kept running until she reached the rotten stairs.

The light hit her eyes, blinding her, sending pain splintering through her head. Shea squeezed her eyes closed, stumbled to the truck, started the winch. She didn't want to see him brought up anyway. That she was the one tormenting him sickened her. Tears were streaming down her face. Shea pretended it was a reaction to the setting sun. Intellectually she knew he had struck at her out of fear that she was deserting him.

The whine of the cable stopped abruptly. Shea felt her way around the truck, opened the tailgate, slid down the ramp, and threaded the cable back through the cab into the shell. The winch loaded the coffin smoothly into the pickup bed. Shea desperately needed her sunglasses for driving, but she couldn't bring herself to get close to him again until it was absolutely necessary. By now he would be in so much pain that he might kill her before she could convince him she was not trying to torture him. She couldn't find it in herself to blame him.

The drive to her cabin took longer than it should have, with her eyes streaming and swollen and her vision blurred. She drove slowly, trying to avoid every rock and bump in the dirt track. As it was, even with four-wheel drive, it was hard going. Shea was cursing softly by the time she backed the truck practically onto her porch.

"Please, please, don't grab me and eat me alive," she chanted softly, a litany or prayer. One more time ripping at her throat and she might never be able to help anyone again. Taking a deep breath, she opened the tailgate and shoved the dolly over the ramp. Without looking at him, she lowered the coffin onto the dolly and wrestled him inside.

He never made a sound. Not a groan, not a sob, not a curse. He was in agony; she could tell by the sweat coating his body, by the white lines around his mouth, the crimson stain on his forehead, and the stark pain reflected in his eyes when it was finally safe to remove the sunglasses.

Shea was exhausted, her arms aching and weak. She was forced to take a moment to rest, leaning against the wall, fighting a wave of dizziness. His eyes were back on her face, simply staring at her. She hated his silence, instinctively knowing that those who had tortured him had not received the satisfaction of hearing his cries. It made her feel like one of them. Movement had to be excruciatingly painful for him.

Working quickly, she got him onto the gurney beside her operating table. "All

right, I'm going to get you out of this box."
She needed the sound of her voice even if he
didn't understand. She had tried several
languages, and he hadn't responded yet.
There seemed to be intelligence, knowledge
in his eyes. He didn't fully trust her, but it
was possible he realized her intention was to
help him.

Grasping her sharpest knife, Shea leaned
over him to get at the thick ropes. Instantly
he caught her wrist, preventing movement.
Her heart sank. He didn't understand after
all. She closed her eyes, steeling herself for
the pain of teeth ripping through flesh.
When nothing happened, she looked at
him, fully expecting to meet his blazing
eyes.

He was examining the long gash on her
arm, his eyes slightly narrowed, lids half-
closed. He turned her arm one way, then the
other, as if fascinated by the long line of
blood from wrist to elbow. Impatient, Shea
tugged to get away. His fingers clamped
down hard, but he didn't look at her face.
He brought her arm to his mouth slowly,
and her heart seemed to stop. His breath
was warm against her skin. He touched her
gently, almost reverently, a long, moist
caress that took the sting from the injury.
His tongue was rough velvet, lapping at the

wound with care. The feel of it sent an unexpected curl of heat spiraling through her.

Intuitively she knew that he wanted to repair the damage he had done. She blinked down at him, unable to believe he was attempting to heal her silly scratch when his own body was so terribly mutilated. The gesture seemed so touching, it brought tears to her eyes. She stroked back his shaggy mane of hair with tender fingers. "We need to hurry, wild man. You're bleeding again."

He released her reluctantly, and Shea slashed through the ropes. "It's okay to yell at me if you have to," she chattered on needlessly. It took an eternity to remove the manacles. Even with a bolt cutter, she was not very strong. When his wrist finally came loose, she grinned at him triumphantly. "I'll have you free in no time." She heaved the heavy chains off him, revealing blackened, charred flesh up and down his legs and across his chest.

Shea swore, furious that such evil existed. "I'm pretty sure the people who did this to you found out about me and my research, too. We may have the same blood disorder." One manacle was finally off his ankle. "It's very rare, you know. A few years ago some fanatics banded together and decided people like us were vampires. But I guess you already know that," she added apologetically.

The last cuff fell away, and she threw down the bolt cutter. "Your teeth seem more developed than mine." She ran her tongue along her teeth, assuring herself she wasn't really like him as she began to rip away the rotting sides of the wooden coffin. "Since you can't understand a word I say, I'll admit I'm glad about that. I can't imagine biting into someone. Yuck. It's bad enough that I need extra blood to survive. There, I'll cut your clothes away and get that thing out of you."

His clothes had all but rotted off anyway. She had never seen a body so battered before. "Damn them for this." Shea swallowed hard at the extent of the damage. "How could they do this to you? And how could you have survived?" She brushed perspiration from her brow with her forearm before bending over him once more. "I need to move you onto this table. I know I'm jarring you, but it's the only way."

He did the impossible. As Shea took the weight of his broad shoulders, attempting to slide him over, in a burst of courage and strength he shifted himself onto the table. Blood beaded on his forehead, trickled down the side of his face.

For a moment Shea couldn't go on. Her body was seized with tremors, and she lowered her head to hide her tears. She could hardly bear to see his suffering. "Is this ever going to end for you?" It took a few minutes of fighting for control before she raised her head to meet the impact of his black gaze. "I'm going to knock you out. It's the only way I can do this. If anesthesia doesn't work, I'll hit you over the head or something." She meant it, too. She was not going to torture him as the others had.

He touched her cheek with a gentle fingertip, removing a tear. He stared at it for a long moment before he carried it to his mouth. She watched the curiously intimate act, wondering why her heart was melting in a way she had never experienced before.

Shea washed thoroughly, pulled on sterile gloves and a surgical mask. When she would have put a mask over his face, too, he warned her off with a silent show of fangs and a wrist lock she couldn't budge. It was the same when she tried a needle. Black eyes blazed at her. She shook her head at him. "Please don't make me do this, not like this. I'm not a butcher. I won't do it this way." She tried to sound tough and not tearful. "I won't do it." They stared at one another, locked in a strange mental combat. His black eyes burned into her, demanded obedience; his rage, always seething, was beginning to surface. Shea's tongue touched her lower lip; her teeth followed, scraping nervously. Satisfaction crept into the black ice of his eyes, and he lay back, certain he had won.

"Damn you for being so stubborn." She cleansed the area around the stake, set up her clamps, all the time wishing for a good surgical nurse and a large mallet. "Damn them for doing this to you." She gritted her teeth and pulled with all her strength. He moved, just a ripple through his muscles, contracting, flexing, but she knew he was in agony. The stake did not budge. "Damn it! I told you I couldn't do this with you awake. I'm not strong enough."

He seized the stake himself and jerked it free. Blood gushed, sprayed her, and she fell silent, working desperately to clamp off every source of bleeding she could. She didn't look at him, every ounce of concentration focused on her work. Shea was a meticulous surgeon. She worked methodically, repairing damage, at a fast, steady pace, blocking out everything around her. Her entire being was centered on the surgery, her mind locking him to her so he would not die.

Jacques knew she was unaware of her fierce hold on him. She was so involved in what she was doing, she seemed not to notice how she merged with him mentally to keep him safe. Could he have been so wrong about her? The pain was excruciating, but with her mind merged so strongly with his, it kept the shattered remains of his sanity together.

Twice she added light for the close work, suturing for hours. So many stitches inside and out, and when his chest was done she still wasn't finished. All his other cuts had to be washed and closed. The smallest laceration took a single stitch, the largest forty-two. It went on and on as the night closed them in. Her fingers were nearly numb, and her eyes ached with strain. Stoically she went on cutting away dead flesh, forcing herself to use soil and her saliva, though it went against everything she had ever been taught in medical school.

Exhausted, hardly knowing what she was doing, she pulled off her mask and gloves and surveyed her work. He needed blood. His eyes were nearly mad with pain. "You need a transfusion," she said tiredly. She indicated the blood transfusion apparatus with her chin. The black eyes stared at her relentlessly. Shea shrugged, too exhausted to fight him. "Fine, no needles. I'll put it in a glass for you, and you can drink it."

His gaze never left her face as she wheeled the table to the bed and, with his help, shifted him into the comfort of clean, soft bedding. She stumbled twice, so exhausted that she was half asleep as she went for the blood. "Please cooperate, wild man. You need it, and I'm just too tired to fight with you anymore." She left the glass on the night table inches from his fingers.

Like an automaton she cleaned up, sterilizing instruments, washing down the gurney and tables, bagging the remains of the coffin, the rotted rags, and the blood-soaked towels for burial at the first opportunity. By the time Shea was finished, dawn was only two hours away.

The shutters were closed tightly to block out the approaching sun. She bolted the door and dragged two guns from the closet. Propping them up near her only comfortable chair, she tossed a blanket and pillow onto the cushion, prepared to defend her patient with her life. She knew she needed sleep, but no one was going to harm this man further.

In the shower she allowed the hot water to pour over her, rinsing blood, sweat, dirt, and grime from her body. Shea fell asleep standing up. Minutes later a strange sensation in her mind, almost like the brush of butterfly wings, jerked her awake. She wrapped her long hair in a towel, pulled on her mint-green robe, and stumbled out to check on her patient. Switching off the generator, she made her way to the bed. The glass was still sitting on the nightstand. Full. Shea sighed. Very gently she touched his hair. "Please do what I ask and drink the blood. I can't go to sleep until you do, and I'm so tired. Just this once, please listen to me."

His fingertips traced the delicate bones of her face as if memorizing her shape, the satin softness of her lips. His palm spanned her throat, fingers curling around her neck. He pulled her toward him slowly, relentlessly.

"No." The single word was more moan than protest. He increased the pressure almost tenderly until he had pulled her small form onto the bed beside him. His thumb found the pulse beating frantically in her neck. Shea knew she should struggle, but she was beyond caring, lying helplessly in his arms. She felt his mouth move over her bare skin, a whisper of movement, an enticement. His tongue stroked gently. She closed her eyes against the waves beating in her head. He was there. In her mind. Feeling her emotions, sharing her thoughts. Heat coiled in her as his mouth moved over her pulse again. His teeth scraped, nipped; his tongue caressed. The sensation was curiously erotic. Searing pain gave way to warmth and drowsiness. Shea relaxed against him, gave herself up to him. He could decide life or death. She was simply too tired to care.

Reluctantly he lifted his head, sweeping his tongue carefully to close the wound. He savored the taste of her — hot, exotic, the promise of passion. There was something terribly wrong with him; he understood that. Part of him was locked away so that he had no past. Fragments of memory seemed like shards of glass piercing his skull, so he tried not to allow them in. She was his world. Somehow he knew she was his only sanity, his only path out of his dark prison of pain and madness.

Why hadn't she come to him right away, when he had first called her? He had been so aware of her presence in the world. He had bent his will and commanded her obedience, but she had waited. Jacques had had every intention of punishing her for forcing him to endure madness and pain. Now, none of it made any sense. She had suffered much for him. Had there been some reason she had resisted his call? Perhaps the betrayer or the assassins had been following her. Whatever the reason, she had suffered greatly at his hands already. It didn't make sense that she had deserted him deliberately, prolonged his agony. He could read compassion in her. He felt her willingness to trade her own life for his. When he touched her mind, he felt only light and goodness. It did not add up to the cruel, treacherous woman he had perceived her to be.

Jacques was weak, vulnerable in his present state, unable to protect either of them. Shea was small and fragile. He had been so alone. Without light or color. He had spent an eternity alone, and he would never go back to that ugly, dark world. He slashed a wound in his chest, cradled her head to him, and commanded her to drink. Binding her to him was as natural as breathing. He could not bear to let her out of his sight. Shea belonged to him, and right at this moment she needed blood every bit as much as he did. The blood exchange had been made. Their mental bond was strong. When his body was healed he would complete the ritual, and she would be irrevocably bound to him for all eternity. It was instinct as old as time itself. He knew what to do and that he must do it.

As small as she was, Shea felt right in his arms, a part of his insides. None of it made sense, but in his narrow world, it didn't matter. Even as she fed, her mouth soft and sensuous against his torn flesh, he lifted the glass and carelessly emptied the contents down his throat. When he had sensed her sleeping as she bathed, he had awakened her, fearful of the separation. Now she would sleep beside him where she belonged, where he might have a chance of protecting her should the assassins find them. He might not be at full strength, but the monster in him was strong and lethal. No one would harm her.

The one bit of his memory that remained, forever etched into his mind, was the scent of the two humans and of the betrayer who had lured him to his living hell. He would recognize the voices of the tormentors and their smell. Demons. God, how they'd made him suffer, how they'd enjoyed his suffering. Laughing, taunting, torturing him until madness reigned. And it still reigned. He knew he was struggling for his sanity.

He would never forget the hunger as they bled him dry. Hunger had burned holes in him, crawled through him, eaten at him from the inside out. To survive he had slept, heart and lungs ceasing so that what little blood his body retained, he kept. He woke only when food was near. Always alone, unable to move, in agony. He had learned hatred. He had learned rage. He had learned there was a place where there was nothing, only stark, ugly emptiness and the burning desire for revenge.

Had these same animals attempted to hunt Shea? The thought of her in their hands sickened him. He fit her close to him so he could feel her reassuring presence. Was she being hunted? Were they close on her trail? If he had unfairly punished her failure to aid him, he would never forgive himself. He had wanted to kill her, had almost done so. Something inside him had been unable to do it. And then she had ceased to struggle, offering her blood, her life for him. He had thought himself hard, impossible to touch, yet something in him had melted at her offering. And the way her fingertips had brushed his hair had sent his heart pounding.

He cursed his weakness, both of body and mind. He needed more blood, hot human blood. It would speed his healing. There was something terribly important eluding him. It slipped in and out of his mind, leaving pain and fragments in its wake. If he could just hold it for a moment he might remember, but it never stayed long enough to do other than drive him mad. It was unbearably frustrating to have his memory taken from him.

Shea groaned softly, the sound cutting through him like a knife. She was shivering, even in her heavy robe. His gaze quickly jumped to her face. She was in pain. He felt it in her mind. Instinctively he laid a hand on her stomach, fingers splayed wide. Something was happening inside her body. Again his head seemed to splinter as he tried to catch the memory. He should know. It was important for her.

Shea rolled over and came to her knees, clutching her stomach. Her eyes were wide with fear. She was extremely cold, as if she would never be warm again. Shivering, she could only rock back and forth as wave after wave of pain shook her small frame. Heat was burning her insides, eating through her internal organs, squeezing her heart, her lungs. She rolled off the bed onto the floor, landing hard, attempting to protect her patient from whatever virus she had contracted. The towel unraveled, and her hair spilled out like dark blood pooling around her head. Her abdomen was on fire. A fine sheen of perspiration coated her body; across her forehead was a faint ribbon of scarlet.

Jacques tried to move, to get to her, but his body was not his own, lying heavy and useless. His arm couldn't reach her. His every movement brought pain rippling through him, but his world for so long had been pain, he knew no other. It had been his only reality in the darkened eternity of the damned. Pain only added to his iron will. He would live for all eternity and find those who had taken his past. He would turn that same iron will to finding a way to help Shea.

Shea's slender body writhed, locked, writhed again. She rolled to her knees, tried to crawl toward her medical bag. She wasn't thinking; the movement was blind, instinctive. She had no idea where she was or what was happening to her, only that the fire consuming her had to stop.

He struggled, raged at his inability to move, to help her. Finally he lay back, crawling into her mind as he had many times before in an effort to save himself. *Come to me, to my side.*

The whisper of sound, the thread of sanity, was in her head. Shea knew he had not spoken aloud. She was hallucinating.

She groaned, rolled over, and curled up in the fetal position, making herself as small as possible. She would not go near him. If this were contagious, he would not survive such a virulent flu.

What if she didn't survive? What if she had brought him here, and, with no one to care for him, she left him to die slowly of starvation? Somehow she had to tell him there was blood in the icebox. It was too late. Another wave of fire beat at her, attacking her internally, spreading to every organ. She could only draw up her knees like a mortally wounded animal and wait for it to pass.

You must come to me. I can help ease the pain. The words penetrated her next moment of lucidity. He sounded so tender, so unlike the way he looked. She didn't care if she was going crazy, if she was making his voice up; there was a soothing quality, like the touch of gentle, cool fingers on her body, to the voice in her mind.

Shea was going to be sick. Something in her, some ridiculous shred of dignity, made it possible to drag herself to the bathroom. He could hear her, fighting to stop the endless stomach spasms. Her agony was worse for him than his own, his rage at his impotence growing until he was consumed with it. Fingernails lengthened to murderous claws, tore holes in the sheets. Outside the wind picked up, howled at the windows, and ripped through the trees. A low growl rumbled in his throat, in his mind, increasing in volume. She was trying to protect him. He was a male of his race, his duty to take care of his own, yet she was suffering the fires of hell and refusing his aid lest she somehow give him her illness. He knew it was hers alone, that the fire twisting her insides was something important. She had to come to him; he did not know why, but every instinct, every cell in his body demanded her compliance.

You must come to me. I cannot get to you. There is no danger to me, little red hair. I must insist on your obedience. It was an imperious demand, the voice a soft yet steely thread of sound. Very Old World, heavily accented. At the same time his voice was brushing at her skin, soothing her, promising his aid.

In the bathroom, Shea splashed cold water on her face and rinsed her mouth. She had a minute or two before the next wave hit. She could feel the wild man's mixed emotions. He was frustrated with his inability to help her, was determined to reach her should she not respond. She was amazed that he needed to help her. It was an all-consuming emotion that vibrated in the air. Shea wanted to do as he commanded but was terrified of infecting him. The way her body was convulsing and pulsing with pain, she was certain it would kill him. Yet she wanted the comfort of another being.

I cannot come to you. You must come to me. His voice was pitched low, black velvet enticement, impossible to ignore.

Shea pushed herself off the wall and stumbled back to the bedroom, her face starkly white, shadows under her eyes. The bruises and wounds on her throat stood out plainly. She looked so fragile, he was afraid she would break if she fell again. He held out a hand to her, the expression in his dark eyes a mixture of demand and gentleness.

"You probably gave me rabies," she muttered rebelliously, but already the fire was eating at her spleen, her kidneys, spreading from tissue to muscle, bones, and blood.

Come now! *I cannot take your suffering a moment longer.* Deliberately he used that same mesmerizing tone, so that she felt an overwhelming need to do as he asked her. The voice seemed to be echoing in her mind, impelling her forward until she made it to the bed, rolling into a ball, burying her face in the pillow, hoping for death.

His hand gently, almost tenderly, pushed

back the heavy fall of hair from around her face, traced his thumbprint on her neck. He made an effort to search inside his mind for information. There was a key somewhere, a way to end her suffering, but, like his past, it eluded him. He was failing her when she had already endured so much to ensure his survival. He wanted to roar at the heavens, tear someone's throat out. They had done this to him.

Two humans and a betrayer. They had taken his past, shattered his mind, and imprisoned him in a living hell. Worst of all they had taken away his ability to protect his lifemate. They had created a monster the likes of which they could not conceive.

He touched her swollen throat, examined her wounds. Shea was beside him, locked in her own world of suffering. This was so wrong. His head ached, splintered. He damned himself and wrapped an arm around her waist, offering her what comfort he could. The dawn was upon them, and he inadvertently did the one thing he needed to do. He issued a sharp command and sent them both to sleep.

Chapter Three

The silence in the cabin was broken by the hum of night creatures singing to one another. The sun was setting, and the land was once more theirs. Air filled lungs, a chest rose and fell, a heart began to beat. The rush of agony always overwhelmed him, took his breath, his mind. He lay still, waiting for his mind to accept the atrocities that had been done to his body. Hunger rose, a sharp, gnawing emptiness that could never be assuaged. Rage flooded, consuming him, a need to kill, to fill the terrible emptiness.

Into the middle of that cauldron of intense, violent emotion suddenly came something soft and gentle. A wisp of memory. Courage. Beauty. A woman. Not any woman, but his woman, his lifemate. All red hair and fire. She walked like an angel where men feared to tread, where even his own kind would fear to venture.

He wrapped a length of her silky hair around one fist, afraid to wake her, afraid she would be in pain. Shea. Why didn't she ever use his name? Reluctantly he issued the command to awaken her and watched as air rushed into her body, listened to the ebb and flow of blood circulating through her heart. Her eyelashes fluttered. She burrowed against his warmth, unknowing for a moment. He touched her mind cautiously, took inventory. Within moments of awakening, her mind had already begun trying to assimilate all that had happened to her the night before, running through a list of diseases and their symptoms. Her body was sore. He found hunger, weakness, fear for his recovery, his sanity, fear of who and what he was. Guilt that she had slept instead of watching over him. An urgent need to complete her work, her research. Compassion for him, terror that he would not heal and that perhaps she had made his suffering worse. Fear they would be found before he was strong enough to go his own way.

His eyebrows went up. *Our way is the same.*

She sat up gingerly, swept back her tangled, wild hair. "You could have said you speak English. How do you do that? How can you talk in my head instead of aloud?"

He simply watched her curiously with his black, fathomless eyes.

Shea eyed him warily. "You aren't getting ready to bite me again, are you? I've got to tell you, there isn't a place on my body that isn't sore." She flashed him a wan smile. "Just out of curiosity, your rabies shots are up to date, aren't they?" His eyes were doing something to her insides, causing a flood of warmth where it shouldn't be.

His gaze dropped to her lips. The shape of her mouth fascinated him, along with the light so clearly shining from her soul. He raised a hand to cup her cheek, to feather his thumb along her delicate jawline; his fingertip traveled up to her chin to find the satin perfection of her full lower lip.

Her heart somersaulted and heat rushed low, pooling into a distinct ache. His hand slid around to the nape of her neck. Slowly, inexorably, he forced her head down toward his. Shea closed her eyes, wanting, yet dreading his taking her blood. "I'd hate to have to feed you every day," she muttered rebelliously.

And then his mouth touched hers. Featherlight, a skimming brush Shea felt right down to her toes. His teeth scraped her lower lip, teasing, tempting, enticing.

Darts of fire raced through her bloodstream. Her stomach muscles clenched. *Open your mouth for me, stubborn little red hair.* His teeth tugged; his tongue followed with a soothing caress. Shea gasped as much at the tender, teasing note as at the feel of his lips on hers. He took advantage immediately, fastening his mouth to hers, his tongue exploring every inch of her velvet-soft interior.

Flames licked at her, swept through her like a storm. Electricity crackled, and Shea knew the full meaning of chemistry. Feeling. Pure and simple. There was nothing else but his mouth claiming hers, whirling her into another world she hadn't known existed. The ground shifted, and Shea clutched at his shoulders to keep from floating to the clouds. He was sweeping aside every resistance, demanding her response, taking her response, all hunger and desire. Then he was in her mind, white-hot heat, possession. She was his, only his, always his. Smug male satisfaction.

Shea shoved at his broad shoulders, then tumbled backward to the floor, wiping at her mouth with the back of her hand. They glared at one another, until amusement crept into her mind. Low, male, taunting. Nothing showed on his face, not a flicker in the ice of his eyes, but she knew he was laughing at her.

It took a moment to realize her robe was gaping open, giving him a generous view of her bare skin. With great dignity Shea dragged the lapels together. "I think we need to straighten something out here." Sitting on the floor, struggling desperately to get her breathing under control, to throw ice water on the raging fire in her blood, Shea was afraid he wasn't going to take her seriously. "I am your doctor. You are my patient. This . . ." She waved a hand, searching for the right words. "This sort of thing is unethical. And another thing. I am in charge here. You follow my orders, not the other way around. Absolutely never, under any circumstances, do that again." Involuntarily she touched her fingers to her lower lip. "It wouldn't have happened at all if you hadn't infected me with some sort of, I don't know, rabies strain." She glared at him.

He simply watched her with his disconcertingly steady gaze. Shea inhaled, wrinkled her nose, desperate to change the subject to something safe. He was supposed to be half-dead. He should have been dead. No one should be able to kiss like that after the agony he had been through. She had never, ever responded to anyone the way she had to him. Never. It was shocking, the effect he had on her.

There was a sudden glint in his eyes, somewhere between a flame dancing and amusement. *No other man must ever make you respond to him. I would not be pleased.*

"Quit reading my mind!" Her cheeks

flushed a bright red; she glared at him. "This is a totally improper conversation between a doctor and a patient."

Perhaps, but not between us.

She clenched her teeth, her green eyes smoldering. "Shut up," she said rudely, a little desperately. She had to find a way to get control back, and he wasn't cooperating. She took a deep, calming breath to restore her dignity. "You need a bath. And your hair could use a good wash." Shea stood up and gingerly touched his thick ebony hair, unaware that the gesture was curiously intimate. "You were number seven. I wonder if any of the others live. God, I hope not. I have no way to find them."

As she turned, he caught her wrist. *What is number seven?*

Shea sighed softly. "Those men, the ones who hunt me, had photographs of some of their victims murdered around seven years ago. Eight bodies were found, though likely there were more victims than anyone knew. People refer to them as the 'vampire' murders because the victims were killed with a wooden stake driven through the heart. The picture numbered as seven was yours. You. It was you."

His eyes questioned her further. Hunger

98

was intruding, becoming a sharp, distracting ache. He was so much in her mind, she couldn't tell if he or she was in desperate need of blood. "Do you know your name?"

There was the impression of confusion. *You know, you are my lifemate.*

Her eyes widened in surprise. "Lifemate? You — you think we know one another? I've never met you before in my life."

His black eyes narrowed. His mind pushed at hers in confusion, in sudden dismay. He seemed certain she was lying to him.

Shea shoved a hand through her hair, the action parting her robe slightly, lifting her breasts. "I dreamed about you. Sometimes I thought about you . . . maybe even felt your presence. But I never actually laid eyes on you until two nights ago." Was it only forty-eight hours? It felt like a lifetime. "Something drew me to that forest, to that cellar, I didn't know you were there."

More confusion. *You did not know?* He was probing her mind. She could feel him sharing her head, and it was strange. He felt familiar to her; she recognized his touch. It was strange, exhilarating, but frightening to have someone capable of learning such intimate knowledge of her. Shea told herself she endured his examination only because

99

he was clearly agitated. She had a physician's need to soothe him, to take away every pain from his body and his mind. The urge had nothing to do with the way he made her feel.

Everything around her seemed so different. Colors were more than just vivid, they were startling in depth. She was uneasy with her acceptance of so many bizarre events, uncomfortable with the facility with which he slipped in and out of her mind. His fingers suddenly tightened like a band around her wrist. *I am Jacques. I am your lifemate. There is no question that I can share your mind. It is my right, as it is yours to share mine. More than a right, it is a necessity for us both.*

She had no idea what he was talking about, so she ignored his statement, worried that he seemed so distressed over her lack of knowledge of him. She found herself needing to touch his hair with gentle fingers. "Can you use your voice at all?"

His eyes answered, impatient, frustrated at his own inability.

Her fingertips found his forehead, calming, soothing. "Don't worry. Your body's been through a lot. Give it some time. You're already healing amazingly fast. Do you know who did this to you?"

Two humans, one betrayer. Rage welled up, and for a moment red flames glowed in the depths of his black eyes.

Shea's heart nearly stopped, and she jerked backward to put distance between them. He moved faster, his arm a blur. His fingers circled her wrist, preventing escape. His grip was unbreakable — she felt his raw strength — yet he was not hurting her at all.

With an effort he pushed down the demons, angry with himself for alarming her. His thumb feathered lightly over the inside of her wrist, making him all too aware of her pulse racing frantically. Very, very gently he tugged until she was forced to his side. *I know little of my past, but almost from the beginning of my imprisonment I have known of you. I waited. I called you to my side. I hated you for allowing my suffering to continue.*

She caught his face in her hands, suddenly anxious that he believe her. "I didn't know. I swear to you, I didn't know. I never would have left you there." Grief clogged her throat that she had not somehow ended his suffering sooner. What was it about him that drew her like a magnet, that captivated her and made her want to ease his pain? The urge was so strong in her, so intense, she could hardly bear to see him lying so vulnerable and shattered.

I know you speak the truth; you cannot lie to me. It was a courageous thing you did, rescuing me. But as your lifemate I can do no other than forbid you to ever take such a risk again. He sounded totally complacent, as if she would do as he said simply because he wished it. Every moment he was awake he became more tyrannical, more possessive. She glared at him, her green eyes smoldering dangerously. "You can quit with the orders, Mr. Jacques whoever-you-are. No one tells me what to do."

His black gaze slid over her calmly. So she had not been part of his life before. The information amazed him. How had she found the courage to save him the way she had? How had she returned to him after he had nearly ripped her throat out? His fingers tightened around her wrist, tugged until she relaxed against him.

You are my lifemate. The words came from somewhere deep inside his heart. He had no idea why he needed to say them, he knew only that it was imperative that he do so; it seemed his entire being forced the words out of his soul. *I claim you as my lifemate. I belong to you. I offer my life for you. I give you my protection, my allegiance, my heart, my soul, and my body. I take into my keeping the same that is yours. Your life, happiness, and welfare will be cherished and placed above my own for all time. You are my lifemate, bound to me for all eternity and always in my care.*

Shea heard the words echoing in her mind, felt a rush of heat, of blood. Fear welled up, stark terror. "What have you done?" She whispered it, her eyes enormous. "What have you done to us?"

You know the answer.

She shook her head adamantly. "I don't. I don't know. But I'm different, I can feel it. Those words did something to us." She could feel it; she couldn't describe it. She felt tiny threads, a million strong binding his soul to hers, weaving their hearts together, their minds. She no longer felt like a single entity but one complete being with him. There had always been a raw emptiness inside her; now it was gone.

He released her wrist reluctantly, traced his fingertips along her high cheekbone. His mind touched hers, found genuine fear and confusion. *I am as much in the dark as you are. I know only that you ended my suffering, that you came to my call, that I recognize my other half. You are the light to my darkness.*

Shea edged away from him, making certain to get beyond his reach. "I'm your doctor, Jacques, nothing more. I heal people." She said it more for herself than for him. Shea had no idea what he was talking about. She worried that his mind was playing tricks on him, weaving fantasies for him. Intellectually, Shea knew no one could tie another to himself with words, yet she *felt* threads binding them together. There were too many things she didn't understand. Jacques was half mad, his mind shattered, his memories coming to him in tiny pieces, yet maybe he was more stable than she was. It was a scary thought.

She was so hungry, the need for blood nearly overwhelming. She had never experienced such a craving. Shea decided she was feeling Jacques' hunger, that somehow she was actually sharing his distress. At once she poured the wild man two pints of blood from her supply and took the tall glass to his bedside. "I'm sorry, I should have realized you'd be hungry. If you let me give you intravenous fluids, it would help." The moment she put the glass down, she retreated to her computer desk.

He ignored her comment. *Why do you not feed?* The question was asked casually, curiously. His black eyes were thoughtful as he studied her.

From her position of safety across the room, Shea watched him. The weight of his gaze alone broke her concentration, took her breath away. She was feeling far too possessive of this patient. She had no right to tangle her life around his. It was frightening that she was reacting so uncharacteristically to him. She had always felt aloof, remote, detached from people and things around her. Her analytical mind simply computed facts. But right now, she could think only of him, his pain and suffering, the way his eyes watched her, half-closed, sexy. Shea nearly jumped out of her skin. Where had that thought come from?

Knowing she wouldn't want to think he was reading her mind at that precise moment, Jacques did the gentlemanly thing and pretended merely a casual interest. It was nice to know she found him sexy. Smugly he lay back with his eyes closed, long lashes dark against his washed-out complexion.

Despite the fact that his eyes were closed, Shea felt as though he witnessed every move she made. "You rest while I shower and change my clothes." Her hands went to her hair in a futile effort to tidy the wild thickness of it.

His eyes remained closed, his breathing relaxed. *I can feel your hunger, your need for blood nearly as great as my own. Why would you attempt to hide this from me?* With sudden insight he let out his breath. *Or is it that you are hiding from your own needs? That is it — you do not realize it is your hunger, your need.*

The gentleness in his tone flooded her body with unexpected heat. Furious that he could be right, she stalked into the bathroom, shrugged off her robe, and allowed the warm shower to cascade over her head.

His laughter was low and taunting. *You think to escape me, little red hair? I live in you as you live in me.*

Shea gasped, whirled around, grabbed frantically for a towel. It took a moment to realize he was still in the other room. The connection between them was growing stronger. She wanted it now, enjoyed it, yet it made her uneasy that she could find such an intimacy with another so natural, so normal, when it wasn't.

It suddenly occurred to her that she was showing no indications of normal bodily functions. As always, her intellect took over to analyze the situation. Her brain began to process information without emotion, sorting through the various changes she found in herself, connecting them with her recent illness and the fire in her internal organs. It was crazy, but she knew she was physically different. Something had reshaped her genetic code.

Shea took her time braiding her hair, fussing over her blue jeans, adjusting her ribbed cotton shirt, allowing her mind time to cope with the new knowledge. It was frightening yet fascinating. She wished she had observed it in someone other than herself. It was hard to accept it clinically when it was her own body she was studying.

Such a nice body.

She nearly dropped her brush. *Will you stop!* Just the low velvet touch of his voice sent heat curling through her body. It was sinful and unfair to have such a voice.

I did not think you would ever speak with me as a lifemate would. I waited long for that impatient comment. There was a teasing note now.

Shea went very still. Her face, reflected in the mirror, visibly whitened. She had not spoken the words aloud, yet he had heard her. Her teeth tugged worriedly at her lower lip. The change was in more than her body. Her capabilities were growing. She could talk to him easily using her mind. It shocked her that she could conceive of such a thing as normal. If she didn't think about it or analyze it, she could almost accept it. She found herself trembling. Extending her hands out in front of her, she watched with annoyance as they shook. She was a doctor; nothing should shake her composure. More than that, Shea knew her own worth, had complete faith in herself.

Her chin went up. She walked into the main room, avoiding looking at him as she opened the refrigerator and took out some apple juice. Her stomach lurched. The thought of swallowing the liquid made her ill. Something inside her had changed dramatically, as she suspected. She needed to take more blood samples, find out just what was going on with her body. Yet for the first time in her life, she found herself reluctant to study data.

What are you doing? He sounded curious.

"Actually, I'm not sure. I thought I would drink juice, but . . ." She trailed off, uncertain what to say. Shea always had a firm direction; now she was seriously floundering. Pouring the juice into a glass, she stared at it helplessly.

You will make yourself ill. Do not touch that.

"Why would apple juice make me ill?" she asked, curious. Did he know what had happened to her?

You need blood. You are not nearly strong enough. I have scanned your body. Although I am not able to help you as of yet, I can see the need for proper nourishment. Your body cannot cope with the demands you make on it.

"I don't want to discuss what I should or shouldn't do." It bothered her the way he sounded so concerned, almost tender. His voice had a way of making her want to do anything he asked of her, including drinking the blood. She could smell it. She could hear his heart, the rush of blood through his veins. For the space of a heartbeat she allowed the sound to echo in her head, to feed the hunger gnawing at her. She bit down hard on her lower lip. She needed to put a little distance between them. His personality was extremely overpowering. Something deep within her, something wild she hadn't known was a part of her, was calling out to him. The chemistry was so strong, she ached just looking at him. Shea unbolted the cabin door, began to open it.

Stop! The command was soft, menacing, yet she caught the hint of desperation. The door seemed to be jerked out of her hand by some unknown force and slammed closed. Shocked, she dropped the glass in her hand. It smashed on the floor. She watched the apple juice spread out in a golden stain, the pattern particularly odd, almost like the yawning jaws of a wolf.

With an effort Jacques calmed himself. It was absolute hell to be so helpless, to be trapped in a useless body. He took a deep breath, let it out slowly, releasing the terror her rash action had caused. *I am sorry, Shea. You did not scan to see if there was danger near. We are hunted. You must never forget that. You must stay close to me so I can be of some use if you are threatened. I did not mean to frighten you.*

She looked up at him, her green eyes bewildered. "I don't know what you mean by scanning." She said it absently, as if her mind was on something else.

Come here to me. His voice whispered over her skin. He held out a hand to her, his eyes eloquent, hungry. He wanted something from her she dared not think about.

"Not on your life." He looked so sensual, so sexy, he took her breath away. Shea felt behind her for the wall, leaned against it for stability.

I am not asking for much. Walk to me. It is only a few short steps. Black velvet enticed her; warmth flooded her mind.

She regarded him carefully. "You know what's wrong with me, don't you? You did something to me. I know you did. I feel it. Tell me what you've done." Her face was pale, her enormous eyes accusing.

We are one, bound together.

There was the impression of puzzlement.

Jacques felt her confusion; he was a shadow in her mind. Yet he was as confused as she was. She truly didn't understand what he meant by scanning, which was ingrained in him just as breathing was. She had no idea what he meant by their being bound together, yet to him it was perfectly clear. Still, he was not certain he could explain it to her adequately. Why didn't she know these things? He was the one damaged. His was the mind shattered, his the memories scattered to the four corners of the earth.

Shea rubbed her forehead with a trembling hand. "You shut that door, didn't you? You took it out of my hands and slammed it closed right from the bed. You did it with your mind, didn't you?" She could do many things, had special gifts, but this unknown man had tremendous powers she could barely comprehend. What was he? What else was he capable of? The pull between them was so strong — had she allowed something outside herself to dictate her own actions? Shea was uncertain of the answer.

At once Jacques sought to soothe her. He didn't know what was upsetting her so much — it was a natural part of his life to move objects with his mind — but his need was to overcome her distress. He sent her warmth and reassurance, comfort. *I am sorry, Shea, I was thinking only of your protection. It is difficult for me to know we are hunted while I am so helpless to protect you, that we cannot leave this place because of my weakness. You are tied to my side, and I endanger you.* He tried as hard as he could to undo the damage his thoughtlessness had caused. She deserved so much more than a half-mad lifemate. She seemed to have no real idea of what they needed to survive. *You have no conception of the monsters we are dealing with. It is always important to scan as you wake, before you leave a dwelling.* He tried to be gentle as he imparted the information. It was easy for him to read her mounting fears.

"I don't know what you mean."

Her genuine puzzlement brought out a protective urge in him so strong that it shook his narrow world. He wanted to take her into his arms and shelter her for all eternity within his soul. She looked impossibly small and fragile, the questions in her mind as easy to read as the worry on her transparent face. His dark eyes widened in sudden understanding. *You do not know the ways of our people at all, do you?*

"What people? I'm an American, of Irish descent. I came here to do research on a rare blood disorder, which I seem to share with

112

you. That's all." Unknowingly she was biting her lip, her knuckles white from clenching her fists, her body tense, waiting for his reply.

He cursed his inability to remember basic things, certain they were of great importance to the two of them. If she was as much in the dark as he was, they were in deep trouble. It was frustrating to have so many gaps in his mind. *You are of this land. I feel your connection to this land. I know absolutely that you are mine, that we belong together.*

Shea shook her head. "My mother was Irish. My father was from this region, but I never even knew him. I arrived here for the first time only a couple of months ago. I swear I've never been here before."

We do not have a disorder, a disease. Our people have existed as they are from the dawn of time. He did not know where that piece of information came from. It was simply there.

"But that's impossible. People do not require drinking blood to live. I'm a doctor, Jacques. I do medical research all the time. I know. This is extremely rare." She could feel her breath refusing to leave her lungs.

You can accept that I remained buried alive for an eternity, yet you cannot accept that our people exist?

Shea bent to pick up the scattered pieces

of glass, needing something practical to do while she tried to hold on to her self-control. What was he really saying to her? That he did not have a blood disorder but was of another race or . . . species? "We don't know how long you were there," she said uneasily, slowly mopping up the juice.

How long ago were you shown the picture of me?

Shea dumped the broken glass into the garbage can. "Two years ago," she admitted reluctantly. "The vampire murders occurred seven years ago. They claimed the photos were of those victims. But it would be impossible, totally impossible, for you to have survived that long. That would mean you were buried with a stake through your body for seven years. It's impossible, Jacques." She turned to him, her eyes enormous. "Isn't it?"

Not if I shut down my heart and lungs. My blood would not run, he explained, choosing his words carefully, afraid of upsetting her.

It had just the opposite effect. "You can do that? Really do that?" Now she was excited. "You can control your heart rate, slow it down, speed it up? My God, Jacques, this is incredible. There are monks who can do such a thing, but not on the scale you imply."

I can stop my heart if need be. You can stop yours.

"No, I can't." She dismissed the idea as nonsense with a wave of a hand. "But is that really what you did? Stop your heart? Is that how you survived being buried alive? Lord, that must have driven you mad. I don't know if I can make myself believe this. How did you eat? You were chained, both hands." Her thoughts and questions stumbled over one another in her excitement.

I woke rarely, only when I sensed blood nearby. I called creatures to me. You must know you can do that. He was pleased that for once he could give her information. *I managed to scratch a hole in the wood to allow them in.*

Shea could call animals to her; she had been doing it since she was a child. And that talent she and Jacques shared accounted for the rat carcasses she had seen buried in the wall with him. "Are you saying there are others who do these things?" She hurried to her computer, turning on the generator so she could work. "What else do you remember?"

She was so excited, he wanted to give her more information, but as hard as he tried to come up with something, his head simply pounded, and memories eluded him. Shea

115

felt his distress, glanced over at him, saw the faint sheen of perspiration beading on his forehead.

Immediately her eyes warmed, her mouth curving softly. "Jacques, I'm sorry. It was thoughtless of me to press you like that. Don't try to think right now. Things will come back to you eventually. I've got plenty to work on right here. You just rest."

Grateful for her compassion, Jacques allowed the fragmented pieces of his memory to escape for a while and leave him in peace. He watched with interest as Shea took a blood sample from her arm and made several smears on small glass squares. Her excitement was so intense, her rush of joy so totally encompassing, that it pushed aside her gnawing hunger. Her mind was consumed with facts, hypotheses, and a bombardment of data. All at once she was far away from him, completely absorbed with her work. Jacques watched her, reached lazily for the glass on the end table, and swallowed the contents to dull his own terrible hunger.

Even after an hour of observation he saw that Shea remained completely focused on whatever she was doing, concentrating totally on her task. He enjoyed watching her, found her fascinating, every turn of her head, the fringe of her long eyelashes in profile. She often shoved at her hair when she was puzzled. Small teeth would worry her full lower lip. Her fingers flew on the keyboard, her gaze fastened on the monitor. Frequently she would consult notes and several books with a slight, all-too-alluring frown on her face. He found he liked that little frown, the habit she had of biting her lip.

Every time he recognized hunger beating at her, she seemed to be able to push it aside. Just as she had temporarily pushed him aside, out of her thoughts. That actually annoyed him a bit, but he also felt a sense of pride in her. Whatever she did, she did wholeheartedly. Still, Shea was ignoring the danger to herself, so absorbed in her work that she blocked out everything around her. Jacques thought about reminding her of the hazards, but instead he opted to remain alert enough to scan their surroundings, slipping in and out of the mortal's sleep.

Jacques jerked himself awake four hours later, then cursed at the clumsiness that sent pain spiraling through his body. He felt hunger, weakness, a swaying dizziness. Black eyes leapt to Shea. She was peering at a notebook, pencil clenched in her teeth.

Her skin was so pale, it was nearly translucent. The intense emotions in the room were hers, yet she seemed not to notice. Her mind fought to merge with his; he could feel it tuning itself, vibrating with need, but Shea was disciplined, strong, and very determined. She brought her thoughts back under control, focusing on her work.

He felt a curious melting in the region of his heart. Ice-cold hatred and fury, the need for revenge, for retribution, had been the force driving him to live. He had not thought himself capable of tenderness, yet Shea managed to bring it out of him. He was first and always a predator. Shea was light to his darkness, radiating beauty as if it shone through her skin from her soul. She had introduced gentler emotions to him.

She needed a break, rest. Most of all she needed to feed. If he was completely honest, he needed her touch, her attention. Deliberately, he moaned softly in his mind, his head back, eyes closed. He sensed her instant alertness, her concern. A rustle of papers signaled she had set her notes aside. Jacques beat down a sense of triumph, concentrating on the pain that encompassed his battered body.

Shea glided across the room, not noticing how silent she was, how efficient her body had become, moving with grace and speed. Her hand was cool on his forehead, soothing. She brushed back his grimy hair, her touch so soft that his heart ached. She bent to examine his wounds with a professional eye. Antibiotics wouldn't work on him any more than they did on her. Perhaps new soil would help. "I'm sorry I can't take your pain away, Jacques. I would if I could." Her voice was filled with concern, with regret. "I'll get you some fresh soil and wash your hair for you. It isn't much, but it can be soothing and might help." Her fingers were drawn to his mane of hair again, then traced his shadowed jaw in a small caress.

Both his hands came up, caught her with surprising strength, his black eyes capturing hers so that she felt she was falling forward into those dark, mysterious pools. *You have not fed.* She could get lost in his gaze for all time. She could hear the sound of her heart tuning itself to his. It was strange yet normal how their hearts seemed to want to beat in the same rhythm.

"I don't drink human blood. I transfuse if I'm desperate, but I can't make myself drink it," she explained quietly. She felt him now, in her mind, his touch calming and gentle. But there was also a hard authority in him. His will was so strong, nothing could resist him when he insisted. She wanted him to understand. "I am human, Jacques. Drinking blood is abhorrent to me."

To try to live for any length of time without feeding is dangerous. You must drink. Although Jacques tried to make it a simple statement of fact, it came out as a soft command. He didn't know where the information came from, only that it was true. It was plain to him she wanted his understanding in this ridiculous regimen she was forcing on herself, but it made no sense to him, and he could not allow such foolishness. He had to find a way to make her realize what she was doing to herself.

She smoothed back his hair, the touch of her fingers stirring interesting reactions in his battered body. Unaware of what she was doing to him, Shea smiled into his eyes. "I accepted a long time ago I would die if I was unable to find a cure. Now, do you want me to wash your hair?"

His hands tightened on her slender shoulders, pulled her down to him. *You know, little red hair, as your lifemate it is my duty to see to your health. My purpose in life is to protect you and see to your needs. You are weak, unable to perform the most basic survival skills. This cannot continue. You must use the blood you are supplying to me for yourself.*

There was something magical in his voice. She could listen to it forever. "There's very little left. As it is, I'll have to visit the local blood bank soon." She had already used most of her units to try to replace the tremendous volume of blood he had lost. "Really, Jacques, don't worry about me. I do this all the time."

Look at me, little Shea. His voice dropped an octave. Low. Compelling. An enticement. His black eyes held her green ones. Warmth flooded her mind; arms surrounded her, held her close. She fell further into deep, dark pools of burning heat. *You will accept my blood, as you are meant to*. He gave the command softly, firmly, holding her mind with his. The strength of his will, shaped by centuries of practice and honed by the fires of hell, conquered hers. Without hesitation he drew her to his chest, cradling her tenderly in his arms.

She seemed so light, so small and fragile. He loved the line of her throat, the satin perfection of her skin, her mouth. With one nail Jacques opened a small wound in his heavy muscles, pressed her to him, and felt heat coil unexpectedly deep within him. His gut clenched, and desire shot through him, piercing and sweet. The feel of her mouth on him was erotic. Their minds were merged as he held her. It was an intimacy he was unfamiliar with. In the midst of pain and darkness, hatred and rage, she had brought light, compassion, and courage. Where there was bleak despair and a weak, empty shell, she had given him the beginnings of strength and power, blossoming hope. Where there was endless pain, an eternity of hell, she was bringing beauty, joy, and an intense pleasure he almost could not comprehend.

Jacques did not want to end their joining, but he needed every drop of blood to try to heal his broken body and mend his fractured mind. He didn't dare allow her to take too much from him. Already his hunger was growing. He needed fresh blood, hot and rich, flowing straight from his prey. Reluctantly he stopped her, felt flames dance over his skin as her tongue caressed him, closing the wound.

For a moment he dropped his head over hers, savoring the closeness of her body, her scent, savoring the beauty of her spirit. He could no longer bear to be alone, separated from her even for a moment. Seven years of darkness, of total isolation, of believing she had deliberately allowed, even prolonged, his suffering. To know it wasn't true, that, indeed, her courage had saved him, had given him back hope, a chance at living. Jacques would never survive her loss. He could not let her out of his sight, out of his mind. He was so fragmented, she alone was holding him together.

He released her will slowly, watching her closely, intently, black eyes burning possessively. Her long lashes fluttered, and the cloudiness vanished, leaving glittering emeralds behind, flawless and mysterious. Cool beauty fired to flashing flame. "What have you done this time, Jacques? You absolutely cannot take care of me. I mean it. You have no idea just how close to death you really are. You cannot afford the loss of blood."

His faint smile was in her mind. *You are my lifemate, always in my care. I can do no other than provide what you need.*

She shook her head slowly. "What am I going to do with you? You need every drop of blood we can get our hands on. I'm used to getting by on tiny amounts."

Getting by is not good enough. He growled it at her, black eyes glittering.

Shea rolled her eyes heavenward. "At least have the decency to try to look guilty. You needn't be so smug and annoying." Her fingers found his tangle of hair again, brushed it from his forehead. "I wonder about you, Jacques. Where your family is."

Confusion reflected in his eyes, a black void suddenly filled with splintering pain. She caught at his hand, reeling under the impact of her mind sharing, even for a split second, the agony in his. "Stop, Jacques. Don't try to force your memory. It will come back as you heal. Just relax. I'll bathe your wounds and wash your hair. It'll be soothing to you."

Her fingers were soothing on his skin, sending coolness into his burning mind. His body responded, relaxing muscles clenched taut, releasing a bit of the pain wracking him. Her touch gave him a flicker of light to follow, hope that the pain would actually end someday. He closed his eyes and gave himself up to her ministrations. The sound of her moving so lightly around the house was comforting. Her natural fragrance and the faint aroma of herbs and flowers that drifted from her skin and hair seemed to surround him like arms holding him close.

Shea touched him gently as she examined his wounds. Her sponge seemed to skim over raw, damaged flesh, leaving a curious tingling in its wake. The warm water pouring over his hair as she cradled his head in her arm felt so good, it was almost sensuous. As her fingertips massaged herbal shampoo into his scalp, he concentrated on the feeling, for a few minutes able to push aside his world of pain.

"You have beautiful hair," Shea said softly, rinsing the suds away with more warm water. Her arm was aching with the effort to hold his head up over the plastic basin, but she could sense she was bringing him a measure of peace. She removed the basin, maneuvered a towel onto his pillow, and helped him slide back to his original position.

As she dried his hair, her hands lingered in his scalp; she enjoyed touching him. "You're very tired. Go back to sleep."

More blood. The husky, drowsy note echoing in her mind turned her insides soft and warm.

Without hesitating, Shea poured a unit into a glass and busied herself dumping the wash water and mopping up the floor. As she moved past the bed, his hand snaked out, fingers shackling her wrist, drawing her close.

"What?" Shea perched on the edge of the bed, a faint smile on her face, her eyes soft, even tender, although she was unaware of it.

His palm slid up her arm; strong fingers massaged her aching shoulder. *Thank you, little red hair. You make me feel alive again.*

"You are alive, Jacques," she reassured him, smoothing back his hair. "Disrespectful but definitely alive. I don't know a single physician referred to as 'little red hair.'"

Her quiet laughter remained in his mind long after he fell into the mortal state of sleeping. On some level he was aware of her closeness as she mixed soil, herbs, and saliva for his wounds, and it soothed him, kept rage, pain, and the terror of his empty, isolated world at bay.

Chapter Four

Shea opened the door to the night and inhaled deeply. The amount of information that flooded her was shocking. Creatures were roaming the forest, and Shea knew the precise location of each animal, from a pack of wolves several miles away to three mice scurrying in the bushes close by. She could hear water roaring in cascading falls and bubbling softly over rocks. The wind played through the trees, the underbrush, and the very leaves on the ground. The stars glittered overhead like millions of jewels radiating prisms of colors.

Entranced, Shea stepped from the cottage, leaving the door open to allow the odor of blood and sweat and pain to seep outside, to be replaced with clean, fresh air. She could hear the sap running like blood in the trees. Every plant had a special scent, a vivid color. It was as if she had been reborn into a whole new world. She lifted her face to the stars, drawing air into her lungs, relaxing for the first time in forty-eight hours.

An owl slipped silently through the sky, its wingspan incredibly long, each feather iridescent to her new sight. The sheer wonder of it drew her toward the deep woods. Droplets of water sparkled like diamonds on moss-covered rocks. The moss itself looked like emeralds scattered along the winding stream and up the trunks of trees. She had never seen anything so beautiful in her life.

Her mind, as always, processed the data flooding into her brain. It was all a huge jigsaw puzzle, but the pieces were beginning to fit themselves together. She had been born to a woman who ate food and walked in the sunshine. Yet she — and others — displayed decided differences in sensitivities, metabolism, nutritional requirements. It was impossible to believe that the vampire legends were true. But could there be a separate race of people with incredible gifts who needed to drink blood to survive? Could they live incredibly long lives, survive the unthinkable, be able to control their hearts and lungs? Their bodies would have to process everything differently. Their organs would have to be different. Everything would be different.

Shea shoved at her hair. Her tongue swept her lower lip, teeth biting nervously. It was something out of a fairy tale. Or a horror film. Impossible. Wasn't it? A man could not survive seriously wounded, buried seven years in the earth. No way. It couldn't happen. But she had found him. It wasn't a lie. She had uncovered him herself. So how could one's sanity remain after seven years of being buried alive, of being in agony every moment? Her mind shied away from that question. She didn't want to dwell on it.

And what was happening to her body? She was different. Many changes had started seven years ago, with sudden pain driving her to the point of unconsciousness. That episode had never been explained. Then the nightmares, so persistent, so relentless, never giving her a moment's peace, had started. *Jacques*. Always Jacques. The picture, two years ago, the human butchers had shown her. The seventh one. *Jacques*. Something drawing her, calling her insistently to that horrible place of torture and cruelty. *To Jacques*. They had to be connected. Somehow, some way. Intellectually it seemed impossible. By every standard she knew it was impossible. Yet wasn't her very existence strange? Her need to transfuse blood wasn't psychosomatic; she had tried everything to overcome it. So maybe there was another explanation, one her human mind and prejudices could not comprehend, even with the facts in front of her.

Shea! The call was loud, a flood of fear and confusion, an impression of strangling, of darkness and pain.

I'm here, Jacques. She sent her answer back so easily it startled her. To reassure him, she tried to fill her mind with every beautiful thing she saw.

Come back to me. I need you.

She smiled at the demand in his voice; her heart somersaulted at the raw truth in his voice. He never tried to hide anything from her, not even his elemental fear of her leaving him to face the darkness alone. *Spoiled brat.* She sent it tenderly. *There's no need to sound like the lord of the manor. I'll be right in.* There was no reasonable explanation for the joy flooding her at the touch of his mind lingering possessively in hers. She shied away from looking at that one too closely, too.

Just come to me. He was more relaxed now, beating back his fear of isolation. *I do not want to wake alone.*

I do need an occasional break. How was I supposed to know you would wake at this precise moment?

She was teasing him. Warmth curled in the pit of his stomach. He had no memory of such a thing before Shea. There was no life before Shea. There had been only ugliness. His world had been torment and hell. He found himself smiling. *Of course you should know when I wake. It is your duty.*

I should have known you would think that way. Shea laughed aloud as she raced across the rough terrain back to the cabin, reveling in her ability to do so, at the sudden surge of strength she had never before experienced. For just a brief moment a heavy weight seemed lifted from her shoulders, and she knew carefree happiness.

Jacques found he couldn't take his eyes from her. She looked so beautiful, her red hair tangled and wild, just begging for a man's fingers to straighten it. Her eyes were sparkling as she came across the room to his side.

"Are you feeling any better?" As always she examined his wounds to see for herself if he was making progress.

He lifted a hand, needing to touch the silk of her hair. *Much.* It was a blatant lie, and she scowled at him.

"Is that so? I'm beginning to think you need a monitor like we have for newborns. I want you to lie quietly. I can tell you've been squirming around again."

I have nightmares. His black eyes never left her face, burning his brand into her heart. No one had the right to have eyes like his. Hungry eyes. Eyes that held fire and the promise of passion.

131

"We'll have to do something about them," Shea said with a slight smile. She hoped her own eyes weren't revealing her confused, unfamiliar feelings for him. She would get over them soon; it was just that he was the sexiest thing she had ever encountered.

No one had ever needed her as he did. Not even her own mother. Jacques had a way of looking at her as if his life, the very air he breathed, depended solely on her. Intellectually she knew that any living person would really do for him, but she wrapped herself up in his hunger and fire anyway. For this time in her life, when she was alone and hunted, near the end of her endurance, and coping with many bizarre happenings, she would enjoy this unique experience.

His black eyes smoldered, a velvet seduction. *I need a dream to rid myself of nightmares.*

She backed away from him, holding a palm outward to ward him off. "Just you keep your ideas to yourself," she warned. "You have that devil's look, the one that says no woman is safe."

That is not true, Shea, he denied, the hard edge of his mouth softening into temptation. *Only one woman. You.*

She laughed at him. "I think I'm very

grateful you're in no condition to move around. The sun is coming up, and I have to secure the cottage for daylight. Go back to sleep. I'll be here when you wake up." Shea patted the one comfortable chair she had.

You will lie beside me where you should be, he informed her.

Shea carefully closed the shutters on the windows and fastened them. She was always cautious in locking her home. During the day she was very vulnerable. Already she could feel her body slowing, becoming heavier, more tired.

I want you to lie beside me. His voice was a sinful caress, enticing, insistent.

"I think you can manage all by yourself," she answered, refusing to look into his dark, hypnotic eyes. Instead, she shut off her computer and the generator and locked the door.

I have nightmares, little red hair. The only way to keep them at bay is to have you close beside me. He sounded very earnest, innocent, hopeful.

Shea found herself smiling as she poured him another unit of blood. She was beginning to think the devil himself had shown up at her doorstep. Jacques was temptation incarnate. "I removed a stake from your heart just a couple of nights ago, and you have a major wound there. If I move around while I sleep, I could easily bump into you and start it bleeding again. You wouldn't want that, would you?"

He took the container from her hand, his fingers curling around the glass precisely over the spot where her fingers had been. He did things like that, intimate things that sent butterfly wings brushing deep within her. *Not my heart, Shea. They did not get me in the heart, as they should have. It is here within my body — can you not hear it? Your heart beats with the same rhythm so that it matches mine.*

"Were you a playboy before they buried you?" she asked him, tossing a mischievous grin over her shoulder. Shea checked her gun to make certain it was clean and loaded. "You need to drink that, Jacques, not just hold it. And then go back to sleep. The more rest you get, the faster you'll heal."

You persist in being my doctor when I so need my lifemate to come and lie beside me. Again his voice was temptation itself.

"Drink, Jacques." She tried to sound stern, but it was impossible when he was looking so desperate for her company.

I am desperate.

She couldn't help but shake her head. "You're outrageous."

134

He made an attempt to raise the glass to his mouth, but his arm wobbled. *I cannot lift this without your aid, Shea. I am too weak.*

"Am I supposed to believe you?" She laughed aloud but crossed to his side. "You were strong enough to lift me off my feet with one hand when I found you. Don't give me that poor-little-boy look, Jacques, because it won't work."

But it was working. He needed to feel her touch, the brush of her fingers in his hair, and she stroked his thick mane without conscious thought. Her fingers lingered as if she enjoyed the sensation as much as he did. Jacques took the gun from her hand and pulled her down beside him, as hungry for the feel of her warmth beside him as he was for the sustenance she provided. Her scent drifted to him — the forest, the flowers, and the night air itself. He wrapped an arm around her and held her to him. She relaxed, allowing her eyelashes to drift down.

Shea slept fitfully, her body cumbersome in the light of the day. Jacques lay beside her, motionless, his arm a heavy weight curved possessively around her waist. Several times she struggled to surface during the afternoon hours, but it was an impossibility. Once she heard a noise outside the cabin, and her heart pounded in alarm, but she was unable to summon up enough energy to do more than clutch the gun beneath the pillow tightly. She knew she was responsible for their safety, yet she couldn't pry her eyes open or force herself to rise and check around the cabin to ensure no one was near.

The sun had long since sunk beneath the mountains before Shea managed to rouse herself. Hunger was a gnawing, relentless ache, but the thought of food made her stomach heave. She struggled to sit up, far weaker than she had ever been. She pushed a hand through her heavy fall of wine-red hair.

Jacques' fingers circled her arm, slid the length from shoulder to wrist. She was small and delicate, yet she had such inner strength. It amazed him how brave and courageous she was, how compassionate. He found her intriguing, mysterious even. The world as he knew it had begun seven years earlier: pain, isolation, and darkness. The monster in him had grown, eclipsed his soul. At first he had had no emotion at all, simply a will that would never die, an icy determination, a promise of retribution made in exchange for his lost soul. He would find them — the betrayer, the human assassins — and he would destroy them. But once he had found his lifemate, despite the distance that separated them, he had begun to feel. To smolder with a black fury that would never cease until he had found a way to retaliate for the loss of his soul. Every emotion he possessed was dark and ugly. Until Shea had changed him. Since the moment he had merged his mind with hers, he had stayed there in that haven, a part of her, a shadow so quiet she didn't always know he was there. He could not bear to be away from her.

Jacques' fist tangled in her thick, luxurious hair. She stirred things in him he had no name for. He would never endure closed-in places again, never endure being alone again. And he would never allow Shea to place herself at risk. Silently cursing his weakened body, he brought the silken strands of her hair to his face, inhaling her fragrance.

"I'm so tired, Jacques," she confessed, swaying slightly as she sat on the side of the bed. She found it strange to have someone to talk to, to wake up and not be alone. Shea should have been uncomfortable in the situation — she had never shared her life with anyone — yet with Jacques there was a weird familiarity, as if she had known him forever.

Her life had always been one of isolation, a certain distance always present between herself and others. Jacques had no respect for that barrier, slipping in and out of her head as if he belonged there. His touch was possessive, even intimate. Shea was bewildered by her own feelings, by her acceptance of their strange affinity. She was excited at her rare scientific find, perhaps holding an answer to the terrible disease that branded those so afflicted as *nosferatu,* unclean. The undead. Her kind was condemned to a life of hiding and loathing, always living in fear of being discovered. It was important to find out whether they were a separate species or whether some rare genetic code had given them a need for blood to sustain their lives.

Shea studied Jacques' worn but handsome face. He looked young, yet ageless. He looked tormented, as if he had suffered greatly, yet he looked like stone. She could see the power in him now; it clung like a second skin. Biting her lip, she drew away from him, her emerald eyes thoughtful. The strength and power in him was growing. His body might be mending slowly, but his unusual capabilities seemed to be recovering at a much faster rate. It occurred to her that she should be afraid of the creature now lying motionless in her bed. It was apparent that he could be extraordinarily dangerous, was capable of extreme violence. Especially with his mind so fractured, his rage so deep.

Jacques sighed. *I do not like that you fear me, Shea.*

"If you wouldn't persist in reading my thoughts, Jacques," she said gently, afraid she had hurt him, "then you wouldn't have to see these things I worry about. You are capable of violence. You cannot deny it. I see it in you."

She stood up with a return of her quick, restless energy, and he allowed her silken hair to slide through his fingers. With half-closed eyes, Jacques watched the transparent thoughts slipping across her expressive face. Shea was incapable of subterfuge. What she was, who she was, was an open book.

"I didn't think things through, you know. I just rushed out and rescued you. I caused you great suffering." Her large green eyes fastened on his face. Storm clouds gathered instantly when she felt his faint, mocking amusement echoing through her mind. "What? What's so funny? Some idiot tried to put a stake through your heart, and he didn't even hit the darn thing!"

For which I am grateful. And I am even more

grateful that you rescued me. I did not like being imprisoned and in such pain.

"I guess I'm glad I rescued you, too, but the truth is, Jacques, I have watched you healing faster than is possible. You're even more dangerous now. You are, aren't you?"

Never to you, he denied.

She raised an eyebrow. "Is that strictly the truth? I've been in your head, too, remember." She had touched his mind and had recoiled at the seething cauldron of raw violence and black fury often swirling within him. "Sometimes I can even read you as well as you read me. You have no idea what you're doing half the time. You have no idea who you are."

Perhaps not, Shea, but I know you are my lifemate. I could not harm you now. His face remained granite, his eyes dark and ice cold. She was right. He was dangerous. He knew it in his soul. His mind was not to be trusted. Her presence kept him tranquil, calm, but his mind was a maze of dark, deadly trails. He had no idea if he would be able to distinguish reality from nightmare if their delicately balanced world tilted in any way. His black eyes went a glittering obsidian, and he looked away from her, ashamed. He should allow her to leave, give her her freedom, but he could not. She was

140

his only sanity, his only path to the surface from the hellish nightmare he lived in. *I have sworn to protect you, Shea. I can only promise it is in my heart to do so.*

Shea stepped away from the bed, suddenly close to tears. He was in a treacherous labyrinth; he walked a fine line between sanity and a world she did not want to try to comprehend. "I will protect you, Jacques. You have my solemn word, I won't let you down. I'll see you through this until you're right again."

And then? His black gaze slid lazily over her. *Do you intend to leave me, Shea? You save me, and then you think to desert me?* There was a kind of dark humor in his voice, a secret amusement that stirred something in her she hadn't known existed. Something that went beyond fear. Terror.

Her chin tilted a little belligerently. "What does that mean? Of course I won't desert you. I'll stay with you and see you through this. We'll find your family."

It was too late. Even if she attempted to put distance between them, she could not break their bond. His blood ran in her veins; his mind was familiar with the path to hers. Their souls called to one another. Hearts were following, and it was only matter of time before he possessed her body. Running would not save either of them. Jacques knew it with a certainty with which he knew few other things. But imparting the knowledge to her would frighten her more. His heart twisted, a funny somersault. His Shea feared death far less than she feared personal commitment. She really had no idea they were already bound together. She would need him, need him close, need him touching her in her mind, in her body.

I feel your need to perform the human functions you seem to enjoy. Go bathe. I am in no hurry to have you examine my wounds.

Shea blinked once, her green eyes thoughtful before she turned away to disappear into the other room. He was making an attempt to put her at ease, but it sent a chill through her. His voice held some note, one she realized was beginning to emerge more and more, one she found disturbing. It was possessive, holding complete authority. She had the feeling Jacques was slowly taking over her life. He was in her thoughts, in her head. He was everywhere, and she was allowing it to happen.

Jacques lay quietly, staring up at the ceiling. Shea was worried about the way she responded to him. Her brain intrigued him, the way she addressed every problem from a scientific or intellectual angle rather than an emotional one. He felt the smile that wanted to tug at the corners of his mouth. He knew her thoroughly; he spent more time in her mind than out of it. He was taking no chances on losing her.

She had been trying to reassure him with talk of his family. He had no family other than Shea. He wanted no other, needed no other. She hadn't accepted her role as yet. Half of her persisted in looking at him as a patient. She was a healer first, a researcher second. He was in her mind. He knew very well she never entertained the idea of a long-term arrangement. She didn't expect to live long, let alone share her life with anyone. The idea was so foreign to her nature, she couldn't yet conceive of it.

He listened to the water running in the other room, knew it sprayed over her bare skin. His body stirred uncomfortably, the beginnings of an unrelenting ache. It amazed him that his body was coming back to life, that he could feel signs of sexual awareness. He had a vague feeling he had not known such a thing in many centuries, let alone with his body so battered and his mind so fragmented. Shea had given him back life. More than life. More than existing. He couldn't wait to see the smile on her face, the way her hair was always such a flyaway mess begging for his attention. He loved to watch every gesture she made, every movement and turn of her head. He liked the way her brain worked, focused and absolute, the way her mind was filled with humor and compassion.

Jacques cursed the weakness of his body. He needed fresh blood desperately. He stilled his mind and body, calling on all of his reserve strength. He lifted a hand, concentrated, and focused on the cabin door. Pain beat in his head. Fire raced along his wounds. Cursing, he slumped back against the pillows. He could use physical powers, yet when he called on his mind for the simplest task, he could not perform it.

He smelled her first, her clean fragrance, the scent of flowers drifting from her hair. She had rushed in to the room so silently he had not actually heard the sound of her bare feet on the floor, but his mind never completely separated itself from hers, and he knew the exact moment she had caught up a towel and run to him.

"What is it, Jacques, did you try to move, tear something open?" There was anxiety in her voice, but her touch was coolly professional as she examined his wounds.

The towel was large, a pale peach sheath of cotton encasing her slender body. As she bent over him, a bead of water ran from her shoulder across the swell of her breast to disappear beneath the towel. Jacques watched the little bead of moisture and suddenly was incredibly thirsty. Her eyelashes were ridiculously long, her lush mouth set in a slight frown as she searched her small, precise stitches for signs of damage. She was so incredibly beautiful, she took his breath away.

"Jacques? What is it?" Her voice whispered over him like a caress.

No memories, no abilities. The simplest task is impossible. His thumb feathered gently back and forth along the inside of her wrist.

"You'll heal, Jacques. Don't be impatient. If you need something, I can get it for you." His thumb was sending butterflies winging through her stomach. It amazed her that she was so susceptible to his charm. She just wasn't like that.

Although his harshly sensual features remained a mask, something inside him melted, and he felt a leap of joy. He wanted to smile in spite of everything. The pain ceased to matter, his shattered memories and impotent body were merely inconveniences he would eventually get over. Shea mattered. *Open the door for me that I might breathe the night,* he said and tried not to devour her with his eyes. He was well aware she was beginning to see that no one — certainly not Shea with her gentle, compassionate nature — could oppose his will, a will honed in the fires of hell.

She did as he asked. "You didn't try to get up, did you? You can't, Jacques. You'll do too much damage. And if you keep adding scar tissue, you'll end up looking like Frankenstein."

He had closed his eyes to inhale the fresh, clean night air. *Carpathians never scar.* It came out of nowhere. He was elated he remembered something. He was even elated he remembered Frankenstein.

Her eyebrows shot up. "Oh, really? Then what's that thin line around your throat? I barely caught it, but it's there."

His black eyes snapped open, a merciless fury burning there. Shea stepped away from him quickly, her heart pounding. She could actually see red flames burning in the depths of his eyes. He looked like a demon, an invincible predator. The impression was so strong that she brought a protective hand to her throat to cover the evidence of the ragged wounds there.

Jacques was unaware of Shea, the room, even his own weak body. The sensation of battle was strong in him. He touched the uneven, faint white scar curving around his jugular. The impression of danger was so strong, he felt the beast in him rage for release. Fangs exploded in his mouth, and his nails began to lengthen. His muscles rippled and contracted, and his power and enormous strength bonded briefly with his will. A slow, venomous hiss escaped him. Then the pain in his body from muscles waiting for release made him aware of lying helpless in a bed. He dimly remembered a woman's anxious face, tears swimming in her large blue eyes. He should know her. He should know. Fists clenched, and he welcomed the exploding pain that drove the fragment of memory from his mind.

Shea saw his hands come up, clutch at his head to try to stop the pain. Instantly she was back at his side, soothing fingers brushing at the hair spilling across his forehead. "Jacques, stop tormenting yourself. It will all come back to you. Believe me, I know what I'm talking about. Things are already coming back." Shea padded across the room to her dresser and pulled out fresh clothes. "You persist in thinking your body can instantly set aside the trauma it suffered. It needs rest to repair itself, rest and care. So does your mind."

I cannot do the things I must. I remember

147

nothing, yet I feel there are things important to both of us I need to know.

She smiled at his frustration. Jacques was a man unused to being ill or injured. "You referred to yourself as a Carpathian. You know you're from this mountain range. You remembered that."

She moved into the other room. He could hear the sound of her dressing, the whisper of silk panties and cotton jeans sliding over her bare legs. His body clenched, burned, the rush of heat adding to his discomfort.

"Jacques?" Her voice was so soft, playing along his skin and nerve endings like the touch of fingers. "Please don't be discouraged. Technically, you should be dead. You beat all the odds." She moved back into the room, towel-drying her hair. "You thought I was one of your people. A Carpathian. Who are they? Can you remember?"

I am Carpathian. We are immortal. We can . . . He stopped, the information eluding him.

Shea leaned against the wall, regarding him with fascinated awe. Her mouth was suddenly dry; her heart slammed hard against her chest. "What are you saying, Jacques? You live forever?" What *was* he? And why was she beginning to believe him? Seven years buried alive. Surviving on the

148

blood of rats. She had seen the red glow in his eyes on more than one occasion. She felt his impossible strength, even injured as severely as he was.

Her hands, clutching the towel, were trembling so much, she put them behind her back. *Vampire.* The word came unbidden to her mind. "It isn't true," she denied in a whisper. "It's impossible. I am not anything like that. I won't believe you."

Shea. His voice was calm, tranquil, as she became more agitated. He needed all his memories, not these shattered bits and pieces that frustrated him so.

"Jacques, you might be a vampire. I'm so confused, I'll almost believe anything. But I am not like that." She was talking more to herself than to him. Every horrible tale of vampires ever told rose up to haunt her. Her hand crept up to her neck as she recalled the vicious way he had taken her blood the first time they had met. He'd nearly killed her. "You didn't because you needed me to help you," she said suddenly, softly. It didn't occur to her that she had become so accustomed to his reading her mind, she simply accepted that he would know what she was talking about. Was he controlling her all the time? Couldn't vampires do that?

Jacques watched her closely, his body motionless, his icy black eyes unblinking. He could taste her fear in his mouth, feel it beat at him in his mind. Even while she was afraid, her brain processed information at a remarkable rate. The way she shoved emotion aside to concentrate on the intellectual was a protection. He had given her a glimpse of the darkness in him, the violence. It was something that was as natural to him as breathing. Sooner or later she would have to face what and who he really was.

Shea felt caught in the trap of his merciless, empty black eyes, like a mesmerized rabbit. As frozen as she was, her body wanted to move toward him, as if under a strange compulsion. "Answer me, Jacques. You know everything I'm thinking. Answer me."

After seven years of pain and starvation, little red hair, after torment and suffering, I thought to take your blood.

"My life," she corrected bravely, needing all the pieces of the puzzle.

He stared relentlessly, the watchful eyes of a predator. Shea twisted her fingers together in agitation. He looked a stranger, an invincible being with no real emotion, only a hard resolve and a killer's instincts. She cleared her throat. "You needed me."

I had no thought but to feed. My body recog-

nized yours before my mind did.

"I don't understand."

Once I recognized you as my lifemate, my first thought was to punish you for leaving me in torment, then bind you to me for eternity. There was no apology, only a waiting.

Shea sensed danger, but she did not back down. "How did you bind me to you?"

The exchange of our blood.

Her heart slammed painfully. "What does that mean, exactly?"

The blood bond is strong. I am in your mind, as you are in mine. It is impossible for us to lie to one another. I feel your emotions and know your thoughts as you do mine.

She shook her head in denial. "That may be true for you, but not for me. I feel your pain at times, but I never know your thoughts."

That is because you choose not to merge with me. Your mind seeks the touch and reassurance of mine often, yet you refuse to allow it, so I merge with you to prevent your discomfort.

Shea could not deny the truth in his words. Often she felt her mind tuning itself to his, reaching out for him. Disturbed by the unwanted and unfamiliar need, she always imposed a strict discipline on herself. It was unconscious on her part, something she did automatically for self-protection.

Jacques, within minutes of her need arising, always reached for her to merge them. She took a deep breath, let it out slowly. "You seem to know more about what is happening here than I do, Jacques. Tell me."

Lifemates are bound together for all eternity. One cannot exist without the other. We balance one another. You are the light to my darkness. We must share one another often.

Her face paled. Her legs weakened. She sat down abruptly on the floor. *Her mother. All of her life she had condemned her mother for living a shadow existence.* If Jacques was telling the truth, and something in her feared he was, had this happened to her mother? Had Jacques sentenced Shea to the same terrible fate?

Shea's hand found the wall. Using it as a support, she pulled herself up. "I refuse to buy into this. I am not your lifemate. I made no commitment, nor will I." She began edging along the wall toward the door.

Shea, do not! It was no plea, rather an imperious command, his harsh features an implacable mask.

"I won't let you do this to me. I don't care if you are a vampire. You can make the choice to kill me, Jacques, because there is no other way."

You have no conception of power, Shea, its

uses or misuses. His voice was a soft menace, the tone sending a shiver down her spine. *Do not defy me.*

Her chin lifted. "My mother's life was a waste and my childhood hell. If the man who was my father was like you and somehow bound her to him, then abandoned her —" She broke off, took a deep breath to regain control. "I'm strong, Jacques. No one is going to own me or control me or abuse me. I will not kill myself over a man's desertion. Nor would I ever leave my child alone in the world while I withdrew and became an empty shell."

Jacques could feel the hurt she had suffered as a child. Her memories were stark and ugly. She had been utterly alone and in need of support and guidance. Like any child, she had blamed herself for her isolation. On some level she thought she was not lovable, too different to be loved. The child had retreated from her emotions — it was unsafe there — and had trained her intellect to take over when she was frightened or threatened in any way.

She stepped backward out the door, her eyes still locked with his. Jacques made an effort to tamp down his dark fury, the promise of retaliation, but it was impossible to hide the swirling emotions from her. She was too close, too aware of him now. Jacques simply withdrew from her, silently. He turned his face away from her. Shea whirled and ran, tears for her mother, tears for herself, running down her face. She never cried, never. She had learned a long time ago that tears never helped. Why had she been so foolish as to think she could tamper with things she didn't understand?

She ran fast, her body sleek and streamlined, making a silent dash over rotting logs and moss-covered boulders. It took some time to realize she was barefoot, and never once had either foot come down on a dry branch or small rock. She seemed to skim over the ground rather than pound on it. Her lungs were fine, no fierce burning for oxygen. There was only hunger, sharp and gnawing, growing with each step she took.

Shea slowed to a steady lope, lifting her face to the stars. Everything was so intensely beautiful. The wind carried scents, stories. Fox kits in a den, two deer nearby, a rabbit in the brush. She stopped abruptly beside a small stream. She had to have a plan. Running away like a wild animal was totally ridiculous. Her hands found the trunk of a tree, fingertips feeling each whorl, hearing the sap running like blood, the very life of the tree. She knew each insect invading it, making its home in the wood.

She sank down in the soft soil, guilt washing over her. She had left him alone, unprotected. She had not fed him. Her forehead slipped into her open palms. Everything was so crazy. Nothing added up. Hunger ate at her like an insidious monster, and she could hear the heartbeats of the animals in the forest beckoning.

Vampire. Was there such a creature? Was she such a creature? Jacques took blood from her so easily, in so practiced a manner. She knew what was in him; he could be utterly cold and merciless, raging with venomous fury. It never showed on his face or in the way he talked to her, but it was there, seething below the surface. Shea picked up a stone and threw it toward the bubbling stream.

Jacques. What was she going to do about him? Her body rippled with discomfort, her mind with unease. She had an overwhelming urge to reach out to him, to assure herself he was all right. Her mind was trying to comprehend, to believe the impossible. He was a creature far different from a human being. She wasn't like him, but her father must have been.

"What are you thinking, Shea?" she whispered. "A vampire? You think this man is an honest-to-God vampire? You're losing your mind."

A shudder shook her slender frame. Jacques had said blood exchanges bound them together. Had he somehow managed to make her completely like him? Shea's tongue ran along the inside of her mouth, explored her teeth. They seemed the same, small and straight. Hunger burned, rose sharp and voracious.

At once she could hear the heartbeat of a small rabbit. Her heart sang with exultation. A fierce, predatory joy rushed through her, and she turned toward her prey. Against her tongue, fangs exploded, sharp incisors, hungry and waiting.

Chapter Five

Jacques knew the precise moment Shea discovered the truth. Her heart beat frantically; her silent cry of denial echoed through his mind. She believed herself to be vampire. She believed him vampire. What else could she possibly deduce with so little information? Her thoughts were desperate, even life threatening. He lay very still, gathered his strength should it be needed to stop any foolish decision she might make. He simply waited, monitoring her thoughts and the telltale signs of her body.

To be alone was a kind of agony in itself. Jacques would not have been able to bear it if his mind was not a shadow dwelling in hers. Sweat broke out, bathing his skin in a fine film. His every instinct was to force her back to his side, and he was gaining strength daily now. But a part of him wanted her to return to him on her own.

What had she said to him? Her mother was Irish. Shea did not believe she was like him. What if she hadn't been? What if he had inadvertently turned her? Jacques had never considered that possibility. Their bond was strong. It had crossed man's boundaries. Jacques had assumed he had known her all of his existence, long before the betrayer had delivered him into the hands of the two human butchers and into madness, into the absence of memory. His suffering, his agony, had been hers. He had felt her with him. He wasn't mistaken about that. He had been certain he had always known her, that she was his lifemate. When she did not come for him, his every waking moment had been spent gathering his strength to bend her will to his in his eternity of hell. What if she had been human? He had been carelessly cruel that first day, wanting her bound to him, under his domination.

Jacques called on his fragmented memories. *Three blood exchanges. Psychic ability.* A human possessing psychic ability might be converted under the right conditions if three blood exchanges were made. He closed his eyes against the guilt and remorse sweeping through his head. If she were human, that would explain her strange feeding habits, her human ways. She never took necessary precautions, never scanned before leaving the cabin. *She didn't know how.* She had said she could not shut down her heart and lungs. She never slept the rejuvenating sleep of a Carpathian.

He cursed himself eloquently. The night

she had been so sick, her body had gone through the conversion. There was no other explanation. She had believed she'd contracted a very virulent strain of the flu. He loathed himself for his inability to remember important information. It came only in fragments, and she was suffering because of his ignorance.

Shea's bond with him had been so strong, it had never occurred to him that she was not Carpathian. He thought her courageous as a Carpathian woman to dare venture into his prison and save him. It was nearly impossible to believe a human female had been so compassionate and brave to return to his gravesite after the callous way he had treated her. She had been terrified, yet she had returned to him.

A scent drifted in with the night breeze. Game, fairly close. It wasn't human, but the fresh, living nourishment would help. If he could feed enough, he could safely make an exchange and try to keep Shea alive. She was refusing food. Or perhaps not refusing. Perhaps she was unable to feed. He focused, inhaled deeply, and sent forth a call. Closer, closer, on the porch, the first step into the cabin. First one, a doe, usually a shy and skittish animal, padded across the floor to the side of the bed, her dark, liquid eyes fixed on him. A second doe and then a third followed, bunched together, awaiting his attention.

Hunger rose. Sharp fangs exploded into his mouth, and he seized the first doe with his enormous strength, found the artery pulsing in the neck. The wildness grew in him, rushed through him, and he welcomed it. Hot blood, pulsing with life, sweet and powerful, poured into his depleted system, swelling shriveled cells. He drank greedily, his hunger insatiable, his mutilated body craving the dark liquid of life.

Shea lifted her face to the stars, felt the tears on her cheeks. Her throat was raw and burning, her chest tight. If her father had been one such as Jacques, contaminating her blood, Jacques had finished what her parent had started. She hadn't mixed up her blood samples with Jacques' because she had been so tired. Her blood matched his exactly.

She made an effort to control her trembling. She needed to think; it was her only salvation. Her brain could overcome any problem. She breathed deeply, calming herself as she always did in any threatening situation. At once she thought of Jacques alone and helpless in the cabin. She couldn't desert him. She would never leave him when he was so helpless. She would set things up for him so he could survive on his own. She would no longer eat or drink anything other than water. She couldn't take any chances until she was certain what she was dealing with.

She wandered downstream, away from the cabin. She felt very alone. This time her mind insisted she had to reach out to him. She needed his warmth, the reassurance of his touch. Shea turned that thought over. Jacques obviously was telling her the truth. She had been alone her entire life. She had not needed anyone, least of all a creature whose mind was shattered, whose nature was that of a killer. Yet she had to know he was not suffering, that nothing had happened to him while she was gone.

Deliberately she waded into the stream, the ice-cold water shocking her, numbing her body but not her mind. Imposing her will, strong and disciplined through a childhood of isolation, Shea resisted merging with him. The water was so cold, she could no longer feel her feet, but it helped to clear her head somewhat.

Jacques released the third deer and inhaled sharply. Shea was strong-willed. He knew she would try her best to resist their bond. Her childhood had been hell, yet she had survived, and it had shaped her into a strong, brilliant, courageous woman. He longed to calm her, to reassure her, but knew she would not welcome his intrusion. She had reason to fear him. He remembered so few things. Betrayal. Pain. Rage. He had been so clumsy in his handling of her conversion, in his handling of everything.

The deer stirred, stumbled to their feet, and, wobbling unsteadily, plodded out to the freedom of the forest. Jacques would have finished them off, utilized every drop of life-giving nourishment he could, but Shea would have thought him a monster. His body tuned itself to hers, craved the sight and scent of her, the touch of her. Perhaps he was a monster. He really didn't know anything other than that he needed Shea.

Shea wandered aimlessly until she could no longer think of anything but Jacques. The emptiness inside her yawned like a enormous black void. Her skin crawled with need, her mind was chaos, reaching, always reaching, so that she was worn out with fighting herself.

What if something had happened to him?

Again the thought crept in unbidden, unwanted, and her sense of isolation increased, threatened to become a terrible thing. Grief welled up, enveloping her, driving away her logic and reason, leaving raw, gaping emotions. Shea could no longer function properly, and she knew it. Whether or not her pride allowed, she had no choice but to go back. It was not only humiliating but frightening, too. Jacques had acquired more power over her in a short time than she had ever thought possible. She had no choice but to accept it for the moment.

She walked slowly, reluctantly, dread filling her, yet with every step back toward the cabin, toward Jacques, the heaviness of her heart lifted. At the edge of the clearing before the cottage, three large deer rested beneath the swaying branches of a tree. She stood for a moment watching them, all too aware of what had transpired. Shea stepped onto the porch, hesitated, and went inside.

Jacques was lying motionless in the bed, his black eyes wide open, fixed unblinkingly on her face. Shea felt as if she were falling forward into those black, fathomless depths. He held out a hand to her. She didn't want to go to him; she went because she had to go. She needed to go to him. A part of her brain analyzed that, how it could possibly be, but she went without fighting the strong compulsion.

His fingers, unexpectedly warm, closed around the coolness of hers, his hand enveloping hers. He tugged at her gently until she had no choice but to sit, then lie beside him. His black eyes never once relinquished their hold on hers. *You are cold, little red hair.* His voice whispered over her skin, mesmerized her mind, dispelled the chaos to replace it with a soothing, tranquil calm. *Allow me to warm you.*

His hand shaped her face, traced each delicate bone, stroked down her throat. Shea blinked, confused, unsure whether she was awake or dreaming. Her body moved restlessly. Again her brain attempted to sort things out for her, but she could not pull away from his hypnotic eyes. Part of her didn't want to. She wanted to be trapped there for all time, sheltered by him, belonging to him.

Ignoring the screaming protest of his body, Jacques shifted so that his large frame half pinned her smaller one to the bed. His hand continued to caress the soft, vulnerable line of her throat, moved to trace the neckline of her cotton top. *Feel the way our hearts beat together.* His hand pushed the concealing fabric aside so that her full breasts gleamed in the silver light of the moon.

His mind felt the protest of hers, his soft voice murmuring to weave her deeper under his spell. In the depths of his eyes was hunger, fire, need. He trapped the emerald green of her eyes in the intensity of his hot gaze. A slash of razor-sharp talons, and cotton floated to the floor. His hand found warm softness, and with his black stare still holding hers, he slowly lowered his head.

Shea's breath caught in her throat as his perfect mouth hovered a scant inch above hers. She burned for him. Burned. Her long lashes swept down as his mouth fastened on hers. She nearly cried out at the rush of liquid heat racing through her body at his touch. His mouth explored every inch of hers, caressing, demanding, gentle, and dominant, a sweet stroking along her incisors, a stark male possession.

His mouth left hers to trail kisses down her throat, her shoulder, lower to find the swell of her breast. Shea's hands found his hair, its rich softness bunched in her fists as his tongue traced a path over her pulse. Her body clenched, waited in anticipation. His teeth nipped gently, moved again so that she shuddered with pleasure as his mouth drew her rich softness into its moist heat. *I want you, Shea. I need you.*

And it was true. His body didn't seem to understand that claiming her was an impossibility. He hurt, a pain to rival all the others. His skin burned and was unbearably sensitive. Reluctantly he released her breast, moved once more to stroke his tongue over her pulse. *Shea.* He murmured her name, and his teeth sank deep.

She gasped at the white-hot lance of pain, the wave of intense pleasure washing over her. Her body arced upward, her arms cradling his head.

It was ecstasy, holding her like this, feeding on sweetness, exploring her softness with his hands. The pleasure was such that Jacques' battered body swelled, every muscle taut, rigid. She tasted hot, spicy, addicting. He needed to bury himself in her as he fed. Every natural instinct he possessed, as both man and beast, urgently demanded he unite them in the way of his people, sealing them together for all eternity. Her breasts were soft, perfect, driving him to the brink of madness. Did her ribcage have to be so small and delicate, her waist so tiny? He didn't just want. He needed. He lifted his head, his tongue stroking across the tiny wound, reluctantly closing it.

Shea's eyes were closed, her body soft and

pliant. *You need, my love.* He kissed her gently. *Kiss me, my chest. Let me feel that your need is as great as my own.*

It was sheer black magic, an erotic whisper of seduction she seemed helpless to resist. Her mouth tasted his skin, lingered, found his throat, the heavy muscles of his chest. Jacques knew he was playing with fire. His body could not take much more. His hand caught the nape of her neck, pressed her head to him. *You hunger, my love.*

Self-preservation interceded, and her body stiffened.

Jacques' voice was purity itself. *You will take what I freely offer. It is my right, and you cannot deny me.* The touch of her tongue sent fire racing through his blood. When her teeth pierced his skin, he cried out with the ecstasy of it. He gave himself up to the sensual pleasure, his hand stroking her hair, encouraging her feeding. He needed this closeness, this erotic intimacy. If he could not have all of her at this moment, he could at least ensure their bond.

He held her, blanketing her body in the age-old dominant way of his people, yet there was tenderness in his hands as they caressed her. Slowly his hand slid over her silky hair, stroked, lingered, moved around to trace the delicate lines of her face. Then carefully he began to insert his hand between her mouth and his chest. *Enough, Shea. Close the wound with your tongue.* His gut clenched hotly, his body shuddered as she obeyed him. He wanted her, needed, even hungered for their union. For a moment he felt that need was far more tormenting than wounds.

He caught her hair in both hands, dragged her head up to his, when everything in him screamed to push her down, to force her to give him some relief. Jacques felt as if he was in hell all over again. His mouth found hers, tasted his own blood. Something inside him raised its head and roared, wild, untamed, something close to breaking free of his tight control. Instinctively his mind sought hers. *Shea!*

The summons was sharp, on the edge of desperation. Shea blinked, found herself tangled on the bed with Jacques, her skin rubbing against his, his arms tight, vise-like bands around her, his mouth taking hers with such expertise that her entire body raged for him. He was aggressive, dominant, the position he held her in one of submission. When she looked up at him, his eyes went from desperation, hungry desire, and tenderness to a bestial glow, that of a wild animal taking what belonged to it. She recognized those red flames leaping, betraying the violence in him. When she stiffened, tried to struggle, a warning growl rumbled deep in his throat.

Shea went very still, forced her mind away from panic and fear, back toward logic. He had called to her in need. The moment she realized that, she relaxed, holding him in her arms with acceptance. He needed her, and she could do no other than help him. His hands were everywhere, rough, hurting even; his teeth bit at her much too hard. *Jacques.* Deliberately she sought the red haze of his mind. She was calm, tranquil, accepting of his bestial nature. *Come back to me.*

He latched on to her like a drowning man, merging his mind with hers. He was breathing hard, in such pain. She could feel the dark desire beating at him, the demand that he claim what was rightfully his. Jacques struggled for control of the monster within him. Shea kissed his throat, the hard line of his jaw, a soothing, gentle touch. *It's all right. Come back to me.*

He buried his face in her neck, crushed her tightly to him. He was exhausted, in pain, afraid he had driven her even further away. It was Shea who stroked his hair, murmured soothing nonsense, Shea who lay soft and pliant close to his heart. Her palm shaped the side of his face, a physical contact; her mind merged firmly, wholly, with his.

I am sorry. Jacques rested his chin on top of her head, unwilling to face the condemnation he feared would be reflected in her eyes.

Ssh, just be still. I should never have left you alone.

You did not cause this. His arms tightened momentarily. *Shea, do not think that. You are not to blame for my madness. My body needs yours. The mating between lifemates is not exactly the same as human mating. I nearly hurt you, Shea. I am sorry.*

You're the one in pain, Jacques, she pointed out gently. She realized she was using their mental link, accepting it as natural. She sighed, reached up to kiss his chin.

They held each other like two children after a terrible fright, taking comfort in one another's closeness. Shea became aware after a time that her skin was against his, bare, sensitive, her breasts pressed into his side. "I don't suppose you want to tell me what happened to my shirt." She lay motionless, drowsy and content. Being so close to him should have bothered her, but it simply seemed normal. Her gaze found the material slashed to ribbons, scattered on the floor beside the bed. "You were in a bit of a hurry, I see," she pointed out, making an effort to get up to get dressed.

When Shea would have pulled away from him, Jacques refused to relinquish his hold. Instead, he reached lazily for the quilt and pulled it around her. His smile was in her mind. *Tell me of your childhood.* He dropped the words into the silence, felt her shock, her pain, her instant withdrawal. *I want you to tell me this yourself, Shea. I could look into your memories, but it is not the same as your trusting me with something so personal.* He had already seen her childhood, the terrible way she had grown up alone. Jacques wanted her to share it with him, to give him the priceless gift of her trust.

Shea could hear the strong, steady beat of his heart, a soothing rhythm. It seemed only fair that she share her nightmare when she had glimpsed the dark stain on his soul. "I became aware something was wrong with my mother at a very early age. She would withdraw for weeks at a time, never noticing if I ate or slept or was hurt. She had no friends. She almost never left the house. She rarely showed interest or affection."

Jacques' hand slid over her hair in a

caress, found the nape of her neck in a comforting massage. The distress in her voice was almost more than he could bear.

"I was six years old when I discovered I was different, that I needed blood. My mother had forgotten me for several days in a row. She just lay in bed and stared at the ceiling. I would go into her room every morning to kiss her good-bye before going to school. She never seemed to notice. As the days went by, I became so weak I couldn't walk across the room. She came to me, and I watched as she cut herself and bled into a glass. She told me I had to drink it — to drink blood often. After she died, I only used transfusions, but . . ."

She was silent for so long that Jacques touched her mind, felt her childhood self-loathing, her fears, and her sense of isolation. His arms tightened, drew her closer to his powerful frame, wanting to shelter her for all time. He knew what it meant to be alone. Totally alone. He never wanted her to feel like that again.

Shea felt the light brush of Jacques' mouth on her forehead, at her temple, in her hair. His tenderness warmed her when she was shivering inside. "My mother wasn't like me. No one was like me. I could never tell anyone, ask anyone about it. She took me to Ireland to hide me because when I was born, my blood was so odd it stirred interest in both the medical and scientific fields. I had to be transfused daily, but I still grew weak. When I was a few years old, two men came to our house and asked her a lot of questions about me. I could hear their voices, and I was afraid. I hid under the bed, afraid she might make me see them. She didn't. They scared my mother as much as they did me. She packed us up and moved us away."

You are certain your mother never touched blood? He probed gently, afraid she would stop sharing what were obviously painful memories. He had no real way to ease her hurt except with the strength of his arms and the closeness of his body.

"Never. She was like a beautiful shadow already gone from the world. She thought only of him. Rand. My father."

The name touched a painful fragment of memory in him. It was so intense, he let it slip away before he could catch it. *You never met him?* The mere thought of the man she called her father brought splinters of glass stabbing through his head.

"No, he was married to a woman named Noelle."

Shocked recognition, an inconsolable

grief, a woman once beautiful, beheaded, a stake through her heart. The memory was so vivid, so intense, Jacques choked, shoved the information far away from him. But he had recognized her. *Noelle.*

Shea lifted her head, green eyes searching his black gaze. "You know her." She shared the memory in his mind, saw the same fragments of images. The glimpse sickened her, the brutality of that death. The woman had been murdered using the ritual "vampire" slaying techniques. Beheaded. The stake.

She is dead. He said it with certainty, with sorrow. *She was my sister.*

Shea's face went white. "Did she have a son?"

A male child.

"Oh, God!" Shea tore herself out of his arms as if burned, leapt up and away from him, her arms covering her breasts, her eyes wild. "This gets worse every minute. My father was probably your sister's husband." She backed away from the bed in horror.

You do not know this. It is a big world.

"How many Rands are there from the Carpathian Mountains, someone like you? Someone married to a woman named Noelle, who gave birth to a boy? It was all in my mother's diary."

Vampire hunters drove a stake through her

*heart. Years ago. Years before they got me. I do
not remember more. Perhaps I do not care to.*

Shea found another shirt, dragged it on.
"I'm sorry for her. I'm sorry for my mother.
This is all so wrong." She waved a hand, encompassed the bed. "We're probably related or something."

*Lifemates are born to one another, Shea.
There is only one for each. What your parents or
my sister chose to do with their lives has nothing
to do with us.*

"Of course it does. We don't know who
you really are. We know virtually nothing
about you. What I'm doing here with you is
against the rules of my profession. We don't
even know if you're married or not."

*There is only one lifemate, Shea. I know this
is all new and frightening to you, but as I must
lie here in frustration, you must have patience.
We are finding out information in bits and
pieces. I cannot remember details I know are
important to us. I ask that you be patient while
we sort these things out.* He shifted uncomfortably.

The movement brought her back to herself, calmed her as nothing else could. "You
aren't taking care of yourself, Jacques. You
can't be moving around." She bent over
him, her hand cool on his burning skin. The
hole below his heart was beginning to heal.

Her long hair fell over her shoulder, brushed his abdomen with fire. The warmth of her breath as she leaned over him to examine the wound was like a dancing flame on his skin.

Jacques closed his eyes as every muscle in his body clenched in response. His reaction to her more than anything else told him that he was healing. His hand knotted in the silk of her hair. *I know you think to leave me, Shea, when I am at full strength.* Her enormous eyes jumped to his face, watched as he crushed her silky hair to his mouth. *You fear me. I can see the fear in your eyes.*

Her tongue moistened her lower lip. She looked thoughtful. Jacques found her mind using its ability to shove her emotions aside as it did when she felt threatened in some way. Her intellect took over, assessing the situation between them. "I don't know what you are, Jacques, or, when you're perfectly well, what you're capable of doing. I know nothing of your past or your future. I'm a medical researcher, and, once you recover, it's very possible we won't have a thing in common."

His black gaze did not leave her face. Hard. Watchful. Even his body seemed utterly still. *You fear me.* He wanted her to face the real issue, not push it aside. *You have no reason to fear me.*

She tilted her head to one side, red hair cascading in all directions. "You think I don't? Jacques, you threaten everything I have ever known about life. You changed me. If I was only half Carpathian, or whatever it is — vampire, maybe, I don't know at this point — you did something to bring me all the way into your world. I'm different now. I can't eat, I have no human bodily functions, and my hearing has increased even more. All my abilities. Everything. You took away the life I knew and replaced it with something neither of us knows anything about." She shook her head, then gave in to the desire to tangle her fingers in his jet-black hair. "I will not be like my mother, Jacques, living only for a man. When he deserted her, she waited only until she thought I no longer needed her, and she killed herself. That isn't love, it's obsession. No child of mine will ever suffer what her sick obsession with Rand put me through."

He breathed in her scent, and again the heat was upon him, scorching him with the urgent demand to bury himself in her, to become truly one. *I need you, Shea. Is it so impossible to think you might actually love me? I feel your complete acceptance of me. I know it is in you. Rand and your mother have nothing to do with us. You saw the darkness in me, the beast struggling for control, yet you remained. My imprisonment may have destroyed whatever I originally was, and I do not know who I am now. But I know that I need you. Would you really leave me alone?*

She felt his despair. "Don't start believing you're a monster. The way you touch me sometimes, with such tenderness, that is no monster." Her body was restless, a need moving over her, through her, a need she had never known before. "You wanted me, Jacques, yet you stopped yourself. You're no monster."

Maybe my wounds stopped me, not my self control. She had stopped him with her acceptance of the beast in him.

"You're tired, Jacques. Sleep for a while."

He caught her hand, his thumb feathering across the inside of her wrist. *I am not a vampire. I have not turned.*

"I don't understand."

He closed his eyes, smiled in his mind. She was back to using her professional, scientific voice. *You were worried that I had turned. Earlier, in the woods, you were afraid I was a vampire. Just now you thought our people might be vampire. We are Carpathian, not the undead. Unless we turn.*

"Would you stay out of my head? Wait

178

until you're invited."

If I waited for an invitation from you, little red hair, I would be centuries old before it ever came about. The smile in his mind was just a little too sexy for her peace of mind. *I was merely attempting to ease your fears.* Now he sounded innocent.

She laughed softly. "Do I have *naïve* stamped on my forehead?"

Has anyone ever complained about your bedside manner?

Shea raised her eyebrows. "I'm a surgeon. I don't need a bedside manner. And in any case, I've never had such an outrageous patient before. Stop calling me *red hair*. And *little red hair*. And all the other things you call me. Dr. O'Halloran is appropriate."

For the first time his sensuous mouth softened, curved into a grin. The effect on her was shattering. It wasn't right for a male to look that sexy. He should be banned from all female company.

Handsome and sexy. I must be getting somewhere after all. His tone was lazy, teasing, a little bit husky.

Shea laughed softly. It was impossible to be annoyed with him when he was in this mood. "You *are* handsome and sexy, but don't let it go to your head. You're also arrogant, dominating, and too ruthless for my taste." She squashed him without a qualm.

Jacques tugged on her hand, drew her close to the bed so that he could bring her palm to the warmth of his mouth. *I am exactly to your taste.*

She yanked her hand away as if he had burned her, rubbing her palm along her thigh. The feeling didn't go away, and neither did the butterflies he had sent winging in her stomach. "How do you know you're not a vampire?" She needed to distract him, distract both of them. "Maybe you forgot. You're certainly capable of acting like one."

This time he laughed, startling both of them. The sound was husky, low, and foreign to his ears, as if he had forgotten what it was like. His black eyes leapt to her face almost in fear.

"Not bad, wild man. First a growl, and now a laugh. We're making progress." Her eyes danced at him, reassured him.

Joy welled up in the midst of pain. Shea. She had created a world where his soul could somehow touch light. *Vampires feel nothing but the momentary high a kill brings. They are amoral, deviant creatures.*

Her chin lifted, eyebrows drawing together in concentration. "A kill?"

They always kill their prey when feeding. They do not place them in a trance. It feeds their high to experience their victim's terror. They do not discriminate between man, woman, or child. The vampire has chosen to trade his soul for fleeting emotion.

"Do you kill?" Her fingers twisted together, and her breath seemed caught in her lungs. Why had she asked him that? She already knew the answer; she had glimpsed the darkness in him on more than one occasion.

Quite easily when necessary, but never my human prey. He answered matter-of-factly, without real thought. It was instinct, his predatory nature.

"*People,* Jacques," she corrected. "We are *people.*"

You are Carpathian.

"I don't even know what a Carpathian is. Do you? Do you honestly know? Maybe you do have a rare blood condition, and somehow it gives you extraordinary gifts." Shea no longer seriously believed there was any hope of that. She was certain he knew the truth: he belonged to another species of people.

Exhaustion was winning the battle with Jacques. Mortal sleep was not rejuvenating, but until Shea became accustomed to her new life, he would not leave her unprotected. He closed his eyes. *I have existed for*

181

over eight hundred years. I existed before Leonardo Da Vinci. The words were slurred in her mind.

She backed away from the bed until the wall brought her up short. Over eight hundred years? Shea pressed a hand to her head. What was he going to do next? Turn into a bat? A wolf? Nothing would surprise her now. *I prefer the wolf, given a choice.* There was a distinct smile in his voice, brushing in her mind. It softened the hard edges of his mouth, giving him that sensual, sexy look she could not resist.

You would, she sent back to him, inexplicable feelings for him spilling into her mind and heart.

There was so much about Jacques she didn't know. Just how powerful was he? If vampires actually existed, had they originated from Carpathians, as Jacques implied? Did that mean a cold, merciless killer nature lay buried in Jacques, waiting to surface? Seven years buried alive should do a great job of bringing any latent hostilities out. Nor could she put aside the possibility that he was completely insane. She felt the madness in him, his struggle to find his memories and the truth, to suppress the violence within him. She sighed softly, touched his hair with a fingertip, her heart melting at the sight of him, so vulnerable, like a little boy. What was it about him that tore her heart out every time she faced the fact that he would get well and she would have to move on?

I am very powerful.

Startled, Shea looked at him. Jacques hadn't moved. His eyes remained closed. "I'm sure you are." Did he need reassurance?

I have no intention of allowing you to leave me.

She laughed softly. "I was just thinking what a vulnerable, boyish look you have in your sleep. Now I think you're a spoiled brat."

I am more powerful than a vampire, little red hair. I hunt them down and destroy them. I will have no trouble keeping you at my side.

"I'll just have to make it my business to annoy you to the point that you'll be happy to get rid of me." She poured the last unit of blood into a glass for him. "I can do that, you know. My patients always are glad to see the last of me."

I may be insane, Shea. I have thought about it for a long while. I know my nature is that of a predator. He sounded very thoughtful, giving each of her worries his strict attention. *But if I am truly insane, then I cannot be*

183

without you. I will need you every moment by my side to ensure the safety of all mankind.

Shea started to laugh, but as his serious tone registered, her smile faded. He was not teasing her. He was being as honest as he could be. Jacques didn't know whether he was insane or not. "Sometimes, wild man, you break my heart," she said softly.

You want to leave me, Shea. I feel the need in you to put distance between us.

"I have spent more time with you than I have with anyone in my life. I've told you more about myself, talked, laughed, and . . . and . . ." She hesitated, blushing wildly.

Jacques opened his eyes, turned his head to look at her.

"Other things," she went on decisively. "It isn't like I'm thinking of deserting you. I just need space now and then, don't you?"

He merged with her immediately. At once she felt stark emptiness. A black void that could never be filled. Her heart beat hard, pounding in near terror. The world was gray and black, dark and ugly. There was no relief, no hope, only the terrible emptiness of total despair.

Her breath caught in her throat. She touched his hair with gentle fingers, ran a fingertip along his jaw in a small caress. "You *really* dislike being alone."

I think the word dislike *is not nearly strong enough,* he answered dryly. *I cannot breathe unless you are close to me.*

"I didn't realize it was so terrible for you. I'm sorry I was so insensitive, Jacques. I wasn't meaning to be. I have a tendency to plan things out far in advance. What you're picking up in my mind is something altogether different. Our situation is becoming desperate. I have to drive into one of the villages and get us some supplies. Blood, clothes for you." She held up a hand. Merged as she was with him, she felt his instant rejection of her plan. "We don't have a choice, Jacques. I'm going to have to leave immediately in order to get down to the village first thing in the morning."

No! It is not safe. I will not allow such a thing. It is too risky.

She ignored his protest. "It is the only way that I can get back here by nightfall. I don't want to leave you alone during the daylight hours, but we need blood, Jacques. You're not healing as fast as you expect because we don't have the amount of blood you need. And as much as I hate to think about it, I know you're supplying me with blood. I was so weak before, but now I'm stronger. You gave me your blood, didn't you?"

You cannot go.

She understood the terrible dread, the empty void he would feel if she left him alone now. The dark, ugly hole that swallowed him when he was without her. Her heart ached for him. To be imprisoned underground all those years, with no memory, only pain and darkness and starvation, had to have left mental scars.

I cannot be without you. His hand found hers, his fingers lacing with hers, a bond. To him it was simple. She was his balance, his sanity, or what little remained of it. She was light to his darkness. She could not leave him. He carried her fingertips to the warmth of his mouth.

She felt the jolt of sensual awareness right down to her toes. His mind was open to hers, the ultimate intimacy, so that she could feel his every emotion, read his every thought if she chose. Dark desires mingled turbulently with stark resolve to keep her close to his side. Isolation yawned like a black, empty hole. So alone. So much pain. Emptiness. Hunger. Always the terrible hunger consuming him. She found tears on her face. Her arms cradled his head, rocked him gently. "You're not alone anymore," she whispered. "I'm right here with you, Jacques. I'm not leaving you alone like this."

It is still in your mind to leave me. You cannot hide your intentions from me, Shea. I have explained countless times to you. You are my true lifemate. There cannot be deceit between us.

Shea laid her head gently over his. The dark emotions whirling within him were becoming alarming to both of them. Violence was mixed with terror. "I have never tried to deceive you. You know that. I don't lie to you, and I don't play games. We need the blood. You won't get better without it. There's no other way."

You cannot leave me, Shea. This time his voice was a demand. He lost the indulgence often present when he conversed with her. All at once he was a being of enormous power, arrogant and commanding.

Shea sighed, her fingers caressing the strong bones of his face. "Don't go getting all bossy with me, wild man. We need to stay focused on our problem. We need blood. And I don't have any clothes that would fit you. Do you have a better idea?"

Wait until I am stronger and can go with you to protect you.

She shook her head. "You keep getting mixed up. I'm supposed to be protecting you. I'm your doctor."

You are my lifemate. There is only one.

You are mine. Only one.

She lifted her head, green eyes searching his face. "You've never lived with a woman? You must have had sex."

Carpathians do not live with any other than their lifemate. Sex is a simple sharing of the body, a pleasure that fades along with emotions after two hundred years if we do not find our lifemate.

"I don't understand. Without a lifemate, Carpathians feel nothing?"

Nothing, Shea. Not affection or remorse, not right or wrong. Certainly not desire. After two hundred years Carpathian males cannot feel.

Color flooded her face. "You feel desire when you're with me. I may not be experienced, but I do have medical training."

His fingers tightened around hers, his breath warm along her knuckles. *I want you with every cell in my body, with my mind and my heart. Your soul is the other half of mine. When you are with me, I feel. Joy, desire, anger, even laughter. You are my lifemate. I have waited over eight hundred years to find you. I could not see color until you came into my life.* His black eyes, worn with suffering, fastened on her green ones. *I cannot lose you. I can never be alone again. Mortals and immortals alike would be in danger should I lose you.*

She didn't want to touch that. She murmured his name softly, brushed a kiss against his temple almost without knowing it.

I cannot exist without you, little red hair. There is darkness in me. The beast is strong. I struggle every moment against loss of control. My lifemate is my anchor. Only you can save me, keep me from walking in complete madness.

Shea brushed the hair from his face with gentle fingers. "How do you know this? You've admitted you can't remember much."

I have opened my mind to you. You know it is true. You anchor me, and I can do no other than see to your happiness.

Shea couldn't help but smile. "You have no idea how arrogant that sounds. You aren't responsible for my happiness. I'm responsible for my own happiness. And at this moment, whether your macho pride can deal with it or not, I am the one responsible for your health and safety. We don't have time to wait until you're better. I have to go now. Every day we wait gives Don Wallace time to find us. When you're able to travel, we'll leave this place." Her hand caressed his thick mane of hair. "I have to go, Jacques. I'm not leaving you, I'm only going for supplies."

He retreated from her for a moment and

as always, it was impossible to read his expression. His black eyes flickered. *I will go with you.*

Shea sat up reluctantly, hating to have to prove her point but knowing she must thwart his resolve. "Then let's try going outside onto the porch. Let me do most of the work."

You think I cannot do this.

"I think your will is strong, Jacques, but your body is weak. Perhaps I'm wrong. I hope I am." She was silent as she made the preparations. She knew he couldn't do it, not without terrible pain. The gurney was narrow and uncomfortable. Shea padded it with a blanket. As she helped him from the bed to the gurney, he broke out in a sweat, but he didn't make a sound. With a sinking heart she pushed him out into the night air. Of course he would tolerate movement silently. He had endured torture and hours of surgery without painkillers or anesthesia. If he made up his mind to do this, he would do so without complaint.

Jacques pushed the pain aside, staring up at the stars, inhaling the night. His world — open air, the rush of wings, the high chirp of bats, the call of insects. He closed his eyes, the better to absorb the smells, the stories. His body resisted the physical exertion, crawled with pain, a dull-edged knife sawing away at his chest.

"Jacques, please don't be stubborn. I feel what you feel."

There is no need, Shea. Do not merge with me. I would not wish this on you.

"Please allow me to take you inside and get you into bed. Just this small amount of movement is hurting you. I won't take you to the village no matter what you say. If the circumstances were reversed, you wouldn't take me."

A slight grin curved his mouth. *If the circumstances were reversed, there would be no need to go to the village. I would call every human in the vicinity to nourish you.* There was a threat in his voice, subtle but still there, and she caught the echo of his censored thought. *No human would ever be safe from him if Shea were hurt.*

Shea touched his forehead gently. "I'm safe, Jacques, and for now, I'm in charge."

He gave the mental equivalent of absolute derision. *This place is familiar to me.* He was surveying his surroundings now, a peculiar glow in his black eyes. *I know this place. Something happened here a long time ago that I should remember.* His hand went of its own volition to his throat, tracing the thin, almost nonexistent white line curving around his jugular. *Only a severe mortal wound can leave a scar.* He murmured it aloud under his breath, as if to himself.

Shea remained very quiet, holding herself still, wanting to allow any memory possible to come to Jacques.

I have been here, some time ago. Perhaps a quarter of a century. His head ached, but the memory shimmered, solidified instead of slipping away. His black eyes moved restlessly over the clearing. *There was a fight here. A vampire, high and powerful from a fresh kill. I had never fought one before; it was my first time. I was not prepared for his strength, his ferocity. Maybe I just could not believe one of my own kind, even turned, would do such evil.* He frowned in concentration, tried to catch more fragments and hold on to them. *I was guarding someone, someone important, someone who could not fall into the hands of the vampire. There are so few . . .*

The last thought seemed to trail off. Shea merged her mind firmly with his, felt his confusion, his frustration at being unable to capture and pin down the information. Shea put a hand on his forehead, wanting to soothe him. Her touch was tender, her green eyes anxious.

So familiar. Not green, but blue. *A woman. Carpathian women are so few. We*

192

must guard them well, protect them. It was a woman I was guarding, and she was special. Our hope for the future.

Her heart nearly stopped. Jacques had fought for another woman, nearly lost his life, if the scar was any indication. *What woman?* Shea was totally unaware she had used the Carpathian lifemate's method of communication.

Through the pain of his body and his pounding head, joy and male amusement washed over him. His little red-haired doctor did not like the idea of another woman in his life. *She had blue eyes, and there were tears in them, such as you have in yours now.* He touched one glittering drop with a fingertip, brought it to his mouth to taste. His body, always voraciously hungry, absorbed that bead as if absorbing her very essence.

Who was she, Jacques? Or who is she? A male like Jacques, so handsome, sensual, intense — of course he had to have a woman stashed somewhere. Shea bit her lip so hard, two drops of blood beaded up.

Jacques tried to hold on to the fragments slipping in and out of his head. He sensed that the information was of great importance to both of them. *She belonged to another. He is . . .* Pain gripped his head in a vise and squeezed hard.

Shea laced her fingers through his. "Let it go, Jacques, we don't need it." She smoothed the hair from his forehead. "It will come in time. Look how much you've already remembered." It was shocking to her just how much of a relief it was to learn that the unknown important woman belonged to another.

If it is not some fantasy. It was half humor, half self-censure. His hand came up, caught the nape of her neck, and pulled her down so that he could kiss her soft, trembling mouth. His tongue swept the ruby droplets from her full lower lip.

"I told you to stay out of my head." She returned his kiss gently, taking care not to jar him. "Let's go in and make you comfortable." It seemed harder for her to bear his pain than it was for him.

Another minute. Listen to the song of the night. The wolves call to one another in joy. Do you hear?

She did. How could she not? A distance away the pack lifted their muzzles skyward and poured out their happiness to one another. It was impossible to contain it within their bodies, and it flowed from their hearts, out their throats into the night. It was so beautiful, so pure, so much a part of their

194

world. The notes, each different, unique to the individual animal, floated through the forest, lifted to the very heavens. She belonged here in this land. She belonged with the wolf pack, the mountains, and the night. She turned her head to look at Jacques, found him clutching his head as memories crowded in, jagged bits and pieces that teased and frustrated, that felt like piercing shards of glass.

I should remember him. Someone important. I remember the fight. His hand went once more to his throat. *The vampire slashed my throat. The woman saved my life. She pretended to be hysterical, but she packed the wound with soil and her saliva as she cried over me. The vampire took her. Why can I not remember the important one?*

"Stop it right now!" Shea ordered sharply as she stroked away the crimson stain on his forehead. "I'm taking you back into the house this minute."

Shea. Her name was a magic talisman, a soothing balm to his tortured mind.

I'm here with you, Jacques. She merged with him immediately, held him close physically. *It will all come in time, I promise you.*

His hand brushed her throat, the raw, ragged wounds and bruises that refused to heal. Without proper blood and the rejuvenating sleep of their people, her body could not heal itself. *Look at you, what I have done to you. And I cannot guard you, as I must, as is my duty. I am of little use to you.*

Shea tugged at his hair, a tiny punishment. "I don't know, Jacques, you're more than adequate at giving orders." She maneuvered the gurney back into the cabin, then took the opportunity to put fresh sheets on the bed before helping Jacques onto it. "You know I have to go," she said softly.

Jacques lay very still, staying on top of the pain, drifting with it, grateful for the comfortable bed and her soothing touch. He loved the feel of her fingers caressing his hair, his forehead, stroking away his pain. *I cannot allow you to go unprotected.* His resolve was fading. She could tell he didn't like the idea, but he knew it was necessary.

"I'll be leaving you unprotected as well. But we can do this. It isn't as if either of us will really be alone. Does distance matter? Our bond is so strong, can't we use it across a few miles? After all, you called me from thousands of miles away."

His black gaze reflected pain, but he was becoming more resigned to the trip. *It is true, we can touch one another at will, but it consumes my energy. Over a distance it may be difficult.*

"Only because I always let you do the work." Shea checked the loads in the shotgun and rifle and laid two boxes of cartridges beside the weapons, near his hand. "I'm getting good at this mind-reading thing. My mother was supposed to be psychic, and supposedly I inherited her gift. Who knows, maybe it's true."

Our bond is growing stronger with each blood exchange, with each passing moment we are together.

"So if we were apart I might stop wanting to be around you?" she teased. "If I had known it was that simple, I would have sat outside most of the time."

He caressed her silky hair. *I will allow you to do this thing, but do not* — he broke off the thought abruptly.

But not before Shea caught the echo of the primitive, territorial male. Her eyebrows shot up. Sometimes he reminded her more of a wild animal than a man. "Less of this *allow* stuff. It offends my independent nature."

She was smiling again, gently teasing him, and Jacques felt surrounded by her light. It seemed to shine through her vivid green eyes and lead him away from the yawning emptiness. She was making perfect sense, and in this moment of lucidity, he could do no other than acquiesce. Still, how was he going to be without her even for a short time? How would he survive as each minute, each second crawled by? Jacques closed his eyes, a fine sheen of sweat coating his skin at the thought of the darkness he would endure. The agony. The isolation.

"Jacques, don't. You said you could shut down your heart and lungs. If you do that, do you feel or think? Dream?" *Have nightmares?*

No, but I dare not sleep in the way of our people. When you are separated from me or you choose the sleep of mortals, I must remain alert.

"I'll be fine. Put yourself to sleep and escape for just a little while. I'll take off and get as far as I can tonight."

You must not allow anything to happen to you, Shea. You cannot comprehend how important it is that you come to no harm. I cannot be without you. You brought me back into this life. I know my mind is not right. You cannot desert me when I need you the most. I would not be able to find my way back from the madness of the beast.

"I have no intention of deserting you, Jacques," she assured him.

Do not forget that you must merge with me this time. There was a trace of fear in his voice.

"I will check in often, Jacques. And you tell me if anything goes wrong on your end. Understand? No more of this chest-beating macho stuff."

Chapter Six

Dawn was streaking the sky by the time Shea managed to make the trip over the rough terrain to the nearest village. She needed fuel, herbs, sutures, various supplies, and, most of all, blood. Whole blood. She had always had to fight off fatigue during the daytime, but now it was more than simple fatigue; she was exhausted. She was terrified of being caught alone in her camper in such a weak state. She knew it would be virtually impossible to protect herself. More than anything else, she feared that something might attack Jacques while she was away.

Shea parked her truck at the village petrol station and slipped from the cab. Almost immediately she was uneasy, not certain why. Few villagers were out and about at such an early hour. She leaned casually against the truck, taking a long look around. She could detect no one, but she felt eyes on her, someone or something watching her. The feeling was strong. Lifting her chin, she forced herself to ignore her overactive imagination while she filled the truck, its reserve tank, and the two tanks for her generator.

The feeling of being watched became so strong, it made her skin crawl. Without warning something pushed at her mind. Not Jacques. It wasn't his familiar touch. Fear slammed into her, but she kept her cool, professional mask, her single-minded purpose to finish her tasks as quickly as possible. Whatever it was retreated, unable to penetrate.

Shea drove down the nearly deserted street and parked close to the small medical clinic. This time, as she slid from the seat, she searched the shadows around her carefully, using every sense she could. Sight. Smell. Hearing. Instinct. There was someone, something. It had followed her, was near. She could feel it, but she couldn't find it.

Jacques? She touched his mind gently, suddenly afraid she was feeling something that was happening to him.

I am awaiting your return. She sensed his tiredness. The morning light was even harder on him than on her. She hated being away from him.

I will come soon. Shea took another deep breath and looked around, determined to find what was making her so uneasy. A man lounged lazily in the shade of a tree. He was tall, dark, and motionless, like a hunter. She felt the impact of his eyes as his gaze casually found her.

Her heart jumped. Who was he? Had Wallace found her so soon? Shea turned away. First, before anything, she had to complete her business. She dragged out her laptop computer and typed in the commands to access the clinic's blood bank. If she had to move Jacques, they would need supplies desperately.

In another moment, Shea felt silly. The door to the small general store across the street swung open. The short, stooped owner emerged, apron tied around his ample middle, a broom in his hand. He waved openly at the motionless figure beneath the tree. "Byron. Good morning to you. Bit early, isn't it?" She recognized the local dialect.

The tall, dark-haired man replied in the same language, but his voice was low, a beautiful tone. He stepped out of the shadows, young, good-looking. He flashed a quick, friendly smile at the grocer approaching him. Clearly they knew one another, were friendly. The dark-haired man was obviously no stranger to the area. Neither exhibited the least interest in Shea. She watched as Byron bent his head solicitously down to the older man, listening intently, his arm circling the shopkeeper's shoulders.

Shea breathed a soft sigh of relief. The

feeling of being stalked was gone, and she couldn't be certain if it had been real or imagined. She watched for a moment as the two men moved deeper into the shade, until they were merely a dark shadow blending with the trees. Laughter floated back toward her. The taller, younger man bent his head even closer to the shopkeeper to hear every word. Hurrying into the store, she purchased from the shopkeeper's assistant an extra blanket and pillow, several blocks of ice, and some clothing for Jacques.

The small hospital was ready with her medical supplies, a friendly clerk asking about her mobile clinic, treating her like a valued client. Feeling slightly guilty, she completed her transactions quickly. She needed to get to her truck and find a dark area to sleep in until it was safe to return to Jacques. She rushed outside.

Light pierced her eyes like a thousand needles. Shea stumbled, then felt a strong hand close like a vise around her upper arm, preventing her from falling. Murmuring a thank you, she fumbled in her pocket for her dark glasses to cover her streaming eyes.

"What are you doing here alone, unprotected?" The voice was pitched low, the dialect and accent eerily similar to Jacques'.

Shea's breath caught in her throat, and

she struggled for release. The tall, dark-haired man merely pushed her into the shadows, her back to the wall of the building, his large frame easily blocking hers. "Who are you?" he asked. "You are small and fair for one of us." His hand caught her chin so that she met the penetration of his sunglass-shaded eyes. "Your scent is familiar to me but elusive. How is it I did not know of your existence?" For just a moment satisfaction curved his mouth. "You are free. That is good."

"I don't know you, sir, and you're scaring me. I'm in a great hurry, so please let me go." Shea used her coolest, most disdainful voice, and she deliberately spoke English. The man was enormously strong, and it terrified her.

"I am Byron." He gave only his first name, as if that should be enough. "I am a male of our race, you a single female. The sun is climbing, and you did not give yourself enough time to seek refuge from the dawn. I can do no other than help you, offer my protection." He switched easily to heavily accented English.

His voice seemed to slide right inside her. He gave the illusion of being a gentleman, so friendly, yet he had not released her or moved even an inch to allow her to get by

204

him. He inhaled, dragged her scent into his lungs. Suddenly his entire demeanor changed. His body stiffened. His fingers dug into her arm. White teeth gleamed a predator's flash of warning. "Why did you not answer me when I spoke to you?" His words were low and menacing. The suave stranger was frightening.

"Let go of me." She kept her voice even, her mind working at top speed, looking for a way out. He seemed to hold all the cards, but . . .

"Tell me who you are," he demanded.

"Let go of me now." She lowered her voice, pitched it to a soft, hypnotic melody. "You want to let me go."

The stranger shook his head, his eyes narrowing, recognizing the hint of compulsion in her voice. He inhaled a second time, drinking in her fragrance. At once his face seemed to go still. "I recognize that scent. Jacques. He is dead these seven years, yet his blood runs in your veins." His voice crawled with deadly threat.

For a moment she was frozen with fear. Was this the betrayer Jacques had spoken of? Shea swung her head sideways to remove his fingers from her chin. "I have no idea what you're talking about. Let go of me now!"

Byron let out his breath in a low, venomous hiss. "If you wish to see another night, you will tell me what you have done with him."

"You're hurting me." He was drawing closer, leaning toward her neck, bending her backward like a bow as she tried to elude him. His breath was hot on her throat, and Shea gasped as she felt needle-sharp teeth pierce her skin. With a low cry she jerked sideways, her heart pounding.

Without warning he caught at the neckline of her shirt to examine the bruises at her throat. She could feel his puzzlement, his confusion. Shea took advantage of his momentary distraction. As hard as she was able, she brought up her knee and screamed for all she was worth. Byron looked so shocked, she nearly laughed. He had been absolutely certain she wouldn't want attention drawn to her. His hiss, a deadly promise of retaliation, was the last thing she heard before he melted away.

And he literally melted away. Shea never saw him move. One moment he was there, his body trapping hers against the wall, and then he was gone. A fine mist was mixing with the layers of fog covering the ground to about knee level.

Two orderlies came running, hearing her

screams. Shea, holding her palm to the trickling wound on her neck to cover it, allowed them to soothe her, to assure her the animal she thought she saw lurking in the shadows was most likely a stray dog, not a wolf. They went off shaking their heads and laughing at how silly women could be.

Shea loaded the supplies into her truck, taking as much time as she dared. If the sun affected her, it had to be just as lethal to her assailant if he was like Jacques. It had never occurred to her that she might have to contend with a vampire. Don Wallace had been her nightmare; she suspected this was much worse. She packed the blood carefully in the center of her large cooler, surrounded by the blocks of ice. She had to find a way to get the blood to Jacques without leaving a trail for the vampire.

She waited, stalling now before she left. The sun climbed higher, touched her skin right through the thin cotton of her clothing. A wide-brimmed hat and her dark glasses provided relief. Still, Shea sensed it was safer to stay among people as long as she could; until her weakness left her she had no alternative but to seek rest in her darkened camper in the shade of the woods.

There was a push at her mind, a familiar path she recognized instantly with relief.

Shea merged with Jacques. He was weak, what little strength he had leeched away with the rising of the sun. Shea was angry with herself for not making the effort earlier to reassure him. She should have known that he would feel her fear even from a distance.

You are well?

Yes, Jacques. I'm sorry I didn't check in. She made an effort to stay calm and hide her alarm from him. The last thing she wanted was for the wild man to attempt to rescue her. And she knew he would. He would kill himself trying to get to her side.

You are in the sun. I feel your discomfort. It was a reprimand of the sort she was becoming used to. The arrogance of command was creeping more and more into his voice as his health improved.

Behind the dark glasses her eyes were streaming constantly. She took a deep breath, let it out slowly, and took the plunge. *There was one of your kind here. At least I think he was your kind.*

His reaction was explosive. Hot fury, fear for her, an almost uncontrollable jealous rage. Jacques forced himself to remain silent and hear her out. He knew his volcanic, intense emotions frightened her. They frightened him. Emotions were unfamiliar to him and could be overwhelming at times.

He recognized your scent, even called you by name. He demanded to know where you are. Please be careful, Jacques. I'm afraid I left you completely helpless. I think he'll search for you.

Did he touch you? Take your blood? The demand was imperious; she felt his black rage beating in her head.

She touched her hand to the oozing wound on her neck. *You would have known,* she replied soothingly.

Some of his helpless fury dissipated. *Where are you?*

I am safe for now, but he'll hunt me this evening, I'm certain of it. I don't want to lead him back to you.

You will return this night to me. Straight to me. He cannot be allowed to touch you, cannot exchange blood.

I'll be fine. It is you who must be careful, Jacques. She tried to reassure him. *I'm afraid for you, afraid I will lead him to you, or while I'm gone he will find you.*

You do not understand the danger you are in. You must get to me.

Shea might not fully comprehend, but she could feel his conviction, his fear for her, and she shivered, remembering the strength in the stranger's grasp, his hiss of deadly promise. *Don't worry, I'll come right away.*

Go to sleep now, Jacques. This is draining for you.

Shea. There was a moment of silence, of longing. *Come back to me. If you believe nothing else I have told you, believe I need you.*

I promise. Shea put her forehead down on the steering wheel. She was so tired, and her eyes were swelling. The tinted windows in the cab helped to prevent blisters on her skin but wouldn't for much longer. Her body was slow and clumsy, nearly unresponsive. She could no longer afford to wait, could only hope the vampire was already in his lair and unable to see where she went.

She drove into the mountains. At first, to save time, she took the road, driving as fast as she dared on the winding dirt track. When the sunlight became unbearable, she made her own road, following a deer trail, always climbing, seeking deep forest. The heavy canopy of trees gave some relief from the unrelenting sunlight piercing her skull. When her body was simply too heavy, she pulled into a particularly heavily wooded area and dragged herself into the camper. She had just enough energy to lock the door and place the pistol beside her hand before her body became lead. She lay as if paralyzed, her heart beating fast, terrified by her own weakness.

She needed Jacques, needed to touch that core of unbelievable power in him. She needed to touch his iron will. Shea pictured him in her mind, found it slowed her heartbeat. If she could just hold him, feel his arms around her. And then somehow, incredibly, she could feel his arms, all corded strength, closing protectively around her, hear his heartbeat, strong and steady, matching the rhythm of hers. Shea brushed his face with her fingertips, her eyes closed, her mind on every detail of his sensual features. They slept apart yet together, the uncomfortable sleep of mortals, always aware of the danger surrounding them, always aware of the leaden paralysis of their bodies. Shea, for the first time, experienced the power of holding a mind merge, of never being alone, the strength that came from two beings connected.

The long day passed slowly, the sun moving across the sky, shining brightly, hotly, then retreating just as slowly toward the mountains, sinking gracefully and colorfully into the sea.

The cave, only a few miles from Shea's cabin, was far beneath the earth. The narrow passage leading to the maze of underground chambers and steamy pools was twisted and nearly impassable in spots. In the smallest cave, beneath the rich soil, a single heart began to beat. Dirt spewed like a geyser, and Byron burst from deep within the ground. There was that brief moment of disorientation, and then his body shimmered, dissolved, became a mist streaming through the passageway and out into the darkening sky. Immediately the mist formed a large bird, and strong wings lifted the streamlined creature into the sky. It circled the vast forest area, high above the canopy of foliage, then took off as if shot from a bow.

Jacques, alone in the cabin, felt the disturbance even within the confines of the four walls. He felt the power vibrating in the air and knew something dangerous was searching for him. He kept his mind perfectly patterned as a human, aware if the other probed, he would believe the being in the cabin was human. He felt the dark, winged shadow pass over him, the swift intrusion of another in his mind, and then the being was moving away.

Jacques? Shea's query was soft, worried.

He is close by.

She read his mind easily. Jacques wanted her with him, close, so he could protect her, so that no other male would presume to claim her as he had. He feared if she returned to him, she would come straight into the vampire's trap, yet Jacques could not bear the separation, could not leave her unprotected. His mind was beginning to crumble, fracture, and his need of her was great.

Shea leapt from the camper and flung herself into the driver's seat. *I will be with you soon.* She felt his smile all the way to her heart. Jacques was beginning to remember humor. *You really like that I go my own way and make my own decisions, don't you?* she teased him, wanting to keep his mind as stable as possible until she was with him to give him an anchor.

Do not bet on that, little red hair. Instant obedience is the ideal.

You wish. Shea found herself laughing in spite of being afraid. It was silly to feel so lighthearted when they were facing danger and a difficult move ahead. Where could they go on such short notice? By the time she reached the cabin, three or four of their precious hours would be lost.

Jacques stretched slowly, cautiously. His body protested sharply. Pain had been his world for so long that he allowed it to wash over him, through him. He could live forever with pain. He could not live without Shea. He dragged himself to a sitting position. The room lurched, spun crazily before righting itself. Almost immediately he could feel warm, sticky blood running down his ribcage, his abdomen. He swore softly, eloquently, in the language of his people. He knew pain intimately, had forgotten gut-wrenching agony. It did not matter. Nothing mattered but that he protect his lifemate.

Shea drove like a woman possessed, finding trails where there were none, over rotting logs and into rocky ravines. Sometimes she made good time, other times she crawled. It was interesting driving at night. She no longer needed headlights. She could see as clearly as if it was day. The moonlight spilled down to bathe the trees and bushes in silver. It was beautiful, all colors of the spectrum vivid and detailed.

Far away, a huge owl banked, circled a large, rambling house built into the cliffs, and approached it warily. As the bird landed on a stone gate column, folded its wings, and shimmered into human shape, the wolf pack in the surrounding woods began to sing in warning. Almost at once a man emerged from the house. Lazily he glided from the fog-shrouded verandah across the grounds to the gates. He was tall, dark-haired. Power emanated from his every pore. He moved with the grace of a great jungle cat, the elegance of a prince. His eyes were as black as the night and held a thousand secrets. Although there was no expression on his handsome, sensual features, there was danger, a quiet menace in the way he held himself.

"Byron. It is long since you have visited us. You did not send a call ahead." No censure roughened the soft, musical, black-velvet voice, yet it was there in volumes.

Byron cleared his throat, agitated, his dark eyes not quite meeting the other's penetrating gaze. "I am sorry, Mikhail, for my bad manners, but the news I bring is unsettling. I came as fast as I could and still cannot find the right words to tell you this."

Mikhail Dubrinsky waved a graceful hand. One of the ancients, one of the most powerful, he had long ago learned patience.

"I was late going to ground this dawn. I had not fed, so I went to the village and summoned one of the locals to me. When I entered the area, I sensed the presence of one of our kind, a woman. She did not look as we do; she is small, very slender, with dark red hair and green eyes. I could tell she was weak, had not recently fed. Using our common mental path, I tried to communicate with her, but she did not respond."

"You are certain she is one of us? It does not seem possible, Byron. Our women are so few, one would not be wandering unprotected, uncared for, at dawn, unknown to us."

"She is Carpathian, Mikhail, and she is unclaimed."

"And you did not stay with her, guard her, bring her to me?" The voice had dropped another octave, so soft it whispered with menace.

"There is more. There were bruises on her throat, ragged wounds, several of them. Her arms, too, were bruised. This woman has been ill-used, Mikhail."

A red flame glowed in the depths of the black eyes. "Tell me what you are so reluctant to reveal." The black velvet voice never hardened or increased in volume.

Byron stood silent for a long moment, then steadily met the direct, penetrating stare. "Jacques' blood runs in her veins. I would know his scent anywhere."

Mikhail did not blink, his body utterly still. "Jacques is dead."

Byron shook his head. "I am not mistaken. It is Jacques."

The black eyes swept over Byron once,

then Mikhail lifted his face, drinking in the night. He sent a powerful call along a familiar path and met emptiness, blankness, a void. "He is dead, Byron," he repeated softly, a clear warning to end the subject.

Byron stood his ground, militarily erect. "I am not mistaken."

Mikhail studied him for a time. "Are you saying Jacques misused this woman? Perhaps turned a human?" There was a low hiss accompanying the question. At once the power in Mikhail flowed from him to fill the air and surround them both.

"She is Carpathian, no vampiress. And she visited the local clinic's blood bank. I do not know her connection to Jacques, but there is one." Byron was adamant.

"In any case, Byron, we can do no other than find this mystery woman and protect her until such time as she is given a true lifemate. I will tell Raven I am going with you. I do not wish her to hear of Jacques." That was spoken in the softest of tones, all the more menacing, an absolute edict.

Beneath the words was a darker promise. If Mikhail ever found Jacques alive, unable or unwilling to answer the call, swift and deadly retribution would follow. And if the woman was a part of it . . . Byron sighed and looked up at the sky as Mikhail dissolved into the fog. Wisps of clouds were beginning to move across the stars, and the land stirred restlessly, disturbed by an unseen danger.

Mikhail emerged from the mist already shape-shifting, his powerful body taking flight as he did so. Byron had never mastered the speed Mikhail had and was forced to change on the stone column before launching himself skyward. The larger bird glided silently toward earth, razor-sharp talons extended as if coming in for a kill. At the last moment it pulled up, wings beating strongly. *The woman, how old?*

Young. Twenty, maybe a little older. It was impossible to tell. She knew our language, I could tell, but she spoke in English. The accent was off. American contractions and way of speaking, yet I heard a hint of Irish brogue. She deliberately drew attention to us. None of their kind would do such a thing. *I was forced to leave her, as she knew would happen. She was able to stay in the morning light longer than I was. I know she is not a vampiress or that would not be so.*

The two owls raced across the darkened sky, carried the breeze with them. A low hiss heralded the building force of the wind. Below them, the trees swayed and dipped toward the forest floor. Small animals scurried nervously to their homes. Clouds drifted in, ominously blotting out the stars.

Shea's arms were beginning to ache as she bumped her way over uneven vegetation. Her fingers had gripped the steering wheel so hard they were nearly numb. She was beginning to suspect she had somehow gotten lost when the truck bounced hard, splashed through a shallow creek, and she suddenly recognized the faint trail that led up to the old cabin. Breathing a sigh of relief, she turned onto it. The grassy track was pitted with holes and rough with rocks, but she was familiar with its twists and turns, and she made good time.

Twice she attempted to merge with Jacques, but he resisted her efforts. It worried her. She told herself he wasn't in danger. She was certain she would know if the one called Byron had found him, yet she couldn't help being afraid something was very wrong. She breathed an audible sigh of relief when she finally spotted the cabin. It took a few moments to pry her fingers loose from the steering wheel and stretch the tightness from the muscles in her legs. When she managed to slide from the cab, she stumbled, her legs unsteady.

The wind was beginning to pick up, tossing leaves and twigs around in tiny whirling eddies. Overhead the branches swayed and danced. Streaks of black and gray crossed the glittering stars, extinguishing them one by one. Clouds began to roll in, heavy looking and dark. Shivering, Shea glanced up, certain the storm was a portent of danger.

Hunger was gnawing, ever present, relentless. It seemed to worsen every day, her weakness growing if she didn't have blood. Right now, though, nothing mattered except getting Jacques to safety. Squaring her shoulders, she moved to the porch. The cabin was dark; Jacques couldn't open shutters or turn on lights. Shea unlocked and pushed open the door, anxious to see him.

Jacques was up, leaning against the wall. He wore a pair of soft cotton jeans and nothing else. He looked gray, gaunt, lines of strain carved deeply into his handsome face. The wound below his heart was trickling a steady stream of blood. His feet were bare, his thick mane of hair wild and tangled. A fine sheen of perspiration coated his body. There was a crimson smear on his forehead, and beads of scarlet dotted his skin.

"Oh, God!" Shea's heart nearly stopped. She could taste fear in her suddenly dry mouth. "Jacques, what have you done? What were you thinking?"

She nearly leapt the distance separating them, not noticing how fast she was able to move. She could feel tears burning in her throat, behind her eyes. What Jacques was doing to himself was making her physically ill. "Why would you do this?" Her hands were gentle, tender, as she examined his gaping wound. "Why didn't you wait for me?" Even as she caught him to her, the silliest thought ran through her head. Where had he gotten a pair of jeans that fit him? But it hardly mattered at that moment.

He will come this night, and I must protect you.

"Not like this you won't. In case you haven't noticed, there's a huge hole in your body. You're putting far too much stress on those sutures. We have to lay you down."

He is coming.

"I don't care, Jacques. We can leave this place, travel all night if we have to. We have guns. Maybe we can't kill him, but we can slow him down." The truth was, Shea wasn't altogether certain she could shoot anyone. She was a doctor, a surgeon, a healer. The thought of taking a life was abhorrent to her. She wanted to patch Jacques up fast and get out of there. Avoiding trouble seemed easier than facing it.

He read her mind, her reluctance, easily.

Do not worry, Shea. I am quite capable of killing him. He swayed against her, nearly toppling both of them to the floor.

"I'm not sure I consider that great news," she said between clenched teeth. Somehow they made it the few steps to the bed. "And if you could see yourself right now, you might not be so certain you could swat a fly."

Jacques stretched his long frame out across the sheets, never once making a sound. He kept his mind firmly closed, not wanting to share his agony with her. It didn't matter; Shea could see it clearly etched in his face, in the white lines around his mouth and the bleak emptiness in his black eyes. "I'm sorry I left you alone." She pushed back his thick mane, her fingers lingering in the blue-black strands. With a sinking heart she began gathering her equipment. Moving was going to hurt him all over again, and once more she would be the one causing him pain.

It is not you torturing me, little red hair.

"I know you think that, Jacques," she answered tiredly, haphazardly securing the red hair falling around her face in a clip at the nape of her neck. "I hurt you when I brought you here, hurt you when I operated on you without painkillers, and I'm going to

222

be hurting you now." Shea shoved her tray of instruments close to the bed. "You're losing too much blood again. Let me stop this, and then I'll give you blood." She bit her lip hard as she blotted the welling red fluid and examined the open wound.

Outside the wind rattled at the windows, howled low, rubbed branches against the walls. The sound was disturbing, raising the hairs on the back of Shea's neck. A soft whisper, like the touch of death against her skin. Jacques caught her arm, staying her hand as she began repairing the damage. *He is here.*

"It's the wind." She didn't believe it, but there was nothing they could do until she had closed his wound.

The wind rose to an eerie scream. Thunder cracked as a whip of lightning danced and sizzled across the sky. The heavy front door splintered, split. Shea whirled around, needle and suture clutched in her bloody hands. Jacques, bleeding and in agony, lying so pale and gray with scarlet beads of perspiration coating his body, attempted to sit up.

Two men filled the doorway. She recognized Byron, but it was the man in front of him who drew her terrified gaze. He was the most powerful individual she had ever en-

223

countered. His eyes glowed a feral red. There was something vaguely familiar about him, but Shea was far too panic-stricken to attempt to identify what. A cry of alarm escaped her. She whirled around and snatched up the shotgun.

Mikhail's burst of speed made him a mere blur. He easily wrenched the weapon from her hands and tossed it carelessly aside, his glowing eyes fixed on Jacques. A slow, venomous hiss escaped Mikhail's throat.

Jacques met that burning gaze squarely, his own eyes filled with black fury mixed with defiant hatred and murderous resolve. He tried to lunge at the heavier man, but Mikhail leapt back, seized Shea by her throat, and slammed her so hard against the wall that it knocked the breath from her body. Never had she felt such strength in a single hand. He held her above his head, pinned to the wall, his fingers literally squeezing the life from her.

The very air in the cabin thickened, heavy and vibrating with violence, with malevolence. Even as Byron roared a warning, a chair, seemingly of its own accord, jerked into the air, hovered, then shot across the room as if to crash against the back of Mikhail's head. At the last possible second the powerful man slipped his head to one side, avoiding the chair, which then slammed into the wall and splintered into pieces very close to Shea's face.

Mikhail turned to face Jacques, dragging Shea in front of him, his fingers digging deep into her neck. "What have you done to him?" he demanded, his voice low and crawling with menace. He shook her like a rag doll. His voice dropped an octave. Low. Insidious. It wrapped Shea in velvet. *Tell me what you did to him.* The voice was in her head, yet not on the same path Jacques used.

With her last ounce of strength she fought him, struggling for breath, struggling to keep him from pushing into her mind. Another chair flew at Mikhail from his left. A slight wave of his hand stopped it in midair. It hovered there for seconds, then dropped harmlessly to the floor. All the while those terrible fingers never left her throat, never let up that vise-like grip. He was crushing her easily, strangling her with one hand.

Shea was gasping, laboring to breathe. The room whirled, turned black, little white spots shooting at her from all directions. Jacques felt her losing consciousness, and the beast broke free, his mind a killing frenzy. He launched himself from the bed, a blurred streak of lethal fury, the need to defend Shea, to kill her attacker, paramount. Mikhail was forced to leap aside, releasing Shea, who collapsed on the floor, unable to do anything but lie there, desperately trying to breathe.

"Jacques." Mikhail's voice was low and compelling. "I am your brother. Do you not know me?" He made several attempts to touch the shattered mind, found only a ferocious need to kill. He glanced helplessly at Byron, a question in his eyes.

Byron shook his head. *Can you control him?*

There is no path, no fragment I can seize. Mikhail had to streak across the room to avoid Jacques' next attack, two lamps hurtling toward his head at bullet speed. He reappeared in a far corner, raking a hand through his heavy fall of hair.

Jacques dragged himself across the floor to Shea, propped himself up in a sitting position against the wall, attempting to shield her body with his. Shea smelled fresh blood, then realized a shower of it splattered her arm and side. She looked around, dazed and confused, before she realized what was happening.

Jacques! She was on him in seconds, clamping hard on the wound, forgetting everything but her need to save him. "You have three choices," she snapped over her shoulder at the intruders. "Kill us both now and get it over, leave us, or help me save him." She heard only silence. "Damn it! Choose!" Her voice was husky and raw from her near-strangulation, but it was clearly that of a professional.

Mikhail leapt to help her. Jacques, perceiving an attack, knocked Shea backward and, growling like a wild animal, placed his body before hers.

"Get back!" Shea spat at Mikhail. She merged herself completely with Jacques. Her heart slammed so hard, she was afraid it might burst. There was nothing there but a red haze of violence, a killing fury she couldn't get through to reach him.

Mikhail instantly dissolved, reappearing some distance away.

Jacques, let me help you. Shea pleaded softly, trying to reach into his mind, trying to soothe him, calm him.

He snarled at her, fangs gleaming, a clear warning to stay behind him.

"He has turned, Mikhail," Byron murmured. "He is dangerous even to the woman. We cannot afford to lose her."

Shea ignored them, whispered soothing nonsense in her mind, trying desperately to anchor Jacques back in reality. Her hands once more found his wound. *They won't touch me, wild man. They'll stay away from us. Please let me help you or I'll have no protection from them. I will be alone.* She refused to lose him to injury or insanity. Outsiders might kill them, but she would never allow his wounds or his madness to defeat her. She was afraid for him, and she was afraid of him, but she would not desert him.

"What do you need?" Mikhail demanded softly.

"My instrument tray," she answered, not looking at him, not even turning her head. Her entire focus was on calming Jacques.

"Your surgery is barbaric. I'll call our healer." He sent the imperious mental summons immediately.

"He'll be dead by then. Damn you, get out of here if you won't help me," Shea snapped furiously. "I can't fight both of you, and I'm not going to let him die because you don't like my methods."

Cautiously, so as not to arouse Jacques' wrath, Mikhail shoved the tray across the floor. It slid within a few inches of Shea's hand.

Jacques never once took his eyes from the two men, staring at them with hatred and the dark promise of retaliation. When Shea moved, he mirrored her movements as if he knew before she did what she was going to do, so that his larger frame continuously shielded her from the others even as it crushed her against the wall.

"Get me fresh soil." Shea's voice was hoarse, but authoritative. She kept her every movement slow and cautious, to avoid alarming Jacques.

Byron shrugged and reluctantly did her bidding, his eyes meeting Mikhail's across the room. It was clear Byron believed that Jacques presented a real danger to all of them.

Shea coughed several times, her throat swollen under the clear imprint of Mikhail's fingers. Slowly rising to kneel beside Jacques, keeping her hands steady, her concentration total, she used tiny clamps and stitches to meticulously repair his reopened wound. It was slow, tedious work, and she fought to maintain her mental link with him as she sutured, dividing her mind between maintaining a constant tranquil, soothing touch to hold him to her and ensuring he did not bleed out. Jacques was a seething cauldron of violent emotions. His eyes, hard and watchful, never left the other two males. Once he lifted his hand, brushed aside her silky hair, his fingertips feathering over the bruise on her temple where he had knocked her against the wall. When his hand fell away, Shea was afraid he took with it her last link to him.

She packed the wound with soil and saliva and straightened slowly. "You need blood, Jacques." She said it softly, gently, an invitation. He had to survive, had to live. Every cell in her body demanded it.

He did not take his soulless eyes from Mikhail and Byron. She had never seen such relentless hatred in anyone's gaze before. He neither looked at her nor acknowledged her efforts. Not once did a hint of pain show on his face.

"My blood is ancient, powerful," Mikhail said softly. "I will give him mine." He glided closer with fluid grace, no sudden moves to alarm Jacques.

Shea felt Jacques' savage triumph, felt him gathering his strength. Before Mikhail was within striking distance she flung herself between them. "No! He'll kill you. He intends to —"

Jacques' grip was terrifying, slamming her back down to his side, his fist in her hair. His fury was a tangible thing. His eyes holding Mikhail's, he bent his dark head and sank his teeth into the side of Shea's neck.

"Don't!" Byron rushed forward, but

Mikhail stopped him with a raised hand, his black gaze locked with Jacques'.

White-hot heat, a burning brand. Shea understood Jacques was furious at her interference, and this display was to tempt the others to intercede, to draw them within his cruel reach. She lay perfectly still, accepting of his violent nature. He was so close to complete madness that one false move would send him careening over the edge. She was tired anyway, and sore, every part of her aching. Her lashes drifted down, a heavy lethargy stealing over her. She would easily trade her life for Jacques'. He wasn't taking anything from her she wasn't willing to give.

"You're killing her, Jacques," Mikhail said quietly. "Is that what you want?" He stood there motionless, his black eyes watchful, thoughtful.

"Stop him," Byron grated between his teeth. "He's taking too much blood. He's deliberately hurting her."

Mikhail's cool black eyes swept over Byron just once, but it was enough of a command, enough of a warning. Byron shook his head but remained silent.

"He will not kill her," Mikhail said in his same quiet voice. "He is waiting for one of us to try to stop him. It is the two of us he intends to kill. He thinks to draw us to him. He will not take the chance of leaving her side, so we will not be idiotic enough to go near him. He will not harm her. Go outside. While you are out there, find something to repair the door. I will follow you."

Byron went reluctantly, waited on the porch for Mikhail to join him. "You are taking a chance with her life, Mikhail. She is no vampiress, and he is clearly abusing her. She cannot afford such blood loss. Jacques was my friend, but what is in that cottage is no longer one of us. He recognizes neither of us. You cannot control him. No one can."

"She can. He has not turned. He is injured, sick." Mikhail said it softly, his black-velvet voice certain.

Furious, Byron turned away. "I should have taken the woman."

"Make no mistake, Byron, as weak as he is, Jacques is still extremely formidable. Before his disappearance he spent many years studying. The last years he hunted. With his mind so damaged, he is more beast than man, a predator, but with the intelligence and cunning of a learned one. And you were not paying attention in there. Whoever the female is, she is fighting to save him at great cost to herself. I believe she has chosen."

"The ritual has not been completed. She has not lain with him. We would know," Byron said stubbornly and began to pace restlessly. "There are many of us without a woman, and yet you allow this risk."

"There is only one lifemate. She obviously belongs with Jacques."

"We do not know that. If he were not your brother . . ." Byron began.

A low snarl stopped him. "I see no reason for you to question my judgment in this matter, Byron. I have had more than one brother, and I have never let fraternity stand in the way of what is just or right."

"It was Gregori who hunted your other brother," Byron pointed out.

Mikhail turned his head slowly, black eyes catching the whip of lightning cracking across the sky. "At my order."

Chapter Seven

Jacques sat on the floor, aware of the wall at his back, the woman lying so still in his arms. Dark, violent emotions swirled; his body shook with the need to kill his enemies. A ribbon of sanity moved through his mind, caught his attention. Both intruders had been familiar to him. *Someone he knew and trusted.* A silent snarl revealed his sharp fangs. *Betrayers sometimes ran in packs.* They thought him weak, but he was faster than all but the ancient ones. He had honed his fighting skills, his mental powers. They would not torture and kill his woman.

Shea. Her name was a soft, clear breeze blowing gently through his mind. *Shea.* A single candle leapt into flame, a light to guide him through the layers of black fury. He felt her then, small and slender in the circle of his arms. Her skin was soft, her hair, against his bare chest, like skeins of silk. He dropped his chin to the top of her head and rubbed gently, tenderly. It took a few moments before he realized her body was limp, cold, nearly lifeless, laboring for blood.

An anguished cry broke from him. He pulled her head back, saw the bruises and torn flesh at her throat. *Shea, do not leave me!* The plea was wrenched from his heart. Had he done this? The fingerprints were not his, but the ripped flesh? Had he done this to her?

A ripple of unease ran through the very land, the ground shifting, rolling. *Do not leave me, Shea.* Jacques tore at his wrist with his teeth, trickled life-giving fluid into her mouth. *Come on, little red hair, try.* His life force ran down her throat. He stroked the swollen column, forcing her to swallow. *You cannot leave me in darkness.* He could not remember attacking her, yet somehow, his heart in his throat, Jacques knew he had done this. He was insane.

Outside the wind rushed through the mountains, and thunder cracked. The dark clouds burst, and rain pelted down in sheets. Out of the trees loped a huge black wolf with pale, burning eyes. As he approached the small porch, the powerful body contorted, stretched, shape-shifted into a heavily muscled man with wide shoulders, long dark hair, and slashing silver eyes. He stepped onto the porch out of the pouring rain and regarded the two men facing him. The tension was tangible between Mikhail and Byron. Mikhail, as always, was inscrutable. Byron looked like a thundercloud. The newcomer's eyebrows went up, and he leaned close to Byron. "The last time someone got Mikhail seriously angry, it was not a pretty sight. I do not wish to attempt to replace major organs in your body, so go take a walk and cool off." The voice was beautiful, with a singsong cadence — compelling, soothing even, yet it clearly commanded. It was a voice so hypnotic, so mesmerizing, even those of their kind were drawn into its power.

Gregori. The dark one. Ancient, powerful, instrument of justice. He dismissed Byron by simply turning his back and addressing Mikhail. "When you sent the call, you said it was Jacques, yet I cannot detect him. I have tried to touch him, but there is only emptiness."

"It is Jacques, yet he is not the same. Not turned, but he has been severely injured. He does not recognize us, and he is extremely dangerous. I cannot restrain him without further injuring him."

"He fought you?" The voice, as always, was mild, even gentle.

"Absolutely, and he would again. He is more wild animal than man, and there is no reaching him. He will kill us if he can find the strength."

Gregori inhaled the wild night air. "Who is this woman?"

"She is Carpathian, but she does not know our ways or respond in any way to our normal means of communication. She seems trained in the human practice of healing."

"A doctor?"

"Perhaps. He protects her, yet he is abusive, as if he cannot separate right from wrong. I think he is trapped in a world of madness."

The silver eyes flickered. There was a latent cruelty in Gregori's dark, sensual features, the clear stamp of a dangerous predator. "You have no knowledge of what happened to him?"

Mikhail shook his head slowly. "I have no idea, no explanation. I did not ask the woman. I attacked her, would have killed her, thinking her my brother's assailant." Mikhail confessed it without changing tone, a simple, quiet admission. "He was in bad shape, in obvious agony, sweating blood, and she stood over him, digging in his wound. There was so much blood, I thought her a vampiress, deranged, tormenting him, trying to eviscerate him."

There was a small silence, only the wind and rain daring to comment. Gregori simply waited, his body as still as the mountains.

Mikhail shrugged. "Perhaps there was no

thought, just reaction. I could not touch his mind with mine. The suffering on his face was more than I could bear."

"The storm is not yours," Gregori stated. "Jacques has grown far more powerful than I realized. There is a darkness in him unlike any I have ever observed. He is not vampire, but he is truly dangerous. Let us go in and see if I can repair the damage."

"Go carefully, Gregori," Mikhail cautioned.

The silver eyes glittered, reflected the driving sheets of rain. "I am known for my careful ways, am I not?" Gregori glided through the broken door; Mikhail, shaking his head over the outrageous lie, followed one step behind.

Jacques' head snapped up, a black fury smoldering in his eyes as he tracked them. A long, slow hiss of warning escaped from deep in his throat. Gregori stopped, held his hands away from his sides in the age-old gesture of a peacemaker. Mikhail leaned against the doorjamb, so completely still, he seemed to become part of the wall itself. He was well aware that he had made a major mistake in his attack upon the woman.

"I am Gregori, Jacques." Gregori's voice was power itself, yet soft and soothing. "A healer for our people."

Shea was lying across Jacques, her head on his shoulder, her eyes closed. She groaned — a low, husky sound that added fuel to Jacques' rage. His fingers brushed the dark smudges along her swollen throat, and he turned a murderous gaze on Mikhail.

"Leave us alone." Her voice was barely a whisper, hoarse and raw. She did not open her eyes or try to move.

"I can help him," Gregori persisted, using his same compelling tone. The woman was so obviously the key to reaching Jacques. It was in the way he held her, the protective posture of his body, the way his eyes moved possessively, even tenderly, over her face. His hands were continually caressing her, stroking her hair, her skin.

At the underlying command in Gregori's beautiful voice, her long eyelashes lifted, and she studied his face. He was savagely beautiful, a blend of elegance and untamed beast. He looked more dangerous than the other two strangers did. Shea made an effort to swallow, but it hurt. "You look like an ax murderer to me."

This one has brains. Mikhail's soft laughter echoed in Gregori's head. *She sees beyond that handsome face of yours.*

You are so funny, ancient one. Gregori deliberately reminded him of the quarter of a century difference in their ages. *Jacques is gathering himself for the attack. Hear the wind pick up outside.* He was silent for a moment, searching every path known to him. *I cannot find a single fragment to reach him, and she is very resistant to mental compulsion. I can use her, but he will know what I am doing. He will fight me, fearing I am taking her from him. She is too weak to survive such a struggle.*

Can you immobilize him? Send him to sleep?

Not in his present state of agitation. He is more animal than man and more dangerous than you can know. Gregori gave a slight bow toward Shea, continuing his conversation aloud with her. "Nevertheless, I am a healer for our people. I can help Jacques, but I will need information."

Jacques' palm slid from Shea's throat, down her shoulder, to tighten around her arm. *Do not listen to him. They speak to one another without our knowledge. They are not to be trusted.* The words were hissed, low and commanding. Already his brief moment of sanity was beginning to slip away with the intrusion of other males so near to Shea.

If he is a healer for your people, he can make you well faster than I ever could. Let's at least listen to him. Shea kept her voice as soothing and as unafraid as she was able. She was tired and wanted to drift away, but she would not desert Jacques.

"You speak with Jacques in the way of our people," Gregori said, "as a true lifemate." His eyes were on the strong fingers circling her arm. "You must not sleep. You are his sanity. Without you we cannot help him."

Shea's tongue darted out, touched her lower lip. Her small teeth bit nervously. "Tell us something about Jacques," she challenged. "Prove you have met him before and are friends to him."

"He is Mikhail's brother, lost to us these seven years. We sought him and, thinking him dead, sought his body. Mikhail, Byron, and I have all exchanged blood with Jacques. It strengthens out telepathic communication. We should have been able to reach him. When none of us could feel him, we all were certain he was dead."

Shea took a deep, calming breath for both her and Jacques. These men were powerful and dangerous. Although the healer looked as if he might be the prince of darkness, there was a sincerity about him. But his words were fanning the smoldering embers of Jacques' killing rage. She tried to keep him as calm as she could. "I found him buried in the cellar of a burned-down structure about six miles from here."

Jacques' grip on Shea tightened to the point of pain. *Do not tell them anything.*

Jacques. She said his name gently. *You are hurting me.*

Gregori nodded. "He lived there on and off before he disappeared. This cabin is Mikhail's. Years ago Jacques guarded Mikhail's wife in this place, fought a betrayer to save her. He nearly died here." He saw a flash of hope in the woman's eyes. Gregori knew her control of Jacques was but a slender thread. He had to reach her, get her on their side. She recognized the truth of something he had said. "After that incident, we left this area for a while. About eight years ago, Jacques returned to his home near here. There was much danger that year and the next. Humans and Carpathians alike were being murdered. Mikhail, Jacques, Aidan, and I were hunting the assassins. Jacques was supposed to rejoin us in three days several hundred miles south of here. When he did not meet us and did not answer our summons, we came to his home. It was completely destroyed. We could not detect his life force, nor did he answer our calls."

Jacques' venomous hiss called him a liar. Red flames leapt and burned in the depths of his eyes. *I called and called, Shea. Do not believe this betrayer.* The strength of his grip on her arm increased, threatening to crush her bones.

Perhaps I can learn from him, something to help us. Shea swayed wearily, was forced to lean against Jacques' chest for support. *My arm hurts.* She was so tired. If she could just sleep . . . Everything seemed to be blurring together, the voices fading as if coming from a great distance.

Gregori's silver gaze met Mikhail's dark one. *The woman is weak, perhaps in more immediate need than Jacques. If we lose her, he is lost to us. There is no doubt in my mind that she is all that is keeping him with us. She is his only link to sanity.*

"Now you tell me more," Gregori prompted Shea as Mikhail nodded his understanding. They were aware of Jacques' terrible grip on her arm. Gregori needed to keep her conscious and willing to aid them. "What of Jacques' wounds?"

"He was tortured, burned. A wooden stake the size of your fist was driven through his body. That is the worst wound. He remembers two humans and one he refers to as a betrayer." Her voice was very weak.

A single sound escaped Mikhail, a low, ominous growl that sent a shiver racing along Shea's spine. *A vampire,* Mikhail hissed to Gregori. *A vampire turned him over to humans to be tortured and murdered.*

No doubt. Gregori was matter-of-fact. He didn't even glance in Mikhail's direction, his entire focus on the woman. He had to keep her from slipping away, and she was very close to doing just that. It was only her determination to save Jacques that kept her from succumbing to the blood loss and fatigue and pain.

"He was chained and manacled at the wrists and ankles. Buried upright in a coffin in the cellar wall." She made a determined effort to speak clearly, but her throat was very sore, and she was so tired. "There were well over a hundred deep cuts on his body and as many shallow ones. He lived a prisoner of the earth, in terrible agony during his waking time for seven years. It has done something to his mind. Jacques remembers very little of his past. Bits and pieces only. Most of his memories are of pain and madness." Shea closed her eyes, exhausted. She just wanted them all to go away so she could sleep. Her heart was laboring, sweat beaded on her body, and her limbs were like lead. It was almost too difficult to keep her eyes open. "The one who betrayed him was someone he knew and trusted."

"Jacques." Gregori's voice dropped even

lower so that it seemed to whisper — low, compelling, beautiful. "Your woman is in need of care. I offer my services as a healer to both of you. I give you my word that at no time will I attempt harm to your woman."

Let him, Jacques.

No! It is a trick.

Shea stirred, tried to sit up on her own, but was too weak. *Look at us, wild man. They could easily kill us. I'm so tired, I can't hang on anymore.*

Jacques turned it over in his mind. He knew something was wrong with him, but he trusted none of them. He gave in only because he sensed Shea's health was even more precarious than his. *Stay close to me.*

Shea's hand came up, fluttered weakly. She pushed the tangled mane of hair from her face wearily. "He says you may help him."

"We will have to get you to the bed, Jacques." Gregori's voice dispelled the thick tension in the room, pushed it aside to replace it with clean, fragrant air. "Mikhail, I will need herbs. You know which ones. Tell Byron to bring me plenty of rich soil from the steam chamber in the caves."

Gregori glided closer to the couple, his graceful elegance failing to conceal the rippling strength of his muscles and the power emanating from his body. He looked totally confident, relaxed, completely fearless.

The soft rumbling in Jacques' throat increased; his fingers tightened possessively, crushing bones and tendon in Shea's upper arm. Gregori stopped moving immediately. "I am sorry, woman, I know you are weak, but you will have to move to the other side of him or he will not allow me to help," Gregori instructed calmly. *What we need, Mikhail, is Raven's calming influence. You look about as reassuring as a Bengal tiger.*

Oh, and you look like a bunny rabbit, Mikhail scoffed.

"You could have brought Raven along," Gregori chided softly, aloud. "You bring her along on every other dangerous thing she should not be involved in." That was a clear reprimand. "You might have brought her where she could actually do some good."

Through the open doorway suddenly stepped a small woman, long ebony hair braided intricately, huge blue eyes flashing at Mikhail. As Byron shouldered his way inside behind her, she gave him a friendly smile and stood on her toes to brush his chin with a kiss.

Mikhail stiffened, then immediately wrapped a possessive arm around her waist.

"Carpathian women do not do that kind of thing," he reprimanded her.

She tilted her chin at him, in no way intimidated. "That's because Carpathian males have such a territorial mentality — you know, a beat-their-chest, swing-from-the-trees sort of thing." She turned her head to look at the couple lying on the floor. Her indrawn breath was audible.

"Jacques." She whispered his name, tears in her voice and in her blue eyes. "It really is you." Eluding Mikhail's outstretched, detaining hand, she ran to him.

Let her, Gregori persuaded softly. *Look at him.*

Jacques' gaze was fastened on the woman's face, the red flames receding from his eyes as she approached.

"I'm Raven, Jacques. Don't you remember me? Mikhail, your brother, is my lifemate." Raven dropped to her knees beside the couple. "Thank God you're alive. I can't believe how lucky we are. Who did this to you? Who took you from us?"

Shea felt the ripple of awareness in her mind. Jacques' shock. His curiosity. He recognized those tear-filled blue eyes. Shea caught a glimpse, a fragment of memory, the woman bending over him, her hands clamped to his throat, pressing soil and

247

saliva into a pumping wound. Shea held her breath, waiting. Jacques' silent cry of despair echoed in her head. She forced herself to move, found his hand with hers, silently supporting him as she regarded the woman kneeling beside her.

You didn't tell me she was so beautiful, Shea reprimanded deliberately.

In the midst of Jacques' pain and agony, his possessive fury and maniacal madness, something seemed to melt the ice-cold core of murderous resolve. The urge to smile at that feminine, edgy tone came out of nowhere. Something snarling to be set free retreated, and the tension in him eased visibly. *Is she?* Jacques asked innocently.

Shea's green eyes touched his face, and warmth spread further inside him. And the beast was temporarily leashed.

"Is this your lifemate, Jacques?" Raven asked softly.

Shea looked at her then, this woman who had been a part of Jacques' life. "I'm Shea O'Halloran." Her voice was husky and ragged. "Jacques has been unable to use his voice since I found him."

Raven touched Shea's bruised throat with gentle fingers. "Someone had better tell me what happened here." Her blue eyes were studying the dark smudges closely.

"Help her to the bed," Gregori interceded, distracting Raven from her study. *You owe me one, old friend,* he sent to Mikhail.

Raven smiled very gently at Jacques. "Do you mind if I help her? Shea is quite weak." Not waiting for his approval, she slipped an arm around Shea's waist, supporting her as she tried to stand.

Instantly Shea felt the ripple of unease coursing through Jacques. The others felt it as the ground shifted and rolled. The flames in his eyes glowed a brilliant red, and a slow hiss escaped him.

Raven glared at Mikhail over her shoulder. He shrugged helplessly. *I am not doing it, little one. Jacques is unstable. He does not like the woman apart from him.*

Temper tantrums seem to run in your family. Raven was careful to keep Shea close as Gregori lifted Jacques in his arms. With his tremendous strength, the healer carried Jacques as if he were a child and gently laid him on the bed.

Jacques didn't so much as look at him. His eyes were always on Shea. Raven made certain Shea was beside him every step of the way.

"Lie close to him, Shea," Gregori instructed. He stepped back so Raven could help her into the bed. The woman was very weak and could not survive another attack. All of them had to take great care not to set Jacques off.

Raven lit the candle Mikhail produced, then lit pungent herbs. Mikhail, Byron, and Raven all joined together, in low murmurs reciting the ancient healing chant in the language of their people. Gregori laid his hands on Jacques, closed his eyes, and sent himself seeking outside his own body and into Jacques'. The physical wounds had begun to heal, with the exception of the one Shea had just repaired. Gregori examined her work, found it flawless. She was a true healer, human or not. Few could have equaled her medical expertise. He began the painstaking project of healing Jacques from the inside out.

Jacques was uncomfortably aware of another's presence in his body, in his mind, of a new burning sensation inside him. The presence was vaguely familiar. The chant, the scent of herbs, and the flickering candlelight also seemed familiar. But he couldn't catch the memories and hold on to them. As fast as they shimmered in front of him, they swirled in a teasing eddy, crystallized, and dissolved.

Automatically, in his frustration and

hopelessness, he reached for Shea, the one path his mind knew and could hold on to. She was drifting, floating, yet she watched Gregori intently, trying to follow his every move despite her physical weakness. As always, information was massing, computing in her brain at a speed that amazed Jacques. He concentrated on her, found she was terribly weak, her blood volume insufficient. Alarmed, Jacques jerked himself from the half-trance the healing ritual had induced and clamped his hand like a vise around the healer's forearm.

Gregori instantly withdrew from the wounds in Jacques' body. The room fell dead silent; the very air itself stilled, thickened. The flames vanished from the candles, plunging the room into the total darkness of night, yet it was no darkness to the group. Little beads of perspiration dotted Gregori's forehead, the only indication of how difficult the healing process was on the healer.

Silver eyes slashed to the hand gripping his forearm, jumped to Jacques' gaunt face. There was the glitter of death in those pale eyes. Jacques met the ice-cold gaze, stare for stare. His mind struggled to tune itself, find a path. When he could not, Jacques reached for his voice. The words formed in his brain but were lost before his vocal cords could find them. Black fury swirled at his own inadequacy, but he pushed it aside. Shea needed blood, needed help. He had caused her enough suffering. "Blood." The single word was more of a growl than anything else, but the healer heard.

Gregori regarded him dispassionately, silent for a long moment. His movements were unhurried as with his free hand he calmly punctured his own wrist just above Jacques' menacing fingers. His silver gaze remained locked with Jacques'. Gregori's blood was powerful, ancient like Mikhail's. It would speed the healing process as no other's could. Rich blood dripped and beckoned as he offered it silently to the Carpathian male lying so battered and torn, yet so willing to do battle.

Hunger rose so swiftly and sharply in Jacques that it was a compulsion. He dragged the proffered wrist to his mouth and fed voraciously, at last finding the hot, rich blood he needed to survive, to heal and grow strong, to pass on to Shea. The liquid nourishment poured into his starved body, spreading to every withered cell. Tissues and muscles swelled with strength. Power surged through him, built and built until he felt alive, really alive. Until colors were vivid, brilliant even, until the sounds of the night beckoned and called to him as one of them. *Creature of the night.*

"Enough." Gregori's voice was a whisper of beauty, of purity, so compelling it would have been nearly impossible to disobey him.

Jacques closed the wound on Gregori's wrist and immediately reached for Shea. He pulled her into the circle of his arms, cradling her light, nearly insubstantial body to him. He focused his attention, blocked out his own pain and merged his mind firmly with Shea's. *You must feed.*

He could feel the ripple of unease running through her body. She turned her face from him. *I can't, Jacques, not with them here. I'm so tired, just let me sleep.*

You must, little red hair. He strengthened the command. *Feed.*

As weak as she was, Shea resisted him, her hand going to her pounding head. *Don't make me do this in front of them.*

The little catch in her words warmed his soul. Her words created an intimacy between them that belonged. He had been insane, a mad darkness taking hold of him, but she had been there, by his side, fighting for him, believing in him. He owed her more than his life, he owed her his sanity. *There is only you and me, my love. Feed now. You must do so to survive, so we both survive.*

There was no way to deny him. Jacques' will was iron, his voice hypnotic, his mind locked with hers and reinforced the command. Shea was weak and tired and hurting. She sank into the compulsion, nuzzling his neck, his throat, her lips soft satin skimming across his chest.

Jacques bent over her to give her what privacy he could from the others in the room. His body clenched hotly, unexpectedly, as her tongue swirled over his pulse. His fingers tightened in her hair, and he glanced up, angry that the intruders were witnessing their intimacy.

Gregori was in a far corner, leaning against the wall, his dark head bent to Mikhail's wrist, clearly replenishing his own blood supply. Raven was on her knees, picking up the shattered glass of a lantern, soaking up the oil with a towel. Byron was working on the door. His eyes alone slid over the couple, dwelt on the curve of Shea's hip, her abundance of wine-red hair.

There was helpless envy in Byron's stare, and Jacques deliberately shielded Shea's face from his view, knowing she still had an aversion to the necessary and natural function of taking blood. Her tongue stroked across the steady pulse in his neck, and his heart jumped in response. His body stirred restlessly, need rising. Soft velvet caress, moist and erotic. His blood surged hotly.

Shea had far too much passion in her to simply yield to compulsion. This was Jacques, and her body craved his. Her natural inhibitions slipped away. Her small teeth barely scraped his skin, but it was enough to send darts of fire racing through his bloodstream. He had to bite back a groan as the white-hot heat pierced his skin and he flowed into her, his very life force, his very soul. Her hand curled around the back of his neck, another intimacy binding them together like the silken skeins of her hair. She didn't simply drink, she feasted. Her mouth moved seductively, her body restlessly, deliberately enticing his. Jacques wanted her with a hunger he had never known. He lowered his head to brush her temple with his lips.

So, Gregori. Mikhail's voice was a mere thread of sound in the healer's mind. *Tell me what you found.*

The woman would have healed his wounds eventually. She is an excellent physician. It is a miracle he managed to keep himself alive until she found him. His mind is completely shattered, Mikhail. Very dark and violent. He has bound the woman to him, and the tie is strong.

255

Gregori's reply was thoughtful.

Why do I hear the inevitable but *in there?* Mikhail, a little weak from donating blood, sat down to rest.

Gregori righted a chair and sat facing him. *I think he turned the woman, maybe accidentally, maybe on purpose. She is Carpathian, yet human. She is weak, as if her internal organs had very recently suffered a trauma.*

How could you know this? You have not touched her, Mikhail pointed out.

His mind never quite releases hers completely. She anchors him. He is extremely dangerous, Mikhail. His rage seethes in him. A good part of him is pure animal instinct. His nature is predatory — you know that. What was done to him has shaped his life for all time. That I cannot change.

Mikhail rubbed his forehead, unconsciously sought to touch Raven's mind with his. Immediately she was there, flooding him with warmth, surrounding him with love. His lifemate could take away every sadness with one melting look from her blue eyes, one touch of her mind to his.

Mikhail mentally laced his fingers through Raven's, even as he turned to Gregori. *Do you think he will turn?*

Gregori gave the mental equivalent of a

shrug. *I think he is dangerous either way. Only the woman can control him. She is the answer to that. If I am correct and she knows nothing of our ways, it will be difficult. She is determined he survive, but I sense she has accepted that it is inevitable that she die. She has no clear idea of what she has been committed to here.*

Mikhail glanced at his brother, saw him gently, even tenderly stroke back Shea's hair. The gesture touched his heart.

Gregori sighed. *It is obvious how he feels, but he does not always know what he is doing. He is quite capable of harming her if something triggers the beast in him.*

Mikhail rubbed the heel of his hand over his forehead. The Jacques he knew and loved was so different. His laughter came readily, and compassion always tempered his predatory nature. Jacques was so intelligent, so easy to love. Long after Jacques had lost his ability to feel his emotions, he had retained the memory of them. He had often helped the older males to recall memories of their own laughter. Who had done this to him? To be forced to sentence another brother to death . . . Mikhail couldn't do it. It was time to step down, time to hand someone else the weight of responsibility for their dying race.

Mikhail felt Raven slip her arms around

his neck. "Jacques is strong, love. He will find his way back to us."

Mikhail turned her palm up, kissed the center gently. *Gregori thinks Jacques turned Shea O'Halloran without her knowledge or consent.* His black eyes met her blue ones, filled with guilt, tenderness. *He does not think the woman has any idea of our ways.*

Jacques will —

No, little one, Jacques remembers very little of anything. Hatred, rage, revenge, the woman — that is all he thinks of. We are not certain he is capable of taking care of her.

Look at him with her, Raven instructed. She repeated it aloud. "Look at him with her."

Jacques wanted the strangers to be gone. So many males pressing close to Shea kept him on edge. He trusted none of these people, with the possible exception of the blue-eyed woman. Jacques could hardly bear to look at the one who claimed to be his brother, the one who had attacked and nearly killed Shea. Strangely enough, it hurt to look at the man. Jacques' head seemed to want to disintegrate every time their eyes met. Memories. Fragments. Pieces of nothing.

Enough, he whispered to Shea, his words a soft command. Her tongue stroked across the wound to close it, a seduction of pure sensation.

Shea came out of the trance slowly, a sweet, coppery taste in her mouth. The terrible gnawing hunger was gone, but her body was on fire, soft and pliant, in such need. Suddenly aware of the others in the room, she burrowed closer to Jacques for protection. If they all were just gone, she could sleep, figure things out later. She could sort through all the data she had and determine just what these people were.

Fear slammed into her, her mouth went dry, and her heart began to pound in alarm. Shea could feel Jacques' hands tightening like bonds on her arms. A hypnotic trance. Jacques had induced it. Her green eyes slowly opened to move over his face in a slow, terrified study. So why wasn't she joyful, ecstatic, that they had found his people, his family? Why wasn't she thrilled at the arrival of a healer?

There was something wrong here. Her only hope was to get out of the situation, leave Jacques to his family. There were now plenty of people to care for Jacques without her. The healer obviously was far more skilled than she was. Shea was shaking, embarrassed that those surrounding them could see how badly she was trembling. She was always in control. She just needed distance to regain it.

No! Jacques' voice was much stronger now and much more frightening. *You cannot leave me.*

Shea knew he was capable of far more power than she could conceive of. And he was manipulating her, had been all along. For the first time she allowed the facts to come together in her mind. Vampire. Jacques was a vampire. All of these people were. Her hand went to her throat. She was probably one of them now.

"Let go of me!" Shea struggled in earnest now, shocked at how physically strong Jacques had become with the infusion of Gregori's blood.

Jacques snarled, black fury rising along with fear of losing her, fear that she could not survive without him, fear of once again being alone in utter darkness. He held her down easily, but the sound of her heart racing was alarming to him, dragging him back to a shred of sanity.

Into the swirl of violent emotions came the healer's voice. "She does not understand the ways of our people, Jacques. You must be gentle with her, guide her, as your brother guided Raven."

Shea fought the compelling voice, a

weaver of spells. "I want to leave. You can't keep me here." *Jacques, please, don't do this. Don't make me stay when we know it's impossible for me. You know me, know me inside and out.*

Stop it, Shea, Jacques pleaded with her, knowing he was holding on to his intellect and reason by a thread. *Nothing has changed.*

Everything has changed. These people are your family. She tried to take a deep, calming breath. *Jacques, I was your doctor, nothing more. I don't belong here. I don't know how to live like this.*

You are my lifemate. The words were firm in her head. *You are tired, my love, tired and afraid. You have every right to be. I know that. I know I frightened you, but you belong with me.* He did his best to keep his voice a soft whisper of sense, but it was difficult with the beast rising and the fragments in his brain confusing him.

She lay looking up at his strong, harsh, uncompromising features, the warning in his furious eyes. *I don't even know what it means to be your lifemate, Jacques. You know I want the best for you, I want you well and whole again, but I can't be with all these people. I need time to sort out what's happened here. What I am. I can hardly breathe right now, let alone think things through.*

She was telling the truth. Merged as he was with her, Jacques could feel the familiar pattern in her brain, her intellect leaping forward to protect her from any overwhelming emotion. She was too tired and drained to succeed at her attempt. He struggled once again to reassure her. *You are my lifemate. It means we belong together, never apart.*

She shook her head adamantly. "No way." Her enormous eyes jumped to the others. All at once they looked sinister, beings too powerful for their own good. "I want to leave this place." It was somewhere between a demand and a plea for help. Instinctively she looked toward Mikhail. His fingerprints were on her swollen throat. She had saved his brother's life. He owed her.

Raven tightened her fingers around Mikhail's, feeling his tension, his indecision. Clearly the woman was asking for help, and Mikhail could do no other than offer his protection. But Jacques was already warning them off, a low growl rumbling in his throat. He sensed Shea was looking to the others for assistance, and it triggered his predatory instincts. At once he was dangerous, violence swirling close to the surface, aggressive toward Shea, clearly demanding submission.

Byron nearly leapt forward, but a show of Jacques' gleaming fangs held him motionless. He glared at Mikhail. "I told you she had not chosen. Take her from him. She must be protected." Hope was shining in his eyes.

"Jacques." Gregori's voice was pure black velvet, a caressing, compelling tone impossible to ignore. "The woman is overwhelmed. She needs rest, a healing sleep. Both of you should go to earth."

Shea's heart nearly stopped. She shoved hard at Jacques' immovable chest, caught the picture of the earth opening, accepting them. Buried alive. A scream of alarm caught in her throat. She flung herself off the bed in an attempt to get away.

Jacques caught both fragile wrists, pinned her to the mattress. *Do not fight me, Shea, there is no way to win.* Jacques struggled to stay in control. Shea was trembling, her mind filled with fear of him and what he was, what he represented. The loss of freedom, the horror of being a vampire preying on human victims for sustenance as portrayed in old novels, the terror of ever needing a man the way her mother had — to survive.

"Take her from him," Byron demanded.

Jacques turned his head, eyes glittering

like black ice. His voice was hoarse, a growling representation of his long-silent vocal cords. He made a supreme effort to stay in control for Shea's sake. She had been there for him; he had to do the same for her. "No one will take her from me and live."

There was no doubt he meant it. Shea lay shocked, unable to absorb that he had spoken aloud. There would be a bloody war here, and someone would die. *Please, Jacques, please let me go. I can't live like this.* There were tears in her eyes, tears in his heart.

Jacques tried to reach her, calm her with his mind, but she was panic-stricken, too petrified to think.

"Send her to sleep. She is weak and worn. You must care for her health." Gregori's voice was always the same, as pure as the sound of crystal-clear water running over rocks.

"No!" Gregori frightened her more than anything. She was always in control. Always. No one had ever taken her decisions out of her hands, not even her mother. She just needed to be alone, have time to think. Shea struggled in desperation against Jacques' hold. "Let me go!"

The purity of Gregori's voice was finding threads of fragments in Jacques' head,

weaving them together. Shea was so frightened, small, and vulnerable lying beneath
him, pinned helplessly. *It is all right, my love.*
Jacques bent his dark head and kissed her
temple. *You will sleep and heal. I will ensure
that you come to no harm. In this you can trust
me.* The command was firm and strong. He
heard the echo of her anguished cry in his
mind fading as she succumbed to his order.

Chapter Eight

The storm moved in slowly, blanketing the land in a peculiar, dreary drizzle. All day it blotted out any chance of sunshine and hid the mountain range in sheets of silvery rain and a shroud of thick fog. In an abandoned shack, three men huddled by the fire and tried to escape the water leaking through the cracks in the roof.

Don Wallace sipped at the scalding-hot coffee and stared uneasily out the window into the gathering dusk. "Unusual weather for this time of year." His eyes met the older man's in a long, knowing stare.

Eugene Slovensky hunched his shoulders against the cold and regarded his nephew with reproach. "The weather is like this when the land is unsettled. How could you allow the woman to slip through your fingers, Donnie?"

"Well, you had her when she was a mere baby," he retorted. "You let her escape you then. You couldn't even trace her mother between Ireland and America. I was the one who did that, nearly twenty years later. Don't act like I'm the only one who bungled this."

The older man glared at him. "Don't take

that tone with me. Things were different all those years ago. We didn't have the advantages of all the modern technology you have now. Maggie O'Halloran had people help her escape with her little demon whelp." He sighed and glanced once more out the window at the fog and rain. "Do you have any idea the risk we're taking coming into their territory?"

"I believe I was the one who tracked and killed those vampires we got a few years back while you stayed safe in Germany," Don snapped, irritated.

"You weren't very discriminating about who you marked as vampire, Don," Eugene pointed out waspishly. "You enjoyed yourself whenever the mood struck you."

"I was the one taking the risks. I should be allowed to have some fun," Don snapped back.

"Well, this time concentrate on why we're here. This is dangerous work."

Don's eyes flattened, hardened. "I was with you when we found Uncle James's body, remember? Happy fifteenth birthday, Donnie. Instead of a real live vampire to stake, I get my uncle's body buried in a pile of rubble. I know how dangerous it is."

"Never forget that sight, boy, not ever," Eugene cautioned. "Twenty-five years it's been, and we still don't have his murderers."

"At least we made them pay," Don pointed out.

Eugene's eyes burned. "Not nearly enough. It will never be enough. We have to wipe them out. All of them. Wipe them out."

Jeff Smith stirred and glanced at Don Wallace. The old man was crazy. If there really was such a thing as a vampire, Jeff wanted to take advantage of the opportunity to become immortal. They had killed fourteen so-called vampires, and Jeff was fairly certain a couple of them had been the real thing. No human could have taken the kind of punishment Wallace had so eagerly dispensed and survived so long. Most of the victims definitely had been human, though, Wallace's enemies. Don had really enjoyed those sessions.

Jeff was also certain Shea O'Halloran was no vampire. He had researched her very carefully. She had gone to a regular daytime school, had eaten in front of other children. She was a bona-fide surgeon, respected in her profession. A child prodigy, all her professors spoke highly of her. Jeff couldn't get her out of his mind. Her voice, her eyes, the fluid, sexy way her body moved. The crazy old man was obsessed with finding her, and Don always did what his uncle said. Don's uncle, old Eugene Slovensky, held the purse strings, and the money was considerable. If they found the woman, Jeff was not going to let them kill her. He wanted her for himself.

"Why do you think she's is this area?" Slovensky demanded.

"She always uses cash, so we can't follow a money trail, but she often leaves her signature behind anyway." Don grinned, an evil facsimile of a smile. "She just has to help people in these isolated villages. It's kind of amusing, really. She thinks she's so clever, but she always makes the same mistake."

Eugene Slovensky nodded. "The brilliant ones never have any common sense." He cleared his throat nervously. "I sent word to the Vulture."

Don Wallace's hand jerked, and hot coffee spilled over his wrist. "Are you crazy, Uncle Eugene? He threatened to kill us if we didn't leave the mountains the last time he saw us. The Vulture is a true vampire, and he doesn't exactly like us."

"You killed the woman," Eugene said, "he warned you not to. I warned you not to. You just had to have your fun."

Furious, Don hurled the mug across the room. "We're hunting a woman right now.

We've followed her for two years, and now that we're close, you call in that killer. I should have put a stake through his heart when I had the chance. He's a no-good vampire like the rest of them."

Slovensky grinned, shook his head in denial. "Not like the rest of them. He hates, Donnie, my boy. He hates with an intensity I have never seen before. And that can always be useful for us. He wants a certain woman this time, the one with the long black hair. He wants her and those close to her dead. He has their trust, and he'll deliver them into our hands. He may be beneath contempt, a snitch, but he is powerful."

"All their woman have long black hair. How am I supposed to know the difference?" Don pouted. "Do you remember the kid? The one about eighteen? He hated that kid. He really wanted that kid to suffer." He smiled with satisfaction. "He did, too. Most of all he hated the last one we caught, the one with the black eyes. He ordered me to torture him, burn him. He wanted it to last forever, and I made sure it did. The Vulture is evil, Uncle Eugene."

Slovensky nodded. "Use him. Let him think you respect him, that he is the one in charge, giving the orders. Promise him the red-haired woman, too. Tell him we'll give them both to him if he will deliver James's murderers. My poor brother James."

"I thought you said we needed to study her, that she wasn't as strong as the others and we had a better chance of controlling her. In any case, she doesn't have black hair." Don got up abruptly and paced across the floor to hide his expression from the others. It had been far too long since he'd had a woman completely in his control. His body grew hot and hard at the memory of his time in the basement with the last one. She had lasted three delicious weeks, and every moment of it she had known he would eventually kill her. She had tried so hard to please him, done anything and everything to please him.

He wanted Shea O'Halloran in his hands for a long, long time. She would learn respect. The icy contempt in her vivid green eyes would be replaced with pleasing, begging. He fought to control himself, cursed the others sharing the small confines of the cabin keeping him from indulging his fantasies. Don turned his head to catch Smith watching him. His mask slipped into place, his friendly smile. Smith was weak, always whining. He got off watching Don perform, but he rarely had the guts to do anything exotic himself. One of these days, Don resolved he would show Smith just how weak he really was. Their longtime partnership was coming to an end.

Slovensky dragged a blanket around his shoulders. In his sixties, he felt the chill of the rain seep into his bones. He detested these mountains and all the memories that came with them. Twenty-five years ago he had brought his younger brother, James, on a vampire hunt with other members of a secret society dedicated to wiping out the loathsome creatures. They had trapped a vampire, but it had killed James.

Shea O'Halloran was the key to all of it now. He would use her to ferret out his brother's murderers and deliver retribution, as they deserved. Donnie would put a stake through the Vulture's heart and rid the world of a detestable worm. And then the society could study the woman, obtain the proof they needed to be finally recognized as scientists, as they deserved.

"How long are we going to be stuck in this hellhole?" Smith demanded.

Wallace and Slovensky exchanged another long, knowing look. Wallace shrugged, pulled out a pack of cigarettes, and shook one loose. "You should know by now never to go outdoors when the land is so unsettled. It means they're out tonight."

"Every time it rains we're locked in? Damn, Don, the least we could have done was get decent accommodations."

"Stop whining," Slovensky snapped. "The last thing we want to do is advertise our presence here. They control the locals, bind them to them in some way so that the villagers are loyal to them."

Jeff turned away from them, staring out at the darkening land. Slovensky was a total whacko. Wallace he had met in college. Don had been everything Jeff was not. Cocky, self-assured, handsome, and tough. Wallace had cornered one of Jeff's constant tormentors, held him, and encouraged Jeff to beat the kid to death. The sense of power was incredible, and the two of them became inseparable. Don was sadistic, violent. He'd enjoyed watching snuff films, shared the experience with Jeff, and eventually became obsessed with the idea of making them. Jeff filmed Don's private performances, each of which became a classroom for torture. At first they'd used prostitutes, but twice they were able to lure a student to their warehouse. Afterward, Don was always mellow for several weeks, a month or two even, if the sessions had been to his liking. Jeff knew

273

that the need to kill was riding Don hard now, and anyone close to him had better keep a low profile.

When the older man went outside to relieve himself, Jeff went to stand beside Don. "You ever think what it would be like, the power we'd have if we forced one of them to make us like them?" He whispered it softly to be sure Slovensky could not possibly overhear what he would consider sacrilege. "We'd be immortal, Don. We could have anything we ever wanted. Any woman we wanted. We could do anything."

Wallace was silent for a few minutes. "We'd need to find out more about them. Most of what I know, the old man and his freaky friends told me, and it's probably all bullshit."

"You sure?"

"Superstitious crap. All the people around here are superstitious. They believe these vampires can direct your mind, even shape-change. If they had all these great powers, Jeff, why didn't they use them when we were having fun with them?"

Jeff shrugged, disappointed. "Maybe you're right. But they just hang on to life so long . . ." He trailed off.

"Hate keeps them alive." Don laughed in anticipation. "They're almost as much fun as women." He looked thoughtful. "But there's the Vulture."

The sun gave up its feeble fight, the storm and the late hour completely obliterating its paltry light. The sky darkened still further, and the clouds grew heavier. The wind began to strengthen, driving the rain so that it pelted the ground hard enough to bruise leaves and vegetation. A low moan rose, echoed through grotesquely swaying branches.

The wind raced northward, howled down a canyon, rushed through the darkened forest, and climbed higher into the steep mountains to find a cabin dark and silent. Inside, away from the sheets of silvery rain and the monstrous wind, two bodies lay motionless, entwined on the bed. Shea was curled up, small and slight, her wine-red hair spilled across the pillow like blood. Jacques' much larger frame was curved protectively around her. Jacques' arm was firmly locked around her waist, holding her to him. His heart began a rhythm, a strong, steady sound in the silence. He drew air into his lungs to inflate them, to resume their normal function.

Jacques waited for the familiar rush of agony his awakening had triggered these last seven years. It would surge through him with the first circle of life, blood heating every cell and nerve ending. The rush didn't come. Instead he was sore, his muscles ached, but he felt strong and alive again. The healer's blood was incredible, his internal healing beyond Jacques' wildest expectations. *Gregori. The dark one.* The words came floating out of nowhere, one of those elusive fragments he could never seem to hold on to. Jacques tried to do so, wanting the information, knowing it was important, yet pain exploded in his head.

It didn't matter. He calmly allowed the fragment to drift away and slowly released his hold on Shea. Before giving her the command to wake, he scanned their surroundings to locate possible danger. There were others of his kind close by. It put him on edge. It was imperative for a Carpathian male to find a female, his true lifemate. If he did not succeed in binding Shea to him, every male in the vicinity would be pressing his suit, hoping against hope his chemistry would match hers. As with all the knowledge that came to him, he felt the truth and rightness of it, knew it was real and not imagined.

A silent snarl lifted his lip, revealing his white teeth. Deliberately, Jacques stretched, a slow, languid movement designed to reacquaint himself with his muscles, with his strength. His body was still a little sluggish, but it was alive again. As he moved, he felt the softness of Shea's body brushing along the hardness of his. His body responded, a sweet ache unknown to him for centuries, now ever present. He turned on his side and stared down into her still, pale face.

His body hardened aggressively. His hand went to the buttons of her shirt, his fingers brushing against her cool, creamy flesh. His heart jumped, and his breath caught in his throat. Such exquisite torment. He'd had no idea anything could be so soft. As he pushed her blouse from her shoulders, he leaned close to her ear. "Wake, little red hair. Wake needing me." He kissed her eyes, took her mouth, tasting her first breath, his hand closing over her breast to feel the way her heart raced into his palm.

Blood rushed, a symphony of sensation sending heat and need and an urgent ache coiling through Shea. Jacques' mouth was magical, reverent, a slow seduction, while his hands traced the contours of her body. He could feel her awakening, her mind opening to his. Her emotions were mixed — longing, need, a reluctant caring for him, overpowering fear of what she was, and a deep sorrow. He brushed his hand down her face to trace every beloved line already committed for all eternity to his mind, to his heart. Her face was damp. Jacques bent his head and followed the trail of tears down the slender column of her neck. Her skin was warm honey flowing up from melting ice, the combination irresistible. His tongue swirled over her pulse, and need slammed into him so hard that his body clenched painfully. Shea made a sound, a soft moan somewhere between despair and acquiescence. Her body was arcing into his, pressure and hunger building to drown out all good sense.

"You are safe with me, little Shea." Jacques used his voice, a blend of heat and velvet. He was willing to utilize every weapon in his arsenal of centuries of experience to bind her to him. "I need you." His body moved restlessly, aggressively, his mouth finding the hollow of her throat while his hand slid down her narrow ribcage, fingers splayed possessively across her flat stomach. "I know you are afraid. I feel it in my mind. Let yourself feel what I am feeling. There is no doubt, no other love for me. I know you are my other half. Give yourself into my keeping." His beautiful husky voice rasped softly, slightly hoarse as the fire began to spread. Flames were leaping, hunger rising, and the beast inside was fighting for freedom. Dark purpose began to swirl as Carpathian instincts fought with the man.

The effort to control the wild cravings, the need for dominance, a frenzied, heated mating, his stamp of possession, was riding him hard. He found her mouth a little desperately, pushed further into her mind, not waiting for complete acceptance, afraid it might never come. Her mind was a mixture of tears and sorrow and smoke and flame and burning desire.

Jacques. His name was a whisper echoing in his head. Her hands were on his, stopping him from pushing the jeans from her hips.

He deepened the kiss, possessive, erotic, deliberately sharing the urgent hunger, the burning desires in his own mind. *You gave me back my life, Shea. Give me my soul. I need you, only you. Make me complete again.* The tension went out of her hands enough that he could slide the jeans from the curve of her hips, down her legs, exposing the beauty of her body to him, to his exploring hands.

Shea heard Jacques' swift indrawn breath, felt his heart jump, his body savage with need, his mind a red haze of burning hunger. The intensity of his emotion was overwhelming to her, threatening to her. She closed her eyes, her arms creeping around his neck, knowing she could not find the strength to refuse such a terrible need in him. Anyone else, but never him.

He inhaled deeply, breathing her scent into his lungs, his hands moving slowly over her body, taking his time with her, fighting off the beast raging to possess her. He had already hurt her too much, taken from her parts of her life he could never give back. He wanted her first time with him to be beautiful, to be as right as he could make it.

"Don't cry, love," he whispered softly into her throat, his mouth resting over her pulse, his tongue stroking the frantic rhythm. His body clenched; pain and hunger rose until it beat at him, at her. His teeth scraped her neck, a sweet torment for both of them. He nuzzled her breasts, marveling at how soft she was, how perfect. Her bones felt small beneath his seeking hands, yet her muscles were firm and her skin like satin.

He was trembling now, a shudder of effort to hold back his wild nature, a fine sheen of sweat bathing his body. Sensations and textures danced with swirling colors and heat. After centuries of no emotion, no feeling, after seven years of damnation and pain, Jacques would never forget the feel of this moment. The way she looked, smelled, and felt to his touch, the reluctant love, the sorrow, the matching hunger and desire in her mind was forever etched into his soul.

Shea felt the change in him, in the way his hands caressed her thighs, the absolute conviction in his mind. She felt his fierce hunger, the burning in his body, his urgent need. His body blanketed hers, imprisoned her, his knee effectively parting her legs. Her body clenched hotly as he pressed against her, hard and insistent. Her heart jolted in sudden rebellion, but his mouth was on her breast, driving out sane thoughts. With every hot pull of his mouth, moist heat throbbed and beckoned him deeper until he met innocent resistance.

His mouth reluctantly released her breast, found her pulse, where his tongue swirled erotically. "You are my lifemate." His teeth scraped her soft, creamy flesh. Liquid heat bathed him invitingly. "I claim you as my lifemate. I belong to you. I offer my life for you." His hands found her small hips, cupped her in his palms. His body was a relentless, savage ache of burning hunger. "I give you my protection, my allegiance, my heart, my soul, and my body. I take into my keeping the same that is yours. Your life, happiness, and welfare will be placed above my own for all time."

"Stop it, Jacques," Shea whispered desperately, feeling every word, every breath weaving them so tightly together that she couldn't tell where he left off and she began.

"You are my lifemate, bound to me for all eternity and always in my care." His teeth sank deep; his body surged into hers. White-hot pain exploded over both of them, leaving shimmering flames leaping high and hot.

Shea's cry was lost in her throat. She wrapped her arms around his head and cradled him to her. Welded together, body, mind, and heart, her life flowing into him, his body took command of hers. He moved — a slow, careful test of her response to him. She was hot and tight, the friction threatening to engulf him in the frenzied, uninhibited sexual mating of a Carpathian male. With effort he controlled himself, savoring the sweet, hot spice of her blood, the velvet fire gripping his body.

He moved gently, tenderly, a long, sure stroke designed to coax her, to calm him. Her muscles clenched around him, and he surged forward, buried himself deep in her very core, his mouth drawing the essence of her life into his keeping. The world narrowed, receded, until she was his breath, his heart, the blood flowing in his veins. There was no darkness, no shadows, only Shea's body with its heat and flowing colors and leaping flames.

Shea's soft little keening cries were muffled against him, yet they echoed in his mind. His body craved hers, more and more, harder and faster and deeper. He drove on and on, reaching for the stars, the universe, reaching for the meeting of their souls. Her blood fed his insatiable hunger, no taste ever better, so erotic and perfect that he indulged himself, giving himself up to lust and greed and wave after wave of unbearable pleasure.

Her body gripped his, shuddered, clenched, and the earth itself seemed to roll and shake. Molten heat coiled around him like a volcano, and he was crying out, his seed spilling into her, his body going up in her flames.

Jacques became aware of her blood trickling between her breasts. In the ecstasy of the moment, he had neglected to close the tiny pinprick he'd made. His tongue stroked gently, tracing the bright trail, and his body reacted as hard and as needy as ever. Her hunger was in his mind, her desire wrapped in age-old need. "Yes, my love," he whispered against her throat. "Need me the way I need you. Let me give to you everything that I am. Take from me what only I can give you."

Her mouth moved over his neck, his throat, and his body raged at him, swelled and hardened to fill her completely. His heart jumped as her lips caressed his chest. Her tongue swirled around his flat nipples, moved over his heart in little nibbling motions. Jacques pulled back, waiting breathlessly, waiting while his body screamed at him to bury itself in her once again, to take her over and over.

"Just once, Shea, say you need me, too," he whispered.

She lifted her head, her green eyes moving over his sensual face, meeting his black eyes. She smiled a slow, sexy, very wicked smile. Then she dropped her head down to his chest, stroked the heavy muscles with her tongue. Her teeth scraped once, twice, teasingly, then sank deep.

Jacques' voice was hoarse in his mind, in the darkness of the room. The sensation was beyond his imaginings. His body plunged wildly into hers as she drank from him. His palm held her head to him, pressed her closer as his body took hers again and again. He could never get enough. Colors whirled and danced, and the earth shook, and he soared higher and higher, taking her with him in body, mind, and soul. In that perfect moment she was his, her life connecting wholly with his for all eternity. Two halves of the same whole, never to be apart again. His release was shattering, Shea with him every step of the way. They erupted into the heavens and floated together to earth, Jacques anchoring them safely.

Shea's tongue closed the wound over his heart, and they lay spent, their bodies locked together, so close that their minds and limbs were still rocking with the after-effects. Little shocks sent shivers of pleasure through them, in them.

Shea lay very still, unable to grasp the wonder of what had happened. She knew it was forever. She knew he had somehow completed the ritual of binding them to-gether. Her body felt as if it didn't belong to her, that he had taken possession of and failed to return some intrinsic part of her. She appeared outwardly calm, but panic was welling up, fear, sheer terror. She had always been alone; she knew no other way.

Jacques' hand stroked the length of her hair, lingered on the curve of her bottom. "I have never experienced anything like this," he said softly, attempting to find the words to fight her panic.

She swallowed hard, listened to the frantic pounding of her heart. "How would you know, silly?" she teased back, trying desperately to appear normal. "You can't remember your past." The pounding of her blood was a roar in her ears. Nothing would ever be the same again. She felt weak. Maybe Jacques had taken more blood than she had exchanged. It was affecting her mind, slowing her thoughts. Unless it was fear paralyzing her ability to think. That had never happened to her before. Her intellect had always dominated. But now her emotions had pushed aside all good sense, and she literally felt lost.

Very cautiously, she eased her body away from his, felt the loss as if it were some terrible sorrow. She wanted him for all time. She needed him with her. She might actually love him. Her throat closed, and Shea felt as if she were suffocating. She had let this happen, let him take control of her. She was as foolish as her shadow of a mother had been. Love wasn't supposed to be a part of her carefully controlled world. Neither was need.

"Shea." He said her name softly, gently,

even tenderly, as if to a wild animal trapped in a corner.

She sat up abruptly, gasping for air, her eyes growing enormous, wild, her heart thumping loudly. She leapt up, long hair swinging around her slender body like a cape. She ran on bare feet toward the bathroom.

Jacques pulled on a pair of jeans, carelessly buttoned them up the front, and padded after her. His eyes never left her slim, fragile figure. Shea looked as if the smallest thing might shatter her. She was going through human gestures, movements. Brushing her teeth, standing in the shower allowing the water to cascade over her, staring out the window. Jacques held the mind touch lightly so that she wasn't aware of his intrusion. Her fear didn't recede with these human activities. Instead, panic was building to overwhelming proportions. Jacques leaned one hip lazily against the wall, his dark eyes watchful, simply waiting for the inevitable.

"I can't do this, Jacques." Her voice was so low, he barely caught the thread of sound. Shea dressed with shaking hands, donning jeans, cotton-ribbed shirt, hiking boots. She didn't look at him.

Jacques waited silently, feeling her confusion and fear, wanting to comfort her but instinctively holding back. Shea was a strong woman, courageous enough to return to save a demon, a madman who had viciously attacked her. Yet the thought of loving Jacques, of needing or wanting him, terrified her.

"I have to leave this place, go to Ireland. I have a home there." Shea twisted the length of red hair into a thick, haphazard braid. Her gaze was jumping from the window to her computer to the door and back again. Everywhere but at him. "You're safe now, with your family and friends. You don't need me anymore."

He moved then, in the way of his people. Silent, unseen, too fast for the human eye. He was suddenly behind her, his body against hers, his palms resting on the wall on either side of her head, effectively forming a cage. Jacques leaned close so that his male scent invaded her lungs, until he was the very air she breathed. "I will always need you, Shea. You are my heart and soul and my very sanity. It has been many years since I have been to Ireland. A beautiful country."

He felt her inhale sharply, fighting for air, fighting a tight, suffocating feeling. In her mind was a strangled denial of his words.

She was desperately searching for a way to dissuade him. Not only was she shaking on the outside, even her insides were trembling. Jacques could literally smell her fear.

Shea's arms crossed her stomach, holding tight against the internal rolling. "Listen to me, Jacques. This . . ." She waved an unsteady hand, turned so that she leaned against the wall, so that it would hold her up. It was a mistake facing him. His hard, muscular body, his sensual features still ravaged by pain, the intensity of his black eyes. The hunger. Desire. Need. She tilted her chin at him, her sorrow so deep that he wanted to gather her close, but it was necessary for her to feel in control.

Jacques crushed down his natural predatory nature, held himself utterly still, her body imprisoned between his immovable one and the wall.

Shea cleared her throat, tried again. "It can't work. I have obligations. I can't afford a relationship right now. And you're looking for something intense, passionate, forever, some eternal bond. I'm just not like that. I don't have all that much to give anyone." Her fingers twisted together in agitation; he felt his heart twist in answer. The smile deep in his soul at her foolish words never found its way to his face.

Shea had a passionate nature, and her need for him was as great as his need for her. She knew it, and it terrified her. More than anything, that knowledge was what made her determined to run from him. She had taught herself to be a solitary person, had no idea how to share her life. She would never, could never be like her mother.

"Are you listening to me, Jacques?"

He moved closer, crowded her slender body. His arms swept her to him, nearly crushing her. "Of course I am listening. I hear that you are afraid. I feel it." His warm breath caressed her neck. The way he held her was completely protective, gentle, tender. "I am afraid, too. I have no past, Shea. Only a living hell that shaped a madman. Those people you call my family mean nothing to me. I do not trust them. Any one of them could be the betrayer." He laid his head over hers, a soothing gesture of unity. "I cannot always distinguish reality from the madness. There is only you, my love, to keep me sane. If you choose to desert me, I fear for myself and any who dare to come near."

Shea blinked back tears, found his wrist with trembling fingers, the lightest contact, a connection between them. "We make such a perfect pair, Jacques. At least one of us should be stable, don't you think?"

He brought her hand to the warmth of his mouth. "You came for me, from thousands of miles away. You came for me."

She managed a smile. "A few years late."

Something eased in the vicinity of his heart. He knew there was no escape for either of them. He might not understand fully, but he knew he had bound them irrevocably together for all time. "Is there not a saying, 'Better late than never'?" His thumb feathered over her wrist, found her pulse.

Her mind was calmer now, more accepting of their union. She rested her head in the niche of his sternum. "I feel so terrible that I didn't listen to my dreams. If only . . ."

His hand covered her mouth, stopping her words. "You saved my sanity. You came for me. That is all that matters. Now we have to find our way together."

She pulled his hand to her neck, held it tight against the satin texture of her skin. "Those men are following me, Jacques. Without me, you have a better chance of escaping. You know that you do."

The beast in him raised its head, fangs dripping triumphantly in anticipation. She could never possibly conceive of his wanting to meet the two humans who had tortured and imprisoned him. She had no concept of his immense power, of his rage, of what kind of dangerous creature he was. She was bound to him, yet she was so compassionate, she could not truly see his nature. She would keep running, avoiding confrontation for all of her life if need be. He preferred to be the aggressor. He would be the aggressor.

"Do not worry about what may happen, little one."

Shea touched his jaw with gentle fingers. "Thank you for watching out for me while I was unaware. You didn't let them put me in the ground."

Again he brought her hand to his mouth. "I knew you would not want such a thing." His dark eyes indicated the far side of the room. He raised his hand, and the door opened at his mental command.

Instantly the wind blew rain into the cabin, a high-pitched moan rising above the scraping branches. Shea shivered, drew closer to the heat and protection of his body. It was wild outside, black fury, the rain driving down in silver sheets. Shea didn't need the flashes of lightning illuminating the forest to see clearly the deep, vivid greens and browns, the drops of rain like thousands of crystals reflecting the beauty of the trees and bushes. She saw with more than the eyes of a human; she saw with the eyes of an animal. She could feel the wildness of the storm in her own body.

Jacques tightened his hold on her as he felt her try to reject such intense and foreign emotions. "No, little one, look at it. This is our world. There is nothing ugly in it. It is clean and honest and beautiful." He murmured the words into her ear, his mouth finding the heat of her skin, his tongue caressing her pulse.

A shiver of excitement, of sensual awareness, rushed through her blood. Everything in her seemed to reach for him. Her body, her heart, her mind. Fear crawled in as she acknowledged her need of him. Her life was different now. She was different. If her father had been like Jacques, his blood had run diluted in her veins. Jacques had somehow brought her fully into his world. She found herself inhaling deeply, drinking in the sights and smells, something wild in her rising to meet the fury of the storm.

"It is ours, Shea. The wind, the rain, the soil beneath our feet."

His words brushed along her skin like a hand in a velvet glove. His teeth scraped seductively along her throat, sent her blood rushing, pooling. "Can we leave tonight?

Now?" The wildness in her was growing, spreading. Her need of him was growing just as strong. She wanted to flee the woods, escape from whatever was inside of her and gaining strength with every moment she was here.

"We will have to make plans for shelter," he counseled softly. "Running blindly without thought will get us killed."

Shea closed her eyes tiredly. "There isn't any place for us to run to, is there?" The part of her that sorted data so perfectly told her she was trying to run from herself.

He folded his arms around her, cradling her tenderly. "You could not have existed for much longer in the half-life you were living. And you were never really happy there. You have never been happy, Shea."

"That's not true. I love my work, being a surgeon."

"You were not meant for a solitary life, little red hair."

"A doctor hardly leads a solitary life, Jacques."

"A surgeon does not need to interact with patients, a researcher even less so. I am in your mind, know your thoughts, and this you cannot keep from me."

Her green eyes glinted at him. "Has it occurred to you that I might not like you running around in my head? You're like a loose cannon. Neither one of us knows when you might go off." Amusement was creeping into her voice, and her body began to relax.

Jacques held back his sigh of relief. She was coming back to him, meeting him halfway. "It is the way of our people."

She turned back to stare out the door into the storm. "All the time?"

The information came easily this time, without the curious splintering pain in his head. "No. All Carpathians can communicate on one common path if they desire it." He rubbed the bridge of his nose. "I am not certain if I am able to do this. I cannot exactly remember the path, only that there is one."

"The others tried to speak to you," she guessed shrewdly.

"Each used a different path when they reached for me. I could feel their touch but could not tune it in. When Carpathians exchange blood, the mental bond becomes stronger. Each individual sharing creates an exclusive path that only the two participants can use." Another fragment of information came out of nowhere. "Males rarely exchange blood unless they have a lifemate."

Why? The question shimmered in his mind. Shea didn't even realize it.

Jacques made the mental equivalent of a shrug. "Once blood has been taken, we can track at will. The closer the bond, the stronger the trail. If it is an actual exchange, each can easily find and 'speak' to the other. Males can turn after so many centuries alone."

"I don't understand what you mean, turn."

"After two hundred years we lose all emotion, all ability to feel. We are natural predators, Shea. We need a lifemate to bring back feeling, to balance us. As the centuries go by, it is easy to give in to the need to feel something, even if only momentarily. A kill while feeding brings a rush of power. But it also turns one. Once a Carpathian turns, he can never go back. He becomes the thing of human legend. A vampire. An amoral killer, cold-blooded, without compassion. He must be hunted and destroyed." A grim smile touched his mouth, did not reach his black eyes. "You can see why lone males rarely take the chance of a blood exchange. It is incredibly easy to be tracked after an exchange, and if one turns . . ."

Shea's white teeth scraped at her lower lip. Beneath his fingers her pulse was racing. "I don't want to believe what you're saying."

"You saved me from such a fate. I know my mind is still in fragments, but I am saved from walking the earth as the undead."

"Those men, the ones who came after me . . ."

"They are human killers." There was contempt in his mind, in his voice. "Those they destroyed were Carpathian, not vampire."

"So the one you called the betrayer . . ."

"Is a Carpathian . . . turned vampire."

Chapter Nine

A gust of wind howled, raced through the room, brought a spray of rain through the door. Jacques gently pushed Shea behind him. "The others come," he warned her.

Shea groped behind her for the wall. These people were definitely a different species. Her father had also been one of them. A part of her was intrigued and excited. If she studied them as a scientist, she would be in her element. But she was stuck in the middle of the drama instead of being able to observe it from a distance. She caught Jacques' wrist. "Let's just go far away from here, away from these people, this place."

"It is important to know as much as possible." His voice was soft and mesmerizing, deliberately tender, wrapping her in the safe cocoon of his protection. "The healer comes with the one who names himself my brother. The woman is with them." He was uneasy not knowing where the third male was. He trusted none of them completely. Somewhere deep inside himself he knew his tormentors had ripped out something precious that he could never fully regain.

Shea's hand crept up his arm. Her forehead rested against the middle of his broad back, a tender, loving gesture of solidarity. Jacques could not bear to withdraw completely from her mind, so it was easy for her to hear the echo of his thoughts when she wanted. She felt sorrow for him, sorrow for both of them. "Whatever was taken from you, Jacques, has only made you stronger. The one who healed you was a miracle-worker," she whispered softly, meaning it. "I've never seen anything to equal it. But it's really your own determination that kept you alive."

Jacques tried to hear that she was consoling him, but instead he heard the interest in her voice, the trace of envy that Gregori could heal so magically, so quickly. The Carpathian had accomplished, in one short session, what she could not. Before he could reply, tell her it was she who had saved his life, the wind was bringing rain and mist streaming through the open door.

The healer, Gregori, shimmered into view, followed quickly by Mikhail, then Raven. Jacques narrowed his gaze, glimpses of memories instantly triggered. Flying in the body of an owl, running in the forest in the body of a wolf, becoming the mist and fog. Behind him, Shea's breath caught in her throat, and she stared at their visitors, at Jacques, awed and intimidated by the display of shape-shifting, the example of power so casually wielded.

Gregori's pale silver eyes examined every inch of Jacques. "You look better. How are you feeling?"

Jacques nodded slowly. "Much better. Thank you."

"You need to feed. Your woman is still pale and worn. She should be resting. If you like, I could heal her bruises." Gregori made the offer in his casual, indifferent way. His voice was so compelling, so beautiful, it was nearly impossible to deny him anything. There was a purity in his voice, a whisper of black velvet. He never raised his tone or appeared anything but calm and unruffled.

Shea's heart gave a leap, then settled into a hard, rhythmic pounding. She found herself listening intently, wanting him to go on speaking, wanting to do whatever he asked. Mentally, she shook her head. Gregori's abilities intrigued her, but he was far too powerful. He had not used any kind of mental enhancement, no compulsion, no hypnotic suggestions. His voice was a weapon in itself. She sensed he was the most dangerous Carpathian in the room. She had not been in such close proximity with so many people in a very long time. She needed to be alone with Jacques, to give herself time to adjust.

"We thank you for the offer, healer, but Shea is unused to our ways." Jacques couldn't remember most of them himself. He was as uneasy in the presence of the Carpathians as Shea. His black eyes glittered like ice, caught and trapped the reflection of a lightning whip as it sizzled across the dark sky. "The other male is not with you."

"Byron," Mikhail supplied. "He has been a good friend to you for centuries. He is aware that you completed the ritual and this woman is your true lifemate. Search your mind, Jacques. Remember how difficult this time is on our unattached males."

Shea's face went crimson under the unearthly paleness. The reference to the ritual had to mean they were aware Jacques had made love to her. The lack of privacy disturbed her immensely. She went to move around Jacques, strongly objecting to the *this woman* label. She did have a name. She was a person. She had a feeling they all thought her the hysterical type. She certainly hadn't managed to show them her normal calm self.

Jacques stepped backward and his arm swept behind him to pin her against the wall. He never took his ev   from the trio before them. He knew he was unstable, still fighting to hold on to reason when his every instinct was to attack. He trusted none of them and would not allow Shea to be put in any danger.

Shea retaliated with a hard pinch. She was not going to cower behind her wild man like some seventeenth-century heroine fainting with the vapors. So she was surrounded by a few vampires. Big deal.

Carpathians. Jacques sounded amused.

If you laugh at me, Jacques, I might find another wooden stake and come after you myself, she warned him silently. "Well, for heaven's sake." Shea sounded exasperated as she addressed the group. "We're all civilized, aren't we?" She shoved at Jacques' broad back. "Aren't we?"

"Absolutely." Raven stepped forward, ignoring Mikhail's restraining hand. "At least the women are. The men around here haven't quite graduated from the swinging-through-trees stage yet."

"I owe you an apology for last night, Miss O'Halloran," Mikhail said with far too much Old World charm. "When I saw you crouched over my brother, I thought . . ."

Raven snorted. "He didn't think, he reacted. He really is a great man, but overprotective with ⸺ people he loves." There was a wealth of love in her teasing tone. "Honestly, Jacques, you can't keep her prisoner, locked up like some nun in a convent."

Shea was mortified. *Jacques, move! You're embarrassing me.*

With great reluctance Jacques stepped aside. Shea could feel the instant tension in the room, the red haze building in Jacques' mind. To reassure him, she took his hand, kept her mind firmly linked to his. The moment she was exposed to the others, she could feel their eyes examining every inch of her.

Raven glanced at Gregori, clearly worried.

Self-consciously, Shea shoved at her hair. She hadn't even looked at herself in the mirror. Jacques tightened his hold on her hand. *Do not! You are beautiful as you are. They have no right to judge you in any way.*

"Jacques," Gregori said softly, "your woman needs to feed, to heal. You must allow me to help her."

Shea's chin went up, eyes flashing green fire. "I am perfectly capable of making my own decisions. He doesn't *allow* me to do or not do anything. Thanks for the offer, but I'll heal with time."

"You'll get used to them," Raven said hastily. "They're really big on women's health. It would help you, Shea — may I call you Shea?" Raven smiled when Shea nodded. "We'd be happy to answer any of your questions. It would be nice to get to know you. After all, we are in-laws of sorts," she pointed out.

The rush of fear-based adrenaline in Shea's body at that simple observation of her commitment to Jacques triggered an aggressive reaction in Jacques. Lightning slashed across the sky, sizzled and danced, hit the ground in thunderous fury. The wind hurtled through the cabin, lashed at the windows and walls. A low, ominous growl rumbled in Jacques' throat. Shea felt the beast in him rising, felt him welcome it, reach for it with murderous intent. She whirled to face him, slammed her palms flat on his chest, and shoved him as hard as she could, walking him backward toward a far corner.

You will not do this, Jacques. I need you sane right now. I'm doing my best to hold it together, but if there's a fight, I'll go crazy, I swear it. Please help me now. Please. There were tears in her mind, a vulnerability Jacques had never seen in her.

Jacques' arms swept around her, cradling her close as he struggled to regain control. Her distress seemed to give him added strength. He lifted his head, black eyes moving warily over the two males. Mikhail and Gregori looked perfectly at ease, yet Jacques sensed their alertness. He forced himself to smile, then shrug casually. "I am afraid my mind has not healed as my body has. You will have to have patience with me. Please enter our home as our guests." The formal words came out of nowhere.

Mikhail swung the door closed. "Thank you, Jacques. We want only to help you and your lifemate." He deliberately seated himself, placing himself in a vulnerable position. Raven perched comfortably on the arm of his chair. Gregori moved across the room with a deceptively lazy stride. He walked with fluid grace, an animal sensuality, but Jacques was well aware that the healer was subtly placing his body between the couple and Jacques.

Gregori. The ancient one. The dark one. The words shimmered in his mind. Gregori was a very dangerous man. "I remember little of my past," he admitted softly. "Perhaps it would be better for all of us if Shea and I kept to ourselves. I am well aware I am unstable, and I would not want anyone to get hurt."

Shea turned in his arms to face the Carpathians. "We appreciate your help. It's just that this is all so new to both of us."

Gregori's silver eyes studied her pale face, seeming to look right through her into her soul. "You are a doctor?"

Shea shivered. The healer's voice was incredibly compelling. The man had far too much power. "Yes, I'm a surgeon."

A smile curved the healer's sensual mouth. He was charismatic, but Shea was well aware that his silver eyes had not warmed in the least. They were cool and watchful. "You are very good. Carpathians do not respond well to human healing. Jacques was healing despite the odds against it. We are all indebted to you."

"You were able to do in an hour what several days of my care could not accomplish." In spite of herself there was a note of admiration in her voice.

"How is it you found Jacques when we could not?" Again Gregori's voice was casual, but she sensed the question was a trap.

Her chin lifted, her green eyes defiant. "Seven years ago, while studying, I was overcome with pain. Pain there was no medical explanation for. The agony lasted for hours. From that night on, I had dreams of a man tortured, in pain, calling to me."

"Where were you?" Gregori questioned.

"In the United States." Shea swept her fingers through her hair, found her hand was trembling, and put it behind her back. Those glittering pale eyes were disconcerting. They seemed to see right into her soul, see every mistake she had ever made. "I know it sounds bizarre, but it's true. I had no idea there really was a man, that he was suffering." Guilt washed over her. "I should have found him sooner, but I didn't believe . . ." She trailed off, tears welling up.

Do not do this, my love, Jacques commanded, his arms tightening protectively. *They have no right to judge you. None of them came for me. You did, across an ocean. And I did not treat you gently.* He touched the warmth of his mouth to her bruised throat. "Yet you returned to me in spite of the way I attacked you." He said the last aloud deliberately, a warning to the Carpathians to back off from questioning her.

"You must have been terrified," Raven said softly.

Shea nodded and sent Jacques a small smile. "He was definitely something I had never encountered in my practice." She was striving for normalcy in a world that was turned upside down.

"You are young to be a doctor," Mikhail observed.

Shea made herself really look at him for the first time. Jacques and Mikhail shared the same powerful build, the thick mane of hair, the ice-black eyes. They both carried the hard edge of authority, self-confidence, and the trace of arrogance that came with it. Jacques' finely chiseled features were more worn from his ordeal. "You look young to be centuries old," she countered, remembering the feel of his fingers on her throat.

Mikhail acknowledged her with a slight grin and a nod.

Beside her, Jacques fought down the snarling beast the memory of Mikhail's attack triggered. Shea ignored him. "A woman named Noelle had a child, a son, with a man named Rand. Do you know where the boy is? He would be twenty-six now," she asked.

Mikhail's features stilled, became a mask. A slow hiss escaped, and Jacques instinctively edged around Shea so that she was behind him.

Be very careful, Mikhail, Gregori warned.

"Noelle was our sister," Mikhail stated softly, "murdered just weeks after the child was born."

Shea nodded. The information confirmed what Jacques had already told her. "And the child?"

I do not like this, Gregori. Why would she wish to know of Noelle's child? Humans murdered her. They have a network with far-reaching tentacles. Perhaps she is a part of it after all. Mikhail's voice shimmered in Gregori's mind.

Jacques would know. Gregori was certain.

Maybe not. His mind is shattered.

He would know. She could not hide it. You fear for your brother. You do not look at her with your eyes and mind open. There is much sorrow, tragedy in her eyes. She is tied to a man she does not know, a man who is extremely dangerous, one who has hurt her on more than one occasion. She is highly intelligent, Mikhail; she knows what she has become, and she is struggling to accept it. This woman is no assassin.

Mikhail inclined his head at his oldest friend's assessment. "Noelle's son was murdered seven years ago, probably by the same assassins who tortured my brother."

If it was possible for Shea to grow any paler, she did. Her body swayed slightly; and Jacques gathered her close. The boy had been his nephew, but Jacques had no memory of the child or the man, so the pain he felt was Shea's. Her half-brother, her only chance at a family.

I am your family, Jacques comforted her

309

gently, his chin rubbing lovingly over the top of her head.

He was the young man in the second photograph Wallace and Smith showed me. I know he was. Shea laid her head wearily against his chest. *I felt such wrenching pain when I saw the photograph.*

I am sorry, Shea. So much has happened. You need time to absorb all this.

Puzzled by her obvious distress, Mikhail glanced at Gregori, who shrugged his broad shoulders rather elegantly.

"What of Rand, his father?" Jacques voiced the question for Shea, although the name sent pain splintering through his head, evoked a black, empty hole where memory should have been.

"Rand went to ground for a quarter of a century. He rose last year, but he keeps to himself. He sleeps most of the time," Mikhail answered.

Shea's fingers curled in Jacques'. "He did not raise his own son?"

When Mikhail shook his head, Shea swallowed the hard knot of protest blocking her throat and glanced accusingly at Jacques. *Children and the women who live with them seem to be left alone rather easily by your race.*

We are not Rand and Maggie. Jacques stated it firmly.

Shea bit her lip as she studied Mikhail. "What does 'go to ground' mean?"

"Carpathians rejuvenate in the soil," Gregori explained, watching her closely. "The human sleep does not allow quick healing or real rest. We may go through human practices — showering, dressing, all the little habits to protect what we are, although there is no real need — but we sleep the sleep of Carpathians. The earth heals and protects us during our most vulnerable hours when the sun is high."

Shea was shaking her head in denial, a hand going to her throat in a curiously defenseless gesture. Her eyes met Jacques in helpless fear. *I cannot. You know I cannot.*

It is all right. Neither would I welcome another burial. And it was true. Jacques had begun to suffocate, to associate the deep earth with pain and torment. *I would not force such a decision on you.*

Raven settled against Mikhail's shoulder. "I sleep above ground in a very comfortable bed. Well, the bedroom is situated below ground, but it's a beautiful room. You'll have to come see it sometime. I don't like to sleep in the ground. I was human, Shea, like you. It feels too much like being buried alive."

"Rand is my father," Shea admitted suddenly.

There was a stark silence in the room. Even the wind stopped, as if nature itself was holding its breath. Mikhail moved then, seemed to flow from the chair, his power unmistakable. His black eyes covered every inch of her. *Gregori?*

If this is true, Mikhail, Rand has done what was thought impossible. Unless . . .

Mikhail caught the thought. Gregori suspected that Shea's mother was Rand's true lifemate. "What you are saying is of tremendous importance to our race, Shea. Your mother is human?"

"Was. My mother committed suicide eight years ago. She couldn't face life without Rand." Her chin lifted defiantly. "She was so obsessed with him, she didn't have anything left over for her child." She said it matter-of-factly, as if she hadn't suffered, hadn't been alone all her life.

"Did he convert her?" Mikhail asked, furious at the unknown woman for neglecting her child, a female child at that. At the very least the woman should have brought the baby to the Carpathians to raise. "Was she Carpathian?"

"No, she wasn't like you, not even like me. She was definitely human. She was beautiful, Irish, and completely withdrawn from the real world most of the time. I knew about Rand and Noelle through my mother's diary."

"Did your mother have any psychic talent?" Gregori asked thoughtfully.

Raven glanced up at Mikhail. She had psychic ability. Shea's answer was extremely important to the future of their race. She would provide the proof of what they had long suspected, long hoped.

Shea's teeth bit at her lip. "She knew things before they happened. She would know the phone was going to ring or that someone was about to stop by. You have to understand, though, she rarely spoke. She would forget about me for days, even weeks at a time, so I didn't know much about her. She didn't exactly share lots of information with me."

"But you are certain Rand is your father?" Mikhail persisted.

"When I was born, my blood caused quite a stir in the medical community. In my mother's diary she wrote that Rand was my father and that he had a strange blood disorder. She thought I had inherited it. She took me to Ireland, hid me, because the doctors and scientists frightened her with their persistent questions. She was certain Rand was dead."

Mikhail and Gregori exchanged a look.

Their race was dying out. The last female child to be born had been Noelle some five hundred years earlier. The men were choosing to end their existence or turning vampire without a lifemate. Mikhail and Gregori had long suspected that a handful of human women, those with true psychic talent, had the ability to become a lifemate as Raven had. There had never before been an instance of a child born half-human, half-Carpathian. The only explanation possible was that Shea's mother had been Rand's true lifemate. Everyone had known he did not have real feelings for Noelle. Yet Rand had not turned Shea's mother. No Carpathian woman would have allowed her child to grow up alone as Shea's mother had. Why hadn't Rand said anything? Their people would have cherished a child.

Rand did not mention suicide when he awakened, Gregori mused. *He stays to himself, but that is not unusual.*

"Is it possible for us to see this diary?" Mikhail asked Shea gently.

Shea shook her head sadly. "I was being hunted. I had to destroy it."

"Your life must have been difficult, with no one to guide you," Gregori said quietly. "You are not without your own unique capability. You are a true healer."

"I studied many years." She sent him a small smile. "I had plenty of time to apply myself."

"You were born a healer," he corrected. "It is a rare gift." Gregori's silver eyes dwelt on her slender figure. "Jacques." His voice dropped even lower so that the sound seemed to seep into one's bloodstream and warm it like a good brandy. "She is growing weaker. Her body trembles. I know that you do not fully understand her importance to our entire race, but I know your instincts are strong and intact. You are her lifemate, sworn to her protection and care."

Shea's hand gripped Jacques' tightly. "Don't listen to him. What we choose to do has nothing to do with any of them."

"Trust me, love, I would never allow him to harm you," Jacques said softly in reassurance. "He is only concerned that you are so weak."

"I am a healer, like you, Shea." Gregori seemed to glide forward. His body flowed without a hint of movement or threat. He was just suddenly closer. "I would never hurt a woman. I am Carpathian. A male seeks only to protect and care for our women." His hand reached out to her neck. The touch of his fingers was astonishing. Light. Heat. A tingling sensation. "You must feed, Shea." The voice was around her, in her, working at her will. "Jacques needs you strong to see him through what lies ahead. Our people need you. My blood is ancient and powerful. It will serve you, heal you, strengthen both of you."

"No! Jacques, no. Tell him no." For some reason she was alarmed at the idea.

"I will feed her," Jacques objected quietly, his voice all the more menacing because of its hush.

The pale eyes slid over him. "You need to conserve your strength to heal your own body. Mikhail will supply you with what you need. There was a time, not so long ago, when you gave freely to your brother."

Jacques carefully inspected Shea. Her skin was so pale, she looked translucent. The bruises on her throat, stark smudges; had not healed. She looked tired, her body far too slender. Gregori was right; she was trembling. Why had he not seen her weakness? He certainly had contributed to it. *His blood is very pure, Shea. It is what aided my healing so quickly. I am not happy with another male seeing to your needs, but he is our healer. I want you to do as he says.*

I won't, Jacques. Shea shook her head adamantly. *I want to go right now. You promised me we could go.*

This must be done, Shea. He is right. You grow weaker every day.

We don't need them to help us. She held out a hand to stop Gregori's advance. "I know you're trying to help us, but I'm not ready for this yet. I need to figure things out for myself and get used to what I have to do to survive. Surely that's not such an unreasonable thing." Deliberately her fingers tangled with Jacques', linking them together. She needed him on her side, to understand she needed time.

"To give you time to slowly die from lack of care? Your health has been neglected for some time. You are a doctor — you know that is so. You made up your mind your life span would be very short. That cannot be," Gregori said softly. His voice was mesmerizing, hypnotic. "Our women are our only hope. We cannot lose you."

Shea could feel Jacques' swift denial of the possibility of such a thing. Violence swirled close to the surface, but he managed to control it. His black eyes centered on her green ones. *I know what he says is true, Shea. I have felt your acceptance of your death on more than one occasion. You were willing to trade your life for mine.*

That's different, and you know it, she said desperately. His hands were on her, trapping her to him. *Don't do this, Jacques. Let me do this in my own time.*

Shea. He ached with wanting to do as she asked him. She could feel it in his mind, the need to give her whatever would make her happy, yet at the same time the idea that she could be slipping away from him terrified him. His every instinct insisted he do as the healer suggested and ensure that she was brought to full strength. He fought to stay in control, to not allow his animal instincts to make the decision. *Please, little red hair, just do this so we can both be strong. Once it is done, we will be able to be on our own together and make our own decisions.*

I'm not ready, Jacques. Try to understand. I need time to comprehend what's happening to me. I need to feel in control. I'm not going to die. I've accepted that whatever you are, whatever my father is, I have become wholly. I know that you somehow were able to bind us together. And I'm trying to deal with all that in my own time and way.

I am attempting to do what is right for you.

How can you know what's right for me? You decided for me. You took over my life without my knowledge or consent. You had no right to do that, Jacques.

No, I did not, he admitted. *I would like to think that if I was not what I have become, I would have courted you as I should, that I could have earned your love and loyalty. I would hope I was not the type of man to force my will on you.*

This is no different, Jacques. Can't you see that?

"She is so weak, Jacques, and so much has happened so quickly." Gregori's velvet voice was seductive. "She cannot make a rational decision. How will you aid her? If you try to supply her with blood, you will be unable to adequately protect her. She needs to be healed. You are her lifemate, Jacques. Reach inside yourself, deep within you. These things were imprinted on you before your birth. The male can do no other than to see to his lifemate's health."

Mikhail, Raven objected. *She's being pushed too far. Don't allow this.*

She is too important to all of us. We need her at full strength, so she can control Jacques while we wait for his mind to fully heal. None of us can do so. We do not wish to be forced to destroy him. In the end she would choose to follow him, and we would lose her also. You can see her first thought is for Jacques and not for herself. She would follow him for certain. We have to do this, Raven. I am sorry it distresses you.

Jacques bent his head to find Shea's temple with warmth and tenderness. His arms closed around her, pulled her resisting body in close to his hard frame. "Shea, I believe the healer is right in this."

I can't believe you would betray me like this. You're siding with them. Why, Jacques? You owe me more respect than this.

Because without you, I am far too dangerous to the world. Because what I feel for you goes far beyond the human emotion of love. Jacques tipped her chin up and forced her green eyes to meet his black ones. At once she could feel his will bending hers to do his bidding. She was falling forward into the depths of his eyes. His voice was murmuring in her head, a low command she tried hard to resist. *You will accept what the healer offers.*

Gregori was already moving forward, his soft voice adding to the power of Jacques'. He bit carefully into his wrist and held it to Shea's mouth. The scent was overpowering, triggering the terrible hunger and need in her. Jacques' palm was pressing the back of her head, forcing her toward the liquid of life, the healing ancient blood that would pour power and strength into her body.

"She is strong-willed, Jacques," Gregori counseled softly. Shea was fighting the compulsion to feed. The rich blood, so potent, flowing into her starving body, did not weaken her resistance, it merely made her stronger. Gregori could see that Jacques was wavering as he watched Shea fight the compulsion. Jacques' mind might be fragmented, he might even be mad at times, but his feelings for Shea were strong and healthy. The healer purposely dropped his voice another octave, using the purity of his tone to persuade Jacques. "Our women are few, the only hope for our people. The one sure way to wipe out our people is to murder our women. They must be guarded at all times. The assassins have returned to our land. The very soil groans under their boots."

"Shea has seen them." Jacques watched warily as Mikhail approached, still not trusting himself with the man who had come so close to strangling Shea. "They have nearly caught her twice."

"Feed, Jacques. I offer my life freely to you as you have so many times done for me." Mikhail slashed his wrist and held it out to his brother.

The moment the richness spilled into his mouth, the taste and surge of power brought a rush of fragments of memories. Mikhail laughing, pushing Jacques from a tree branch playfully. Mikhail's body crouched low, protectively, in front of his as a vampire with brown-stained teeth began to grow long, dagger-like nails. Mikhail holding Raven's limp body, a river of blood, the earth and sky erupting all around them while Mikhail looked up at Jacques with the hopeless resolve to join his lifemate in her fate.

Jacques' eyes jumped to Mikhail's face, examined every inch of it. This man was a leader, a dangerous, powerful predator who had skillfully steered their dying race through centuries of pitfalls. One whom such as Gregori chose to follow. Something stirred inside Jacques, the need to protect this man, to shield him. *Mikhail.*

Mikhail's head jerked up. He heard his name echo clearly in his head. The path had been there for one heartbeat, familiar and strong; then just as quickly it was lost.

Jacques was so distracted by the pieces of memories floating in his mind, his hold on Shea slipped. Shea felt his inattention and gathered herself, waiting, waiting. The moment the compulsion lifted, she wrenched her head from Gregori's wrist and leapt away. Jerking the heavy door open, Shea fled into the fury of the storm.

The air in the cabin stilled, thickened with a kind of malevolent darkness. Jacques' features were a granite mask, his black eyes flat and hard. He took one last swallow of the powerful liquid, carefully closed the wound, and lifted his head. "I thank you for your assistance, but I must ask you to leave. Perhaps tomorrow night you will try your hand at mending my mind, healer." His gaze was on the night, a dark purpose creeping into his tone.

"Jacques . . ." Raven ventured hesitantly. This stranger was more beast than man, not the gentle brother-in-law she had known. At one time, Jacques had been filled with lazy amusement, with laughter and boyish pranks. Now he was a being without mercy, dangerous, insane perhaps.

Mikhail silently pulled her from the cabin, his body already beginning to lose form. *They have to work it out themselves, my love.*

He seems so dangerous.

He cannot harm his lifemate. Mikhail tried valiantly to believe it. There was a darkness in Jacques, a truly frightening void none of them could breach.

Gregori hesitated in the doorway. "Take precautions when you sleep, Jacques. We are hunted." He, too, shimmered, dissolved, and streamed into the night.

Gregori, will he harm her? In spite of his reassurance to Raven, Mikhail felt he couldn't take any chances with Shea's health. If anyone could assess the damage to Jacques' mind, it was the healer.

He thinks to punish her impetuous behavior, Gregori replied softly, *but I can feel his mind turning to hers, taking in her overwhelming emotions. He tries to be angry with her, but it will not stay in his mind.*

The blood from the ancients had given Jacques his full strength. He felt his immense power, savored it once again. On bare feet he padded across the room to the door and inhaled deeply. Despite the storm, he knew exactly where Shea was. He was in her mind at all times, never separated. He could feel her wild emotions, her panic and desperation, her need to escape the mountains, the Carpathians. To escape him.

You will return to me, Shea. It was a clear order, and he hoped she would obey him, hoped he would not have to force her.

Shea leapt over a rotting log and stopped abruptly under the canopy of a huge tree. The command was stark, impressive in its absence of emotion. She recognized anger in herself. It was new to her. Brand new. She couldn't remember being angry before. Shea was usually careful not to feel anything at all. She preferred to analyze things.

Please try to understand, Jacques. I won't be a part of this.

I will not argue long distance with you. Come to me now.

For strength Shea clutched at an overhead tree branch. Jacques' lack of inflection frightened her more than his anger could have. She sensed a power in him, a total confidence. *I won't come back. I can't. Just live your life, Jacques. You have it back now.* If Jacques had really felt no emotion in centuries, then he would be struggling just as she was to stay in control. Everything seemed so intense. She wanted the calm, tranquil world she understood, where her brain ruled and emotions could be pushed aside.

You cannot possibly win this battle, Shea. It was a warning, nothing less. The tone was devoid of any feeling whatsoever.

Why does it have to be a battle? You need to accept my decision. I have the right to leave.

Come to me, Shea. There was iron strength in his command. This time he exerted a subtle but frightening pressure.

Shea pressed both hands to her head. *Stop it! You can't force me.*

Of course I can. Even as the words echoed in his mind, he realized they were true. He could do almost anything. He stepped off the porch into the driving rain and stretched his muscles lazily, reveling in their response. He was truly alive again. He could easily bring her to him, bend her will to his. She needed to learn that Carpathian women were under their lifemate's protection at all times. She never took precautions, never scanned her surroundings; she never took care for her own protection.

Was that the kind of man he had become? Had he always been so? Someone willing to force his will on the one person who cared for him, risked her life for him? Was it so much to ask that he give her time to adjust? Jacques rubbed the bridge of his nose thoughtfully.

She was so fragile, so vulnerable. Shea could brave the wildest river or highest mountain. She had the strength to handle any crisis, but not her own emotions. His competent little redhead was terrified of her feelings for him. Her childhood had been a nightmare. He could not allow her life with him to become the same thing.

Jacques actually felt the curious melting in the region of his heart, the surge of heat that rushed through his bloodstream. *Little one, why do you persist in fighting me?* His voice, whispering so softly in her mind, was filled with tenderness. *Do you know what will happen to you without me?*

Her entire being responded to the velvet caress of his voice, the rising tide of love. If he had continued to argue and chastise, she would have had a chance, but the moment he spoke in that tender, caressing way, she was lost. At once she felt overwhelming despair. She could never be free of him, never.

Is that such a terrible fate, love? His voice turned her heart over. *To be with me?* This time there was a single thread of hurt. *Am I truly such a monster then?*

I don't know how to be with you. I feel trapped, like I can't move or think. Shea pressed her fingers to her temple, her back to the tree. *I don't want to need you. I don't want to be with any of them.*

He was moving steadily toward her, not fast, not slow. The rain drove down on his broad shoulders, glistened off his back. The coolness only added to the gathering heat in his body. She seemed small and defenseless. With each step into the night, with the soil beneath his feet, and the ancient's blood flowing in his veins, his strength grew.

I need you just to breathe, Shea, he admitted starkly. *I am sorry that terrifies you. I wish that I had more control, but I cannot be alone like that, not ever again. I try to keep my presence in you but a shadow. Perhaps with time I can let go a bit. Being with me terrifies you, but being without you terrifies me.* A note of amusement crept in. *We are so compatible.*

Shea knew he was coming toward her; she could tell by the way her heart pounded in anticipation, the way her body came alive. She buried her face in the crook of her arm, hanging on grimly to the branch above her. *You don't know me, Jacques.*

I am in you. I know you. You are afraid of me, of what I can do. You are afraid of my instability, my power. You fear what I am and what you have become. Yet you are strong and determined that no harm shall come to me. You know your brain is excited at the possibilities of the existence of our race. His laughter was soft and inviting. *I am your lifemate, bound to treasure you, cherish and protect you. Always see to your happiness. And you have the same abilities as I.*

Your first thought was to force me back to you, she accused him.

Shea, my love, you never think to scan, never check for danger. And you cannot exist without me. It is my duty and my right to protect you.

What happens to me if you die? What happens to you if I die? She knew the answer; she had watched her mother's empty life. *This is obsession.* She said the words aloud so that the wind could carry them through the mountains. "I won't be like her." She lifted her face to the driving rain so that the drops ran down her face like tears. It was too late.

She couldn't survive without Jacques. Wasn't she just like her mother after all?

He came out of the night so beautifully male that he took her breath away. His black eyes moved over her possessively, curiously predatory.

Shea shook her head. "I'm not strong enough, Jacques." The wind whipped at her, nearly drove her sideways.

"Choose life for us, Shea, for our children. I will not be easy to live with, but I swear to you, no one could love you more. I will do anything to make you happy."

"Don't you see? You can't make another person happy. I'm the only one who can do that for myself. And I can't do this."

"You are just afraid. We both have some problems, Shea. You fear the intimacy and I lack of it. It is simply a matter of meeting somewhere in the middle."

His voice was so soft, she felt it on her very skin, as if his fingertips were skimming over satin in the lightest caress. Jacques stepped closer, beneath the tree's canopy, his dark eyes intense. "Choose me now, Shea. Need me. Want me. Love me. Choose life for us."

"It shouldn't be like this."

"We are not human. We are Carpathian, of the earth. We command the wind and the rain. The animals are our brethren. We can run with the wolf, soar with the owl, and become one with the rain itself. We are not human, Shea. We do not feed on flesh as humans do, and we do not love as humans do. We are different."

"We are hunted all the time."

"And we hunt. It is the cycle of life. Shea, look at me."

Chapter Ten

Shea lifted her emerald gaze to the disturbing intensity of Jacques' black eyes. He was so close that she could feel the heat of his skin reaching out to her. His fingertips brushed the curve of her cheek, her mouth. His need of her was as elemental as the storm itself. It burned in him like the hot sizzle of electricity, like the slowly spreading heat of molten lava. "Need me, Shea." His voice ached with it. "Need me the same way I need you. I would give my life for you. Live for me. Find a way to live for me. Love me that much."

Her eyelashes swept down, raindrops glistening on the ends of the feathery crescents. "You don't know what you're asking of me."

His hands framed her face, thumbs brushing her frantic pulse. Each light caress sent flames dancing through her body. Her gaze once more reluctantly found his, her eyes filled with a kind of hopelessness. "Of course I know what the cost is to you, little one. I feel your reluctance, your revulsion of our feeding habits." His hand slid to the nape of her neck, drew her close.

"I've tried to make the adjustment," she protested. "I need more time."

"I know that, Shea. I should have found another way to help you heal. I am trying to find out what kind of lifemate you have. I want to be what you need, someone you can respect and love, not someone who imposes his will and takes the expedient way out. There are ways, little love, to feed you without revulsion." His mouth found her pulse, felt it jump under the velvet rasp of his tongue.

His lips moved to her chin, the corner of her lips. His voice was husky, aching. "Want me enough, Shea. Want me with more than just your body. Let me into your heart." His mouth fastened on hers, not gently but wildly, hungrily. The hunger was in his eyes when he raised his head to look down at her. "Open your mind to me. Want me there, as you want me in your body. Want me coming to you wild with a need only you can satisfy. Take me into your soul and let me live there." His mouth was roaming every inch of her face, the column of her neck, the hollow of her shoulder.

His body burned and ached and needed. His heart tuned itself to the rhythm of hers. His mind was a haze of desire, erotic pictures, and sensual needs. It was filled with tenderness and love, an intensity that scorched her as much as the hunger in him.

The heat of his mouth found her breast through the thin cotton of her shirt, claimed her. His body reacted savagely, painfully, his jeans tight and uncomfortable.

Jacques dragged her closer, the storm in him, around him, a part of him. "Make me whole, Shea. Do not leave me like this. Want me back. Need my body in yours. Have to touch me as I have to touch you."

Shea could feel it in him, the raging, wild desire, the dark, sensual hunger. His eyes held so much need, there was no way she could possibly refuse him. Her hands were already sliding over his defined, sculpted muscles, the wildness in her erupting every bit as stormily as the weather around them.

Her mouth fed on his; her hands pushed at his clothes, at hers, to rid them of the unnatural encumbrances. She couldn't get close enough to him; skin to skin was not going to do it. Jacques drew her shirt over her head, tossed it aside, nearly bent her backward to feed hungrily at her breasts. His hands slid up and down her sides, her narrow ribcage, the tiny waist.

"Let me into your heart, Shea," Jacques murmured along the creamy swell of her breast, against the frantic rhythm beating in tune to his. "Right here, little one, let me in." His teeth scraped her satin skin, his tongue caressed and stroked.

He dragged the jeans from her waist, pushed them down the curve of her slender hips. Dropping to his knees, he circled her hips with his arms, nuzzled the silk panties, burrowed deep. Shea cried out his name, and the wind whirled the sound and roared it back to her, surrounded her with him, with his scent and the strength of his desire.

"Want me, Shea. Like this. Like it is meant to be. Just like this. I have to have you. Out here in the middle of this storm. I have to have you right now." He ripped the silk panties aside, clutched her to him, feeding on flowing, honeyed heat. Her body rippled with pleasure, and she writhed against his attacking mouth, but he didn't stop, instead sending her over and over the edge.

Shea could only grab hold of his thick charcoal hair with her fist and hold on as the world rocked under her feet and the rain crashed to earth. Jacques somehow managed to do away with her shoes and drag the jeans from her body. She stood naked in the driving rain, so hot she was afraid the water would sizzle when it hit her skin.

"Do you want me, Shea?" This time his voice was hesitant, as if for all his strength, for all his power, one word from her would bring him crashing down. He was kneeling at her feet, his beloved face — so ravaged by torment, so beautifully male, so sensually Carpathian — staring up at her. He was lost without her; it was there for her to see. Raw. Stark. His total vulnerability. For just one moment the wind seemed to cease, and the storm held itself still as if the very skies were awaiting her answer.

"You can't possibly know how much I want you, Jacques, even if you're reading my mind." She pulled him to his feet, leaned forward to brush his lips with hers. "I want you in my heart. I always have." Her breath was warm on his chest. Her tongue tasted his skin, felt the answering jump of his heart. Her hands went to the buttons of his jeans, then slowly freed him from their tight confines.

A whip of lightning cracked across the sky, and for one moment his profile was lit up. His dark body, the taut muscles and his terrible need of her, was revealed starkly in the night. His eyes never left her, black and intense and so hungry. Shea's arms circled him lightly, and she touched her mouth to his flat, hard stomach. Jacques jumped as if she had burned him. Her palms followed the carved contours of his buttocks, lingered for a moment as if memorizing him.

Then she was on her knees, her hand cupping him, stroking and caressing the velvet shaft. Her every movement sent a shudder of pleasure dancing through his body, a rush of flames leaping to engulf him.

Jacques caught a fistful of her red hair, soaked and darkened by the driving rain. He urged her forward, thrusting his hips aggressively, consumed with need for her touch. She was laughing softly, tauntingly, as the heated, moist interior of her mouth slid over him. He groaned and held her to him, lifted his face to the wild storm.

"You have to mean it, Shea. You cannot do this and not mean it." The words were torn from him, raw and hurting, as if from his soul.

She tightened her hold on him, followed his unintentional thrusting, deliberately enticed him further. He dragged her up, buried his face in her neck, breathing deeply to maintain a semblance of control. Hands spanning her waist, he lifted her.

"Put your legs around my waist, love." He was biting her throat gently, his teeth urgent, his tongue easing every ache.

She wrapped her arms around his neck, settled herself over him, felt the hard thickness of him pushing aggressively for entrance. He felt far too big, so hot she was afraid both of them would go up in flames. Before she could ease herself over him, he thrust upward, spearing her, filling her so completely that she cried his name. The sound was lost in the violence of the storm raging around them.

The rain ran down her face, off her pale shoulders, down her full, gleaming breasts to form beads at the peaks of her rose-colored nipples. Jacques caught the water in his mouth, his body thrusting hard into hers. Flames burned them, consumed them, leapt between them. She was fiery heat gripping him, holding him to her, drawing him deeper and deeper into the magic of her spell.

Jacques' mouth found hers again, a little brutally, feeding voraciously, dominantly, laying claim to her, branding her for all time. "Open your mind to mine." The whisper was once again against her throat.

She felt his mouth at the hollow of her shoulder, his teeth, the heat and beckoning hunger. "Give me your mind, Shea. Let me in and keep me there." The whisper was a sorcerer's web. He was weaving a spell so strong, she had no thought to deny him anything.

He surged into her body, pushed through the barrier into her mind, and claimed her heart. At once everything was different. He felt her pleasure, so intense she was nearly on fire with it. She felt his pleasure, reaching for the very stars, his body gathering strength, his wanting her fulfillment above his own. He wanted the world for her, ached to have her love him as he was, damaged and broken and nearly a madman. She could see into his soul, the barely leashed beast always striving for dominance, never quite conquered. She could see his fear of losing her, of being forever vampire, loathed and hunted by his own kind. And she could see his terrible need to protect her, keep her safe, and his need to please her. He wanted to earn her respect and love, be worthy of it. He made no effort to hide the demon in him, dark and ugly, so hungry for revenge, so in need of a keeper.

Shea allowed her childhood, stark and lonely, to flow into his mind, her fears of sharing her life, her need for control and discipline, her total desire for him and her secret dreams of children and a family.

Jacques' arms tightened, and he laughed softly, triumphantly. She had faced the worst in him, and her body was meeting his every thrust with a tight, fiery friction. Her mind was consumed with hunger and need for him and a fragile commitment she was determined to see through. He took her mouth as he took her body, wild and crazy and completely uninhibited. Thunder rolled and boomed, and she keened softly, clutching at him as her body clenched around his and exploded into the stars. His hoarse cry was lost in the fury of the storm as his entire body seemed to disintegrate, to soar and erupt with all the explosive power of a volcano.

Exhausted and sated, Shea lay her head on his shoulder as he leaned against the barreled trunk of the closest tree. The rains cooled the heat of their bodies, finally penetrated the wild desire and hot hunger that had shielded them from its onslaught.

Very gently Jacques lowered her feet to the ground, retaining possession of her waist to help her trembling legs hold her up. Shea raised a hand to push back her rain-slick hair. He caught her fingers and raised her palm to his mouth. "You are the most beautiful sight I have ever seen."

She smiled, shook her head at him. "You're crazy, you know that? This is one of the most magnificent lightning storms I've ever seen, and I didn't even notice until now."

He grinned at her suggestively, rubbed the bridge of his nose. "Says something."

"Exactly," she agreed. "You're crazy, and I must be, too."

His hands cupped her bottom, drew her close against his hard frame, his face buried in the hollow of her shoulder as he savored the moment. He would never forget how he felt, how she looked, so wild and beautiful in the storm, and her complete acceptance of him with his shattered mind and leashed demons. "This will never go away, Shea, what we feel for one another. It never goes away. It gets stronger with each century. You never have to worry about losing this intensity."

He felt her smile against his bare skin, the small kiss she pressed into his chest. "I might not survive. I'm not sure I can stand up on my own."

"I can help you with that." There was a teasing, insinuating note in his voice, and she felt him press her closer, felt him thicken and harden against her stomach.

"You really are crazy. I hate to be a wet blanket, but it's raining all over us." She was laughing as she protested, her body moving subtly against his, unable to believe they could possibly do more than cling to one another after such a wild encounter.

He turned her so that she was against the tree, his large frame shielding her from the driving rain. Jacques' palms cupped her face, and he bent his head to hers, his mouth tender, loving, as he kissed her slightly swollen mouth. "I will never get enough of you, not if we live centuries." His palms moved over her breasts possessively, down her flat stomach to rest there, fingers splayed wide. "I cannot wait to feel our child growing within you." His eyes darkened to black ice. "I never thought I could share you with anyone, but the thought of our child makes me want you even more."

"Slow down, wild man, I think we need to get to know one another better first. We're a couple of emotional cripples, and that doesn't make for great parenting."

He laughed softly against her mouth before he kissed her again. "I know what is in your mind and heart, little one. It is not so scary for me anymore. Once you make up your mind, you stick to it like glue. It is what makes you such a good researcher."

"Don't think you're going to get around me with sex. Just as you were in my mind, I was in yours. Don't think I didn't notice your tendency to want to dominate."

His hands were delving into shadows and hollows, finding all kinds of secret, sensitive places. His mouth slid down her throat, a burning trail as he lapped up the water until he came to her breasts. "You do not think sex is a good idea in these situations?" His tongue swirled over her nipple; his teeth scraped lovingly along the contour of the creamy swell, followed it into the valley over her heart. "But you taste so good." His hand cupped springy curls, pushed against moist heat before his fingers tested the fire in her waiting sheath. "And you feel so good."

"You are so crazy." She couldn't help but laugh, pushing against his hand, using her own to stroke and caress and arouse him further. "I swear, Jacques, neither of us is going to be able to stand." She should have felt the cold, but the rain only added to the erotic moment, feeding the intensity of the flames growing between them.

Laughing, happy, Jacques backed her toward a fallen log, turning her around so that she faced away from him. Placing her hands on the moss-covered log for stability, he bent her forward so that he could place a kiss at the base of her spine. The light brush sent a shiver of excitement spiraling through her, a shudder of pleasure as his fingers assured him she was ready for him.

Catching her slender hips in his large hands, Jacques paused for a moment, marveling at the perfection of a woman's body,

Shea's body. Her bottom was round and firm, well-muscled and inviting. "You are so beautiful, Shea, unbelievably beautiful." He pushed against her, prolonging the moment of entrance, watching the rain slide down her pale satin skin to meet the hard length of him.

"Jacques!" Shea pushed back against him excitedly, her body soft and yielding, wet and welcoming.

He drove into the tight, hot, velvet sheath so perfectly fitted to his body. The feel of her was ecstasy all over again, an experience he would never get enough of. Jacques thrust forward, hard and deep, wanting to fill her completely, needing to hear her soft, keening cries. It drove him wild, those little sounds coming from her throat, the way her body pushed back to meet his. The rain seemed a part of it all, surrounding them like a veil, sliding over their hot bodies, sensitizing their skin. He felt her around him, a part of him, one body, truly together, with the earth moving around them and the heavens ripped apart by their passion. He could feel every muscle in his body taut and ready, waiting, waiting, the perfect moment with her body clenching around his, taking his seed from him as he surged into her again and again, a torrent of color and beauty and miraculous pleasure. He felt her open to him, her mind and heart and soul, softly feminine, exquisitely woman, all his. Her pleasure matched his own beat for beat, shudder for shudder. He had to hold her to keep himself on his feet, and they collapsed together into the soaked vegetation.

Holding each other, the rain cooling their bodies, they laughed like children. "I expected steam this time," Jacques said, crushing her to him.

"Can you do that?" Shea fit the back of her head into the niche of his sternum. One hand idly slid over the heavy muscles of his chest.

"Make us so hot we turn the rain to steam?" He grinned boyishly down at her, for the first time so carefree that he forgot for a moment the torment he had suffered. She made him invincible. She made him vulnerable. Most of all, she made him alive.

"No, really — what they did, those others. They were like fog or mist. Can you really do that?" Shea persisted. "I mean, you said you could, but I thought maybe you were delusional."

His eyebrows shot up. "Delusional?" Jacques flashed a cocky grin, held out his arm, and watched as fur rippled along the length of it, as the fingers curved and extended into claws. He had to make a grab for Shea as she scrambled away from him, her eyes enormous. Jacques was careful not to hurt her with his strength.

"Stop laughing at me, you brute. That's not exactly normal." A slow smile was beginning to curve her soft mouth. She couldn't help but be happy for the innocent joy he found in each piece of information that came to him, each new memory of his gifts.

"It is normal for us, love. We can shape-shift whenever we like."

She made a face. "You mean all those hideous stories are true? Rats and bats and slimy worm things?"

"Now, why would I want to be a slimy worm thing?" He was openly laughing. The sound startled him; he couldn't remember laughing aloud.

"Very funny, Jacques. I'm so glad you find this amusing. Those people actually formed themselves out of fog, like something in a movie." She gave a punch to his arm for emphasis. "Explain it."

"Shape-shifting is easy once you are strong. When I said we run with the wolf, I meant it literally. We run with the pack. We can fly with the owl and become the air." He pushed back the wet hair framing her face.

"Why is it you are not cold?"

Shea sat up, astonished at the notion. She wasn't cold, not really. She became cold when she thought about it, but she hadn't been. "Why wasn't I?"

"Carpathians regulate their body temperature naturally. Illusion is also an easy thing to master. Clothes do not have to be bought unless we wish it. Most of the time we are very careful to follow human ways." He kissed the top of her head. "You can pretend to be cold if that will make you feel better."

"I don't like the idea of staying here, Jacques, staying so close to the others. I feel like I can't breathe. But maybe it's only because I don't exactly see people turning into fog every day. Maybe we should stay a little longer and learn a few things from them."

"I can teach you how to shape-shift." He sounded annoyed.

Shea nipped his throat. "I definitely do not want to learn how to shape-shift. I'm still on square one, learning to share my life and my body with another person. But if I ever do want to be a rat or something like that, I promise only you will teach me. I'm talking about other things, like how the healer made you well so quickly."

Jacques swallowed his protest quickly.

She actually sounded excited, not scared. He didn't like the idea of another man near her, another man spending time with her. But she was a healer, and Gregori could teach her much. He wanted her to be happy.

He reached for his memories. *Gregori. The dark one.* Ancient and powerful. Solitary. "He is always alone." Carpathians whispered of his power, rarely used his name or spoke it aloud. "The healer always roams the earth seeking knowledge. He does not stay among our kind. There is none more dangerous, yet none more dedicated to preserving our race. Mikhail is his friend. They understand and respect one another."

Shea burrowed closer to Jacques' body, a protection from the storm. "I can't believe you're remembering all of this. It's amazing, Jacques. Does your head ache?"

He rubbed his forehead even as he shook his head to deny it. The truth was, the pain was splintering and cracking the inside of his mind. For her, he could endure anything. "His one apprentice was only half a century younger than Gregori and Mikhail. He was different even in appearance. A loner like Gregori. He, too, searched for knowledge. He spoke most languages like a native and served as a soldier in many different armies. He was tall and broad-shouldered, with the same heavy muscles Gregori has. His hair was long and blond, very rare among our people. His eyes were gold, pure gold. Gregori allowed him to learn the art of healing from him. They were seen together on and off over a number of years all over the world."

"Who is he? Is he still alive?" Shea was intrigued.

"He is named Aidan, and he has a twin. He often hunted with us." His head was throbbing and threatening to explode if he continued.

"Hunted what?" Shea held her breath, afraid of what he might say.

"Beautiful women, little one, and I was the one who found you after all." His white teeth gleamed at her, a definite leer.

"Don't put me off like that." She had already taken advantage, sliding easily into his mind and picking out the pictures of danger and revulsion. Fear even. Not so much of their adversary, but of themselves turning into the very thing they sought to destroy.

Jacques, unprepared for her entrance into his mind, had been confident he could keep the grimmer side of their existence watered down for her. Shea had always been reluctant to enter his mind; it hadn't occurred to him that she would do so whenever she wanted.

His expression was so rueful that Shea burst out laughing. "Where I grew up, that's called being caught with your pants down."

He looked down at his body, glistening with the rain. His grin was self-mocking, his black eyes amused. "Literally."

"So where is Aidan now? Was he killed?"

Jacques' mind refused to relinquish the information at first. He had to go over and over the pieces to the puzzle, looking for an answer. Because it was hurting him, Shea rubbed lovingly at his arm. "Don't try anymore."

"The United States. The last I remember, he and his people went to the States to control the vampire problems there. Vampires no longer stay here in the mountains where they are easily hunted. If Aidan is still alive, or if he has not turned" — he frowned over the possibility — "then he must still remain there, far from our land."

"What do you mean by his people? A lifemate? A child?"

"He had no lifemate the last that I knew of him. As he is almost as old as Gregori and Mikhail, the danger to him has increased. The older the Carpathian male, the more difficult he finds it to maintain civility."

"Then Gregori is a risk also." Shea found

herself shivering at the idea.

"Gregori is the biggest danger of all, and Aidan is not far behind him. Yet Aidan has a family of sorts. Humans, generations that have served him faithfully. He has given them a fortune, yet they choose to stay with him. Mother to daughter. Father to son. He is the only Carpathian I know of that has such a family."

Lightning flashed, and on its heels thunder crashed almost overhead. Shea stiffened, the smile fading from her lips and eyes. Her open palm went to Jacques' chest, held him away from her. All at once the welcoming forest and wild storm were no longer a sensual playground but a dark and sinister world. Shea scrambled to her feet, swiveling around, inspecting the darkened woods. Jacques rose with fluid grace, circled her waist with his arm protectively.

"What is it?" Instantly he was scanning the area around them, seeking outside himself to reveal his enemies. He stepped in front of Shea to block any threat to her. He found nothing that alarmed him, but Shea's mind held real fear.

Shea stepped away from him, eyes anxiously sweeping the forest around them. She caught up her shirt, held it protectively against her body.

"The others are far away," Jacques said, but he moved again to place himself squarely in front of her in an effort to protect her from the unseen enemy.

"There is something out there, Jacques, something evil watching us." She dragged her shirt over her head quickly. "I know. I always know. Let's get out of here."

Jacques waited for her to pull on her jeans before stepping into his own. His every sense was flaring out to the night, searching for anything to prove her right. He could detect nothing, yet her uneasiness was beginning to seep into his bloodstream. He could feel himself bristle like a wolf ready for attack. "Describe what you feel to me. Let me into your mind fully." It was an imperious order.

Shea obeyed without thought. Dark, malevolent, something not human, not Carpathian, crouched in the storm, watching with red, feral eyes, watching and hating. She had the impression of sharp, dripping fangs and unsheathed claws. Not animal.

Vampire, Shea. He is out there now. The words were a soft whisper in her mind. Jacques "saw" through her mind, caught the impressions that identified the killer stalking them. *You must obey me at once, ev-*

351

erything I say. Do you understand?

Yes, of course. Where is he?

I do not know. I can neither smell him nor hear him. But what is in your mind is vampire. As you have never seen one before and the impressions are so strong in your mind, I can do no other than believe this is real. Stay close to me. If he attacks, run.

I would never leave you. Her chin went up, and she looked mutinous. *I'm perfectly capable of helping you.*

He would use you to defeat me. I have fought them before. His body was crowding hers, urging her back down the trail toward their cabin. He was not looking so much with his eyes as with his entire being.

Shea moved quickly, tried to concentrate on the strong feeling inside her.

Whatever was tracking them so silently through the dense forest was exuding a black hatred that made her feel weak. Her heart was pounding in alarm. The thing was sinister, so evil and perverted she could feel the heaviness in the clean, rain-soaked air.

To their right, a strange fog glowed eerily, streamed through the rain and wound through the trees. It moved forward at knee level coming straight toward them now.

Shea felt her heart in her throat. She touched Jacques' back for reassurance. He stopped, seemingly relaxed, his muscles coiled and ready, like a panther awaiting its moment. She could feel it in him, his readiness, so still and confident.

As the fog grew closer, only several yards away now, the moisture began to stack itself higher and higher, the droplets connecting and forming the shape of a man. Shea wanted to scream with fear, but she stayed very still, afraid of distracting Jacques.

Byron's form shimmered for a moment. She could actually see the tree behind the mist, and then he was solid, standing with the curious elegance of the Carpathian male. He lifted his eyes from the ground to meet Jacques' icy-black gaze. "We have been friends for centuries, Jacques. I cannot remember a time in my life that we did not run together. It is strange and sad to me that you can look at me and not know me."

Shea, behind Jacques, stirred uncomfortably. Byron's sorrow appeared more than he could bear. She wanted to reach out to him, make an attempt to ease his obvious suffering. *Do not!* The command was sharp in her mind, clear and in a tone that brooked no argument. Jacques remained motionless, as if carved from stone. Byron's words did not appear to move him in any way.

Byron shrugged, his face twisted with

pain. "When we thought you were dead, we searched for your body. Months, years even. You were never out of our thoughts. You were my family, Jacques, my friend. It was hard to learn to be completely solitary. Gregori and Mikhail and even Aidan survived the centuries because, as alone as they had to be, they had a bond, an anchor to keep them strong through the bleak centuries. You were mine. Once you were gone, my struggle became immense."

When Jacques remained silently on guard, Shea pushed at his back. *Can't you hear his grief? He's reaching out to you. Even if you can't remember him, help him.*

You do not know if he has turned or not, Jacques reprimanded her. *You felt the presence, and here he is. A vampire can give the illusion of purity, of anything he chooses. Stay behind me!*

"I just wanted to tell you I am glad you are back, and I am happy for you that you found your lifemate. It was wrong of me to be envious. I should have been more cautious about judging what I did not understand." Byron raked a hand through his dark hair. "I am going away for a while. I must to gain the strength to get through the years."

Jacques nodded slowly. "I am going to the healer to try to repair the damage done to my mind. I have noticed Gregori's relationship with Mikhail seems to be strong even though Mikhail has a lifemate. I would wish that if all that you say is true, when I am healed, we can resume our friendship."

The wild winds were dying down. The rain beat down in a steady drone, and the air seemed heavily oppressed. Byron nodded tiredly and managed a wan smile that did not light his eyes. "I wish the best for you both, and I hope that you have many children. Try to make them female for my sake."

"When will you return?" Jacques inquired.

"When I am able." Byron's form began to waver, to fade, so that they could see through the transparent shape.

Jacques' body crouched lower in readiness, a fluid movement that was barely discernible. Instinctively Shea moved back to give him more room. It seemed a good idea to err on the side of caution. Jacques had never once let down his guard, where Shea would have rushed to comfort Byron compassionately. She inhaled the night, suddenly depressed. On the wind came the oppressive hatred the forest seemed to reek of. She searched Jacques' impassive face. He didn't seem to notice, his attention on the mist streaming away from him. Did he feel it? If it wasn't Byron causing it, why hadn't Byron felt it? Her analytical mind examined the question. She had assumed Jacques couldn't feel the presence because his mind was so fragmented.

"We will return using a different route, Shea. We cannot stay in the cabin." Jacques caught her hand in his and pulled her through the trees. "It is no longer safe."

Shea had the vague impression of a twisted, malevolent smile. Silent laughter, grimly amused. She shook her head to rid herself of the image, afraid she was hallucinating. *Jacques?* Her voice trembled with uncertainty.

His fingers tightened around hers. "There is no need to worry, we will find suitable shelter. I would never allow you to be harmed." He drew her hand to the warmth of his mouth with remarkable tenderness. "You feel the undead one. Is it Byron?"

"I don't know if it's Byron. I just know it is something very evil. Let's leave this place, go to a city with bright lights and lots of people."

He tucked her protectively beneath his shoulder and matched his gait to hers. Instinctively he knew they would be vulnerable in a city. They were Carpathian, not human. He took a deep breath, letting it out slowly to give himself time to search for the right words. "If a vampire is marking us for his attentions, we will only be placing innocent humans in harm's way. They have very few defenses against the undead."

"He is watching us, Jacques. I know you can't feel him, but he's out there."

Jacques believed her. Once again he sought the pictures in her mind, heard the eerie sound of taunting laughter echoing in her head. He swore softly. "When Byron found you in the village, are you certain he did not take your blood?"

"I would have told you. He bent his head toward mine, I could feel his breath on my neck, and his teeth touched my skin, but I jerked away from him. He barely pierced the skin." She reached up and covered the spot where the pinprick had been. "In any case, he apologized to you. Couldn't you see his sadness? It broke my heart."

His arm tightened for a moment, and he dropped a kiss on the top of her head. "You are so compassionate, love, and very trusting. A vampire can appear to be the epitome of beauty, of genuineness itself."

She skipped a little to keep up with his ever-quickening pace. "I don't think so, Jacques. I recognized beauty in you when you appeared to be a monster. I knew there was something beyond what I could see. I think I would recognize evil just as well."

"It was the call of our souls to one another that you recognized. We are lifemates, bound together even when apart."

"Call it anything you like, but I think I would know if Byron were truly the vicious creature I feel watching us. It hates."

"Only Gregori gave you blood. And I."

"If I were you, I would not bring up the fact that you forced me to take that spell-casting healer's blood." She twisted away from him, annoyed all over again. "How could you betray me that way?"

With great male superiority he glanced down at her face. "Your health comes before your pride." The truth was, he was ashamed he had forced such a choice on her, yet he was grateful it was over and she was not nearly as weak as she had been.

"Says you. I hope he bled a long time before he closed that wound. And don't talk to me anymore, because you're being arrogant, and I can't stand you when you're arrogant." She stumbled, her legs already tired.

"If you had done as I said, you would be at full strength, your body healed from its ordeal," he pointed out, smug male amusement deliberately in his mind to tease her.

She stopped walking so abruptly, his arm jerked her forward. "Do you have any idea where we're going? I'm lost out here. Everything is beginning to look the same to me. And stop with that cute little grin you always get in your mind. You think you can get around me with it, but you can't."

He tugged at her arm, his black eyes restless, searching the forest around them. He could still feel the dark malevolence through Shea. "I can always get around you, little red hair," he answered tenderly. "You are not capable of holding a grudge."

The feeling of hatred was oppressive. Jacques' gentle teasing was comforting, and she was oddly grateful for it. She tucked her fingers into the crook of his arm. "Don't count on my good nature, Jacques. You do remember what they say about people with red hair."

"That they are great lovers?"

She laughed in spite of the waves of black malice washing over her continually. "You would think that."

At her laughter, the air thickened around them so that for a moment she was choking on hatred. Unable to stand it another minute, not thinking of the consequences, she whirled around to face the murky forest behind them. "If you want us so badly, you coward, come out into the open and introduce yourself!" She tilted her chin at Jacques. "There. He can come or not. I don't feel like being hunted down like some animal."

Jacques could feel her trembling beside him. It worried him that he had inadvertently forced her into a position of accepting too many new things at one time. His hand cupped the nape of her neck, dragged her close, the black eyes burning down into hers. "No one will ever harm you. Not ever. They may attempt to do so, but they will not survive." He took a deep breath before his confession. "I was not aware that you were not Carpathian. I was not capable of knowing much at all at that time. I inadvertently converted you. I would like to say I am sorry, but in truth, I am not. I did not know what I was doing, and I hope I would have done it differently had I known better, but you are my life, Shea. There is no existence for me without you. I would have nothing to live for except revenge, and I would become the undead. I do not want to be vampire, preying on humans and Carpathians alike. You are my salvation."

She pushed him away from her. The rain

swept over her face as she lifted emerald eyes filled with laughter to his. "That's it? That's your big apology? I can see you're not going to be a candy-and-flowers man." She set off quickly. "Don't talk to me, you uncivilized maniac. I don't even want to hear the sound of your voice."

Jacques forced back the smile that seemed so ready to curve his hard mouth. Shea had a way of making even dangerous situations seem a game where laughter was always close at hand. She managed to find ways to make his madness, the terrible, unforgivable way he had treated her at their first meeting, seem casual. "Can I put my arm around you?" Even while his eyes scanned, they held a gleam of merriment.

"You're talking. I said don't talk to me." Shea tried sticking her nose in the air, but it felt ridiculous, and she dissolved into undignified giggles.

His arm curved around her slender waist and locked her under his shoulder. "I am sorry. I did not mean to speak when you asked me not to. Turn here. I'm going to have to carry you up."

"Don't talk. You always get your way when you talk." She walked with him a few more yards and stopped, staring up a sheer cliff face that seemed to go up forever.

There had been no division between the forest and the rock face to warn her. "Up what? Not that." The dark, malevolent feeling had faded away. Whoever it was no longer was watching them. She could tell.

"I feel another argument coming on." His mocking amusement might not have shown on his face, but she could feel it in her mind. Jacques simply lifted her and tossed her over his shoulder.

"No way, you wild man. You aren't Tarzan. I don't like heights. Put me down."

"Close your eyes. Who is Tarzan? Not another male, I hope."

The wind rushed over her body, and she could feel them moving fast, so fast the world seemed to blur. She closed her eyes and clutched at him, afraid to do anything else. His laughter was happy and carefree, and it warmed her heart, dispelling any residue of fear she carried. It was a miracle to her that he could laugh, that he was happy.

Tarzan is the ultimate male. He swings through trees and carries his woman off into the jungle.

He patterns himself after me.

She nuzzled his back. *He tries.*

He could hear the love in her voice, the tenderness, and his heart turned over. They had a long way to go before knowing one another fully, before accepting one another, but the love between them was growing stronger with every moment they were together.

Chapter Eleven

The passage into the cave was so narrow, Shea had to hold her breath to squeeze through. It seemed to go on forever, the rough walls scraping her skin, the oppressive feelings of tons of rock over her head, surrounding her body, waiting to crush her. She couldn't look at Jacques, who had somehow made his large body thin and weird looking. Carpathians were capable of doing things she didn't want to think about. How had she gotten herself into this mess?

Sex. A good-looking intense man with black, hungry eyes, and she fell like a lovesick calf. Sex. It ruined many otherwise sane women.

I can read your thoughts. The amusement was soft and caressing, wrapping her up in strong arms.

I was perfectly sane and sensible until I met you. Now look at me. I'm crawling around inside a mountain. Suddenly she stopped and held herself perfectly still. *I'm hearing something. Tell me you are not taking me into a cave full of bats. Say it right now, Jacques, or I'm out of here.*

I am not taking you into a cave filled with bats.

Shea relaxed visibly. She was not squeamish about very many things, but bats were creatures that were on the earth to remain a safe distance away from her. Miles away. Bats were one of those things she could stare up at in the night sky and think how interesting and wonderful they were, as long as they stayed high above her and nowhere close. Her nose wrinkled. The sounds she was trying to ignore were getting louder. Her heart began to pound in alarm. The walls of the passageway were so narrow, she had no way to move fast. All at once she felt trapped, as if she was suffocating.

I'm going back, Jacques. I'm not a cave person. She did her best to sound firm and matter-of-fact, not at all as if she were seconds from screaming her head off. She turned her head cautiously to keep from scraping her face on the jutting surfaces.

His fingers circled her wrist like a vise. *There must be no disturbance. If any creatures exit the cave or warn others of our existence here, we could be found.*

A piece of paper couldn't fit in here, certainly not a person. No one is going to look for us here.

A vampire would know the moment bats flew from the cave.

Bats can't fly out of here if there aren't any in here, now, can they? She was sweetly reasonable.

Trust me, little red hair, it is only a short distance farther.

You aren't going to make me sleep in the ground, are you? Because I won't do it, not even if there are ten vampires stalking us.

Vampires cannot stand even the dawn, Shea. Killing his prey does something to the blood. The sun would fry him immediately. He might betray us to the human servants he is in league with if he marked the entrance to this cave. Or they might be watching for just such a sign as bats flying unexpectedly into the early sun.

You're telling me there are bats in here.

He tugged at her wrist. *Stop being such a baby. I can control the bats, and they will serve to warn us of any danger.*

Shea made a face but followed him. With every moment Jacques' abilities, his knowledge and power, seemed to be growing. He was confident almost to the point of arrogance. Sometimes it grated and made her want to throw something at him, but she was proud of his growing strength.

The passage began to widen and slowly move downward, as if they were going into the very bowels of the earth. Shea could feel sweat beading on her body and her lungs laboring. She concentrated on breathing, the only thing that would keep her sane.

Jacques realized she was trembling, her

fingers twisting nervously in his. His mind pushed through her natural barrier and found her uneasiness, her ridiculous fear of bats and closed-in places. She was uneasy with the Carpathian ability to shape-shift. Even his thinness, as he moved through the cave, made her uncomfortable. Used to being in control of every situation, she was finding it hard to follow his lead so blindly.

I am sorry, little one. I am introducing you to things that seem so perfectly natural to me yet must be confusing and frightening to you. His voice was a soft caress, sending warmth curling through her body.

Just his voice could give her strength. She straightened her shoulders and followed him. *There's a bed in here somewhere, right?* She tried to inject some humor into the moment.

The passageway widened enough to allow Jacques to resume his true form. He immediately did so, hoping to alleviate Shea's distress. He also sought a comfortable topic for conversation. "What do you think of Raven?"

"I thought we had to be quiet." Shea was looking in every direction for bats.

"The bats know we are here, Shea, but there is no need to fear them. I will keep them away from you." He spoke calmly as if it was an everyday occurrence to control the movements of bats. His fingers curled around the nape of her neck as much in reassurance as to prevent her from fleeing. His thumb caressed her satin skin, found her pounding pulse, and stroked gently, soothingly.

"Raven seems very nice, even if she's married to another wild man like you." *She probably has lousy taste, just like me.* She tacked the thought on deliberately.

"What does that mean?" He tried to sound indignant, to keep her talking, to help her sustain her sense of humor. Jacques appreciated her courage and her unfailing determination to keep up her end, no matter how difficult it was on her.

"It means she can't have much sense. That man is dangerous, Jacques, even if he is your brother. And the healer is positively scary."

"Did you think so?"

"Didn't you? He smiled and talked so gently and calmly, but did you ever look into his eyes? It's evident he feels no emotion whatsoever."

"He is one of the ancient ones. Gregori is the most feared of all Carpathians."

"Why is that?" Because Gregori was far too powerful, his voice alone able to make strong men, Carpathian males, do his bidding?

"He is the most knowledgeable in all the ancient and modern arts. He is the most lethal and the most relentless. He is the hunter of all vampires."

"And he's ancient enough and solitary enough to turn at any moment, right? Makes me feel really secure. And you forced me to drink his blood. That is going to take a long time to forgive." She stumbled, not realizing how tired she was.

A scream echoed up through the very soil, through the earth's crust. More felt than actually heard, it struck terror, a frozen, helpless grasp on nerve endings. The sound vibrated through their bodies, through their minds, and passed back into the earth itself. The rocks picked up the scream and echoed it back and forth.

Jacques went very still, only his icy black eyes moving restlessly. Shea clutched at him, horrified. That sound was of a creature in terrible need, in tremendous pain and suffering. Without conscious thought she sought outside herself, feeling for the source, trying to fix on the location.

"The betrayer," Jacques said in a venomous voice, a low sound of hatred and promised retaliation. "He has another victim in his hands."

"How? You are all so powerful, how can he trap any of your kind?" Shea tugged at his arm to bring his attention back to her. He seemed a stranger in that moment, a predator every bit as lethal as the wolf, as the vampire.

Jacques blinked rapidly, searched his mind for the answer. He had been trapped by a betrayer, hadn't he? How that had happened was locked somewhere in his damaged mind. Until he could find and repair the fragments, all of his kind were in danger.

Shea rubbed her hand down his arm. "This is not your fault. You didn't cause this to happen, Jacques."

"Did you recognize the voice?" His tone was completely devoid of expression.

"It sounded like an animal to me."

"It was Byron."

Shea felt as if he had knocked the breath from her body. "You can't be certain."

"It was Byron." He said it with absolute conviction. "He came to me to ask for friendship, and I refused him. Now the betrayer will turn him over to the human assassins."

"Why doesn't the vampire keep him for himself?" She was struggling to understand, her mind already formulating plans. She could not leave Byron or anyone else in the hands of butchers, murderers. She had lost a brother she never knew to these madmen. She had nearly lost Jacques. "If he hates all of you enough to want you tortured and killed, why doesn't he just do it himself?"

"The vampire must seek the earth before the sun rises. Unlike us, he cannot take even early sunlight. Dawn would bring his destruction. It limits his reach."

"So he was in the woods watching us, just as I feared, and must have followed Byron and somehow trapped him. And he has to turn Byron over to the humans before dawn. The humans must be close."

"Gregori said the very soil groaned under their boots."

"So this betrayer cannot help the humans as long as the sun is up."

"Absolutely not." He said it with conviction.

"But the dawn does not have such an effect on us. We can stand it, Jacques. If we move now, we can find them. All we have to do is get Byron back and hide him until around five or six this evening when we are strong again. We can do it, I know we can. There are only so many places he could be. We can stand the early-morning sun, and no one will be expecting us. The humans who have him can't come into this cave; they can't go into the earth. They have to have shelter somewhere. You know this area, and if you don't, the others do. Let's get Byron back. The vampire might get so angry he'll quit hiding, make a mistake, and the others can get him." She was tugging at his arm, trying to drag him back toward the entrance to the cave.

"I will not expose you to these men."

"Give it a rest, Jacques. I mean it. We're in this thing together. I hate to brag and put you at an obvious disadvantage, but I can take more of the sun than you."

His hand caressed the nape of her neck. "That doesn't mean I will allow you to be exposed to danger."

Shea burst out laughing. "Just being with you is dangerous, you idiot. *You're* dangerous." She shook back her hair, her chin lifting a bit defiantly. "In any case, I can feel the vampire and you cannot. Neither, it seems, could Byron. Maybe the others won't be able to either. You need me."

Reluctantly Jacques was allowing her to pull him toward the cave entrance. "Why do I never win an argument with you? I cannot allow you to be in danger, yet we are walking into the dawn and facing brutal killers when we are at our lowest strength.

In the afternoon, Shea, we will be completely vulnerable, at their mercy, at the mercy of the sun. Both of us will be."

"Then we'll just have to be in a safe place by then. Contact the others, Jacques, tell them what's going on."

"I think you just want to get out of this cave. You would rather face a vampire and human killers than a few little bats." He tugged at her wild mane of hair.

She flashed him a grin over her shoulder. "You've got that right. And don't you ever turn into a bat." She shuddered. "Or a rat."

"We could get kinky and see how bats and rats make love," he suggested in a whisper, warm breath against her neck.

"You are a sick man, Jacques. Very, very sick." The passage was narrowing again, taking her breath. At least Jacques was complying, even if he was grousing a bit.

Jacques separated his mind from his body, thought of Gregori, the way he moved, the way he felt when his essence moved through Jacques, healing mortal wounds from the inside out. He built the feeling and sent a mental call.

Hear me, healer. I have need that you hear me.

Your trouble must be great that you reach out

to those you do not trust.

The voice was startling clear in his head; the answer came so quickly that Jacques felt a surge of triumph. He was much stronger, so much more capable than he had been even the day before. Gregori had given him blood; it flowed in his veins, pumped through his heart, restored damaged muscle and tissue. He had forgotten how easily one could communicate. *I heard Byron scream. The betrayer has taken him. He must turn him over to the humans before dawn.*

Dawn approaches now, Jacques. Gregori sounded calm, undisturbed by even such news as this.

Then we must find him. Do any of you have the ability to track Byron? Has he exchanged blood with any of you?

Only you made a pact with him. If he turned and was unable to seek the dawn himself, he wanted you to hunt him, and vice versa. You did not want your brother or me to have the responsibility for your destruction.

I cannot find the path for him. Jacques could not keep the frustration and self-loathing out of his voice.

You are certain this scream was Byron's?

Without a doubt. We had been talking together only minutes earlier. Shea became distressed; she said someone was watching us. I

374

could detect no one, and Byron showed no un-easiness.

Jacques and Shea were moving through the narrowing rock passage upward toward the entrance. Jacques felt the normal rest-lessness of his kind at the approaching light. *We will do our best to seek him as long as we are able.*

Mikhail's woman can sometimes track those we cannot. She is very gifted. We will meet you at the cabin. Do you both have dark glasses and protective clothing?

Shea does, and I can fashion mine easily enough. She is still too weak to attempt shape-shifting, and she will not go to ground. Nor will I. Jacques heard the echo of Gregori's deri-sion. Women were to be protected from their own foolish desire to be in the thick of conflict. *When you find your lifemate, healer, your own clear thinking perhaps will cloud,* Jacques defended himself.

The dawn was streaking across the sky, pressing through the clouds. Rain was still coming down in sheets, and winds were whistling fiercely through the trees below them. In the opening to the cave they were sheltered, but once they moved away from the cliff face, they would be hit with the full force of the elements.

Jacques leaned close to Shea's ear. "The

storm will lessen the effects of the sun on us. I can feel the healer's touch in this squall."

"There is no sun. Will the vampire be able to be out in this?"

Jacques shook his head. "He cannot see the dawn, not even through the cover of clouds. We often use weather such as this to move in the early and late part of the day. It allows us to blend better with humans, and our eyes and skin take less punishment."

He felt her shiver and immediately swept her beneath his shoulder. The weather didn't bother him; any Carpathian could regulate body temperature easily. Shea had so much to learn, and she needed to overcome her aversion to feeding to gain her full strength. "The healer is right, you know. This is far too dangerous to allow you to do. I do not know what I was thinking."

"The healer can mind his own business." Shea sent Jacques a haughty, over-the-shoulder glare. "The healer may be an intelligent miracle-worker, but he does not know the first thing about women. Don't make the mistake of listening to him in that particular department. Even with your memory lost, you know far more than that idiot."

Jacques found himself laughing again. His mouth brushed the nape of her neck, sent a shiver rushing the length of her spine. "How easily you get around me." He couldn't help the surge of possessive triumph sweeping through him. Shea might admire the healer for his abilities, might even wish to learn from him, but his attitude definitely grated on her independent nature. Jacques found he was particularly fond of that independent streak in her.

"You're a mere man, what do you expect?" she asked straight-faced. "I, however, am a brilliant surgeon and a woman of many talents."

"The bats are beginning to get very nervous. I am not certain I can keep them from charging us," he teased wickedly.

An involuntary shiver ran through her, but she simply tugged at his hand, assuring herself he was close, and returned to the matter before them. "Think of where we can take Byron when we find him."

"The cabin is too dangerous. It will have to be a cave or the ground itself. We can turn him over to the healer and find a safe place to rest, perhaps make it back here."

"That thrills me, it truly does."

"Where did you learn to be so sarcastic?"

Jacques meant the question to be teasing, but a bitter smile curved her soft mouth, and her eyes reflected pain. "You learn fast to protect yourself when you're different, when you don't dare bring a classmate home because your mother forgets you exist, forgets the world exists. Sometimes she stood at the window for days, literally days. She wouldn't even acknowledge me." She stopped. "Could I be like her, Jacques? Because I'm with you, could I be like her?"

"Not in the same way," he answered as honestly as could. "Some things are so fragmented in my mind, I have to piece together information. I do know most lifemates choose to live or die together. But if a child was in need, the lifemate remaining would see to its well-being, emotionally as well as physically." He did not tell her of those children given to other couples to raise because the remaining lifemate could not face existence without the partner. They knew the child would be well looked after, well loved, because most Carpathian women miscarried or lost their newborns within the first year of life. "And I know you, Shea. No matter how difficult something is on you, you always see it through. You would not abandon our child the way your mother did you. Our child would be loved and guided every moment of its life. I know that absolutely."

She caught his arm, preventing him from stepping out into the rain. "Promise me, if we have a child together and something happens to me, you will stay and raise it yourself. Love it and guide it as someone should have me. Promise me, Jacques."

"A Carpathian child is protected and loved above all things. We do not mistreat children."

"That is not what I asked of you."

He closed his eyes tightly for a moment, unable to lie to her. He had been alone too long. He would never want to remain without her. "Lifemates happen to us only once, little red hair."

"Our child, Jacques. If it should happen, I don't want a stranger raising it."

"Sometimes, Shea, another couple, one hungering for a child, is a better choice than a remaining, grief-stricken lifemate."

Her swift indrawn breath, the slam of a mind block so strong it was frightening, made him realize this was no small matter to her. "Did it never occur to you people that the child might also be grieving? That a parent to comfort it and see it through such a time would be of more value. This need you have to choose death when there is a child or other family members left behind is selfish and morbid."

"You persist in judging us by human standards," he said gently. "You have no idea what our bond entails." His strong fingers laced through hers, and he turned her knuckles up to brush the warmth of his mouth along her soft skin. "Perhaps we should save this discussion for a more appropriate time, when we are safe and we know Byron is also."

Her eyes refused to meet his. "I'm sure you're right, Jacques." Tears burned, and Shea chose to attribute them to her sensitivity to the dawn, not to their conversation.

She followed Jacques down to the timberline without a murmur, carefully keeping a strong block up so that he could not read her mind. She could understand why he felt he would have to choose death should something happen to her. He had been too long alone and could not face life without his anchor. Maybe he was right; maybe he would be too dangerous to the world. But if she had to accept that, she knew that there could be no children in their future together. Eternity was a long time to live with such knowledge. But she could not bring a child into the world, given how Jacques felt. She would never take such a risk.

Shea bit her lip, stumbled a little in weariness. Automatically she grabbed at Jacques' waistband for support. For one moment she'd thought she had a chance at a normal life, perhaps not normal as others knew it, but with a family structure, a child and husband.

Do not, Shea. I do not have the time now to comfort you properly, to allay your fears. Leave this.

Startled that he had penetrated her block, she looked up at his face, so mesmerizing, so handsome and seductive, yet ravaged by torment no human could imagine. His eyes, unprotected by the dark glasses he held in his hand, moved over her face. She could see love there, and possession, a dark promise for all eternity.

His fingers brushed her chin, sending a dancing flame spiraling along her spine. His thumb touched her bottom lip, and a shiver of sexual awareness curled in the pit of her stomach. *You belong with me, Shea, two halves of the same whole. You are the light to my darkness. I may be twisted, even mad, but I know in my heart, in my very soul, that I cannot exist without you.* His mouth brushed her eyelids gently. "I am not easy to kill, red hair, and I do not surrender what is mine. Lying in torment these years has given me a strength of will not easily matched."

She rubbed her face along his side, wanting to burrow close for comfort. "We are so far apart, Jacques, in every way we think. It's easy to say in the heat of passion that everything will be fine, but living together may be extremely difficult. We're so different."

His arm circled her waist, urging her forward into the comparative shelter of the trees. Rain was slashing down, soaking them. Clouds, dark and massive, swirled above them. But he could feel the first pinpricks of the sun as it began to climb above the clouds. The early morning light always made him uneasy, always made him aware of his own terrible vulnerability. Replacing his dark glasses, he pushed forward with quick, long strides. If only she had taken nourishment from the healer, they could shape-shift and be at the cabin in an instant.

Jacques knew she had thought her mind block sufficient to keep him out, but he never was able to quite let go of her. Some part of him always dwelled in her mind, quiet, like a faint shadow, but there all the same. She had always dreamed of having a child, to give it the love she'd never had. Now she felt there was no hope of such a thing. The question of the child had been very important to her, but lifemates could not lie to one another, could not cheat on one another. He could only pray he would choose death instantly, without a qualm, without a doubt, if something happened to Shea. Otherwise he feared he would become the monster lurking inside him, so close to the surface, a monster the world of humans and Carpathians alike had never known. There was something very wrong with him, and only Shea stood between that something and the rest of the world.

There was no way for her to break their bond. He knew that with his every instinct, and it brought him a measure of comfort. The rage, always so close, so deadly, was leashed and under control for the time being. As long as Shea was with him.

But now he had to find Byron; he owed the Carpathian that much. The drive in him to do so was strong, almost overwhelming, as if some part of him, not his mind but something deep within him, remembered their shared friendship. He should have placed Shea in a trance and demanded that she sleep while he did this thing, but the truth was, he simply couldn't bear their separation, and he wanted her close, where he could protect her. And he wanted her happy. *Women!*

Shea heard his disgruntled complaint clearly in her mind. A small smile tugged at the corners of her reluctant mouth.

"Am I complicating your life, Jacques?" she asked sweetly, hopefully.

He stopped so abruptly that she was jerked to a halt. Jacques caught her wet hair in his fist and pulled her head back so that the rain ran along her soft skin like honey. "The truth is, Shea, you make me feel so much, I do not know if I can stand it sometimes." His mouth found hers almost blindly, desperately, feeding voraciously as if he might devour her, take her into his body forever. *Nothing can ever happen to you!* His hands were biting into her skin, his body taut with tension, his mind a whirling confusion of fear and determination and so much hunger.

Almost without thought Shea reacted instinctively, her slender arms circling his neck, her body soft and pliant against the aggression in his, her mind calm and loving, a warm, safe haven for his fragmented, tortured mind. She kissed him without reservation, pouring every ounce of love and support she could into her response. He lifted his head reluctantly and rested his forehead on hers.

"Nothing is going to happen to me, Jacques. I think you're having anxiety attacks." She tousled his hair as if he were a small boy, gave him a teasing grin. "Do

Carpathians have shrinks, too?"

He laughed softly, astonished that he could do so when he had been so terrified only moments earlier. "You are as disrespectful as a woman can get."

"I'm not just any woman, silly, I'm a doctor and terribly brilliant. Everyone says so."

"Do they now?" He held her tight against his hard frame, thinking to take her into his very body, his arms protectively sheltering her.

"Is this going to be too much for you, Jacques? Facing those horrible butchers again? Are you certain you can do this?"

He raised his head so that she couldn't see the wolfish smile that didn't reach his ice-black eyes. "I am looking forward to renewing our acquaintance."

Shea touched his mind with hers, found a grim satisfaction at the thought of a confrontation, but Jacques was too strong to allow her to see the rage and hatred welling up, threatening to spew forth violence and revenge. Shea was a healer, a gentle woman who could not conceive of an evil such as he had seen, such as he himself possessed. She took his hand, her fingers lacing tightly with his. She might not ever have a child, but she had Jacques. She wanted him far away from pain and torment, far from men or creatures who might try to destroy him again. She was very determined to see him safe.

Chapter Twelve

Raven stood in the comparative shelter of the porch, her face turned up toward the sky, eyes closed. Tiny beads of perspiration dotted her forehead, and her fingers twisted together compulsively over her stomach. She was not with the others, rather somewhere out of her body and concentrating on attempting to find Byron's location. Beside her stood her dark, intimidating husband, his mind obviously locked with hers. Mikhail was so like Jacques that Shea could not tear her gaze from him. As she moved onto the porch a step behind Jacques, she could clearly see that Mikhail was furious. He was seething with anger, violence swirling very close to the surface, yet his posture was purely protective. He had placed himself between Raven and the ferocity of the storm.

Gregori was as still as a statue, his face a blank mask, his silver eyes as empty as death, yet Shea gave him a wide berth. There was something dangerous in his utter stillness. Shea felt she had no way to sorting out the complexity of the Carpathian male's nature. Gregori was watching Raven through narrowed, restless eyes, eyes that saw far too much. Suddenly he cursed, low and vicious, startling from someone of his stature and power. "She should not put herself at risk. She is with child."

His eyes met Jacques', silver lightning and black ice. Total understanding between the two men. Shea merged her mind with Jacques' quickly to try to understand the hidden currents. Raven's pregnancy, if she was pregnant, changed everything as far as the men were concerned. Shea could see no evidence of a child — Raven appeared as slim as ever — but she couldn't believe the healer would be wrong. He seemed so infallible, so completely invincible. The child was everything, all-important to the men. It surprised, even shocked her, the way they regarded the pregnancy. It was a miracle to both of them. The baby was more important than any of their lives. Shea was confused. Despite Jacques' fractured memories, his protective streak was extremely strong.

"He's aware of his surroundings, but he can't move. Even his mind is locked and still. He is paralyzed somehow." Raven's voice startled Shea, brought her back to the stormy weather and their rescue mission. Raven was clearly speaking of Byron. "He can't move or call out, not even mentally. It is dark and damp, and he knows he will suffer greatly before they are done with him." Raven swayed, her hands protectively covering her stomach.

The healer moved, a blur of speed, catching her arm and wrenching her out into the driving rain. Gregori snagged Mikhail's shirt, too, and yanked him into the fury of the storm. "Break off now, Raven," Gregori commanded. He shook her, shook Mikhail. "Let go of him now!"

Jacques leapt forward, grabbed his brother, and hit his face, once, twice. "Come back!" It was a hoarse cry.

Shea bit her lip, suddenly terrified. The couple seemed somehow bound, caught in the vampire's trap with Byron. Gregori pulled Raven farther into the driving rain. Jacques pushed Mikhail after them. It was Mikhail who recovered first. He blinked at his brother, looked around him as if unaware where he was. Then, instinctively, he reached for Raven.

"Bring her back, Mikhail. Go after her. Guide her back. This is too dangerous for her. Even with my connection to her, she is trapped," Gregori said. "We are dealing with more than just any vampire. This one is skilled in the black arts and the use of herbs and power stones. I know what he has done and how he is doing it."

Mikhail pulled Raven tightly against him,

his black eyes hard with mental strain. Raven blinked, looked around her, seemed surprised to find herself in the rain. Her hand went to her temple in a gesture of pain. "Stop staring at me. I feel like some kind of freak show." She sounded hurt, hid her face on Mikhail's chest.

His arms circled her, drew her into the shelter of his body, his head bent lovingly toward hers. It was such an intimate gesture, Shea had to turn away. To her dismay, she found the healer studying her. Shea moved closer to Jacques, unconsciously seeking protection from the scrutiny.

"You need nourishment." The healer spoke gently.

"When I'm hungry, I'll eat," Shea told him haughtily. "You don't need to worry about all of us. I know how to care for myself."

The silvery eyes slashed through the lie. "Your hunger radiates from you, and your weakness could place all of us in jeopardy." He turned his powerful stare on Raven.

Raven squirmed visibly. "Oh, shut up, Gregori," she snapped, her blue eyes flashing fire at him.

A faint smile curved his mouth, failing to light his eyes. "I did not speak."

"You spoke volumes, and you know it."

Her chin went up belligerently. "Your male sense of superiority is enough to make a woman want to scream. Honestly, Gregori, all that cold logic makes a person crazy." She allowed Mikhail to lead her onto the porch.

"Logic works, unlike emotional women," Gregori returned unruffled. "Your first duty is to protect your child. Our first duty must be to protect you." His silver gaze clearly censured Mikhail.

"You don't know for sure if I'm pregnant."

"Do not play games, Raven. Sometimes your rebellious ways grow tedious. I know you are with child. You cannot hide such a thing from me. Mikhail knows it to be true, and he knows he cannot allow your dangerous involvement in this mission to continue with you in such a condition."

Raven flung out her ebony hair. "No one allows me to do anything. I decide. I was born and raised human, Gregori," she pointed out. "I can only be myself. Byron is my friend, and he is in desperate trouble. I intend to help him."

"If your lifemate is so enthralled with you that he would allow you such foolishness," Gregori replied softly, menacingly, "then I can do no other than protect you myself."

"Don't you talk about Mikhail like that!" Raven was furious.

You really know how to stir up the hornets' nest with the women, do you not? Mikhail demanded, even though he understood Gregori completely and felt him justified.

Gregori did not look at him but stared out into the storm. *The child she carries is my lifemate. It is female and belongs to me.* There was an unmistakable warning note, an actual threat.

In all their centuries together, such a thing had never happened. Mikhail immediately closed his mind to Raven. She could never hope to understand how Gregori felt. Without a lifemate, the healer had no choice but to eventually destroy himself or become the very epitome of evil. The vampire. The walking dead. Gregori had spent endless centuries waiting for his lifemate, holding on when those younger than he had given in. Gregori had defended their people, lived a solitary existence so that he might keep their race safe. He was far more alone than the others of his kind, and far more susceptible to the call of power as he had to hunt and kill often. Mikhail could not blame his oldest friend for his possessive, protective streak toward the unborn child. He spoke calmly and firmly, hoping to avoid a confrontation. Gregori had held on for so long, this promise of a lifemate could send him careening over the edge into the dark madness if he felt there was a danger to the female child. *Raven is not like Carpathian woman. You have always known and accepted that. She will not remain in seclusion during this time. She would wither and die.*

Gregori actually snarled, a menacing rumble that froze Shea in place, put Jacques into a crouch, and had Mikhail shifting position for a better defense. Raven pushed past Mikhail's strong body and fearlessly laid a hand on the healer's arm. Everyone else might think Gregori could turn at any moment, but he had held on for centuries, and she believed implicitly that he would no more hurt her than he would her child. "Gregori, don't be angry with Mikhail." Her voice was soft and gentle. "His first duty to me is to see to my happiness."

"It is to see to your protection." Gregori's voice was a blend of heat and light.

"In a way it's the same thing. Don't blame him for having to make adjustments for what you consider my shortcomings. It hasn't been easy for him, or for me, for that matter. We could have waited to conceive until I'd had time to become more familiar with Carpathian ways, but that would have taken more time than you have. You're far more than a close friend to us — you're family, a part of our hearts. We weren't willing to risk losing you. So we both pray this child is a female and that she grows to love and cherish you as we do, that this is the one who will be your other half."

Gregori stirred as if to say something.

Do not say anything! Mikhail hissed in the healer's head. *She believes the child will have a choice.*

Gregori bowed his head mentally to Mikhail. If Mikhail chose to allow his wife the comforting if false thought that the female child would have a choice in such a matter, then so be it.

Shea was astonished that a man so powerful, obviously such a leader as Mikhail, could calmly allow another man to snarl at him and rebuke him as Gregori had. She was beginning to suspect that Jacques' brother was a man of strong character, and the love and emotion apparent in both him and Raven brought tears to her eyes. This was Jacques' family, his legacy, and there was real love, real affection, among them, making them capable of great sacrifice. She slipped her hand into Jacques' and clung to him, feeling she had something in common with Raven.

Raven's blue eyes were steady on Gregori. "If you wish to examine me to determine the sex of the child, you may do so." Her chin lifted. "But as you wish me to accept you for yourself, for your predatory nature, you must accept me as I am. My heart and soul may be Carpathian, but my mind is human. I will not be put on a shelf somewhere because you or my husband deems it necessary. Human women moved out of the dark ages a long time ago. My place is with Mikhail, and I must make my own decisions. If you feel the need to add your protection to Mikhail's, I will be most grateful."

There was a long silence, and the red glow faded slowly from the slashing silver eyes. Gregori shook his head slowly, with infinite weariness. This woman was so different from his kind. Reckless. Compassionate. Unaware of every taboo she broke. His hand went to her stomach, fingers splayed. He focused, aimed, sent himself out of his body. His breath caught in his throat, and his heart seemed to melt. Deliberately he moved to surround the tiny being, merging his light and will for a heartbeat of time. He was taking no chances. This was his lifemate; he would ensure it with every means at his disposal, from blood bonding to mental sharing. No one was as powerful as he. This female child was his and his alone. He could hang on until she came of age.

"We did it, didn't we?" Raven said softly, bringing Gregori back to his own body. "She's a girl."

Gregori stepped away from Raven, holding on to his composure with his great strength of will. "Few Carpathian women carry to full term. The child rarely survives the first year of life. Do not be so certain we are out of the woods. You must rest and be cared for. The child comes first. Byron would say so also. Mikhail must take you far from this place, away from the vampire and the assassins. I will hunt and rid our people of the danger while your mate looks after you." Gregori's voice was low and pitched in silver tones, tones of light that beckoned and danced. Nearly impossible to resist. So calm and soothing and reasonable.

Raven actually had to shake off the compulsion to do as he wished. She glared at him. "Don't even try that with me, Gregori." She included Mikhail in her stare. "And you, you big lunk, you would have gone along with him like the tree-swinging macho man you are. Watch these guys, Shea, they're impossible. They'll do anything to get their way."

Shea found herself smiling. "So I've noticed." It was reassuring to see that Raven had learned to hold her own with the men. Shea was every bit as strong.

"I can't leave Byron out there to suffer the same fate as Jacques," Raven insisted stubbornly. She looked beyond Gregori to Shea for support. "*We* can't."

Shea had seen firsthand what the human butchers were capable of, and she could no more leave Byron to such a fate than she could walk away from Jacques. She nodded in agreement. "Once we have Byron's location, you men can go after him. I'll stay with Raven, and we'll wait for you here. The vampire can't come out with the sun up, and we have guns if the humans show up."

"In any case, Mikhail, you know you could protect us from humans, even from a distance," Raven reminded him.

"Shea is right, healer." Jacques suddenly threw his support to the women. He owed Byron. He could not allow anyone to suffer as he had. He glanced at Gregori. "You knew Raven and Mikhail were in trouble when their minds were connected to Byron's. What is it? How does the vampire trap us?"

"He ensnared Raven and me through

Byron, a monumental feat," Mikhail admitted. Then he rubbed his jaw ruefully. "Is it possible, little brother, you enjoyed hitting me just a bit too much?"

Jacques' teeth gleamed white in the semblance of a smile. He could not help but admire Mikhail's coolness in the midst of a threat as lethal as the healer's and the vampire's combined. To be able to joke, to put aside the ego of the Carpathian male, was nothing short of a miracle. Fragments of memory rushed over him, memories of greatness, of a powerful being dedicated to the preservation of their people. His arms crept around Shea, his anchor to reality, his bridge from his lost past to the present. Shea responded at once, so in tune with him she needed no second hint. She leaned into him immediately, flooding his mind with warmth and soothing comfort.

"There is a root," Gregori explained. "One can grind it into a fine powder, mix it with two types of berries and sage. It is boiled until it becomes thick, all liquid evaporated, and the remaining gel is then mixed with the venom from a tree toad. I am positive the vampire is using it. The recipe is an ancient one and lost to all but those of us who studied alchemy and black magic. I know of only two others besides me who would have this knowledge."

"Aidan," Mikhail said softly. "Or Julian."

"It cannot be," Gregori denied. "I would feel their presence in our land. Even changed, I would know either of them."

"What exactly does this drug do?" Shea asked. The identity of the vampire seemed secondary; she was far more intrigued with the results of such a mixture as Gregori described. She had studied plants and herbs extensively. Common ones like foxglove and rhododendrons could produce paralysis. She knew, too, that toad venom of itself could be lethal. Certain tribes in various parts of the world had discovered its properties and used it to tip their darts, spears, and arrows. Somehow the blend of root and berries and toxin must paralyze the nervous system, even affect the mind. "How is it administered?"

"It has to be in the bloodstream," Gregori said.

"Who could get close enough to inject a Carpathian? Even a vampire cunning enough to disguise his true self would not have the strength to overcome someone of Jacques' stature. It is inconceivable," Mikhail said. "Jacques was a hunter, a dispenser of justice. At the time the murders were decimating our people, he would have been doubly cautious."

"The vampire tricked him. It is the usual weapon of a deceiver, is it not?" Gregori informed them calmly. "Dawn is here. We must hurry."

The rain beat down into the silence; the wind shook the trees. Jacques stared sightlessly into the forest. Fragments of memory teased and whispered at him. "Blood. So much blood." The words came out of their own accord. His fingertips stroked absently over his neck, a frown creasing his forehead. "It was a hunter's trap, a crude, nearly invisible wire. It cut my throat."

Nobody moved or spoke, not wanting to break Jacques' concentration. Shea found herself holding her breath. Memory was so important to Jacques, and right now it might save Byron's life. She could feel the pain splintering through his mind, felt him blocking it out, focusing his will to remember. He rubbed his thumb back and forth across an eyebrow, then frowned slightly. "I was weak. He came then, offered his blood. I did not want to offend him, but I was reluctant. He was . . . he disturbed me." Jacques broke off, gripping his temples hard with his fingertips. "I cannot see him." He looked at Shea with desperate, anguished eyes. "I do not know who he is."

She wrapped her arms around him both mentally and physically, hating the worn, tortured lines etched into his beautiful face. *Two days ago you could barely stand, could not remember anything. This is a miracle, Jacques. What you've accomplished is a miracle.* She tried to reassure him, reading accurately that he loathed the fact that he could not eke out another detail.

"It is enough to piece it together," Gregori said, his voice a soothing balm. He touched his fingertips to Jacques' temples, inhaled slowly, and focused, sending himself outside his body.

Shea could actually feel the pain melting away, leaving Jacques whole and calm. The healer's power was extraordinary. She wanted it, felt it moving within her, rising to follow where the healer's light led.

Gregori's voice broke the spell. "You must have accepted his offer. The poison was in the betrayer's blood."

"What prevents the betrayer from being paralyzed?" Mikhail hissed it, a venomous sound that sent a shiver through Shea. There was something very lethal about all these men, something far different from their human counterparts. They accepted violence as easily as the animals in the surrounding forest did. They were predators. It was in the way they moved, in the way they held themselves, in their very thoughts.

Gregori made a slow circle of the porch. Shea found it interesting that all three men had positioned their bodies between the dawn and the women. "There are ways, but we have no time for such a discussion, for we must act now if we are to do this. Raven, while you were connected to Byron, could you get a sense of direction, anything at all?"

"He was not alone. He was somewhere underground, a cave maybe. It was damp, musty. He was not so very far from us." Raven looked up at Mikhail with sad eyes, afraid she had not come up with the information they needed to find the Carpathian in time. One day in the company of the two human butchers and Byron was surely going to die a hideous death. Mikhail laced his fingers through hers, brought her knuckles to the warmth of his mouth in understanding and unity.

"The cellar, Jacques," Shea suddenly said, excited. "They took him to the cellar. They can't know this land very well, and they would go where they had already been successful. I know what they're like, very arrogant, particularly the one called Don

Wallace. It would be just like him to use the same place, thinking he was thumbing his nose at all of you."

"It would be damp and musty all right, but they would find Jacques' coffin gone. They would know the place had been disturbed recently," Mikhail argued thoughtfully.

"True, but wouldn't the vampire tell them Jacques is alive? He saw Jacques and me in the forest earlier with Byron," Shea said. "They would feel safe because you're all supposed to be under cover during the day, I'm telling you, this is exactly the kind of thing a man like Wallace would do. He believes you're all vampires and can't move in the daylight hours."

"This Wallace," Mikhail said softly, "he is the nephew of Eugene Slovensky, enemy to all Carpathians. We have met briefly before. I believe the young lady is correct. He believes he is smarter and more cunning than we."

"Aidan would have done our race a huge service had he killed him when he had the opportunity," Gregori observed. "We were hard-pressed that night, with Mikhail injured and Raven in the hands of madmen."

"Maybe this Aidan had already turned?" Shea speculated.

Gregori shook his head slowly. "He had not turned then, nor has he turned now. He is powerful, such as Mikhail and I. The world would know if one of our stature had become the most feared creature of all. No, it is not Aidan. In any case, he has a twin brother, one even more powerful, who would know instantly had Aidan turned." Gregori's voice was low and smooth, filled with certainty.

Shea shook her head to rid herself of the hypnotic effect. Gregori's power frightened her. His voice alone could do just about anything, produce any reaction in any of them. No one should have that kind of power.

"So why can we not detect the vampire when he is near?" Mikhail asked no one in particular. "I have scanned the area and can detect none of our kind, not even Byron."

"Shea was able to detect the vampire when I could not," Jacques said. "I was not certain I believed her at first, but I could feel as she did when we merged."

Shea lifted her chin in challenge. "Do you think you can explain how all this was done, healer? How anyone could have done it?"

Gregori turned the full power of his magnetic silver eyes on her. "I can make the earth shake beneath your feet and bring lightning from the sky to do my bidding. I can close off your airway with a thought. I am all things from a mouse to a wolf running free. Is this not enough for you to believe?" he inquired softly.

His voice was a black-magic weapon. That was what Shea believed. She shivered and moved closer to Jacques. They all trusted Gregori, yet wasn't he one of the ancients? They had all told her a vampire could hide itself, appear normal. None of them even suspected him. It was agreed he was the most dangerous, his knowledge acquired unceasingly through the centuries. And he was their healer, had given blood to all of them. Her brain worked at the pieces of the puzzle.

It is impossible. Jacques caught her thoughts.

Why? Shea demanded.

Mikhail would know. I do not know how I know this, but Gregori could not hide this from Mikhail.

She gave an exasperated little sigh.

Jacques hid his grin at her feminine petulance. She really had an aversion to the way Gregori dictated to the women.

"There is one human a few miles away," Mikhail stated. "I can detect no others. He is in the direction of Jacques' old home. Do we go?"

Light was streaking the sky now, gray patches despite the dark, roiling clouds and the steady drizzle of rain. "Go, Mikhail," Raven insisted softly. "You have to. Otherwise I would always feel I killed him. If you do not go, it will be because of me."

"You have to," Shea added, looking into Jacques' black eyes. He did, too; Shea felt it with great conviction. There would come a time when Jacques would remember his childhood, his great friendship with Byron, and how he had backed away from Byron's attempt at reconciliation. He needed to do this for the sake of his own sanity.

I know. His reply was a soft assent in her mind as he shared her thoughts. "I will go, Mikhail," he said aloud. "You stay and protect the women. It is the only way."

"It could very well be a trap," Gregori cautioned. "More than likely it is a trap. Otherwise this would be very careless on the part of one so cunning."

"That's why all of you should go," Raven said. "Shea and I will wait here. We can destroy all evidence of her research while we wait."

Shea could not prevent the gasp that escaped her. She lifted her chin defiantly. She was not going to be intimidated by these powerful creatures. Her eyes flashed from one to the other. "I spent several years of my life gathering that data," she said hotly.

Raven caught her hand and squeezed it in warning. She tugged Shea away from Jacques and right up to the door of the cabin. "All right, Shea, we'll talk about it."

"You are to leave this place and go to safety if the hour becomes too late or you receive warning from us," Mikhail cautioned his lifemate. "No playing the heroine. On this I will have your word."

Raven smiled into his eyes, an intimate, tender acknowledgment. She nodded. "I would never endanger our child, my love."

Mikhail reached out and touched Raven's face, trailing his fingertips tenderly down her skin even as his form wavered, contorted, began to snap and pop. Fur shimmered along his arms, his back. His powerful frame bent, and he leapt away, landed running, a large black wolf.

Shea's eyes widened, astonished at the quick change. Seeing the man become a wolf was incredible. Her heart was slamming so loudly she was afraid it might burst. She was uncertain whether it was from excitement and awe or from sheer terror. *Jacques!*

It is all right, my love. To calm her he leaned close, brushed her forehead with his mouth. *It is the way of our people to utilize the animals around us. It is natural for us. And it helps to protect our skin and eyes from the sun.*

I'm fine now, wild man. It was a shock. Shea breathed deeply to overcome her trembling. She found she was clinging to Raven's hand and self-consciously dropped it.

Jacques dropped another kiss on her forehead before he deliberately walked off the porch and into the dense forest, making sure he was out of her sight before his body began to change.

Gregori's silver eyes moved over both women, then settled on Shea. "The child must be protected. It is no use appealing to Raven for logic, as she has none, and Mikhail is so besotted with her that he does not see his first duty, so it is up to you. For the sake of all of us, you must protect this child. Do you understand?"

Shea felt ensnared by those molten eyes. She might not fully comprehend his reasons, but she felt his genuine urgency. She nodded. "I'll watch over her, healer."

"It is not for my sake only, but for humans and Carpathians alike. This child must live, Shea," he reiterated. "She must."

Shea clearly felt the warning, the plea from his otherwise damned soul. This child was his only hope. For the first time she believed he was not the vampire, that his fear of turning was great, the child his only chance of survival. She nodded, meeting his eyes steadily so that he could see she comprehended the dangers.

Out of respect for her, Gregori, too, walked into the forest out of Shea's sight before shape-shifting and loping away toward the ruins of Jacques' old home.

Raven opened the door to the cabin and stepped out of the storm into the shelter of the room. "You'll get used to it. When I first met Mikhail, I didn't have a clue what he was. I thought he was a psychic like me. Believe me, it was a real shock when I found out. I had no idea such a species even existed."

Shea managed a small smile. To be back in her cabin was comforting, with all her familiar things around her. "I'm still not certain I believe any of this. I keep expecting to wake up in my office back in the States." Snagging a towel, she tossed it to Raven and caught up another for herself. Her hair was dripping wet. It was soothing to her to do something so mundane as towel it dry.

"We live relatively normal lives, Shea. Mikhail and I have a beautiful home in this breathtaking land. Mikhail has several businesses. We have friends, good friends. We travel. What happened to Jacques was a terrible tragedy for all of us. I'm glad he has you now, all of us are." Raven curled up in a chair. Daylight was taking its toll on her pregnant body.

Shea leaned against the bed and studied Raven. She was a beautiful woman, a little pale, with unusual blue-violet eyes. "Jacques is still quite ill. He's struggling to remember his life. It's difficult." She paced restlessly. "I worry about him. He doesn't believe he is always sane. There is such torment in him."

Shea? You need me? Jacques' voice was clear in her mind, anxious, as if he had caught her thoughts.

She realized that Jacques was unable to release her completely. She should have felt resentful, cornered, but the truth was, she felt safe. Already she was becoming accustomed to their closeness. *I'm fine, Jacques. Just take care of yourself.* It was an exhilarating feeling that she could talk across time and space, that she could touch him whenever she wanted or needed, that he would always know when she was troubled.

Shea watched Raven and, noting her elevated breathing, automatically walked over to her to take her pulse. Raven laughed and pulled away. "My husband is being naughty. He likes to keep me thinking about him while he's away from me. I'm fine. They'll drive you crazy, but they're always intriguing and usually lots of fun. It's a good thing, as they have long life spans. Wouldn't it be hell to be stuck for centuries to someone you found incredibly boring?"

"How dangerous is the healer?"

Raven inhaled sharply. "The truth is, Gregori is the most dangerous of all Carpathians. Mikhail thinks Gregori is more powerful than he is, and that's saying quite a bit. He knows things, more than any other. Mikhail fears for him all the time now. If he turned vampire, we'd all be in grave danger. Mikhail loves him. We both do. That's why we decided to try for a baby now rather than later. To produce a lifemate for him. Carpathians never have female children anymore. No one knows why, but the children that are born rarely survive the first year of life. Mikhail and Gregori both believe a human lifemate can produce them a female child, and I guess they're right, since Gregori says this child is a girl. He would know."

"That's why my father wanted a female child so much. My mother never got to tell him she was pregnant, but in her diary she said he had been disappointed when Noelle gave birth to a male child."

"I met your father briefly," Raven said softly. "He was very distraught over Noelle's murder. He wanted to hunt the assassins, but Mikhail told him it was too dangerous, he was too involved. He was sent to sleep for several years."

"He just went to sleep?" Shea was furious for no reason she could actually name. To think of the man sleeping while his wife lay murdered, his mistress pregnant and alone, and someone else raising his son, made her very angry. She had a feeling she would not like her father very much.

"You need to understand these people, Shea, the kind of power they carry, the kind of devastation they're capable of. They can command the land, cause an earthquake that could destroy whole cities. Control is a huge issue with them at all times. Someone like Gregori is a time bomb. He knows it, Mikhail knows it, all of us do. Rand was so distraught, he was dangerous to everyone around him. Mikhail did what he thought was right for the protection of humans and Carpathians alike. Rand obeyed because Mikhail is their chosen leader. He never seemed very attached to anyone, least of all his son. Even now, he is a loner rarely seen. He spends most of his time in the ground."

"And Rand neglected to say anything about my mother to anyone," Shea said bitterly. "My mother's life was destroyed. He could have prevented that."

"I'm sorry, it must have been terrible for you growing up. If your mother was Rand's true lifemate, then she would have been unable to live without him. It is a bonding of the soul." Raven sighed, looked away from the distaste on Shea's face. "Noelle was not Rand's true lifemate. I would like to think she loved him, but by all accounts she was simply obsessed with him. I have no idea why Rand went along with it. Noelle was a foolish woman not to have waited for her true lifemate. Rand is a very good-looking man. She mistook lust for love."

"I have wanted to tell Rand what a worm he is from the first day I ever read my mother's diary. And I don't want to feel about Jacques the way she felt about Rand. Not to the extent that I would neglect a child, live as if I was already dead, just waiting until she was old enough to be on her own."

"Not everyone is strong, Shea," Raven counseled gently. "Look at how long Gregori has lasted without his lifemate. Mikhail and Jacques, Aidan and his brother Julian, have all lasted far longer than most of the others. There have been so many over the years that have turned, not strong enough to hold out. Why? Why Gregori and not this vampire? What happened to your mother would not happen to you because you are not the same person. You're very strong. And your mother had no way of knowing what was happening to her."

Shea paced the length of the room, suddenly restless. The conversation was giving her a knot in her stomach. Was Gregori really capable of creating an earthquake that could destroy cities? Keeping the unborn child safe was even more important than she'd thought. Hundreds, perhaps thousands of lives could depend on it. That was what Gregori was trying to convey to her. He needed this child in order to survive much longer without turning vampire.

"I'm sorry, Shea, you've been thrown into deep water and told to swim without a lesson. I wish I could help you," Raven said softly.

"I feel as if I've been afraid for so long now, I don't know any other way of life," Shea confided. "Jacques depends on me to keep him sane, and now all this is happening. I hope you're right, Raven. I hope I'm very strong."

Chapter Thirteen

Jacques reached the edge of the meadow at the timberline to find Mikhail pacing carefully across a patch of earth. "Wolf traps," he said tersely and continued his inspection.

"Watch for thin wires, perhaps not visible to our eyes," Jacques cautioned. "He must be able to do something to hide the wires from us."

Gregori's form shimmered into solidity. He stood very still, inhaling the early-morning air. "This is one giant trap, my friends. I am very uneasy finding only one human with Byron."

"If Byron is even inside," Jacques agreed. "Where are the others?"

"The vampire must be in the ground, away from the sun," Mikhail said. "There is nothing that could allow him to see the light of day once he has turned."

"So where is the human's partner?" Jacques asked aloud.

Mikhail shrugged uneasily. "I suggest we approach soundlessly and invisible to the human eye."

"Spread out so we can help one another should there be need."

"The wire." Gregori's voice was a mere

thread of sound. "It is strung crisscrossed throughout the meadow at various heights. A thin, garrote-like affair meant to slice through the throat, but also hung in such a way as to cut us in many places, making us weak. Obviously no thought was given to other humans or animals who might venture near this place."

"Ah, yes, I see them now. Very clever, our vampire," Mikhail said. "We are definitely expected, though not, I should think, until tonight. Perhaps his human friends have gone for supplies, thinking they have the entire day to torment Byron without fear of interference."

"I do not know, Mikhail. Something here makes me uneasy," Gregori warned. "Something not quite right."

"I feel it also," Jacques agreed, "although I cannot explain what it is exactly. It is as if this is all prearranged, and we are walking into a spider's web. I know this place. I can feel the pain and torment as if it was happening all over again." And he was, his insides writhing and his gut clenching. It was difficult to maintain his outward calm when his flesh crawled and pain tore at him, splintering his mind so that he didn't know what was real and what was part of his never-ending nightmare.

"Perhaps you are feeling Byron's pain," Mikhail suggested with concern. Jacques' face remained impassive, but the lines in his skin deepened, and crimson smeared his forehead.

Jacques, are you hurt? I will come to you. Shea's soft voice swirled in his mind, caught fragments of his thoughts and seemed to piece him back together. She was, as always, his one and only anchor to reality.

Stay there, but stay connected to me, Shea. Being so close to this place is disorienting me. I need you to keep me together. He was begging, but Jacques had no choice. She was his lifemate, and her presence in his mind could mean the difference between success and failure to their mission. He did not want to be the cause of the others' deaths.

A grim smile touched Gregori's sensual mouth, his silver eyes humorless and pierced with dangerous light. "They mean to capture us, Mikhail. Us, the two most powerful of our kind. Perhaps they need a real demonstration in power."

Jacques glanced at Mikhail uneasily. Maybe it was the way his body was remembering every burn, every slash. With age the pain became more intense, if one could feel. Unlike a vampire, a Carpathian was capable of tremendous sensation. Jacques had suffered what no man, human or Carpathian, should have endured. It wasn't even in the name of science, just a sadist bent on inflicting as much pain as possible.

Come back, Jacques. Shea's voice was filled with concern.

I cannot. I cannot leave Byron to suffer my fate.

I can feel your pain, Jacques. You are having a hard time concentrating on what you're doing. Your mind is very scattered. Of what use are you to Byron if you get caught? Come back to me.

I will get him out of there. Just stay with me, Shea. Jacques concentrated on her, held her strength and warmth in his mind to fight the growing pain. The ground seemed to roll beneath his feet; the rain pounded down on him. His flesh was burning; he could smell it. Cuts opened up and bled freely. He caught at his chest as pain ripped through him, tearing muscles and bone. His throat closed off; breathing became impossible. His heart pounded until he felt it had to explode.

"Jacques!" Gregori gripped his arm. "It is part of the trap set for you specifically. The vampire knew you would come, and you are caught in the web. He is amplifying your own fears and the pain you suffered. He is not here; it is merely a warp you are trapped in. Know it is not real, and fight your way out."

"I do not understand." Pinpricks of scarlet dotted Jacques' body, stained his shirt. His eyes were alive with pain and madness.

I do. Shea snatched at the information in his mind. She wrapped him in the warmth of her love. *Feel me, Jacques. Concentrate only on me and what you feel when we touch, when we kiss.* She pictured it in her head, him holding her so possessively, so tenderly, his mouth finding hers hungrily. The way she felt, hot and silken with heat, needing and wanting him. Her mouth as hungry as his. Her hands tangled in his thick hair. *Feel me, Jacques.* Her whisper moved over his skin like the touch of her fingers.

Jacques narrowed his focus until he blocked out everything but the smell and taste of her, the touch of her fingers, her soft, sexy voice. She became his world, was his world, would always be. Nothing else was real. She was his heart and his very breath. Her breathing regulated his back to a steady in and out. Her heart brought the rhythm of his slowly back to a normal pattern. His skin was on fire, but with sensual hunger rather than the pain of torture.

Her breath seemed to warm his ear, his mind. *I love you, Jacques. Do what you must, then hurry home to me.* She released him with great reluctance, the warmth of her love lingering behind.

Jacques shook his head to bring himself back to the present situation. Almost at once the earth moved beneath his feet, and the pain tried to hammer at him. But the vampire would not snag him twice in the same trap. He wrenched himself forward, concentrating on the way Shea's mouth tasted, the curve of her hip beneath his hand, the way her eyes lit up just before she laughed. He held her close to his heart, kept the vision of her wild mane of hair in front of him as he pushed his way through the warp and out into the open land.

"Good," Gregori approved. "But this one is very adept. I am uneasy over the way this is going, Mikhail. Let us take to the air above the wires and approach from different directions. I will go in first. Our people cannot afford to lose either of you."

"Gregori," Mikhail reminded him softly, "if the child is your lifemate, and you do something careless, you are condemning her to death. Keep that in mind when you enter this place of madness."

Gregori's silver eyes slashed at his old

friend. "Do you think I would chance harming her in any way? I have waited several lifetimes for her. These humans are nothing. They have persecuted our people for far too long. I mean it to stop."

Mikhail nodded, his dark eyes, so like his brother's, black ice. "You are up to this, Jacques?"

Jacques' smile was a humorless promise of retaliation. "Have no worries about me. I am looking forward to this."

Mikhail sighed. "Two bloodthirsty savages thinking they are in the dark ages."

Jacques exchanged a humorless grin with Gregori. "The dark ages were not such a bad time. At least justice could be dispensed easily without worrying about what the women would think."

"You both have gone soft," Gregori snickered. "No wonder our people have such problems. The women are ruling, and you two besotted idiots just follow along."

Jacques' solid form wavered, became transparent. "We will see who proves to be the soft one, healer." His body completely disappeared from sight.

Mikhail glanced at Gregori, shrugged, then followed suit. None of this was to his liking. Gregori was a time bomb waiting to explode. And only God knew what Jacques was capable of. It seemed the worst possible time to confront an enemy, just as they were weakening from the light of day.

Gregori waited until Mikhail and Jacques had disappeared before allowing his body to dissolve. He launched himself skyward, wincing as the sun's light, penetrating the dark clouds, hit his eyes. He cursed silently. Raven was alone with a woman who knew next to nothing about their people's capabilities. She was very weak. The child was his only hope, and it was stupidity to rescue a Carpathian male who was on the verge of turning. A few more years and Gregori would be hunting him.

Jacques moved across the meadow, high above the gleaming wires. Water danced off the thin strands like crystal droplets. He moved around the blackened ruins in a slow circle, looking for the entrance hidden in the ground. It bothered him that he didn't know exactly where it was, or that the others might know before him. It made him feel as if he were ill, totally incompetent.

Soft laughter sent warmth curling through his body. *Since when have you ever been incompetent? You made me crazy even when you were lying allegedly helpless, in bed. The first time you kissed me, I forgot my own name. That is not incompetent.*

Jacques found the tension easing out of his body. Shea had a way of doing that for him with just the sound of her laughter, her warmth. *I am looking for the entrance to the cellar. The ground appears to be completely undisturbed.*

As I walked across the meadow and approached the burned area, the stone fireplace was on my right. I circled the perimeter from the right side. The door was buried in the dirt. I couldn't see it, but I felt it with my hand. I remember the fireplace was to my right by about ten feet or so.

Thanks, little red hair. Jacques crouched in the rain, ran his hand along the mud-slick soil.

"There is something over here," Mikhail said softly, his eyes searching for a hidden trap. His body hovered over the area as he examined the ground. "There are marks on the ground, as if a branch has been dragged over it. Dirt and rocks have been scattered over the spot."

"Do not touch it!" Jacques ordered sharply. "The fireplace should be to your right and farther out."

"You remember this?" Gregori asked skeptically.

"Shea remembers. It must be another trap. The rain would have removed those marks."

"They did not have much time to set such traps," Mikhail observed. "Byron was taken no more than an hour ago, if that."

"Perhaps we are underestimating this vampire, Mikhail. I could manufacture such traps, and so could you. Aidan and Julian could do so, and no doubt Jacques. Who else do we know who has this kind of power?" Gregori asked softly.

"There are few others over the age of six hundred years," Mikhail said.

"Perhaps this is a crime of hate more than of age," Jacques ventured. "What was done to me was done with the idea of causing as much suffering as I could take before death claimed me. That is a crime of hatred, one of revenge."

Gregori and Mikhail exchanged a quick, knowing look. "Of course, you have to be right, Jacques," Mikhail agreed for both of the ancients. "A vampire would avoid us, not try to draw us to him. So whom did you anger enough to warrant this much hatred?"

Jacques shrugged calmly. His own hatred was deep and smoldering, a rage so ingrained that he knew the demon would rise within him the moment he encountered any of those involved in his torture and imprisonment. Whoever hated him so much had created a like feeling within him, hatred that not only matched but surpassed anything the vampire might feel. "You know more of my past than I do, but it really does not matter, as long as he believes I wronged him," Jacques said. "It is here. The door is here."

"The human is dozing." Mikhail probed the mind of the unseen man carefully. "He is supremely confident that he will be undisturbed."

Gregori, too, was probing the human. "I like none of this, Mikhail. It seems too easy. The vampire knows we can travel in the early morning hours. Our powers might not be at full strength, but even diminished, we can handle humans easily."

"You stay out of sight, Gregori, watch our backs," Mikhail cautioned. "I will instruct the human to open the cellar and allow us in. Jacques and I will test for a trap."

"Jacques and I will go inside, Mikhail. We cannot risk your life. You know that." Gregori did not wait for a response. He had spent most of his life guarding Mikhail, the dispenser of justice for his people. Even with his lifemate so close to existence, Gregori would not back away from this duty. He seized the human's mind with ease, demanding information.

Jeff Smith woke abruptly, a pain in his

head, uneasiness gripping his very soul. In his mind was something that did not belong to him, something powerful that demanded every detail of the past few days, insisted on a blow-by-blow replay of the past few hours. He tried to resist, but the thing was far too powerful to ignore. He went over every detail. The vampire bringing the paralyzed Carpathian, Donnie burning and slicing the victim, Slovensky laughing and egging him on. The vampire standing emotionless, watching with empty eyes and frankly scaring the hell out of Jeff. Donnie and Slovensky going for supplies, whispering to each other and the vampire.

The vampire promised no one would be able to find them; his spells would safeguard the makeshift dungeon until nightfall. The other vampires would be trapped in the ground until night. Jeff was safe and could torment their victim at will. Smith wished he had the woman, the red-haired doctor. He had delicious thoughts of what he would do with her for long hours at a time.

Jacques made a sound, not aloud but in his mind, and immediately broke all contact with Shea. She could not witness the demon rising in him. Already fangs were exploding in his mouth, and the red haze demanding a kill was spewing upward with violent, murderous intent. A low, warning growl escaped him, and he hissed at Gregori to warn him off his kill.

Mikhail moved to intercept his brother. "We have need of this man."

Gregori placed himself firmly between the two Carpathians, recognizing immediately that Jacques' tattered mind was focused on only one thing. *Do not try to interfere, Mikhail. He will attack you. He is not healed, and he is very dangerous. We cannot control him, and he has shut out the woman. She is his only hold on reality. We cannot save this human.* He shrugged as if to say it didn't matter to him one way or the other. And it didn't. If Mikhail had not been with them, Gregori would have already dispensed his own brand of justice.

Smith felt something take a firmer hold on his mind. This was not the same as the demand for information. This was an attack by an alien being, a grip of steel that felt as if it would crush his very skull. Smith cried out, whirled to face the broken man lying so seemingly helpless before him. The eyes were open, staring at him, pain-filled, malevolent even, but his victim appeared near death. The vampire had assured Jeff that this one was quite paralyzed in body and mind, that he could feel the pain inflicted upon him but could not cry out for help to others of his kind or harm the humans in any way.

Smith picked up a knife, still crimson with the victim's blood, and took a step toward the bloody coffin. Instantly he was slammed against the wall by an unseen force, and the knife twisted toward him. Screaming, Jeff dropped the weapon. His head buzzed with pain. Whatever it was, was outside, demanding that he open the door. He clapped both hands to his head, trying to resist the compulsion, but his feet were already moving, obeying the unseen dictator.

The being snarled in impatience and applied more pressure. Jeff knew he was letting in his own death as he made his way up the rotting stairs to the heavy door. His every step brought those razor-sharp teeth closer and closer to his throat. But he couldn't stop himself. The being sent the clear picture to his brain, yet he couldn't stop himself. His hand was on the door. He shoved.

The wooden door exploded upward, and two clawed hands seized him, dragged him into the pouring rain. Thunder cracked, and a bolt of lightning hit a tree, split it in two with a deafening sound. A shower of sparks erupted. The earth fell away as Jeff was jerked skyward. He recognized the face now, the man he had once tortured for days. The man they had purposely buried alive seven years earlier.

Those black eyes had promised death, had haunted him for years, and now they were ice and fire, rimmed with red. Teeth gleamed white, sharp and dripping. Jeff screamed as the hot breath burned his neck. He felt the teeth tearing into his flesh, exposing his jugular. Hot liquid spilled down his chest, and he looked down to see his own blood spraying out. And then the creature was consuming him while his heart stuttered to stay alive and his mind cried out for another chance.

All around him the ghosts of the women he had raped and killed, the men Donnie had encouraged him to torture, floated into his mind. The rain beat down on his upturned face. The creature dropped him into the mud with a sickening thud. Jeff squirmed, tried to crawl, turned his head to see a wolf approaching from the timberline. He tried to make a sound, but there was only a gasping wheeze.

Jacques crouched down and looked him in the eye, completely dispassionate, watching the glaze creeping into the depths of Jeff Smith's staring eyes. "You go to a hell you deserve, human," he whispered contemptuously into the dying man's mind.

Jacques stayed crouched beside the man, red flames burning in his eyes, the demon in him roaring and hungry for retribution. He knew Byron was trapped in the cellar, that this human and his friends had tortured the Carpathian male just as they had tortured him years earlier. Adrenaline and power pumped through his body.

Mikhail paced back and forth nervously. Jacques was more animal than man, acting on the age-old instinct of the predator. Low growls continually rumbled in his throat, something Mikhail was certain his brother was not even aware of.

Jacques bent low, caught the bloodstained shirt, and dragged the human closer, his need for death erupting. The call was wild and strong. Every word Shea had spoken concerning this man and his partner and what they had promised to do to her echoed in his mind. The need of the Carpathian male to protect his mate and the hunger for retribution urged him to feel every moment of the taking of life.

Mikhail could see the war raging in Jacques. It would be a difficult thing for him to live with, the taking of blood during a kill. Gregori and he had both done it, but the rush was addicting and dangerous. In Jacques' state, it could be forever damaging. He approached cautiously. "Jacques, do not do this thing. You have too much to lose."

Jacques whirled on him, baring teeth, a warning rumble bringing Gregori to once again insert his body between them. "Leave him, Mikhail. If he makes the kill and consumes the rest of the idiot's blood, it is only what they owe him. He is no longer a child you must protect."

Mikhail swore, angry with Gregori for dismissing the urgency of the act. Too many had been lost at just such a moment. Mikhail had thought Jacques lost to him once; he did not want it again. He also knew Gregori well enough to know he would have to try to go through the ancient's body to get to his brother. Gregori believed Jacques a danger to all of them. With a sigh he resigned himself to the inevitable.

Gregori watched the fight go out of Mikhail and turned his attention to Jacques, simply waiting for the decision to be made.

Jacques smelled the beckoning blood. His hunger was sated, but the taste of fear and adrenaline, the need for revenge, were burning in him. The rushing high consumed him, yet the cool wind that was Shea anchored him to reality. His body shook

431

with the need to consume while he killed, to feel the life seep out of the man. Reluctantly, he allowed the man's shirt to slip from his fingers. Jeff Smith could die at his own pace, and Jacques would forego the ultimate power of the kill. He took a slow, deep breath and moved away from the broken body, watching his brothers, the wolves, move toward his victim. He shook off the demon, fighting every inch of the way to get himself back under control. It took long moments before he was able to see the two Carpathians as friends instead of enemies.

Gregori nodded at him, then turned and entered the cellar cautiously, inhaling the stale air, careful of any hidden traps. The place smelled of blood and fear, sweat, and the stench of burned flesh. Byron lay in a blood-splattered coffin, his body a thousand cuts and raw, charred flesh. His eyes found Gregori immediately, became anxious and desperate. Gregori tried to reach him on the common path of Carpathians, but Byron's mind was frozen; it was impossible for him to move or communicate. But for the desperation in his eyes, Gregori would have dismissed the cellar as harmless to any of their kind.

Jacques entered the place of death uneasily, the stench sickening him. He caught the warning Gregori silently sent him and did not approach the form in the coffin. It was too easy. The vampire had known they would come, and Jeff Smith had been an unsuspecting sacrifice. The other two humans had probably known it also.

What do you think? Gregori wanted to know.

Jacques had to fight to keep himself under control. His body shook continually, and the need to kill was still burning brightly in him. It was hard to think, to concentrate. He was aware of the wolves outside and the joy in them as they tore into the carcass. He felt connected to their simple way of life. They called to him to join them, to hunt and feed.

What do you think, Jacques? Deliberately Gregori used his name to call him back from the need to run wild, to hunt and kill and be truly free.

Something is not right. Jacques had no idea what it was, but he was certain there was hidden danger.

Byron's eyes were eloquent, obviously trying desperately to communicate something. As Gregori stepped closer, he seemed more agitated, the blood spewing from his wounds.

"Be calm, Byron, go to sleep. No vampire is going to catch us in his trap. Mikhail waits outside. There are three of us." Gregori's voice was beautifully pitched, pure and soothing. "Drift off, slow your heart, and allow your body to hibernate. I will take you somewhere safe to heal. My blood is powerful. You will heal quickly."

The blood pumped out as Byron became even more upset. Gregori's voice softened until it was the wind and the water, the earth itself. "Jacques has exchanged blood with you many times. He can give you his if you prefer to safeguard your pact with him. Do not fear for us; there is no trap the vampire can devise that I cannot unravel. Sleep now, and let us get on with it." The voice was a command.

Although Byron's mind was impossible to control, the voice made anyone hearing it want to comply. Byron was exhausted and wracked with pain. He felt his hold on consciousness slipping away. His life was draining away, and he couldn't convey to them the monstrous, diabolical plot the vampire had outlined to him as he lay so helpless. He could only hope they would figure it out in time. Byron shut down his heart to stop the draining of his blood. His lungs labored for a moment, then, with a little sigh, gave up, and he lay quiet, as if dead.

Gregori breathed a sigh of relief. "I could feel his pain."

"I have felt it before," Jacques replied grimly. "He is better off not feeling or knowing until we can see to his wounds."

"He does not want my blood," Gregori pointed out in his soft, calm tone. Nothing ruffled him; nothing moved him to emotion. He killed or healed as calmly as he talked.

"I am aware that I have entered into a pact with him. I will honor it," Jacques said. "Let us find this trap so we can take him out of here. This place is evil."

Gregori was examining the coffin itself, looking for hidden trip wires or a bomb of some kind. He ran his hand carefully along the outside of the crude wooden box. "The human left here knew nothing; they set him up as expendable. This has to be a death trap." Very cautiously Gregori inspected the body lying so still. "He is in bad shape. He should have put himself to sleep immediately. He must have wanted to die quickly, or he knew they were expecting us and wanted to warn us. Whatever the answer, the day is creeping upon us fast, and we must get him to a cave where we can supply him with blood and the healing earth he needs."

"Stand back, healer, and allow me to lift him. He is my friend, although I do not remember him. I can do no other than honor my commitment to him."

"Go slowly, Jacques. The bomb, if there is one, must be beneath him." Gregori, instead of moving away, moved closer so that he could grab anything that looked harmful and dispense with it if needed.

Hurry, Gregori. The light grows stronger, and I am uneasy, Mikhail instructed from outside.

Jacques very carefully felt under Byron's body, a slow, cautious sweep, taking his time as if the morning light was not affecting any of them. The smell of blood assailed his nostrils, and the stench of charred flesh made his stomach lurch. Near Byron's hips he felt the smallest of resistance. Instantly he stopped. "It is here, Gregori, a trip wire, razor sharp. It is cutting into my wrist. Can you see it? I dare not move until we know if it is connected to some kind of explosive device."

Gregori crouched low and examined the intricate wiring. "A crude bomb, rather pointless. The vampire knows how easy it would be for me to dismantle it."

"Perhaps this is a present from the two humans. It is a rather human trap, after all," Jacques commented, waiting patiently for Gregori to deal with the problem. His superior strength allowed him to hold Byron's dead weight with one hand and not notice any strain. "Is there a second device? Perhaps the first one is really a dummy."

Gregori was more than uneasy now. He was a master of deceit, of cunning. This was far too elaborate a plot to have been set up in a matter of an hour. This had been planned for a long time. Someone had waited for the opportune time to carry it out. For what purpose? Mikhail felt uneasy also, as did Jacques. Something here was very wrong, but what was it? Puzzled, he examined the device again, not wanting to miss anything.

Chapter Fourteen

Shea stared out the window of the cabin into the driving rain. The droplets looked like tiny silver threads streaming from the gray sky. She shivered for no reason and crossed her arms protectively across her breasts.

"What's wrong, Shea?" Raven asked softly, not wanting to intrude.

"Jacques just cut himself off completely from me." Shea swallowed hard. All this time she had been so certain she needed her freedom from the continuous bond between them, but now that Jacques had withdrawn, she felt almost as if she couldn't breathe. "I can't reach him. He won't let me."

Raven sat up straighter, her face going very still. *Mikhail?*

Leave me for now, he ordered. Raven caught the impression of fear for Jacques' sanity, the swirling, violent rage that had welled up in the Carpathian males just before Mikhail broke the mind contact with her. She cleared her throat cautiously. "Sometimes they try to protect us from the harsher aspects of their lives."

Shea whirled around to face her, eyebrows up. "*Their* lives? Aren't we bound to them? Haven't they done something to irrevocably bind us to them so that there is no way to leave them? It isn't just *their* lives. They brought us into this, and they have no right to arbitrarily decide what we can and can't know."

Raven swept a hand through her blue-black hair. "I felt the same way for a long time." She sighed. "The truth is, I still feel the same way. But we persist in judging them by our human standards. They are a different species of people altogether. They are predators and have a completely different view of right and wrong."

Raven shoved a hand through her hair, frowning as she did so. "I wanted to wait to have a baby. But Mikhail has been noticing differences in Gregori, and we both knew he needed some hope to continue. It worries me, though, because I still have such a hard time fitting into their world."

Shea crossed the room and sat on the bed beside Raven's chair. She could hear the fear in the woman's voice, and something in her instantly responded. "At least there are two of us now. We can gang up on them."

Raven laughed softly. "It's such a fight all the time, maintaining any kind of control in my life with Mikhail. I have this feeling he's only going to get worse with this pregnancy."

"And you're obviously going to have the healer on your back," Shea pointed out. "He's more daunting than Jacques' brother."

Raven sighed. "I wish I could say that wasn't true, but he's going to be horrible, really horrible. I can't blame him, though."

"I don't understand what he meant exactly, but I could tell it was imperative I take good care of you."

Raven tucked her feet beneath her. "Carpathians rarely have children. There's something that prevents them from having a female child when they do conceive."

Shea's mind instantly focused on amassing data. "Can you tell me more?"

Raven obliged. "About eighty percent of all children conceived are male. No one knows why. Only about seventy percent of pregnancies are carried to term. Most miscarry, and it isn't even within the first three months. It can happen at any time. Of those children born, only a handful survive the first year. Again, no one knows why. The last female child to survive was born over five hundred years ago." Raven sighed. "The men are desperate. Mikhail and Gregori have a theory that only human women with true psychic ability can make the change and have the right chemistry to be a lifemate. Even if they're right, you can see the magnitude of the problem. Without women and children, the species cannot survive. The males turn vampire because they have no hope."

"Perhaps it's nature's way of population control. They're able to live so long," Shea mused, more to herself than to Raven.

"The species will be extinct soon if they can't find out what's wrong," Raven said sadly. "Gregori is a great man. He's given so much to his people and suffered for so long. He deserves a better fate than turning vampire and being hated and feared by the world. Out of respect, Mikhail would never allow any other to hunt and destroy him, yet doing so himself would be agony. I'm not even certain anyone could actually destroy one such as Gregori alone. It would be a terrible thing for Gregori to be hunted by the very people he protected and healed."

"Gregori must have researched the mystery of why there've been no female children for centuries. Surely he must have found a reason after all this time. At least he must have a few ideas." Shea itched to come up with a hypothesis of her own. She suddenly wanted to talk to Gregori, hear all the data he had collected over the centuries.

"He certainly has worked on it. Maybe it

will help for the two of you to get together and hash it out," Raven said tactfully. "But you know, Shea, none of the information on our people can fall into the wrong hands. Any documentation on our race can be dangerous. For the good of our people, you must destroy all your research."

"It isn't as if I came up with any data on Carpathians, Raven. I never even considered such a race of people. I was looking for an answer to a blood disorder. I knew people in this region had long been accused of being vampires. I think a lot of legends have a grain of truth in them somewhere, so it stood to reason something was going on here. That and the fact that my father was from this area made me decide to come here and see what I could find out. Honestly, Raven, there's nothing in my records to indicate a separate species of people with the kind of power these Carpathians wield. Everything is purely medical."

"It's still dangerous to us. If it falls into the hands of these so-called scientists, they might figure things out." Raven put a hand on Shea's arm. "I'm sorry, I know your records probably represent years of work, but, really, the work was for yourself, and you have the answers to your questions."

"The work was for all those people who

442

have the same blood disorder as I do."

"It isn't a blood disorder, and they don't need a cure. They're a totally separate species, not human, and they have evolved into a very efficient species. They work hard and contribute much to society, but they would never be accepted by the human race. If you want to do medical research, then research a real problem, like why we can't carry babies to term. Why our babies die. Why our women don't conceive female children. That would be an invaluable service. Believe me, all Carpathians would be eternally grateful. I would be grateful." She put her hands protectively over her stomach. "If I do carry this baby to term, I couldn't bear to lose her after her birth." Raven suddenly sat up straight. "I bet you could do it, Shea — find the answer for all of us. I bet you could."

"Do something Gregori has failed to do after all these years? I doubt it. He seems very thorough to me." Shea was skeptical.

"Gregori was the one who came up with the idea about human psychic women, and I'm certain he's right. You and your mother support his theory. He also thinks there's something in the Carpathian woman's chemistry that makes it nearly impossible for the female chromosome to beat out the male."

"Wouldn't you know he'd think it was the woman," Shea sniffed contemptuously. "More than likely the men determine the sex, just like in humans, and they just can't produce girls." She grinned at Raven. "The men bring about their own destruction."

Raven laughed. "Mikhail would never let me speak to you again if he could hear us. He thinks I'm too independent and disrespectful already." She shrugged carelessly. "It's probably true, but it's a lot of fun. I love the way he gets that pained look on his face. He's so cute."

"Cute? I'll bet he likes that description." Shea got up and restlessly paced the floor. She was feeling uneasy without Jacques' touch and didn't want Raven to notice it. He had withdrawn only a short time ago, yet she felt uncomfortable, more than simply uneasy. She longed for the comfort of his mind touch. "Maybe you're right. Maybe I should destroy these papers. I'd hate to think that disgusting Don Wallace would find a way to use them against anyone. That man is a sociopath. I mean it, Raven, he's truly sick."

Reluctantly Shea began to gather up reams of paper and carry them to the fireplace. Her notebooks she hesitated over. She had collected a tremendous amount of folklore, beautiful stories really, along with scientific data. She hated to lose them. Taking a huge breath, she tossed them into the hearth as well and threw a match in after them.

She had to fight back tears. They seemed to burn her eyes and clog her throat until it was nearly impossible to breathe. And she knew it wasn't just losing the papers; it was Jacques' absence from her mind. She felt utterly alone, desolate. She found it harder and harder to concentrate without his presence. *When had she become so needy?* She hated the feeling of emptiness, barrenness. Where was he? Maybe something had happened to him. Maybe he was dead and had left her completely alone.

"Shea!" Raven said sharply. "Snap out of it. You aren't alone. Nothing is wrong with Jacques. It's amazing his silence is affecting you so severely when you've only been out of contact a short time."

Shea rubbed her arms, suddenly cold. Her stomach was rebelling, and it was still hard to catch her breath. "I guess it's because Jacques never leaves me. He can't take being alone."

Raven's eyes widened. "Never?"

Shea shook her head. "I thought it would drive me crazy at first. Most of the time I didn't recognize it, but he would know things I was thinking, and I would realize he'd been in my mind the entire time. He was alone so long, he needed constant contact with me to keep him sane."

"This must be terrible for him," Raven said. "To break contact with you, he must be in the middle of something big. Mikhail is blocking me out, too, and so is Gregori. But don't you worry, we'll be fine together. And we would still know if something were to happen to them."

Shea powered up the generator so she could turn on her computer. She felt very uneasy, restless, even alarmed. "Raven, you don't feel something is wrong, do you?" She typed in her password and waited for her files to appear on the screen.

"No, but I'm used to touching Mikhail occasionally for reassurance and letting him go. We've been together long enough to develop a kind of routine. I touch him, and whether or not he allows me into his mind, I know he's there. You could try that."

Shea concentrated for a moment on giving the commands to destroy her data. With a sigh she paced back to Raven. "It's not that kind of uneasiness. It's something else. At first I thought it was because I wasn't touching Jacques' mind, but I don't think so anymore. I have the feeling something evil is watching us."

Raven sent her mind seeking, scanning the surrounding woods carefully. There were deer a mile away. The three Carpathian men were even farther afield. "Rabbits, fox, wolves several miles out, but nothing scary that I can detect," she assured her softly.

Shea picked up the shotgun and cracked it open to make certain it was loaded. "I feel almost sick, Raven. Something's out there."

"It's the separation from Jacques. The first time it happened with Mikhail and me, I almost didn't make it through the night. Honestly, Shea, separation is very difficult at the best of times, let alone in the morning hours when we're growing weaker and we know the men are in danger. We may have been human, but we are their lifemates. Naturally we miss their mind touch."

Shea wanted to believe her, but, just as she had felt an evil presence in the forest, she felt they were in danger now. She looked at Raven. This woman was important to all of them. Shea had promised Gregori she would keep Raven safe, and she was not about to be unprepared. "Maybe," she agreed softly. Nevertheless, she walked to the door, opened it, and stepped onto the porch to survey the woods.

Nothing. The rain drove down harder, and in the distance Shea could hear the rumble of thunder. Lightning flashed in the sky. She found herself shivering, and her finger absently sought the trigger on the gun. Annoyed with herself, she went back inside, set the shotgun beneath the window, and worked at controlling herself. Her behavior was unacceptable to her. She could not believe she needed Jacques so much that she would be physically ill and have such an impression of danger because she was without his mind touch. Shea did not want to think it was an illusion, a trick of her mind, yet it seemed the lesser of two evils.

"You're very pale, Shea. You need to feed," Raven said carefully, knowing from her own experience what a touchy subject it could be.

Shea swallowed hard. She was dizzy with weakness. Maybe that was what was wrong; maybe it had nothing to do with Jacques. "I know. I just can't face it yet. I know I have to come to terms with it eventually, but it's still all too new."

"You can't see yourself biting someone's neck, is that it?" Raven laughed softly. "I can't do it either. Yuck. Well . . ." She blushed, a faint pink stain spreading across her creamy skin. "Mikhail has a way of making it . . ." She trailed off.

Shea found herself blushing, too. "Yeah, I know what you mean. Jacques seems to have that same way about him." Her hand curled around the stock of the gun again, and she tried to quiet the pounding of her heart. Her mouth was dry with fear.

Shea stole a glance at Raven. She was curled up peacefully, almost serene. Silently Shea cursed. Something was terribly wrong; she knew it deep within her, yet she couldn't explain it adequately to herself or to Raven. "Have you ever tried to leave Mikhail?"

Raven glanced up, startled. A soft smile curved her mouth. "You can't leave your lifemate. One, he knows what you're thinking, and two, he can find you wherever you are. Besides, you can't be away from him for very long — it's too uncomfortable, both physically and mentally. If you left Jacques, what you're feeling right now would not stop, it would only get worse. You can't leave him, Shea. You have to learn how to live with him."

"I know. I don't really want to leave," Shea admitted. She was close to tears. The feeling of dark malevolence was becoming stronger, yet she still couldn't explain it. She felt very mixed up. She wanted Jacques close to her, but this world was so frightening and bizarre. She was completely out of her element.

Raven immediately jumped to her feet and put an arm around Shea, misunderstanding her distress. "He doesn't hurt you, does he?" She was examining the faded bruises and wounds on Shea's neck. "He did this, didn't he?"

Self-consciously, Shea put a hand to her throat to cover the marks. "He didn't mean to. He doesn't always know what he's doing. But he isn't the type of man to abuse a woman. I'm in his mind enough to know that. I'm not a woman who would take it, either." She let the other woman hug her, needing the comfort. "It's just that I'm afraid all the time. Afraid of everything. That isn't like me at all. And I cry. I never cry." Whatever was stalking them was very close now. She wanted to scream for Jacques.

"You've been through a traumatic time, Shea, and so has your body. You're worn out, and you need sustenance." Raven released her and took a step away. "Gregori is a great healer. I know you think he could be the vampire — it's there in your face when you look at him — but he would give his life for you, for me, for Mikhail. He's a great man. He could help you so much if you'd let him."

"He's the scariest man I've ever met," Shea admitted. "If I had a child, a daughter, I would not want that man to be her husband."

"But then, you don't know that much about lifemates. If my daughter is his lifemate and chooses him — and it will be her choice, despite what my husband and Gregori think — she'd be the safest woman in the world. And once she learned to manage him, the happiest."

"You have more faith than I do."

"That's because I've known them longer. Give yourself some time, and for heaven's sake put that gun down. There's nothing out there," Raven admonished. "You're just nervous because Jacques isn't with you."

Lightning crashed close, and the cabin shuddered beneath a deafening roar of thunder. Raven swung around and paced to a chair. "Something's going on for sure. That's one of ours doing that."

Shea's hand went to her throat. She could not shake the feeling of impending doom. She turned to Raven. "What do you mean, one of ours?" Why had she agreed to stay and protect Raven? Something evil was watching them, and she couldn't ferret it out. *Jacques, where are you?*

"The lightning and thunder," Raven replied easily. "One of our males is upset."

"Great. Tantrums, that's all we need," Shea said moodily. Jacques hadn't answered her. Where was he? Couldn't he feel her need?

Raven laughed. "They are great for that, aren't they?"

The door banged open, the wood, so recently repaired, splintering. Shea swung around, instinctively taking a stride to place herself between the entrance and Raven. Framed in the doorway was Don Wallace, a scattergun in his hand, an older man behind him. Shea heard the maniacal laughter of the two men and saw the malice and loathing in their eyes.

Jacques! She screamed his name even as the orange blossom burst from the muzzle of the gun. The wicked stings hitting her arm and shoulder spun her around, and she reeled into Raven. Raven took the main burst of the gun and was flung backward nearly into the wall. Shea landed in a pool of blood. It was everywhere, beneath her, on Raven's chest and stomach, leaking onto the wooden floor. Raven was still and lifeless, her face white, her pulse nonexistent when Shea tried to find it.

Don Wallace seized her by her hair and dragged her away from the body. He was laughing as he contemptuously kicked Raven's leg out of his way. "I knew I'd get you, Doc. Small world, isn't it?"

Jacques! My God, he's killed Raven! Gregori! I'm sorry, I couldn't save her. Shea was fighting, kicking and punching, and didn't even realize it until Wallace hit her repeatedly in the face.

"Shut up! Stop that screaming or I'll knock you out." He hit her twice more. "Damn vampires think they're so smart. It was so easy, wasn't it, Uncle Eugene?"

Shea was sobbing uncontrollably, almost immune to the pain of Wallace dragging her by her injured arm. Warmth stirred in her mind. *Shea? We need you to look at the man holding you, look around the room slowly and picture everything exactly the way you see it.* Jacques' voice was calm and unruffled, no hint of rage or anger, simply a cool wind of logic. *We are all three linked and can aid you.*

Raven is dead! They shot her! she cried hysterically in her mind, afraid to move or call further attention to herself, lest she endanger Jacques in some way.

Just do as I tell you, love. Look around the room. Study your enemy and picture every detail in your mind so that we can see him. Jacques was tranquil, breathing steadily and slowly to help her control her own breathing. *Block out everything else. What they say does not matter. What they do does not matter. Give us the data we need.*

Shea took a deep breath, closed her eyes, and tried to do as Jacques had instructed. It was difficult to overcome the horror of Raven's violent death, the loss of the all-important baby. She blocked out the sounds of the malicious laughter, the sexual threats and innuendoes. Wallace was standing over her, one hand twisted in her thick mane of hair, the other hand deliberately digging into the bloody wounds in her arm. She pushed aside the pain of her injuries, the throbbing in her face.

Shea opened her eyes and looked first at Raven's broken body. The blood lay like a thick red pool around her. Her blue-black hair lay across one cheek like a shawl. Shea made herself move on. Her gaze swept the room, settled on Eugene Slovensky. He was kneeling beside Raven, examining her to assure himself she was dead. He stood up, backed away two feet, cleared his throat, and spat at the body. He reached behind him for a canvas bag and yanked it open. Gleefully he seized a thick, pointed stake and held it out for her to see.

"Spawn of the devil," he whispered insanely. "Bride to the one who killed my brother. You die this day while he sleeps unaware. I am fortunate that the Vulture hates you and the one that created you as much as I hate you both. I don't know why he wants the other female alive, but again, our wishes coincide."

"Not quite, Uncle Eugene. We keep this one for ourselves. You promised we would kill the Vulture like the others this time," Don Wallace protested.

Slovensky lifted the stake higher, poised it over Raven's breast. "This gives me more pleasure than you will ever know."

"No!" Shea attempted to launch herself at Slovensky, unable to bear the thought of them defiling Raven's body with a crude wooden stake.

Focus! Gregori snapped, his voice so powerful, even over the distance, that it brought Shea up short, where all Don Wallace's slaps and punches had hardly fazed her.

Shea stared at Slovensky, the picture etched in her mind. She saw the glee in his face, the hatred, the sick, perverse pleasure he was deriving as he held the stake aloft above Raven's body. Then suddenly she saw his expression change from pleasure to alarm. His face grew crimson, then a dark shade of purple. He coughed, and blood trickled from his mouth, his nose. He coughed again, and his arm fell to his side, the stake dropping from nerveless fingers.

"Uncle Eugene?" The grin faded from Wallace's mouth. He took a step toward his uncle. "What is it?"

Slovensky tried to speak, but the only sound that emerged was a wheezing groan. More blood bubbled up around his mouth. Red foam dribbled onto his chin.

Shea looked away, her stomach lurching.

Look at him! Gregori made his order impossible to ignore. One of the most powerful ancients alive, he forced her compliance without a qualm, holding her mind focused exactly where he wanted it. Jacques and Mikhail had thrown their strength and power squarely behind him.

Shea's terrified gaze returned to the older man as bidden. He was gray, his body swaying unsteadily. Suddenly he fell to his knees.

"Damn it, old man!" Wallace sounded scared. "Don't do this to me. What the hell is wrong? Are you having a heart attack?" He didn't go near his uncle. In fact, he backed up, dragging Shea with him, looking wildly around as if afraid they weren't alone.

Slovensky was strangling, choking on the blood pouring from his mouth, literally drowning in it. He clutched his throat, trying to pry imaginary fingers from around it. Then his hands went to his heart as his chest began to literally rip open.

Shea cried out but could not look away with Gregori forcing her to obey his command. Then suddenly, as Slovensky's heart exploded violently out of his chest and he slumped forward, face down onto the floor, she was released.

Wallace made strange sounds, little mewling noises interspersed with curses. He dragged Shea to her feet, forced her with him toward the door. Her back was to him, and for a moment Shea was curiously thankful. She had never killed or injured another human being in her life. She had taken an oath to save lives. Every instinct in her was to go to Raven, see if there was anything she could do. Even to go to the sick old man and try to aid him. Killing was utterly out of her realm.

You did not kill him, Jacques said soothingly.

I was the instrument you used, she protested. As Wallace dragged her outside, the light hit her eyes, and she cried out as a thousand knives seemed to pierce her skull.

457

Look at this man, his hand on you, anything I can use, Jacques ordered gruffly. He could feel her horror, her reluctance.

I can't, Jacques. I can't think. It was true. Her mind was consumed with grotesque images of blood and death.

This time it was not Gregori who took charge. Jacques gripped her mind in a hold of steel, forcing her compliance. He was far stronger than she had ever imagined him to be, and supremely confident in his abilities, even in the morning hours. The Carpathian men were coming closer, too. Even with the burden of protecting Byron, they were moving rapidly as a group toward the cabin.

Mikhail reluctantly split off from the rest of them, Byron a dead weight in his arms, his path away from the forest and toward the cave of healing. But his concentration on his wife and child was total. He had no room for any other emotion. He kept their waning life force flickering in his mind, held them locked to him, giving them no chance to die before the healer was there to aid them.

Jacques concentrated his venom on the man who had so cruelly tortured him, who now had Shea in his loathsome hands. His hatred was all-consuming, complete, and he focused it and aimed it through Shea. She could see the red haze of killing desire, the need and hunger for it, the pleasure he took in it. He aimed and focused on the only part of Wallace Shea could see.

Don Wallace felt a sudden burning sensation, glanced down, and saw his arm smoking. It burst into flames, red and orange. The smoke whirled up, shaping itself into a malicious, laughing face. Wallace knew that face, had created every tormented line in that face. He screamed and shoved Shea away from him, slapping at his arm with his other hand to try to stop the fire racing up his flesh. He could smell himself charring like so many of the victims he had enjoyed torturing.

Shea fell heavily, clutched at her arm, wanted to remain lying on the ground with her eyes closed tightly. The compulsion to turn and face Wallace was too strong. She sat and stared at him helplessly.

Don Wallace found himself floating in the air, his scattergun on the ground below. The flames died as suddenly as they had begun, but his arm was a mass of charred flesh. Still screaming, he struggled with his one good hand to pull his revolver out of his shoulder holster. He was horrified when it seemed to take on a life of its own and slowly pointed itself at him. His own finger found the trigger and compulsively settled over it.

Shea made a sound in her throat. This was a scene from a horror film, yet she couldn't look away. A huge black wolf burst from the underbrush, running flat out. It leapt into the air, its gleaming jaws closing around Wallace's leg. Bones snapped like twigs as the wolf pulled the man to the ground and thrust its fangs at his exposed throat.

Shea was released from the mind hold and scrambled to her feet, rushing at the wolf tearing at the struggling man. "Jacques! No! You can't do this!" For one bizarre moment the wolf turned its head to look at her, and time stood still. She recognized Jacques' icy eyes and felt his triumph raging in her mind.

Gregori yanked her arm as he emerged from the woods running, still half wolf, half man, changing as he ran. "Come on, we have no time. Damn it, Shea, I need you. You are a doctor, a healer. Come with me." He did not release her arm, and she was forced to sprint with him up the steps into the cabin.

Gregori shoved Slovensky's body out of the way with a boot. "Listen to me, Shea.

We will have to do this together. Raven has shut down her body as much as she dared. Mikhail is keeping her and the child alive, but she is very weak, and the child is in trouble. You have to repair the damage done to Raven, and I will save the child."

Shea was shocked. "She's still alive?" She attempted to back away from Gregori. "I only know human medicine. I have no knowledge of how you do what you do. I might kill her."

"It is in you. Healers are born, not taught. You can do this. I will instruct you as we go. We have no time to argue, Shea. I cannot do this alone. Mikhail says Raven will lose the child in another few minutes. She has to allow her heart and lungs to continue, but her blood will pump out. And life will cease for all of them. Raven, the child, and Mikhail — we will lose all of them," he reinforced. His eyes challenged her. "Do you do this with me?"

Shea was trembling, but her chin went up. "Tell me what to do, and I'll do it."

Gregori nodded approvingly. "You have to block out everything you are. Everything. You are light and energy, nothing more. Once you see yourself as light, you can enter the body and find the worst wounds. Heal from the inside out. The most important thing will be to first stop all bleeding, then repair damage to vital organs. It is very difficult, and you are weak. You will need to feed at some point. Jacques will return to supply you when he is done with his work. You cannot fail us, Shea. I know you can do this. If you need my help, I will be in your mind."

There was no point in protesting that she could not do this thing he expected of her, somehow become light and energy. She had no choice but to try. Gregori believed she could do it, and she had to believe it also. She owed Raven and her child a chance at life. In any case, she was first and foremost a doctor. It was in her nature to heal.

"We do it together," Gregori instructed softly, his voice a cool, soothing balm in the chaos of her mind. She could feel herself respond to that beautiful pitch, the tinkle of silver, the purity of goodness. Shea sank to the floor beside Raven's still body, closed her eyes, and sought a calm place in her mind to center herself. At first everything seemed to intrude, but somehow Gregori was there with her, showing her how to adjust her thoughts and refocus. First the room seemed to drop away, then time and space. Her heart jumped wildly at the odd sensation, but Gregori's soft chanting allowed her to remain calm and float above the earthly chaos. Gradually her body diminished, becoming smaller and smaller until all that remained was her soul. Light and energy. Power.

"We go together. Keep your attention on Raven and her wounds. You cannot think of yourself or what could happen. Believe in yourself. If you begin to falter, reach out to me." Gregori's powerful light seemed to bathe her soul with trust and warmth.

She found only the healer in him. All else was pushed aside. There was so much selflessness, so much purity of soul, Shea could only marvel. She followed his lead without reservation. He was the very epitome of what she had always striven to be. A true healer, with a gift so rare and precious, she felt humbled in his presence. Later she could remember that Gregori was a powerful ancient, that he could make anyone believe and see anything he wanted.

Chapter Fifteen

Shea seemed to float above Raven's body. Her world narrowed until it was only the woman lying so still on the floor. At first it seemed as if Raven was dead, as if her life force was completely gone. Slowly, in her own stillness, with new awareness, Shea could feel the low energy seeping from Raven. Colors seemed to pulse around her, but they were pale and seemed to be fading.

"Now, Mikhail," Gregori ordered.

The words were spoken aloud, yet in her head. Shea realized she hadn't seen Mikhail. He was somewhere with Byron, holding Raven alive from a distance. She wanted to ask his forgiveness for allowing this to happen, but the light that was Shea was already positioning herself over Raven. She felt mild surprise that she seemed to know what to do, but then she realized she wasn't alone. The ball of pure white light beside her was guiding her movements. Her every thought focused on Raven's body; nothing else mattered. She felt Mikhail give Raven the command to awaken to mortal unconsciousness.

Blood spurted, poured from the wounds. Raven's heart was loud, echoing through

Shea's light. She found herself streaming through the blood, white-hot heat cauterizing the worst of the wounds. She worked quickly, in deep and complete concentration, to stem the flow of Raven's life force before she expired. Shea's brain assessed the internal damage to each organ even as she worked. The repairs were done through thought. Every stitch was meticulous, every extraction of bullet fragments precise and careful. It was no different from operating physically, except it was more draining. Maintaining the level of concentration necessary for such a prolonged period was exhausting. Still, there was little sense of time passing. Just as she was in the operating room, Shea was caught up in the job at hand. She even felt as if she were sweating, as if a nurse should wipe her brow for her.

This was the world Shea knew. Her world. She had the patience to deal with extensive injuries. She had the knowledge and skills. More than that, she had the sheer determination. She would not lose her patient if there was any possibility of success.

The damage was horrific. Shea was shocked that Raven had survived as long as she had. Even a trauma center could not have saved her life; there were far too many mortal injuries. And the baby . . . How could the baby possibly survive?

Gregori approached the tiny being cautiously. The extent of the trauma was enormous. The baby was fading as blood gushed from its mother's body. He could feel its willingness to slide away from the pain and outrage of the assault. He could only hope Shea would stop the bleeding quickly, as he had to concentrate on the child. She was so tiny, almost nonexistent, yet he could feel her pain and her puzzlement. She knew fear before she was born, knew pain, and now held forever the knowledge that life was not safe, even here in her mother's womb.

Gregori murmured softly, reassuringly, to her. He had bathed her in his light once before, and she recognized him now, moved toward him, seeking comfort. Very carefully he attended to the wound in the artery that supplied her with nourishment. Very soon he would give her his own blood, sealing her fate, binding her ever closer to him. There were several tears in the placenta, which he meticulously sealed. She was afraid as his light floated closer, so he provided waves of reassurance and warmth.

There was a laceration in her right thigh. It hurt, and blood was seeping into the fluid surrounding her. With the lightest of touches he closed the wound, his touch lingering to calm her. His chant, the low pitch of his voice, echoed in her heart, in her mind, invading her soul. Gregori talked to her as he worked, the purity of his tone beguiling her, soothing her, so that she stayed with Raven rather than simply letting go, fading away with the steady trickle of blood.

Gregori could feel the strength in her, the determination. Without a doubt, she was Mikhail and Raven's daughter. If she chose to go, she would do so, but if she chose to stay, she would fight with every breath left in her body. Gregori made certain she wanted to fight. He whispered to her in his most beguiling voice, promised a fascinating future, lured her with the secrets and beauty of the universe awaiting her. He promised her she would never be left alone; he would be there to guide her, to protect her, to see to her happiness.

Before he could complete his work, he felt Shea tremble, felt her suddenly become aware of the pain of her own wounds. Reassuring the child that he would return, he worked his way out of Raven's body, taking Shea with him. She was swaying on her knees, so pale and drained she was gray. Although the injuries to her shoulder and arm were not critical, she had lost more blood than she could afford.

Jacques was supporting her, holding her against his chest, his arms keeping her from toppling over. She didn't really seem to notice, only pushed ineffectually at him. "I'm not finished. Why did you bring me out, Gregori?" she protested, annoyed. Her one thought was to get back to her patient.

"You must feed or you will not be able to continue," he counseled softly. "And Raven needs blood." The healer's silver eyes went to Jacques', and he nodded.

Jacques thrust his mind into Shea's without hesitation, commanding that she feed. She was so tired and drawn, she could barely turn up her face to the hollow of his neck. At once his body clenched with her breath so warm against his skin. He drew her closer, felt the scrape of her teeth, a slight nip on his neck. Jacques nearly groaned aloud, cursed the depth of Carpathian sexuality that could send his body into hard, painful need when there was blood and death all around them.

Shea whispered something against his pulse, something soft and sighing that invaded his body and left him hungry for her intimate touch. He covered his moan of urgent need as her teeth sank into his neck. Hot flames danced through his bloodstream, darted along his muscles and nerves. His hands found her waist, her back, cradled her head to him. His body needed to sate itself with hers. Never had the heat been so burning and the need so great.

Gregori's teeth tore at his own wrist. His mind merged with Mikhail's, and together they forced Raven's reluctant compliance. She was still a fledging, a mere quarter of a century old, yet she was already strong. It took both of them to force her to feed from other than Mikhail. She resisted for a moment.

For our child, little one, Mikhail whispered softly, lovingly, bending her will to his. *You must do this for our child.*

Gregori added his own reinforcement. *I have never asked anything of you, Raven, of our friendship. This I ask.*

Raven pushed down her revulsion and allowed Mikhail and Gregori to put her into a trance so that she was able to accept the life-giving fluid that both she and her daughter needed so desperately.

Gregori concentrated on connecting with the child. It was so helpless, so tiny, so afraid. A living, thinking being already. He could feel the confusion and its sudden awareness of being alone. He sent waves of reassurance. His blood, flowing into the small body, would strengthen their bond, ensure that her chemistry would match his.

He had spent a lifetime preparing for this moment, the time when he would have the opportunity to choose his mate. He had always known it would be a child of Mikhail's. When Raven had been attacked and mortally wounded years before, Gregori had made certain he had supplied the blood to heal her: His ancient blood was powerful and strong, and he had sent with it the rudiments of the first bonding in the hopes that Raven, a human woman, would conceive a female child. Now he was able to reinforce that bond, seal the child to him for all time. She was bound to him, body and soul, as he was to her. For the first time in centuries he felt hope. And to a male Carpathian on the verge of turning vampire, hope was the only thing left.

Shea closed the wound on Jacques' neck with a sensuous stroke of her tongue, then blinked up at him with eyes slightly glazed and cloudy. Almost at once her expression changed, and she shoved Jacques away. It wasn't that he had taken her free will; she would have fed to save Raven and the child. It was the way he had forced her to help him kill their enemy. Calmly, without emotion, he had commanded it.

You have always known I had demons in me, red hair.

Shea brushed a hand over her face, then shoved her wild hair aside as if to push him along with it. *I always thought you would behave like a man, not a wild animal wanting to kill.*

It is in our nature to kill. We are predators.

Even if you were trying to save my life and felt you needed to kill Wallace, you did not have to use me to do it so viciously. Go away. I have work to do, and I'm very tired.

Jacques did not move from her side. Despite the rain, it was light outside. Even with the intense storm he was generating, the light was beginning to affect all their eyes. They had very little time to finish; soon their bodies would demand the sleep of their kind. He could convince Shea later that he was no monster. Right now his job was to protect all those present while they worked.

He scanned their surroundings continually. He built the storm and kept it roiling and frenzied above them, making the area unsafe to travel within. He supported Shea's swaying body and kept an eye on the healer, who was looking gray and gaunt. What they were doing was a mystery to Jacques. He was proud that Shea was able to

471

perform such a miracle, and he was secretly pleased that the healer needed her help.

Jacques knew Mikhail must be worried sick and feeling helpless. He had been the logical choice to take Byron to the cave of healing and place him in the ground until the healer could get to him. That meant that Mikhail had to keep Raven alive from a distance, a feat that was wearing after a time. And he would want to be the one to supply his own mate with blood and protect her from further harm.

Jacques swore softly to himself. Three Carpathian males should never have allowed humans to fool them. Why hadn't they detected the presence of the men nearby in the forest? Why hadn't the threat to Raven and Shea been ferreted out?

He looked at Shea's arm, red and raw with open wounds, and cursed again. He was sworn to protect her and keep her happy. So far he had done a poor job of it. How was he going to take away the trauma of this day and show her the beauty of their life together? For the first time he became aware of the body of Eugene Slovensky. He sighed and moved away from Shea to hoist the carcass onto his shoulder and toss it outside to the wolves. The last thing Shea would need when she finished the grueling operation was to see any grisly evidence of their kills.

Jacques shoved a hand through his hair, suddenly realizing how tired he was. Everything about his relationship with Shea had gone wrong. He had inadvertently brought her over without her knowledge or consent. He had not even helped her through the difficult process. Worse, he had abused her whenever his mind fragmented. And now, to add to his long list of sins, he had viciously, joyously eliminated an enemy using her as his guide. He wasn't very good at being a husband.

Jacques tried to use his newfound powers to search his memory for the time Mikhail had brought Raven over. Mikhail, too, had done so without her consent, without her knowledge of the existence of Carpathians. He had done it hastily, to save her life, and none of them, even Mikhail, had known if it would work. Raven had been forced to learn a new way of life.

A slight sound sent him whirling around to face Gregori, who staggered away from Raven's body. Shea slumped down beside the woman and didn't move. The two healers appeared drained and nearly helpless.

"You have need of blood," Jacques said to

Gregori. "You gave Raven too much."

"She had need," Gregori answered wearily. He stretched out on the floor, one arm flung over his eyes to protect them.

"Allow me to provide for you. I have fed well this day," Jacques offered formally. The sun was climbing steadily despite the severity of the storm.

"I thank you, Jacques, but I am just too damn tired. This is Mikhail's old cabin. Find out where his chamber is hidden."

Jacques tested his strength, searched for the lost connection to his brother. *Mikhail? They are far too tired to continue. You will have to guard Byron, and I will take care of those here. In this cabin you must have a private resting place. Where is it?*

Beneath the table is a trapdoor that leads to the area under the house. Take care, it is not that well hidden. But if the house were to be discovered or set afire, you could close the earth above you and survive.

The healer will not accept blood this day. He is in need.

There was a short pause as Mikhail touched Gregori to assess his condition. *He will survive. Just get them to safety.*

Feeling like a true Carpathian male once more, Jacques made his way to the hidden chamber. It was unusual for Carpathians to share a sleeping chamber, to even allow others to know where they rested. Entirely vulnerable during the afternoon hours, they were cautious to conceal where they slept. Jacques was uneasy with the arrangement and knew the healer would be even more so.

With his strength waning as the sun climbed higher, Jacques carefully carried Raven's broken body to the chamber below and settled her on a blanket. After locking the cabin, securing the windows, and shutting off the generator, Jacques swung Shea's slight body into his arms. She gave a soft murmur of protest, but her arms crept up around his neck, and her body settled into his trustingly. She was in a light sleep by the time he took her below to the underground chamber.

Gregori stumbled after them, far too drained to bother with floating. He lay across the entrance to the lair and remained there. With Jacques he uttered the words commanding the earth to close them off from the day and cast spells to safeguard them from intruders. Before he slipped off to sleep, he remembered the meadow with the wire strung across it and sent off a silent warning to anything that might try to venture into it. Later he would dismantle the dangerous traps.

Jacques packed healing earth and saliva over Shea's wounds and then Raven's. Only then did he curl his body protectively around his lifemate's before committing himself to sleep.

The rain continued throughout the day. The precipitation was natural and fell in a steady drizzle that cast the land in a gray, depressing hue. Few animals ventured out under the relentless downpour. The storm had been far too long, unpredictable, and dangerous. Around the small cabin in the woods, an uneasiness warned all life forms away from the area. Few humans frequented the deep forest there because of its wild lands, wild animals, and wild legends.

In the chamber below the earth, Gregori roused himself several times, always on guard, always aware, asleep or awake, of those around him and the region surrounding them. In his mind he sought the child. She was brave and intelligent, a warm, living creature shedding a glow of light into his unrelenting darkness. His silver eyes pierced the veil of sleep to stare up at the dirt above his head. He was so close to turning, far closer than either Raven or Mikhail suspected. He was holding on by his fingernails. All feeling had left him so long ago that he could not remember warmth or happiness. He had only the power of the kill and his memories of Mikhail's friendship to keep him going. He turned his head to look at Raven's slight form.

You must live, small one. You must live to save our race, to save all of mankind. There is no one alive on this earth who could stop me. Live for me, for your parents.

Something stirred in his mind. Shocked that an unborn child could exhibit such power and intelligence, he nonetheless felt its presence, tiny, wavering, unsure. All the same the being was there, and he latched on to it, sheltered it close to his heart for a long while before he reluctantly allowed himself to sleep again.

Jacques came alert the moment the sun faded from the sky. Gregori was already gone, racing across the sky in search of prey. Jacques joined him in the hunt, needing the nourishment. They would be working with Byron today, and that meant Jacques would have to feed several times. He soared across the sky, his heart pumping and the blood rushing through his veins. He felt very alive.

We cannot leave the women unguarded for long, Jacques. Gregori's voice shimmered in his head. *The vampire will be angry that his goal was not achieved.*

Jacques sent out a call across the gray sky. It echoed silently for miles. A small cabin tucked into a grove of trees held three hunters huddled together beside a fire. He changed course immediately when he felt their presence. Gregori glided beside him. Hunting was automatic, easy, calling prey to them normal. But in this instance it was more expedient to simply go where it was.

Shea became aware of a voice. She lay silently, not certain where she was. For a moment it seemed as if everything was some far-off echo of a nightmare. But when she studied her surroundings, she knew she was in an underground chamber. Beside her, Raven lay like death. Someone had scattered earth and sweet-smelling herbs over her body.

Cautiously, testing her strength, Shea sat up and shoved impatiently at the hair spilling around her face. Her arm was sore and stung in so many places that it seemed like one massive ache. She touched her shoulder, and her hand came away sticky with blood and dirt. Wincing at the contact, Shea bent to examine Raven.

There seemed to be no pulse, no heartbeat. Her face was white and serene, very beautiful. Shea sighed. She looked the way

Jacques had every time he went to sleep. Unable to do anything for the other woman, Shea stood up and stretched. She felt uneasy without Jacques and wanted to reach out to him, but she knew instinctively that he needed to feed. She studied the chamber until she figured out where the entrance was.

First she tried to find a hidden mechanism to open it. She ran her hands over every square inch. Feeling claustrophobic, her heart beginning to pound, she sank back and thought about it. Jacques would never allow her to be buried alive. There had to be a way out. She glared up at the dirt above her head and focused on it.

Open right now! The picture was vivid in her mind, and the command was strong. Still, she was totally shocked when the earth above her parted and she could see the floorboards of the cabin.

Excited, Shea climbed out of the chamber and resealed the entrance with another sharp command. Feeling proud of her new-found powers, she entered the cabin using the trapdoor. She needed the human act of taking a shower to give her the illusion of normalcy. She doubted she would ever be able to give up her human ways entirely.

Far away, Jacques lifted his head in alarm.

Blood gushed in a warm trail down the hunter's neck to his shoulder. Cursing, Jacques bent once more to feed. How had Shea woken without his permission? Was she really so strong that she could resist his commands? She should still be asleep, yet she was outside the protection of the chamber. He had to hurry.

Shea stepped off the front porch dressed in clean clothes, her hair still damp. It was impossible to find a sign of the life-and-death struggle that had taken place the morning before. She could only conclude that Gregori and Jacques had cleaned things up. It occurred to her that the Carpathians had been doing so for hundreds of years and were probably experts at it.

The thought turned her stomach, and she wandered out under the trees. The leaves collected raindrops and dumped them on her head, but she didn't mind. It made her feel a part of nature. She didn't want to go too far in case Raven needed her protection, so she walked along the pathway to her herb garden. She bent to touch a leaf, battered and bruised by the pounding storm. A shadow crossed her mind, dark and sinister. She found herself shivering uncontrollably. She straightened quickly and whirled to face the tall, pale stranger as he emerged from the forest.

He was physically beautiful, breathtaking. Shea had never seen a more handsome man. His eyes were deep set and sad, magnetic. It was impossible to tell his age. His smile held sorrow. "I am sorry I startled you. I can hear your heart beating."

Shea took an involuntary step backward, mainly because she wanted to step closer to him. His pull was strong, and she felt caught in a spell. "Who are you?" Her voice was a whisper of wonder.

"Do you not know me? I have searched the length of the world for you. Why did you not answer my call?" His words were mild, but they held a hiss of anger.

Shea held her ground, but her mouth had gone dry. "I'm sorry, I don't know you. I've never seen you before in my life."

"You woke to my call. You came here to me. You are my beloved Maggie. If your desire was to punish me with your silence, you have done so thoroughly. Now you must forgive me and come away from this place and from the one whose stench is all over you." This time, his voice dropped to a low snarl.

Shea fought down the desire to call for Jacques. "Are you Rand?"

He stepped closer to her, and her stomach

lurched in protest. "How is it you do not know me? Were you injured? Has the dark one destroyed your memories and planted his own?"

Shea pressed a hand into her protesting stomach and took another step into the forest to put distance between them. "I don't understand. Why do you call Jacques the dark one? I thought that expression was reserved solely for the healer."

The hiss was deadly. "He is evil, Maggie. He and his brother tried to destroy us. I thought they had taken you from me, and I was right. The crazy one plotted his revenge, and he lured you to his place of death, and now you are trapped in their web of lies." He advanced again, and, like a macabre dance partner, Shea retreated.

Was this her father? Was this Rand? Had he really been searching for Maggie, believing her alive all this time? He seemed so tormented, so sincere, she wanted to comfort him, wanted to put her arms around him and hold him, yet something held her back. "I think you're confusing me with my mother. I am Shea O'Halloran. If you are Rand, then you are my father."

"You have been with him, Maggie. You know he is capable of twisting your mind, bending you to his will. He placed memories in your head, memories you think are real. It is not so. He wanted revenge for the death of his sister. They blamed me because I loved you. They forced me into the ground and punished you by keeping us apart. It is the truth. They even took my son from me and gave him to another to raise. They turned him against me so that he was loyal only to them."

Everything seemed so hazy, her mind confused and sluggish. He was stalking her now, following her every backward movement with a forward one, bending his head closer toward her throat. She should allow him to feed, shouldn't she? Even if she wasn't Maggie, she was his daughter, and he was so alone and tormented. She could feel his hot breath on her neck, his will pushing at hers, his hunger beating at both of them. She didn't want this. What was happening to her that she was standing so still, waiting for him to take her blood, when every cell in her body shrieked at her to run?

Shea! God, love, get away from him. I do not know what he is doing, but you are in danger. Do not let him take your blood. Jacques' voice was strong in her mind.

Shea leapt away, putting distance between herself and the tall, handsome man. "You're scaring me." As always when emo-

483

tions threatened her, she forced her brain to take over, find a way out for her. "I don't know what to believe anymore. You're saying Jacques and Mikhail planned to keep us apart because you didn't love their sister?" Shea held up her hands imploringly, her large green eyes shamelessly pleading.

He halted a few feet from her, visibly relaxing now that she was seeking answers from him. "They believed me responsible for Noelle's death because I left her unprotected while I was with you. She was murdered by Slovensky and his friends."

"Did you know Slovensky?" she asked quietly, holding her breath. Could her father be responsible for all the deaths? Could he be the vampire?

"Had I ever met the man, I would have broken his neck on the spot. He and he alone is responsible for Noelle's death. I may not have loved her, but she bore me a child." He tilted his head, and it was easy to get lost in his dark, mysterious eyes.

Shea felt behind her for a solid tree trunk, needing to touch something real. This was all some gigantic spider web, so sticky with intrigue that she had no idea where to turn. Something wasn't right. She was becoming confused, her mind playing tricks on her. Deliberately she pressed her palm into the bark of the tree in an attempt to focus on something that might break the spell he was weaving around her.

I am your lifemate, my love. I am the one you turn to when you are afraid and in need. Jacques' voice was firm, and she sensed him close by.

Shea mentally shook herself. It was like being tugged in two different directions. She knew she was Maggie's daughter. Rand might believe what he was saying, but she knew who she was. Didn't she?

Rand gave a gentle sigh. "All of us are capable of planting memories, Maggie. It is reasonable to assume they would say you are your own daughter. That way they would be able to say there was no chance we could be together. Do you not see the brilliance of such a deception, of such a revenge? It would last a lifetime."

"A Carpathian has only one lifemate. I am Jacques'." She pushed at her hair, found her hand trembling, and put it behind her back.

"He has had plenty of time to work on your memories. Years. He worked his way into your mind and then took you over. Do you really believe he could have lived all those years in that cellar?" His voice was soft and reasonable.

Her head hurt so badly, Shea could barely

think. She closed her eyes for a moment, and when she opened them, Rand had glided closer, was bending once more to her throat.

Get away! The words were so sharp and clear, Shea scrambled away, lost her footing, and fell across a fallen log. Jacques was furious, and his rage was a hideous thing. He dropped like a silent phantom out of the sky to reach her before Rand could. His fingers closed around her arm, possessive and unyielding. As he helped her to her feet, he thrust her body behind his and faced her father.

"What are doing, Rand?" he snapped. His voice was low and ominous.

Rand smiled gently, calmly. "And do you now kill me, too? You are a bloodthirsty one, are you not? You claim I am her father, yet you are eager to slay me." He looked directly into Shea's eyes. "Does this make sense?" His voice was low and sad. "That he might want to destroy your father?"

"You are deliberately trying to confuse her." Jacques' face, worn and lined, was hardened with anger. Shea found herself studying its every beloved detail. All at once she didn't think Rand quite so handsome. There seemed something sinister about his perfect good looks and his thin-lipped smile. Rand seemed without emotion, almost lifeless, his sorrow unreal, while Jacques' powerful form was trembling with volcanic emotion. His mind was a red haze of swirling anger and fear that he might lose her, that he had inadvertently placed her in danger. The rage was toward Rand that he would betray his own daughter.

Rand sighed softly and shook his head. "How easily you allow yourself to be tricked by this dark vampire. Your own neck holds the answers you seek. The wounds there are torn and ragged. Who but a vampire feeds so carelessly? Does a loving lifemate abuse his woman in this manner? When he killed this morning, using your innocence and your very mind and soul to aid him, was he not feeling joy? When you begged him to stop, did he not continue? And when he came to you with blood on his hands, could you not see the dark desire and hunger in his mind, in his eyes, in his body? Could you not see the dark compulsion of the kill? Vampires are very clever, my dear, and you have fallen under his spell."

Jacques regarded the older man with black, empty eyes. "Do you challenge me?"

Shea gasped. Jacques and her father? She pressed both hands to her head. She couldn't stand this confrontation, being

487

fought over like some dog's bone. She didn't even know what was true and what wasn't anymore.

Yes, you do, little red hair. He is attempting to bewitch you. He thought me occupied with Byron. He thought he could lure you from the safety of our people. He will not accept a fair challenge. Jacques attempted to reassure her. She was fighting to stay calm, but Shea had suffered far too much trauma in the last few days. Jacques was certain Rand had not only planned for that but also counted on it to sway her.

Rand's smile was calm. "I would not wish to cause Maggie any further grief. But be warned, dark one, you would be hunted and destroyed if Mikhail were not your brother. You have deceived and hurt this woman I love, and I will not allow you to get away with it. But I would not be the cause of her further distress."

Jacques bared his fangs. "I was certain you would say something of that nature. You prefer to do your dirty work through trickery."

Rand raised an eyebrow. "Listen to him, my dear. Next he will be accusing me of associating with the human murderers. Are you going to say I tried to kill Byron? What about Noelle? Perhaps I was responsible for what happened to you and my own son, too. You are the vampire, Jacques, and you are powerful enough to deceive one such as Gregori. I would be a fool to fight you when you are holding Maggie hostage."

Shea clutched at the back of Jacques' shirt. "Rand, you're wrong about him. I look like Maggie, but I'm your daughter. And I would know if he was truly a vampire."

Rand looked at her with sad eyes. "How many times have you asked yourself what he is? Did you not feel his joy in the kill? He wanted it, welcomed it, and he fed voraciously. You cannot deny this is so. Who better than Jacques to set this entire thing up? Noelle was his sister, and he adored her. He led the others away from you and from his brother's woman. He killed the humans because they could identify him." He bowed his head tiredly. "I cannot convince you, I know this, but in time you will see that I am right. Tell me, Maggie, did you not see me differently when he arrived? Perhaps more like a villain? I wonder who projected that image to you? I doubt that I would have done so myself."

"Her mind was calmer and able to see more clearly with my presence, as you well know. Be gone, Rand, back to the hole you crawled from." Jacques gestured, his face dark with anticipation, his body poised and ready should Rand attack.

Rand simply faded from their sight, his soft laughter sending shivers down Shea's spine. Instantly she stepped away from Jacques, her green eyes not meeting his.

With gentle fingers he tipped up her chin, forcing her gaze to meet his. "I love you, Shea. I have no way to combat the lies he has told until we can be free of my debt to Byron. Reserve judgment until I am able to talk this out with you."

His voice was so loving, his touch so tender, it turned her heart over. She found herself drowning in the mesmerizing depth of his black eyes. She wanted to do whatever he wished. Her body responded to his, to the tormented look of him, to the desperate hunger in him. Her body flared to life and called to his, going soft and pliant with anticipation. Her breasts ached, and she burned for his touch.

Shea jerked her gaze away, stepped back so that his body heat could not affect hers, so that the electricity crackling and arcing between them was broken. Shaken, she shoved a trembling hand through her hair. "How are you going to convince me, Jacques? With sex?"

He was smoldering with need, a dark hunger that never ceased. Once it had risen, it had grown until the urgency nearly overwhelmed him. She was essentially human and could not understand, did not even know of the heat that rose between lifemates. "Love, you are smart enough for the both of us. You can figure out for yourself who is telling the truth. Rand is sick. I wish it was not so, but if he truly believed you to be your mother, he would have attacked me immediately. A lifemate can do no other than guard his woman. That has been our way for all time. No other man can be with her. He is trading on your ignorance of Carpathian ways. I do not need to convince you of what is in my heart or of what is in yours. I know I am damaged. You know it, too. But you would feel it if I was truly evil. You would know it. There would be no way I could hide it." He held out a hand to her. "Just think it through with that logical brain you have. I trust you to come up with your own answer."

"Jacques." She hesitated, wanting to touch him, needing to touch him, but afraid of being lost in the sexual lure she couldn't seem to resist. "How do I know if I'm the one thinking for myself when you're always with me, always sharing my mind?"

"You will have to figure that out for yourself, Shea." His black eyes moved lovingly over her face. "You know me better than anyone, and I have never tried to hide anything from you. If you brand me a monster, even I will believe you." His smile was gentle and reassuring.

Shea took a deep breath and laced her fingers with his. It felt right and natural. The sparks jumped from his skin to hers, and her pulse raced, but she walked quietly through the woods with him, content just to be by his side. Jacques seemed so much a part of her, the air she breathed. She accepted it because he made her complete.

Chapter Sixteen

Gregori was an impressive figure. Shea watched him as he knelt beside Raven, his entire attention seemed to be concentrated on the woman lying so still. "Have you attended to Shea's injuries?" The soft inquiry startled Shea. He addressed Jacques, asking the male, as was his irritating way.

"The wounds are closing," Jacques assured him. *Rand drew Shea alone into the woods. He is the betrayer, healer. I walked away from him because he is linked to Shea. He could make her feel whatever I did to him. He is very dangerous. I cannot be the one to bring him to justice. Shea would never forgive me.*

"Don't do that, Jacques," Shea said with a little bite in her voice. She was exasperated with him. "I know you're talking to Gregori. If you have something to say, say it out loud so that I can hear you. You think Rand is the vampire, don't you?"

The thought was in her mind also, and it made her feel disloyal. She knew something was wrong with Rand; perhaps Maggie's death had twisted his mind so he was living in the past. But something Rand had said in the course of their strange conversation was niggling at her brain. Something she couldn't put a finger on.

Gregori passed a hand over Raven's stomach, his fingers splayed wide. His touch lingered for a moment, a surprisingly tender gesture, then he turned to Shea. "Jacques knows his duty to you, Shea. This man, Rand, the one who is your birth father, was never in your life. Hold on to what is real, not to your childhood fantasies."

"You don't know the first thing about my childhood, fantasy or not," Shea snapped, goaded beyond endurance by his unruffled, superior attitude. Gregori definitely grated on her. She suspected it was because he was always using logic. *She* was the one who was supposed to do that. "I have my own mind, Gregori, and it is a perfectly good one. Perhaps the first couple of times we met gave you a false impression. I am not a hysterical woman who runs at the first sign of danger. I don't faint at the sight of blood, and I can make my own decisions."

"If I gave you the idea that I thought those things of you, then I must apologize," Gregori said gently, courteously. "It is not my impression of you at all. You have much courage, and you are a natural healer, but you have little knowledge of our way of life. It takes much to maintain proper health. You have the human aversion to taking blood, as Raven does."

Her chin lifted. "I am well aware I have a problem in that area. In my own time I will deal with it. But there are other much more important things going on at the moment." Beside her Jacques stirred as if to protest, but he remained silent.

"That is where you are wrong. Nothing is more important," Gregori replied, his voice velvet soft, a whisper of power. "Your health is essential to every member of our race. You are a woman. You are able to create life within you. You represent hope to every male who has no lifemate."

"I have no intention of bringing a child into the world."

There was complete silence. Gregori turned the full force of his silver gaze onto her face. His eyes slashed and burned through every barrier until she felt as if he could see every secret in her soul. He let out his breath slowly. "I understand why you would feel this way now, Shea. What was done to you was an abomination. I see the pain in you at this decision. If you can find it in yourself to wait for Jacques to heal completely before you give up such an important dream, I believe you will find that our race loves and cherishes our children, knowing them for the treasures they are. It is the same way we feel about our women."

"Is that why Rand abandoned my mother? Is that why he allowed someone else to raise his own son? Or are only female children cherished by your race?"

Gregori sighed. "All of our children, male and female, are loved and protected, Shea. I do not understand Rand, I never have. At the moment I believe he is very dangerous, and something has to be done about him. In the meadow he set up wires murderous not only to our kind but to humans and animals as well. I spent some time dismantling his traps. He cannot be allowed to continue this mad behavior. You know it, you just do not want to face it."

"Just like that? You can pass judgment on him and not even know for certain? How can you be sure it's him?" Shea found herself twisting her fingers together, trying to find a way out for her father. She remembered all too vividly his breath on her neck, but she pushed the memory away quickly, feeling disloyal again.

"Because none of us felt his presence in the forest," Jacques answered her gently. A shadow in her mind, he could clearly see the conflict between her brain and her emotions. "Only you felt him, Shea. He was able to wake you despite my command to sleep.

He deliberately lured you into the forest and tried to take your blood to strengthen his hold on you."

"Maybe he's ill. Maybe he's confused. He could have forced me. Why didn't he force me, Jacques? He certainly could have," she pointed out. "He's quite a bit stronger than me, and I felt as if I was in a dreamlike state. Why didn't he simply force me, if he's really a vampire?"

"Because a lifemate cannot be forced to choose. It must be a true choice. Otherwise a true bond is not formed. He knows that." Jacques reached out to her. "It is ingrained in him, imprinted before birth."

Shea stepped away from him, rubbed at her throbbing temples. "Why is everything with you people so darned complicated, Jacques? Nothing like this ever happened to me while I was human."

"You were half-human, Shea," Jacques reminded her gently, "and you know you were in danger even then. Your mother had the presence of mind to hide you from the fanatical society that was pursuing you."

Shea shivered and rubbed her arms to warm herself. "I just wish we could go somewhere, Jacques, and sort all this out. I need to find a way to forgive you for using me to kill those men."

Mikhail's form shimmered into solidity right before Shea's eyes, nearly stopping her heart. He smiled at her. "I must thank you for returning my love to me. Without her, my life would be worthless. You are a great asset to our people. It is unfortunate that you have been cast into our world without any preparation to make the transition easier. These are hard times for all of us." He touched her arm gently. "Please forgive us for using you to stop Slovensky and Wallace. We could not allow them to kill Raven or snatch you, as was their intention. Raven could not help us, so we turned to you. It was wrong to use you without your consent, but time did not allow the luxury of asking your permission. Your lifemate could do no other than protect your life, and from that distance it is impossible to do anything without 'seeing' through another's eyes."

Mikhail was eloquent and sincere, and Shea could not be angry with him. She sighed and bit her lower lip. "I wish it hadn't happened that way, Mikhail, but I'm glad Raven is alive."

"I do not understand how those two humans were able to disguise their presence from us. I monitored Raven continually," Mikhail said. "The two of you should never have been in any danger. I scanned the surroundings; Gregori scanned, as did Jacques. A vampire might be able to confuse us, but certainly the humans could not."

"I, too, scanned." Raven stirred weakly, her voice a thin thread. "I detected no danger to us, yet Shea was uneasy and certain we were not alone almost from the beginning. I dismissed her fears, thinking her separation from Jacques the cause."

"It was only Shea who could detect the vampire in the woods," Jacques said.

Shea found herself the center of attention. Instinctively she moved toward Jacques. He wrapped an arm around her waist, his body protective toward hers. "I know you're all thinking it was Rand. I don't want it to be him. I want to have a family."

"You have a family," Mikhail said gently. "I am your family. Raven is your family. Our child will be, and of course you have Jacques. Someday you will have children." He sent a slight grin in Gregori's direction. "You can even claim the healer as family. We do, although he dislikes it intensely. We are together, and we are close. These past several days are not a real example of what our existence is like. We are under attack, and must defend ourselves. Most of the time our life is much like that of the human world. Do not judge us by recent days. These are exceptional times."

"Maybe Byron can tell us who betrayed him," Shea suggested desperately. "Can't we wait for what he has to say before we condemn Rand?" What was it that bothered her so much? And what was it Rand said had?

Jacques held her close. "No one *wants* it to be Rand, little red hair, and you can be assured no one will act without certain proof."

Shea knew he was seeking to reassure her, even as he believed implicitly that her father was the betrayer. Some part of her knew it to be true. Away from Rand, she was able to see things more clearly. He wasn't just a man confused and tormented by her mother's death. He could be a calculating, cold killer.

Shea closed her eyes, unable to face where her thoughts were going. Jacques could not be the one to take Rand's life. He just couldn't. Warmth flooded her mind, and his arm tightened protectively around her. *There is no need for me to hunt Rand should he prove to be the vampire preying on our people. The others can take care of it. We can go far from this place if that is your desire, my love.*

If Rand was the vampire, the betrayer,

Jacques would have more reason than anyone to want to ruthlessly destroy him. Yet she could not bear the idea. *Thank you, Jacques. I don't want you to be the one to take his life if it really comes to that.*

Let us go to Byron, and I will do as I promised. Then we will find a place to rest.

Shea nodded, her head brushing his chest. She could hear the reassuring beat of his heart, feel the heat in his body rising to meet hers. He was solid and real, and she owed it to both of them to take things slowly and make rational decisions. Right at this moment, Shea was not certain she was capable of such a thing. Her brilliant brain seemed to be malfunctioning lately.

"We go to Byron, healer — do you follow?" Jacques asked.

Gregori reluctantly left Raven to Mikhail. A woman could not be possibly be claimed before her eighteenth birthday. Every moment of the healer's existence would be an endurance test, living in hell until the child came of age. He would hunt and feed and resist the kill unless he was called on to dispense justice. That would be the most dangerous of all times, walking away from the power of taking a life. And somewhere, close by, Rand was waiting.

As Gregori turned to follow Jacques and

Shea, Mikhail stopped him. "Could the humans have found some kind of chemical to cloak their presence from us? If they have done so, we are all in grave danger, and we must move to meet this new threat."

"Anything is possible, but it is more likely the vampire is using a shadow spell. It is ancient and all but forgotten. I came across it in the lost book of Shallong. He buried it with his evil tokens in the mountain of souls. I thought no other had dared to travel there." Gregori glanced after Shea to assure himself she was out of hearing.

"It is entirely possible," Gregori continued, "even probable, that Rand rose more then seven years ago, found Shea's mother already dead, and turned. In his hatred he would blame you and Jacques. He could have studied the ancient arts and returned to lead Slovensky and his nephew to kill our people seven years ago. None of us knew he had risen, so he was never a suspect. Jacques thought he knew the betrayer, was close to him at one time. Rand was his family through Noelle."

"Do you believe Rand would have his own son tortured, mutilated?"

"Noelle's son, Mikhail. If Rand is as twisted as I suspect, he was the one who aided the humans in their murders seven years ago. We are all in danger, particularly Jacques. The only one who might escape death is Shea, and she would suffer greatly."

"He knows we will hunt him now. He will try to run."

Gregori shook his head. "No, he has worked too hard for revenge. This is hatred, Mikhail. He lives to kill, and we are the ones he must seek. He will stay here and continue to try to lure Shea to him."

"You will warn Jacques."

"There is no need. Jacques knows. He will keep Shea close to him. Jacques is dangerous, Mikhail. You persist in thinking him the younger brother you need to protect. He has grown to great power. Rand will underestimate him. He does not recognize the monster he himself created."

"I am not certain I like you referring to my brother as a monster." There was a trace of humor in Mikhail's voice.

"You should hear what I call you behind your back," Gregori said, even as his arms spread to accommodate the wings forming.

Mikhail's laughter echoed as the bird soared into the night sky.

The cave of healing was smaller than most of the other chambers in the maze of underground tunnels. The soil was rich, dark, and fertile. It smelled pleasant, with the aroma of herbs mixed with the natural fragrance of the earth. Shea's hand found Jacques' back pocket and slipped inside, a link between them as they surveyed the extent of Byron's injuries. Shea felt a helpless sense of déjà vue. Smith and Wallace had not had as much time to torture him as they had Jacques, but nevertheless his body was blackened with burns and covered with cuts.

Shea found Jacques' hand, twisted her fingers in his, hardly daring to look at him. The sight of Byron's tortured body must bring back such hideous memories. She attempted to be cheerful. "Well, at least they're consistent in what kind of damage they do. So we know I can help him, based on past experience."

Jacques did not want her touching the other man. The emotion was sharp and ugly and overwhelming. Loathing himself, Jacques took a deep breath and let it out, instinctively placing his large frame between Byron and his lifemate.

Shea touched his face with gentle fingers. "What is it?" Her voice was so beautiful, so clear and cool and soothing, that Jacques wanted to cringe from the truth, ashamed, but he could not lie to her.

"I do not know. Only that I cannot bear

for you to touch him. God, Shea, I hate myself for this, but you cannot." His hands cupped her face, his black eyes filled with sorrow. "You cannot do this."

"What do you think will happen if I touch this man? Do you believe Rand's stories now? Do you think you influenced me somehow, and our chemistry is not real?"

"I only know that if you touch this man, I will not be in control. The demon in me will rise, and my mind will shatter into so many fragments, I will never be able to put myself back together."

Shea could feel his loathing for his unreasonable jealousy, his fear that she would ignore his plea and something terrible would happen. She realized she still knew precious little of Carpathian ways, that Jacques was edgy and more animal than man at that moment. Her fingers curled around his arm, and she smiled up at him. "I guess we wait for the healer."

Jacques could feel the tension drain from his body. "It might be the best idea."

Shea reached up to trail her fingertips over his neck. The massage was suggestive and reassuring at the same time. He reacted by crushing her to him, his mouth hard and dominating as he captured hers. He kissed her possessively, his body as demanding as his mouth. "I need you right now, Shea. My body is going up in flames, and I hurt like hell. We have to be alone soon or I might die."

Her laughter was muffled against his chest. "No one has ever died because they wanted to make love." But she wasn't sure. Her own body was burning and begging for the connection to his.

Gregori suddenly materialized, made a soft, sighing noise, and sent them a clear frown. Like guilty children they broke apart.

The healer spoke. "He will be weak, Jacques. He may even attempt to resist you. He is close to turning and has been for some time. Tell him of Raven's child, of your belief that Shea might be able to provide a female child." Gregori gave the advice softly. "You must take control of him. I felt his resistance to our intervention."

Jacques nodded. He wished Shea away from Byron; and she moved to the end of the chamber, reading his mind. He sent her thanks and turned his attention to his former friend.

Shea watched him, feeling suddenly proud of him. He might not be able to bear her touching another man yet, but he didn't like himself very much for it. And she could sense his determination to save Byron. She knew he could not bring himself to lie to her in order to make himself look good in her eyes. He didn't try to hide his darker side from her but rather wanted her to find a way to love him in spite of it.

And she did. She might not understand, but she loved all of him. He didn't run from the things he had to do. He faced the demon in himself every day. It had all happened so fast, one thing after the other. Shea had taken a long time to assimilate all the information, but the one consistent thing was the way Jacques was with her. He was honest about everything, even his terrible need of her.

Byron groaned, bringing her attention to the men bending over him. Gregori was as still as a statue, his concentration completely on the ravaged body. Jacques was forcing his wrist to Byron's mouth. Shea's stomach lurched, but she didn't look away.

Byron resisted, his eyes imploring.

"You must take my blood. The women are safe; the trap you warned us of failed." Jacques' low voice seemed to be notes of music dancing in the air. Shea merged with him to increase his strength. She could feel Jacques' surprise as her will joined with his to force Byron's compliance.

"Mikhail's woman carries a female

child," Jacques said softly. "Shea is from the human race and capable of providing female children. There is hope now for a future, Byron. We want you to join with us to find those human women of psychic ability our people need. You cannot throw your life away. What if, through our bond of friendship and blood, you are the lifemate to my daughter? What would become of our child? Take what is freely offered, old friend, and save yourself. You are strong. You will endure while we rebuild our race."

Byron looked into Jacques' black eyes for a long time, seeking something he evidently found. He closed his mouth over the offered wrist and drank willingly. For the first time, Shea did not find the act repulsive. There was something beautiful in the way Jacques gave his blood so freely to Byron. It was far more personal than the way humans donated blood.

Her body clenched with hot desire, and without thinking she bathed Jacques' mind in her heat. She saw his body hunch, as if someone had physically punched him. Guilt stirred for a moment, but then he was stroking her throat, his mental touch every bit as exciting in her state of arousal as his physical one.

Gregori straightened up slowly and inhaled sharply, turned to glare at Jacques. *Take your woman and find a place away from us. You know how dangerous Carpathian men can be at such a time. See to your needs, Jacques.*

I have little memory of these parts. If you recall, our home was invaded, and the vampire knows where it is.

Go deeper into the earth. The cave continues until you find the very core, the hot springs. You will be safe there. And alone.

And Byron?

He cannot speak. As yours was, his voice is paralyzed. I doubt if he can recall his betrayer. I will put him in the ground to heal. And I will seek out Rand. Our prince has passed sentence upon such a betrayer. Make no mistake — I will make certain he is the one before I destroy him.

Jacques reached down and touched Byron's shoulder. "Go to the sleep of our earth, Byron. I will return each day to see that you are fed and your wounds are healing. Do you trust me to do this?"

Byron nodded wearily and closed his eyes. He welcomed the solace of the healing earth. Already the blood was flowing through his veins, giving him strength to heal. He felt better knowing he had somehow warned the others of the trap the vampire had set. He had been used to lure the men away from the women. The vampire had even whispered to him of the plan to sacrifice Smith while Slovensky and his nephew killed Raven and took Shea. The earth opened, and his weightless body floated into the cradle. All around him the rich soil reached out for him, welcomed him. He gave himself up to sleep and earth.

Jacques nodded in a slight salute to Gregori and reached out to Shea. The moment his fingers closed around hers, the electricity arced sharply and cleanly between them. He pulled her out of the chamber and into the tunnel. To her horror, instead of going back up toward the forest, Jacques drew her down toward the very bowels of the earth. The tunnel was wide enough that they could walk together, but she didn't move fast enough to suit him. With every step he took, Jacques' body became tighter and more painful. His breath was coming in hoarse gasps. He swung her into his arms and raced down the tunnel's twists and turns.

"What are you doing, Jacques?" Half laughing, half concerned, Shea held on tightly, her slender arms around his neck.

"I am getting us to a place where we can be alone." He was decisive about it. He had wanted her for hours, for days, for a life-time. He had to have her this minute.

Shea buried her face in the hollow of his shoulder, her body responding to the urgency in his voice, to his labored breathing and rapid heartbeat. Her mouth touched his pulse, her breath warming his skin. She felt him shiver with awareness and gently probed the spot with the tip of her tongue. "Mmm, you taste good."

"Damn it, Shea, I swear if you keep that up, we will not make it to the springs."

"I never heard of any springs," she murmured absently, stroking the beating pulse again, her teeth playfully nipping. Her mouth wandered farther up his neck to his ear.

"Hot springs. It is only a little way farther," he groaned, but he leaned his head toward her attentions.

Her hand slipped down the front of his shirt, played with his buttons, slowly sliding them open so that her palm could rest on his hot skin. "I think you're hot enough, Jacques," she whispered wickedly into his ear, caressing his earlobe with her tongue. "I know I am."

He stopped, leaned against the curved wall, and allowed her feet to touch the ground. There were no words to describe the hunger, the urgency of his body, or the chaos of his mind. He bent over her, forcing her slender body backward as he took control of her mouth. His hand spanned her throat, tipping up her chin for better access.

Shea experienced a curious shifting of the earth beneath her feet. Colors whirled in her head, and flames licked at her body. She could hardly bear the feel of clothes against her sensitive skin. Her breasts swelled and ached, her nipples pushing into the material covering them.

Jacques was on fire, his jeans so tight, he could no longer breathe. He tore at them, freed his body from the restrictive fabric and ripped at the cotton covering hers. "I have to have you right now, Shea," he said hoarsely. His hands were everywhere, cupping her firm breasts, his thumbs caressing, arousing, bringing her nipples to peaks of temptation.

His teeth scraped the vulnerable line of her throat, followed the path lower to the creamy swell of her breasts. At Shea's quick indrawn breath he feasted, hungry and aching with need. His hands bit into her small waist as he held her still. Her cotton top gaped open, giving him glimpses of her narrow ribcage. She was making little wild, husky noises that only added to his frenzy.

"You're out of control, wild man," Shea whispered softly, her hands urging him on. They were a living flame, heating the very air around them.

Jacques yanked at her jeans, dragged her to the ground, his body covering hers as he did so. "You think?" His hands pinned her hips, lifted her so that he could drive forward, burying himself deep. The pleasure was somewhere between exquisite and pain, relief and pure joy. She was so hot and ready, clenching at him, surrounding him with fiery velvet. He felt her mouth against the heavy muscles of his chest, her breath, her soft little murmur of wonder. His body tightened in response, moved faster and deeper. White-hot heat spread, piercing pain that moved to sweet ecstasy as her teeth found his pulse. He flowed into her, sensual and spicy, his body taking possession of hers in the dominant way of his kind. Wild. Hungry. Urgent.

He moved slower, faster, deep and shallow. They connected in every way, their hearts and souls flying free. He never wanted to leave her body, a haven of pleasure that would last an eternity. His heart was pounding, his brain whirling with erotic indulgence. His fangs exploded into his mouth, needing all of her. Even as she fed, he bent his dark head and took possession of her neck.

Shea cried out as his teeth sank deep, as his body surged into hers, as the friction grew and colors danced. Her tongue stroked across his chest, and she caught at him for an anchor as he took them soaring into the night. Jacques' arms wrapped her tightly, his body penetrated hers deeply, his muscles welded to hers so perfectly, minds and hearts met like halves of the same whole. It was impossible to tell where one started and the other left off. He caught her mouth in his, sharing their life force as they fell over the edge and tumbled through time and space.

Shea lay spent in his arms, aware of nothing but the beauty and peace of their surroundings. The earth beneath her felt welcoming and soft, the curving tunnel above like a sanctuary for them. Jacques' body, muscled and hard, was a welcome anchor in the turbulent storm of their love-making. For once, her hunger was sated. In the heat of the moment she had fed well, taking what Jacques so freely offered. She realized this was what he had meant when he told her that there were ways to get around her dislike of their feeding habits. She brushed a hand lovingly over the well-defined muscles of his back, inhaled their combined scents. For the first time in days, she felt real peace.

Jacques held her close, grateful that the urgency and painful ache had left his body. He lifted his head and stroked back her hair in a tender caress. "We did not make it to the pools."

"What pools?"

Her voice was drowsy and sensual from his lovemaking. His heart turned over, and his body tightened in anticipation. "The tunnel leads to hot springs, a beautiful spot where we can rest for a time. I was taking you there when you seduced me."

Shea laughed softly. "Is that what I did? If all it takes is opening your shirt, we're in for a wild time together."

Jacques nuzzled the warmth of her neck, lazily slid his attentions lower to the invitation of her full breasts. "Do you have any idea how beautiful you are?"

"No, but you can tell me if you want," she encouraged, circling his neck with her slender arms. She closed her eyes, savoring the feeling he was inducing with his tongue caressing her nipple.

"I do love you." He said it suddenly, raising his head so his black eyes could meet her startled green ones. "I mean it, Shea. I do not just need you, I love you. I know everything about you, I have been in your head, shared your memories, shared your dreams and your ideas. I know you think I need you and that is why I am with you, but it is much more than that. I love you." He grinned unexpectedly, traced her lower lip with the tip of a finger. "What is more, I know you love me. You hide it from yourself, but I found it in a little corner, tucked away in your mind."

Shea stared up at the teasing smile on his face, then pushed at the solid wall of his chest. "You're making that up."

Jacques moved off her, then reached down to pull her to her feet. His clothes were scattered everywhere, and he made no move to retrieve them. Shea's shirt was still hanging open, and her jeans were down around her ankles. Blushing, she pulled them up. His hands stayed hers, preventing her from fastening them. "Do not bother, Shea. The pools are just ahead." He walked a few feet, then looked back over his shoulder. "I did not make it up, and I know you are staring at my backside."

Shea tossed her mane of red hair so that it flew in all directions. "Any woman in her right mind would stare at your particular backside, so you don't need to add that to your arrogant list of virtues. And stay out of my mind unless you're invited." She was staring, but she couldn't help it. He was so beautifully masculine.

Jacques reached behind him and captured her hand, lacing their fingers together. "But I find the most interesting things in your mind, my love. Things you do not have any intention of telling me."

Shea could hear a sound now. Not the drip of water seeping from the earth into the tunnel, but a dull roar that began to boom louder with every step they took. She looked carefully around her, afraid the roof of the cave might come crashing down. Jacques tugged on her hand, urging her forward.

Around the next bend he ducked into a small entrance, and Shea reluctantly followed him. The moment she straightened again, the sight nearly took her breath away. The room was huge, with rock crystals lining the walls, sparkling in the steamy chamber. Pools tiered one another, separated only by symmetrical rock walls. Steam rose from the various pools, giving the chamber an ethereal appearance. A long, steady fall of frothy water tumbled down the far wall into the deepest pool. Large boulders and long, flat rocks divided the pools, forming natural berths for sitting or lying down.

Shea stared at the underground paradise in awe. "This is so beautiful. How come no one knows about it?"

Jacques laughed softly. "You mean humans?" He turned to her, cupped the back of her neck, and bent to take possession of her mouth because he had to do it. She was far too tempting with her disheveled clothes, wild hair, and look of bemusement.

Shea's body instantly went pliant and soft, melding with his harder, more muscular frame. Her mouth was hot and inviting, her breasts pressing into his bare stomach. Jacques lifted his head, his thumb trailing over her lip, her throat, to the tip of her right breast. "These caves are deep and go on for miles. It is easy to get lost and simply disappear. Few humans come near this place. It has a reputation of being dangerous." His hand caressed her soft skin. "Take off your jeans."

She smiled up at him. "I can see it is dangerous. Now, why would I want to do something that is obviously going to get me in big trouble?"

His hand stroked her waist, traced each rib under her satin skin. He could feel her tremble in answer. "Because I want you to. Because you want to please me."

Shea laughed out loud, her eyebrows winging upward. "Oh, really? That's what I want to do?"

He nodded solemnly. "Above all else."

She moved away from him, deliberately enticing him. "I see. I didn't know that. Thank you for pointing it out."

"You are welcome," he countered gravely, his eyes following her every movement. Shea was graceful and seductive, a siren beckoning him to follow. His body stirred, and ruefully he decided the pools might be a safer place to watch her. He entered the nearest hot springs, wincing as the bubbles added to the sensation of fingers stroking his sensitive skin.

Her taunting laughter followed him, brushing provocatively at his nerve endings with the very tip of a flame. Shea felt an unexpected rush of power. Jacques was such an invincible being, yet she could see his body trembling, hear his heart beating even over the roar of the falls. All for her. Deliberately she slid her jeans low, exposing her slender body, the fiery red triangle beckoning him, teasing him. Her shirt floated to the ground, and she lifted her arms skyward, a seductress tempting the heavens.

Jacques' body tightened in anticipation. His black gaze didn't miss one graceful sway, not one rhythmic movement of her shapely form. Shea waded into the pool slowly, allowed the bubbling water to lap at her body like a sensuous tongue. She moved out into the middle of the water and finally slipped under the surface like a sleek, gleaming otter. Jacques sat on the edge of a rock, his legs under the water, bubbles lapping around his hips. He watched her swim toward him, away, her body flashing in the water, breaking the surface, disappearing once again.

Shea's head emerged, her green eyes enormous as they moved over his body. He was utterly still, as if carved from the very stone itself. His muscles were etched and defined, and his body was ready and aggressive. A small smile touched the corners of her mouth. She swam toward him slowly. "So you think I want to please you."

"Definitely." The word came out a low growl. He was finding it hard to breathe.

She smiled at him, a sexy, provocative, very feminine promise. "You're right, I do want to please you. But how do I know you haven't done your hypnotic thing on me, and it's all your idea, not mine?"

He had to reach for his voice, and when he found it, it was gravel. "I would not mind hypnotizing you to do my bidding, but somehow I think you can please me without such help." He was finding it difficult to think straight, his mind a cloud of erotic desire. Water lapped at his hips as she moved closer.

Her breasts brushed his legs, sending ripples of fire through his bloodstream. She pushed against his knees so that he was forced to open them to accommodate her. Her chin nudged his lap. "I have to think of the best way I might please you. You have all sorts of interesting ideas running around in your head. I need to find the best one, don't you think?" Her breath was warm silk, breathing more life into his rigid body. Her tongue caught a drop of water, savored it.

Jacques groaned at the pleasure shooting through him. His legs circled her naked body, drawing her close so that her soft mouth was level with the throbbing velvet tip thrusting toward her. Deliberately he inched his body forward. Bubbles frothed and burst around him; her hair washed over his legs, tangled around him, weaving them closer together. He found he was holding his breath, no longer able to get air.

The touch of her mouth was like hot silk. Jacques' mind seemed to dissolve, his body trembled, and his heart exploded in his chest. He felt as if his very insides were coming apart. His body was no longer his own, no longer under his control. Shea was playing him like a musical instrument, all throbbing notes and building passion. He could only watch her helplessly, ensnared in her web of beauty and love.

He caught her head in his hands, bunching wet hair in his fists. No one, nothing, in all the long centuries had prepared him for the intensity of emotion she brought out in him. He knew what it meant to know he would gladly die for someone.

Jacques' thumb raised her chin so that her green eyes met his black gaze, so that she could easily see into his soul. For all his faults, for all his clumsy handling of their relationship, she had to see what he really felt inside. He lifted her easily into his arms, holding her close, holding her with exquisite tenderness, cradling her with leashed strength, wanting her to be sheltered for all time within his heart.

His mouth moved over her satin skin collecting little beads of water. "Love me back, Shea, love me like this. You are the air I breathe. Do not be afraid of this." His hands shaped her slender form to the hardness of his, caressed every line of her body, found every secret shadow and hollow.

As he lifted her closer, water poured from

her body onto his, hot and steamy. Her mouth was at his throat — small, loving kisses designed to drive him wild. He was gentle and tender this time, taking his time, enjoying his ability to touch her, to take her whenever they wanted, however they wanted. Water splashed up all around them; bubbles frothed and burst. Steam enveloped them, wrapping their bodies like a blanket.

Jacques stroked back her bright hair, kissed her eyelids, her high cheekbones, the corners of her mouth. Every inch of her was his, and he worshipped it tenderly. When at last his body took possession of hers, her eyes held the same message as his, her soul branded forever with his name, his touch.

Chapter Seventeen

Jacques stirred languidly. He didn't want to move, but hunger was growing, and he needed nourishment desperately. He had to sustain Shea, Byron, and his own healing body. He would have to feed often to keep up with the demand. He carefully unwound his body from Shea's. She moaned softly, and her long eyelashes lifted.

"You can't possibly want more." He had made love to her often and thoroughly throughout the last few hours. She wasn't altogether certain she could move.

He ran a teasing finger down her flat stomach. "I always want more. *Insatiable* is the word." He sighed and reluctantly stood and stretched. "I want you to stay here while I go feed. You will be safe."

One eyebrow lifted. "How do you know that? Don't all Carpathians know of this place? I should go with you." She wanted to keep him safe from any harm. If Rand was the vampire, he hated Jacques above all others.

Jacques made certain no expression showed on his face. Shea had the illusion she was still taking care of him. Her protective streak sent unexpected warmth flowing through him. He loved that in her. He wasn't stupid enough to give away his knowledge that she wouldn't harm a fly. "If you made the effort to learn how to scan, you would know if any Carpathians were in the vicinity. Because we are here, no others would invade our privacy," he said gruffly.

"The vampire can cloak himself, or have you forgotten?" she asked suspiciously. "I think it is more likely that you are going out hunting."

Jacques ruffled her hair gently. "I am going to feed, little red hair. It is not my job to hunt the vampire. Gregori has been chosen for that. I do not envy him the job. As for the vampire bothering you, I can find no trace of him when I scan, and you display no uneasiness. Stay here and wait for me. I already know where I can find food. It will take only minutes."

Shea glared up at him. "You had better not be deceiving me."

"It is impossible for lifemates to lie to one another." He stretched again and bent to kiss her upturned face. "Do not wander off, Shea. And stay in touch with me. I do not want any nasty surprises when I return. In any case, if you stay in touch with me, you will see that I am telling the truth. I go only to feed."

She stretched out beside the hot springs and dangled her fingers idly in the water. Her body was pleasantly sore. The truth was, she didn't want to move. "All right, wild man, but it isn't me who's constantly finding trouble. And if you run into Rand, just leave." She turned over, completely oblivious of offering up her body to him. "He may be my biological father, and like any child I may have had my fairy-tale fantasies about the perfect daddy, but I don't want you to take any chances. I've been thinking a lot about this."

"About what?" he encouraged, wanting her to sort it out for herself.

"The reason I can feel the vampire even though he can cloak himself. The reason I felt the humans when Raven couldn't."

"We should have been able to detect them," Jacques said, inviting her to tell him more. He hunkered down beside her. Shea had an exceptional brain, and, given sufficient time, he knew she would be able to put her emotions aside and contribute much to the solution to their problems.

"Blood. Isn't that how everything works? All the bonds and mental telepathy? Don't you track each other through blood exchanges? Isn't that why the men rarely exchange blood? Rand hasn't exchanged with any of you, has he?"

Jacques shook his head. "No, he was very careful never to do such a thing. But then, he had a lifemate. He did not need to share; and there was no chance of his turning."

"But Noelle wasn't really his lifemate, was she? He always knew it, even if no one else did. Later, perhaps, you all realized he couldn't be her true lifemate, but he had already established a habit of never exchanging blood. He knew there was always the chance he might turn, so he protected himself." Shea felt she was redeeming her mother. "Maggie was his lifemate. Mikhail told us Rand had risen only a couple of years ago and kept to himself. That was after the vampire murders had taken place."

"If that is so, then Rand could not possibly be the guilty one."

"If it is so. Suppose he had risen before that time and found my mother dead. You said a widowed lifemate normally chooses death. What happens if they don't? What happens if they keep existing?"

There was silence as Jacques digested what she was saying. "Mikhail thought Rand would be all right because Noelle was not his true lifemate. But if Maggie had been, and she was already dead when he rose, then he would turn. Yet he had his son. He may have stayed to protect him." He inhaled sharply. "But to be able to weave a cloaking spell . . . There are only a few with that kind of power."

"Like?" Shea prompted.

"Mikhail is the oldest living Carpathian. Gregori is only a quarter of a century younger. Aidan and his twin brother, Julian, are perhaps half a century younger. Byron and I are the next oldest. A couple of others are close in age, but they have lifemates and are not suspect. There is Dimitri, but he is far from this land. Only an ancient is powerful enough to cloak his presence." Jacques didn't realize how much he was remembering, but Shea did, and it made the sorrow of Rand's betrayals easier to bear.

"But Rand could have found a way to do it," Shea insisted. "It makes sense, Jacques. I don't have to like it — in fact, I hate it — but I share his blood, and there isn't another explanation. I sensed his presence in the forest because we share the same strain of blood. It has to be that."

"You were so opposed to the idea before, Shea." Jacques' hand spanned her flat stomach. He couldn't help himself, he had to touch her, reveled in his right to do so.

"I didn't want to face it, Jacques. But I've had some time to think about this. It's the only rational explanation. He wants me to be, and he's hoping to keep me for himself, but he knows I'm not really Maggie. And he has to kill you. He wanted you dead and he wanted Raven dead and most likely Mikhail also." Shea took a deep breath. "And Rand said something that bothered me, but I couldn't remember what. I just put it together. He mentioned Byron. He shouldn't have known that Byron was the one the humans had tortured. No one had told him, and Byron couldn't communicate with him. So how did he know?"

Jacques' black eyes glinted like obsidian. "I did not catch that. You are right. He did know of Byron. He named him."

Shea shoved a suddenly shaking hand through her hair. Her eyes held endless sorrow as she looked up at him. "God, Jacques, do you know what that means? He must have been responsible for bringing my brother to Don Wallace and Jeff Smith. He was responsible for their torturing and killing his own son. Is that possible? Could someone really be that insane, that cold-blooded?"

"I am sorry, Shea. A vampire is not capable of any real feeling. The undead has chosen to give up his soul. He is wholly evil." Jacques could feel an unfamiliar lump blocking his throat. He could feel the heaviness in her heart. He admired the courage it took for her to voice her conclusions to him. "The reason the humans have such legends from the old times is because a few have experienced what a real vampire is capable of. I wish it was different. I would give anything to spare you this heartache."

"I wish things were different, too, but I don't think they are. And I think you're in real danger. Even if Rand isn't the vampire, he's definitely a sick, bitter man, and he hates you. Please be careful. I don't want him to hurt you." Her large green eyes were alive with anxiety. She sat up, her arms circling his neck. "I want to put you on a shelf somewhere where no one can ever hurt you again."

Jacques hastily broke the connection of their minds. Shea persisted in thinking him at risk. It simply did not occur to her, even after what she had experienced with him, what she had witnessed, that he could be the aggressor in the upcoming battle. That he might welcome the battle with his betrayer. That he would enjoy it. For all her knowledge of him, she still could not take in that he was a predator by nature. If that was what it took for her to accept their relationship, he was willing for the knowledge to come to her in slow stages.

To Jacques, that was the beauty of a lifemate's bond. Everything was there for the taking, but it was up to the partner to do what they wanted with it all. Jacques knew he would fly to the moon and haul it down for her, walk on water or swim through hot lava if that was what it took to make her happy. Shea was his life, and they had centuries to get to know one another properly. She did not need to confront his killer instincts with her every waking breath.

His palm cupped her face, moved lovingly to her slender neck, his thumb feathering over her soft skin. He ached with love for her. "I promise to be careful."

"Really careful," she insisted.

He found the hard edges of his mouth turning up. "Really *really* careful," he clarified.

Her fingertip traced his smile. "I'm sorry I was so crazy about the healer giving me blood, but I really can't stand it yet, even thinking about it. When we're together, it seems different, something beautiful and natural, but the thought of anyone else —" Her stomach lurched, and she broke off.

Jacques' mouth skimmed her face, settled on her lips for a brief, disturbing moment. "I understand. I am stronger now, little red hair. I can care for you properly."

Her eyebrows shot up, and she frowned. "That isn't exactly what I meant. Don't go all macho on me. That would make me sicker than finding some cute human male to feed off."

She was teasing him. Intellectually he knew it, but for a moment a red haze of jealousy clouded his mind. Rage welled up, and he forced it under control. He knew immediately that he was lucky she didn't want to take sustenance from another man. Something in his fragmented mind, or perhaps it was his possessive nature, would not stand for it. No man, human or Carpathian, was going to be completely safe until he learned to control his fear of losing her. Jacques raked a hand through his hair. "I have a long way to go before I will be normal again."

She burst out laughing. "No one has said you ever were normal, Jacques."

He felt the flood of warmth at her teasing and basked in it. "Stay here, little red hair. Stay safe for me."

She lay back, lazily reclining on the flat rock. Her bright red hair spread out around her like strands of silk. The clean lines of her nude body, her full breasts and tight, fiery curls beckoned to him. Jacques backed away from her. He was going to have to learn a lot about self-control over the next few hundred years. He turned abruptly and walked away.

Once through the small passageway leading back to the tunnel, he shape-shifted as he hurried through the maze of pathways. His body compressed, smaller, even smaller, until he was the very creature Shea was terrified of. Small wings took him gliding quickly through the network of tunnels, upward to the shortcut. It was a tiny chimney cut by centuries of water constantly trickling through solid rock. He charged up it and out into the night sky. Almost instantly his body reshaped itself in flight, taking on the larger, more powerful, and much more formidable shape of an owl. Razor-sharp talons and hooked beak, thick feathers and eyes that easily pierced the night, served him well. He winged his way over the forest canopy toward the cabin housing the three hunters.

Jacques had deliberately ordered their compliance. They would stay the night, unable to figure out why it was so important but unable to defy his hypnotic suggestion. He had taken their blood, directed their minds, and could call them to him at will. The hunters had not intended to stay, as the land was inhospitable to them and they were beginning to believe the superstitions of the locals. He knew the memories he had implanted would remain for as long as he wanted and that they would always answer his bidding if he so desired.

The beauty of the night, seen through the owl's eyes, was incredible. Far below, on the forest floor, small animals scurried for cover. The green canopy blanketing the trees swayed and danced in the wind, a beautiful ballet. The breeze caught at feathers, lifted them and rushed at him with a feeling of sheer joy and power. He spotted the cabin below and swooped down toward it.

Almost immediately he realized something had to be wrong. No smoke came from the chimney, and on a night like this the three hunters would need warmth. The owl banked sharply and glided in, talons extended. He landed as a man, on his feet, his senses alert to any impending dangers, flaring out to scan the area. He caught no signs of life, but he smelled death. The stench was in his nostrils, along with the pungent scent of terror. Someone had died violently, and had known it was coming. Jacques moved carefully, cloaking himself against the sight of humans. He detected none in the immediate area — but then, he hadn't found Smith or Wallace either. He could find no threat, yet he continued to move warily toward the darkened cabin.

He found the first body beside the porch. The man was mangled, his throat torn, the wound gaping and brutal, as though a huge animal had attacked and killed him. He was drained of blood. Jacques stood beside the hunter's body for a moment, angry with himself for exposing the human to danger needlessly. Of course Rand would know he would need to feed often; he would look for Jacques' source and cut it off.

Jacques remained very still while he took stock of his surroundings. The kill was fresh, minutes old, the body still warm. The vampire was somewhere in the immediate vicinity, waiting for him. Jacques had no doubt he was next on the vampire's list. Jacques could not detect any evidence of him, yet he knew with a certainty he was being stalked. He inhaled sharply and allowed the demon inside to awaken with an ugly roar. Jacques could feel the faint stirring in his mind, the gentle, warm inquiry. *Do not attempt to contact me, Shea. The vampire is attempting a trap. I cannot be distracted.*

Then I will come to you! Shea was very alarmed.

Jacques could almost see her face, the

enormous green eyes wide with worry, her chin determined. *You will do as I bid, Shea. I cannot worry about both of us and succeed.* He used his firmest voice, sending a reinforcing push toward her.

He could feel her reluctance to obey him, but she did not protest further, believing she might endanger him. Jacques moved up the stairs stealthily. The door was slightly ajar, the wind pushing it gently to and fro. The hinges were old and rusty and squeaked with each shift of the wind. Jacques slipped inside to the smell of death and fear, the overwhelming scent of blood.

The floor was a pool of dark, nearly black liquid, sticky and thick. The two bodies had been flung carelessly aside after the vampire had sated himself on the adrenaline-laced sustenance. He had deliberately drained the rest of the blood from the bodies so that the smell of it would further trigger Jacques' need to feed. He also made certain there was nothing left for Jacques to use to ease that biting, gnawing hunger. It was growing in him every moment, weakening his body, preying on his strength.

No, it's not, Jacques. Shea's voice was a soft, clean note in his head. *You are not weak. You are strong, very strong and healthy. The vampire has set another trap for you. Get out of the house, get into the open air. You are young and strong. There is nothing he can do to you.* In her mind there was complete confidence in him, not so much as a shadow of worry or doubt. She believed in him. Jacques could do no other than to follow her lead and believe in himself.

Very carefully he searched the interior of the cabin, looking for hidden traps. When the feeling of doom persisted in creeping into his mind, he reached for Shea's reassuring presence. She was always there, utterly loyal, determined to make him see himself as she saw him. Her belief in him enabled him to see how the vampire's trap was preying on his mind. He found himself smiling grimly, without humor. He acknowledged the vampire's power and expertise in illusion, but Shea had broken the spell with her unfailing belief in him. Jacques was strong enough to deal with the undead; it was only a matter of perceiving the traps for the illusions they were.

Jacques made his way outside into the cool night air. The wind tugged at his clothing, raked at his long hair. A lone wolf howled, endlessly calling for a mate. The sound caught at him, touched a spot in him, and he lifted his head and crooned softly into the night. The wolf was wandering far from its companions, alone, an outcast to those who did not understand its predatory nature.

A sound alerted him, a mere rustle in the underbrush, but it was enough to draw his mind away from the wolf and back to the enemy stalking him. He lowered his body into a crouch, centering himself for the attack. When he turned his head, Rand moved out into the open. He was smeared with blood, his fangs exposed, his eyes red-rimmed, and his nails long, clawed tips. His skin, flushed from his recent kills, was stretched taut against his skull so that he had the look of death clinging to him.

"I knew you would leave your bride to feast upon the humans. You could not resist when blood was there for the taking," Rand said in a voice edged with contempt.

Jacques' eyebrows rose a fraction. "You seem to help yourself to whatever you desire. Does that include other men's lifemates?"

Rand's mouth twisted into an ugly snarl. "You took my lifemate from me. You and your brother. Yet now both of you have found the very thing you would never allow me to have. I will destroy Mikhail and his woman, and I will take back from you what is rightfully mine."

"Maggie is dead, Rand, and only you are responsible. You left Noelle to the human butchers while you rushed out to see your lifemate, yet you did not have the courage to bring her before Mikhail and announce her as such. She would still be alive if you had."

"Noelle would have murdered her. She threatened to do so many times."

"Mikhail would never have allowed such a thing, and you know it. It was your own lack of courage that killed her. Any Carpathian male worth anything will stand up for the one he chooses for his lifemate. Is it possible, Rand, that you were so warped with all your womanizing that you simply did not want to make a full commitment to Maggie? Perhaps you liked having the two women, liked to taunt Noelle. Perhaps the two of you had a twisted, perverted relationship, and you could not quite bring yourself to give it up for something so right and pure."

Rand roared, his head back, the sound issuing forth one of anger and agony. "You go too far, dark one. You think I cannot see what you really are? You are a killer. It is plain to those of us who see you with clear eyes. Do you not feel the need to destroy? Do you not enjoy the power? You are one with me, whether you choose to see it or not. Your nature is dark and ugly, like the world you and your brother forced me to occupy. I do not need to destroy one such as you — you will do so on your own. The woman will see what you are eventually."

"Shea knows exactly what I am, and she is willing to live with me. You chose your own life and your own fate, Rand. You rose before your time —"

"I felt the rending tear when my lifemate chose death!"

"That does not excuse your responsibility in the matter. She would not have chosen death had you been man enough to take her before Mikhail and show the world she belonged to you. And you could have chosen to follow her to her fate, but again you left her to face the unknown by herself. Instead you blamed others for your inadequacies and set out to revenge yourself. Tell me, Rand, why did you deliver your own son into the hands of those butchers? He was a boy, a mere eighteen. What had he done to deserve such a terrible fate?"

Rand's face twisted into a snarling mask of hatred. "I gave him a chance to join me, to seek retribution for what Mikhail and you had done to me. I went to him, his own father, and explained my plan. He was so brainwashed by you, by Mikhail, that he called me vampire. I could see you had twisted his mind. He would not listen to me. I could not allow such a traitor to live. My slaves dealt with him. They thought they controlled me, but I put thoughts into their heads at will. They named me Vulture and thought to destroy me after they had used me. It was amusing to turn them against one another, to force them to set each other up for the kill. Wallace and Slovensky were evil men and easy to ensnare. Smith was weak, a follower, a good sacrifice."

"You had them torture and mutilate your own son. And what of the others? Why the others?"

Rand smiled, a wicked, humorless parody of amusement. "For the fun, of course, for the practice. Gregori thinks he is the only one who can use the dark secrets, but he is not as smart as he thinks."

"And do you plan to kill him also?"

"I do not have to take that chance. He will turn soon." There was a wealth of satisfaction in Rand's voice. "He will not choose death, as you all think he will. He has battled too long, and he is far too powerful. He will rip this world apart. And he will squash like bugs those who seek to destroy him. Aidan and Julian together might have a chance, but they, too, are close to turning.

Together we will rule, as our race should have from the beginning. It is your brother who has kept our people from their rightful place. Humans are cattle to be used to sate our hunger, to serve our needs, yet we hide from them like cowards. The others hate me now, but soon all the ancients will join me."

"And what of Shea in this master plan?"

"She will become one of us after your death. Her blood is Maggie's blood, and she belongs to me. You had no right to her."

"And you believe that you can defeat me in battle?" Jacques' head was up, the demon in him struggling for freedom, wanting the joy and thrill of the fight. Hatred rose for this man who had destroyed his innocence, his family, his memories, his beliefs. Savage hatred for this man who had created a dark, dangerous being in the place of a gentle Carpathian rose and began to spread like a dark stain across his soul.

"You will defeat yourself, dark one. Your woman is tied to me. When you strike me, she will feel the pain. Every slash, every cut, it will be the woman who bleeds, not just me. She will also feel your joy in the act. She will know you for what you are, and she will know your need to inflict pain and death. She will finally see you as the monster you really are. She will see you kill her father, see your joy in the act, and she will feel each blow."

Pain exploded in the region of Jacques' temples as he desperately tried to remember if what the vampire was saying could be so. Would Shea feel pain inflicted upon Rand? Was her father's blood in her veins sufficient to cause such a thing? He needed the answer immediately. Rand had him backed into a corner with this revelation.

Before Jacques could send off an inquiry and resolve the dilemma, the vampire launched himself, moving with supernatural speed, a blur of claws going for the jugular. Jacques leapt out of the way, felt the burn across his throat as the tips of Rand's nails caught him and opened a shallow cut. Jacques retaliated without conscious thought, raking his own talons down the vampire's face.

Rand screamed with pain, a cry of fear and hatred. Jacques kept at him, whirling in and out of visibility, inflicting lacerations across the vampire's chest to drain him of his strength. He kept his mind firmly from Shea's. He could not think she was in danger, that this savage fight could somehow affect her. The joy in him increased until his mind and body were alive with power. The vampire fell back under his onslaught. With one last desperate attempt to turn the battle in his favor, Rand disappeared, fled to the tree line, calling on the sky to do his bidding.

A bolt of lightning slammed to earth, scorching the area close to Jacques' body, singeing the tips of his hair. A second bolt hit the precise spot where the Carpathian had been standing, but Jacques was already overhead, high in the trees above Rand. Wings beat the air strongly as he launched himself.

Rand screamed as the razor-sharp talons ripped into his chest, sought his pulsating heart. "Shea! Hear me! Join with me! Save me now! I am your father! You must join with me to save me from this monster tearing insanely at my flesh!"

Jacques reached for the organ, tore it free, and flung it far from the vampire. "You are dead, vampire, and you go, I hope, to some semblance of peace. The crimes you have committed against me and my family are avenged. You go to meet your God and his mercy. I feel none toward you. You would have taken her with you had you been able to do so. Carpathian justice has been dispensed."

Rand staggered forward, his gray face slack, tainted blood flowing freely. His mouth working convulsively, he fell to his knees. Jacques leapt back from the thrashing body, careful that the grasping claws did not touch him, that not one speck of the dark blood splattered on him. His hand was burning as he wiped it clean in the shriveling grass.

The air around them stilled, the wind completely silent. The earth seemed to groan. An eerie steam rose from the wriggling body, mixed with a noxious odor. Jacques instinctively moved farther away from the spectacle. Vampires died hard; all fought to overcome death with every trick they had. The tainted blood trickled across the ground toward Jacques' boots, guided by the dying vampire's last evil thoughts. Jacques watched without emotion as the vampire crawled toward him, inched his way closer and closer, his face twisted with depravity, with hatred.

Jacques shook his head. "You hated yourself, Rand. You hated yourself all these years. All you had to do was find the courage to follow her. Maggie would have saved your soul."

Low, pitiful growls escaped from the hideous mouth, blood spewed forth, and Rand collapsed in front of Jacques, still reaching for him, still determined in his last moment to kill.

Jacques inhaled sharply, caught his first whiff of fresh, clean air, and knew the vampire had fully expired. With a little sigh he carried the bodies of the hunters to an open area and carefully collected what dry branches he could find. There could be no evidence left of this night. The vampire, too, had to be completely consumed by the fire so that there was no chance the tainted blood could find a way to revive him. The power of the vampire's blood was incredible.

Weakness was becoming an increasing concern for Jacques. The fight had used up his last energies, and he still had to create and maintain a huge conflagration in the midst of a rain-soaked forest.

The wolf howled again, this time much closer, obviously loping toward the scene of death and destruction, perhaps drawn by the smell of blood. Jacques scored the earth with a lightning bolt, directing it along the river of blood. No creature needed the madness of that fluid in its belly.

An unusually large, rare, golden wolf trotted out of the timberline, circled the area warily, and sat down on its haunches only feet from Jacques. It watched him steadily with its strange golden eyes, completely unafraid. It seemed not to be affected by the fire, the lightning, or the Carpathian male. Jacques watched the animal equally intently, certain he was facing more than a wolf. The creature did not make an attempt to use the common mental path to communicate. It simply watched him, taking in the bizarre scene, the golden eyes never wavering.

A humorless smile curved Jacques' hard mouth. "If you are looking for action tonight, I am too tired to oblige you, and far too hungry."

The wolf's shape contorted, stretched, shimmered in the smoke of the fire, and soon a large, heavily muscled man was facing Jacques. His long, shaggy mane of hair was blond, his eyes golden, his body perfectly balanced. "You are Jacques, brother to Mikhail. I heard you were dead."

"That is the story going around," Jacques assented warily.

"You have no memory of me? I am Julian, brother to Aidan. I have been away these last long years. The far-off mountains, the places without people, are my home."

"The last I heard, you were fighting wars in distant lands."

"When the mood is upon me, I fight where it is needed," Julian agreed. "I see you do also. The vampire lies dead, and you are pale beyond imagination."

Jacques' smile was grim. "Do not allow my color to fool you."

"I am no vampire yet, and if ever I fear turning, I will go to Aidan, and he will destroy me if I cannot do so myself. If you wish to take blood, then I offer it freely. The healer knows me; you can ask him if I am a reliable resource." There was the slightest of smiles, a self-mocking humor.

"What are you doing in these parts?" Jacques asked suspiciously.

"I was traveling through, on my way to the United States, when I heard the butchers were back, and I thought I would make myself useful to our people for a change."

Jacques found himself admiring Julian's answers. This was a man not in the least worried about anyone's opinion or impression of him. He was self-contained, at ease with himself. It didn't bother him at all that Jacques was suspicious, that he was firing questions at him.

Healer, hear me. I have need of blood, and this one before me, Julian, the golden twin, has said you will vouch for him.

No one can vouch for one such as Julian. He is a loner, a law unto himself, but his blood is untainted. If Julian turns, it will be Aidan or I

548

who hunts him, no others. Avail yourself of what he offers.

"Did he give me a good recommendation?" Julian's smile was frankly sardonic.

"The healer never gives good recommendation. You are not his favorite, but he agrees there would be no harm."

Julian laughed softly, put his wrist to his mouth and bit, then casually reached out to offer his life-giving fluid to Jacques. "I am too much like him, a loner, one who studies too much. I dabble in things better left alone. I fear Gregori has given up on me." He didn't sound worried about it.

Jacques nearly staggered as he moved to take the proffered wrist. His mouth clamped tightly over the ragged wound. The blood flowed into Jacques' withered, shrunken cells. The surge of strength and power was incredible. He had not realized how depleted his system was until the nourishment flowed into his body. It was an effort not to be greedy, to feast at the rich supply.

"Do not worry, I have no duties to perform this night. Take what you need, and I will hunt in town before moving on." Julian made the offer casually.

Jacques forced himself away from the flowing supply. He closed the wound carefully and looked up at the handsome, weathered face. There was intelligence there, coolness, self-possession, and something else. Jacques could read the dangerous stillness in him. Julian was a man always ready for the unexpected.

"Thank you, Julian. If you ever have need, I expect to return the favor," Jacques said sincerely.

"I will finish up here," Julian offered. "It is a shame these three men had to die this night. When they do not return and no search party can find their remains, it will only feed the legends of vampires stalking this country and these parts."

"I should have expected Rand to use them against me; he knew I would keep them to feed." Jacques regretted their deaths bitterly.

"You did not kill these men, the vampire did. And you rid the world of one of our monsters. Both humans and Carpathians are indebted to you. Think only of that, Jacques. I wish you good journey and long life."

"Good journey and long life to you, Julian," Jacques answered formally.

Chapter Eighteen

Jacques entered the maze of tunnels, his body moving with supernatural speed. He could hear every sound, the water dripping, then roaring, the high squeak of the bats, even the slight shifting of the earth itself. But he could not detect what he wished to hear most. There was no sound coming from the pools. No ripple of water, no humming, no soft breath from sleeping. No heart beating.

Shea was lying motionless on a rock when Jacques entered the steamy underground chamber. He stood very still in the entrance, afraid to move or speak. She had not responded to his telepathic call to her. If she were lost to him, the monster that was Rand would win after all. No one would ever be safe again until Jacques was destroyed. He shook his head. No, if she were dead, he would not leave her to face the unknown without him. Rand would not win. Jacques would follow her, find her. They would spend their life in the next world together.

He cleared his throat carefully, noisily, wanting her to turn to face him. She didn't move, her body utterly still. Jacques inhaled sharply and caught the faint scent of blood. He cleared the distance between them in a single leap, his speed so great, he was almost unable to stop before plunging headlong into the pool. As it was, he teetered precariously on the rim of the boulder before regaining his balance.

There was blood smeared on the rock beside Shea's naked body, a faint crimson ribbon over her breasts. Jacques cried out, dropped to his knees beside her, gathered her up to press her against his chest. Her heart was not beating. He could not feel a pulse or find a thread of life. "No!" He shouted it hoarsely, his voice echoing through the chamber eerily. The voice was lonely and lost, his heart ripped out, like Rand's.

Jacques? The voice was faint and far off but unmistakably Shea's.

Jacques held his breath for a moment, afraid he had truly lost his mind. "Shea?" He breathed her name, a whisper of silk like the feel of her hair on his body. That light. "Where are you, little love? Come back to me."

Jacques pressed his forehead to hers, his hand over her heart. He felt the first strong beat in his palm, the first rush of blood through her veins and arteries. He captured her mouth with his to take the first breath from her lungs. His own heart could beat, his own lungs could work. He felt tears on his face and held her close.

"What happened to you out there?" she asked softly, clinging to him.

"The vampire and I fought," he said into her mass of red hair. He caught a strand on the tip of his tongue, ran it through his mouth, needing the feel of her close to him.

"I know. It was Rand. I felt you hit him. I could feel his hatred. It was terrible, like something alien in my body. When you struck, I could feel his pain. Right away I began to bleed. I knew he would use it against you somehow, so I tried to do what you said all Carpathians could do." She looked ruefully around her at the smears of blood. "It took a while to figure things out, but eventually I was able to put myself to sleep."

She took his breath away with her bravery. "Why did you not contact me?"

"I was afraid it would distract you, Jacques. I knew you were in a fight for your life. The last thing you needed to do was worry about me."

"You are still bleeding," he pointed out softly, holding her away from him so he could examine her.

"It doesn't really hurt all that much, now that you're back and safe," she assured him.

"I'm sorry it was your father. I know how much having a father, some member of your family, alive would have meant to you." He bent his head to the angry cut across her left breast. His tongue lapped at the wound gently, the healing properties in his saliva instantly closing the laceration. Her skin, recently so cold and lifeless, was suddenly beginning to heat. Steam rose all around them, enfolding them in its embrace. "My family will have to be your family," he added softly. "We will make our own family."

Shea rubbed her face against his chest like a kitten, her mouth wandering up the column of his throat. "We have a strange family, Jacques, every one of them. I guess we'll have to be the sane ones."

He loved the laughter in her voice. As sad as she must be at this moment, with the man who was her father responsible for so much death and hatred, she still found it in her to try to make him feel better. His arms tightened protectively. "I suppose we cannot tell them we feel this way."

"Better not. I think they're under the mistaken impression that something is a little off with us." Shea moved her head, swinging the silky hair away from her neck, exposing a long, deep scratch for his attention.

Jacques instantly bent his head to accommodate her. His tongue tasted the sweet spice of life, caressed and teased, moved up her neck to find her ear. His teeth nipped gently. He could feel the responsive shiver run through her. Her skin was soft and warm, bringing life to his own. "And we can create our own family eventually, Shea. Our child." When he felt her stiffen, he held her closer, his voice a velvet soft whisper. "Not now, Shea, later, when you are strong in our world and sure of yourself, and I am completely healed. Our child. Children. Your dream has become my dream. We can have it, Shea."

"Don't, Jacques," Shea said.

"We can, my love. I am remembering things much faster now. I know as we grow together, I will be able to feel as you feel. I want our child. I want you happy. I want to give you a family. Do not close out the idea from your mind. We have centuries to come to this decision, but know this: I want it, too."

"When you can promise me you will remain and love and guide our child should something happen to me, then I will gladly agree."

His teeth touched the side of her neck. "Thanks to you, I have faith in myself. I will someday be able to give you such a promise. I will also tell you, if such a thing should occur, that the child would be my hope on this earth, and when she or he had a family, then I would gladly join you."

She could feel the tears swimming in her eyes. "Then I am truly happy, Jacques. You could never give me a more beautiful gift than you already have. Even if you never reach that point, I will always love you for wanting to reach it and striving to do so."

"Your happiness is of great importance to me."

"You smell different, Jacques." Shea inhaled his scent sharply, pulled back so she could look into his eyes. "Why do you smell different?"

He laughed softly. "It is not a woman, red hair. Why are you so suspicious? I met another one such as myself in the forest. I was in need, and he offered his aid."

"And you took it?" She was astonished. Jacques had certainly come a long way from the wary, dark, dangerous man she had first encountered. "He was a total stranger, yet you allowed him to help you?"

"You were a total stranger, and I allowed you to do more than simply aid me," he teased, his mouth warm against the corner of hers. "In fact, you gave me all sorts of interesting ideas on how you could further aid me."

"I did not. As I recall, I told you I was your doctor, nothing more, and you would not listen to me. You know, Jacques, that's a very bad habit of yours, not listening to me."

His mouth wandered back to her ear, his breath stirring her blood. "I promise to remedy the situation as soon as humanly possible," he whispered with a sorcerer's magic.

Shea could feel his breath right down to her toes. Then she saw an ugly slash wound marring his shoulder. She lowered her mouth to heal it and tasted the unique flavor that was Jacques. She felt his involuntary response and deliberately squirmed closer, bringing her body right up against his. She tasted his essence, she tasted the adrenaline, the primitive joy of battle, she tasted his pain. "*Humanly* possible, huh?" she mused. "I don't know if I like the way you put that. It seems to me you'll be able to get around that one fairly easily." Shea circled his neck with her arms and pulled his head down to hers. Blindly, unerringly, she found his mouth with hers. She put everything into her kiss, her love, her fear, her acceptance of his ways. Her desire for him, her need of him, all of it rushed from her to him.

Jacques' arms tightened possessively. His mouth was hungry against hers, needing to feed on her sweetness, her purity, to wipe out the remnants of the lingering demon. Her body was pliant and welcoming, her mouth as hungry as his. He flung his clothes in every direction and moved to gather her even closer. He felt her shift her weight, felt them both teeter, and then they were tumbling into the pool beneath them.

Locked together, they went to the bottom, their mouths clinging to one another, their shared laughter in their minds. He kicked his legs strongly as she wrapped hers around his waist. Their heads broke the surface, sending rings of ripples skipping over the water. She was laughing, catching his face in her hands. "You are so incredibly romantic, Jacques, I can barely catch my breath here."

His hands moved up to cup her buttocks, to massage suggestively. He raised one eyebrow. "Are you saying this was my fault? Woman, I never lose my balance. I needed to follow you into the water to keep you from embarrassing yourself."

Her hand found the back of his waist, caressed the intriguing little niche there, and moved to follow the line of his hip. "I think, wild man, you need me very much." She pressed her body closer to his, found the hot, thick evidence of his desire. "Very, very much." Shea tightened her legs around his waist and settled herself over his aggressive length, taking the thick weight of him into her.

His breath exploded as velvet fire seemed to enfold him. His teeth found the slim column of her neck, holding her pinned and still for his invasion. There was such beauty in the moment, he felt suspended in time, caught in another dimension. Her hair floated around them like silken sea kelp, and her full breasts pushed into the heavy muscles of his chest. She was soft and pliant, flowing around him like warm honey, yet her muscles were firm and moving convulsively to keep him within her body.

Water splashed up around them with the movement of their bodies, brushed their sensitive skin like fingers, a warm, loving caress. She was his world in that moment, the true meaning of living to him. Colors were dancing around them — not the gray, bleak world he had existed in for so long, but true colors, vivid and real. Feelings were strong, emotions deep, his heart thudding with wonder, his protective instincts and great capacity for love stealing into his soul. In contrast to his world of pain and rage, of utter coldness and despair, this love for her was a miracle. She would never understand what she truly meant to him, not even reading his mind, because the depth of feeling was so great. He had hungered and needed for so long, with no hope, yet now she was in his arms, her body one with his, her heart and mind in tune and rhythm, her soul locked irrevocably with his.

Jacques knew, as his body moved gently and lovingly into hers, as his hips thrust forward and he buried himself ever deeper, that his life was changed forever. He would have a home, a family, children; he would have love and laughter surrounding him all the days he chose to remain on earth. He would have her body, her heart, her purity and goodness to temper his predatory nature. His hell had become a paradise that he had somehow, through all his mistakes, managed to reach.

Because she could read his mind so easily, because he rarely left her completely, Shea could glimpse his feelings. She laid her head on his shoulder, closed her eyes, and allowed the building explosion to overtake her. Her arms tightened around Jacques, around her anchor, her security. Whatever happened in the future, whatever they were forced to face and deal with, they had one another, and that was all anyone could ask.

Jacques lifted them to the heavens, and they soared there together while the water in the pool splashed and receded around them. He framed her face gently with his large hands and looked into her vivid green eyes.

"I love you, Shea. I always will," he vowed softly.

"I love you too, Jacques," she whispered back.

He found her mouth, the warm sweetness only she could provide, and took it hungrily. They slipped deeper into their embrace, and the water closed over their heads. Laughing, coughing, they broke apart and swam to the surface, the horrors of the day drowned in the depth of their love.

About the Author

Christine Feehan

I live in the beautiful mountains of Lake County, California. I have always loved hiking, camping, rafting and being outdoors. I've also been involved in the martial arts for years — I hold a third degree black belt, instruct in a Korean karate system, and have taught self-defense. I am happily married to a romantic man who often inspires me with his thoughtfulness. We have a yours, mine, and ours family, claiming eleven children as our own. I have always written books, forcing my ten sisters to read every word, and now my daughters read and help me edit my manuscripts. It is fun to take all the research I have done on wild animals, raptors, vampires, weather, and volcanoes and put it together with romance.

Please visit my website at www.christinefeehan.com.

The employees of Thorndike Press hope you have enjoyed this Large Print book. All our Thorndike and Wheeler Large Print titles are designed for easy reading, and all our books are made to last. Other Thorndike Press Large Print books are available at your library, through selected bookstores, or directly from us.

For information about titles, please call:

(800) 223-1244

or visit our Web site at:

www.gale.com/thorndike
www.gale.com/wheeler

To share your comments, please write:

Publisher
Thorndike Press
295 Kennedy Memorial Drive
Waterville, ME 04901